The Butte Girls' Club

a novel

Lois Paige

This book is dedicated to friends who've always been there for one another, day after day, year after year, and who've kept each other laughing through all of it.

Thanks to my parents, Rose Paige Taylor and Mervin Leo Paige,
who inspired this novel
and

To the people of Butte who make up so many wonderful memories...where the deer and the elephants roam.

DEAR READER,

Welcome to *The Butte Girls' Club*. This story is a work of fiction set in Butte, Montana, during the tempestuous decade of the 1960s. It spans the time of a cultural revolution in America, with changing social attitudes and the counterculture movement, where music played a significant role in challenging established norms. It was an era where change was as constant as the copper in the mines, and rebellion brewed in the youth like a frothy Butte beer.

While the historical backdrop is authentic, specific events and characters are a combination of fact and fiction. The fictional characters in this story are composites of many people and not based on any one individual. For readers who lived in Butte during the 1960s, please note this account may differ from your personal memories. Our recollections of the past are varied and unique, shaped by our own experiences, and each perspective is different. I've also changed the names of some entities for privacy considerations.

With that said, I hope you enjoy this story, along with some of Butte's vibrant history during this transformative decade.

—Lois Paige

Chapter 1
Daughters of the Tempest

May 25, 1968, in the present at Canyon Ferry Lake, Montana
It's funny what flashes through your mind when you're fighting for your life in a sea of chaos. Your brain can't comprehend it, so your world tilts. While everything spins around you at killer speed, your view from the inside out slows to a crawl.

Then you remember you aren't alone.

While the storm unleashes its fury, I surface after plunging into the icy water. My mammalian gag reflex has me gasping for air while frantically searching the frothy waves for my mother and my best friend. A tourniquet of fear constricts me as I cough to purge the lake from my lungs. I tread water like a crazed animal caught in a flash flood.

"Mom? Maggie?" I sputter against a clap of thunder. "Where are you guys? Mom!"

How can this be happening?

The aluminum skiff glints in a lightning flash as it bobs upside down on the waves. I swim toward it, grasping the gunwale, clinging to it for dear life, coughing up water.

"Mom! Maggie, where are you?" I shriek, my tears melding with the rainwater. As I search for them, my vision narrows to pinpricks, the edges blurring with each frantic turn of my head.

Torn between survival and my urgency to find them, my brain cancels itself out. When helping swimmers as a lifeguard, my mind works like an efficient, life-saving machine. Now it's a useless mass of lime Jell-O.

"Mom! Mom!" I scream. "Maggie! Answer me!"

Lightning flashes. I spot something rising and falling like ghosts in the pelting rain. Mom's and Maggie's neon orange life jackets become beacons in the roiling waves. They're a short distance away, but they may as well be a mile, because I must leave the boat to get them.

Our swim coach trained Maggie and me in her water safety classes: *never leave your overturned boat in a body of water!*

But my mother never learned to swim.

I have no choice. I don't want to leave the boat, but I must. Arms slapping water in an American crawl like I've done in dozens of pool races, I swim toward them. Spluttering a disjointed Hail Mary, I battle the devil as he tries to end me with another churning wave. Frothy water invades my mouth when I rotate my head to breathe.

When I reach them, Maggie has my mother. Her face contorts, and she spits water. "Jo! Something's wrong with my arm!"

"Thank God you found Mom!" The words rush out as a wave slaps my face like an angry nun. "What's wrong with your arm?"

"I sprained it or something," Maggie sputters back, rain splashing on her water-soaked face as we bob in the waves. Her hair sticks to her head as if she'd glued it. "Where's the boat?"

"Somewhere behind me!" The lake water whips us around like a washing machine, and I tighten my grasp on Mom's life jacket. "Mags, we gotta keep Mom's face out of the water. Don't worry, I've got both of you. Hang onto her with your good arm."

"I am." The fright in Maggie's eyes turns my insides to ice, but at least she isn't panicking. It bolsters my will to hang on, for all of our sakes.

"Mom, wake up!" I wail as rain pummels her face. Life jackets keep us on the surface, but I struggle to keep us together in the forceful waves. "I can't tell if she's breathing!"

I tighten my grip on Mom's life jacket, sucking gulps of air as I pull the water toward me with my other arm. The relentless attack of rainwater blurs my ability to see. Desperate to clear my vision, I swipe at my eyes. My forehead hurts.

Panic ignites every cell as reality slams home: we're on our own in the middle of a lake that is intent on killing us. My heart pounds against my ribs, and my throat constricts, making each breath a ragged gasp. Tendrils of fear creep up my spine while bile rises in my throat, mixing with the lake water I'm forced to swallow.

Dozens of images flicker along with the lightning, as my life rolls by like a filmstrip in our eighth-grade classroom—and I haven't had the chance to live it. Thank God Maggie talked me into taking swim classes in the sixth grade, or we'd be screwed. Never dreamed I'd be in this situation with my best friend and my mother's lives hanging in the balance.

"Wait for lightning, then find the boat!" hollers Maggie.

When a flash of lavender lights up the water, I madly search for our skiff. I don't see it, but I see something else.

"There! On shore!" I gurgle, pointing with my sculling hand. My head bobs underwater. I frantically resurface to glimpse a dim light rising and falling behind the waves. I spit out another mouthful of lake.

Dog-paddling through windswept waves, I lock onto the bobbing light through my water-logged eyeballs. I pray I can swim us to the light.

"What a stupid idea this was!" I splutter. A camping trip two weeks before our eighth-grade graduation from St. Michael's sounded fun at the time. *Not now!*

"Oh, God, my arm," cries Maggie, gasping.

"Hang on, Mags, I'll get us there!" Each pull of water feels like the last, a sickening fusion of adrenaline and terror coursing through my veins. "Please let Mom be breathing! Please, God!"

What if she doesn't make it? What will I do?

My arms are lead weights as I struggle through the waves to get all of us to shore. Thank God someone left that light on! Just when my arm can't pull any longer, my feet strike bottom.

"We made it, Mags!"

Somewhere I lost my Keds, and stumble onshore barefooted. Maggie's arm has blood on it. She helps me with her good one to drag my mother from the lake where she lies face up on the grass. I kneel beside Mom, placing my ear next to her mouth.

Nothing.

"Mags! I don't think she's breathing!"

"Give her mouth to mouth, like the 'Y' trained us," orders Maggie, plopping onto the grass. She struggles to unclasp the straps of her life jacket, but she's shaking so hard she gives up.

"You're bleeding." Maggie points to my neck.

"I don't care," I croak. "I have to help Mom."

Lightning flashes, and I see people running toward us. Hands shaking, I fight the clasps on Mom's life jacket, then place my ear to her chest. It's raining so hard I can't tell whether her heart is beating.

I roll her onto her side, giving her several karate chops between her shoulder blades to force the water out of her lungs. Never in my life have I struck my mother. I sob with each blow.

"Mom, breathe! Please!"

A sudden rush of water spurts from her mouth and she coughs.

"Thank God!" cries Maggie.

Mom inhales and exhales, but her eyelids stay closed. She says nothing.

The woman and man reach us, bombarding us with questions. "What happened? Are there others in the lake? Are you girls okay?"

"No others. Only us," rasps Maggie. "Please help me get this life jacket off. I cut my arm."

"You poor dears! Thank goodness you all made it to shore." The woman helps Maggie with her life jacket, pressing her hand to the laceration on her forearm. "We must control this bleeding." She pulls off her own jacket, tying a sleeve around Maggie's arm.

My gut twists as I stare at Mom's still face. "My mother won't wake up. I think she needs an ambulance," I choke out, my throat raw from coughing up water.

"I'll call for one. Let me get that life jacket off you." The woman unclasps it, motioning to the man. "Tom, let's get them inside the house."

The woman inserts herself between Maggie and me to help us walk, while Tom picks my mother up in a threshold carry, hurrying toward the house.

Once we're inside, he deposits Mom on a davenport, while the woman rushes to a phone, lifting the receiver. Maggie and I sink to the floor, so we don't soil their white recliners. My hand goes to my forehead. I wince when I discover a humongous bump.

The woman hangs up the phone, telling us an ambulance is on the way from Townsend.

The walls rush in and out as my eyes swim out of focus. Colors blur into a hazy smear. I blink hard, trying to bring Maggie and the others back into focus, but their faces are fuzzy. I slump down onto the carpet and everything fades into darkness as I'm pulled under.

I WAKE INSIDE AN AMBULANCE with Maggie sitting next to my head. Two paramedics work on my mother, who lies beside me. The doors close and the vehicle lurches forward.

"We're on our way to the hospital," says Maggie. Her arm's in a sling, with a blanket around her shoulders. "You scared me when you fainted. They said you might have a concussion."

"Oh," I say hoarsely, reaching for my best friend's hand. She squeezes it.

A paramedic places a mask over Mom's face while our ambulance pulls onto a highway, siren blaring.

I try to lift my head for a better look. "Will my mother be okay?" I choke out.

"Don't worry, we're taking good care of her," responds the paramedic.

Maggie coughs so hard I expect a lung to fly out. She looks like a drowned rat, but I'm glad she's okay. I'm glad we all are, but I'd feel even better if Mom were awake.

When we arrive at the emergency entrance, we're rushed inside. The paramedics immediately wheel Mom through two double doors that swing shut behind them. One nurse whisks Maggie away to who knows where, while another leads me to a corner of the emergency room. She pulls a blue wraparound curtain around us for privacy.

The nurse helps me climb onto a narrow table, telling me to lie down. I wince when she jabs a needle into the top of my hand to connect it to a bag of liquid. The bright lights burn my eyes. The air is thick with the smell of rubbing alcohol mixed with disinfectant, adding to my discomfort. Squeaky wheels and hurried footsteps echo off the linoleum floors.

My fingers explore the golf ball bump on the left of my forehead as pain throbs my temples, and I feel nauseous. "I have to throw up."

The nurse hands me a plastic bin, and I cradle it in my arms. Out comes half the lake, colored dark green. She takes the bin and leaves the curtained room.

As I lie back, I realize I'm alone. I struggle to breathe; my heart races. The room spins. I grip the sides of the narrow table to steady myself. Tears sting as exhaustion crashes over me.

My world fades once again into darkness.

Chapter 2
Another Kind of Tempest

May 26, 1968, the next morning

Someone lifts something off my forehead. I open my eyes to a nurse bending over me, taping a new bandage into place. Every muscle in my body quivers when I move, so I lie still. My arm is a dead weight as I try lifting it to touch my forehead.

"You had a nasty bump on the head, so leave this dressing in place," says the nurse, smiling down at me. "I'll check on you in a bit." When she leaves, I roll my head to the side to take in the hospital room. Maggie lies in the bed across from me.

"Mags, are you awake?" My gravelly voice makes me sound like a smoker.

She turns toward me and relief flushes through me. "Yeah. How are you feeling?"

"My head hurts." I look around. "Are we at the Butte hospital?"

"No, we're still in Townsend. The doctor says you and I will be released later today, and they'll take your mom in an ambulance to Butte. Your Aunt Daisy drove here when she heard what happened."

"Where is she? Jeez, this feels like *The Twilight Zone*." My eyes roam the unfamiliar room.

"She left to go eat lunch, but she'll be back later to take us home. The doctor told me the boat must have clobbered us when it flipped." Maggie points to her arm. "They put a bunch of stitches in my arm."

"Oh, Mags, I'm sorry." I hesitate. "How's Mom?"

Maggie shifts her blue gaze away from me. "She isn't awake yet."

Alarm pings me. "What do you mean, she isn't awake? She hasn't opened her eyes at all?"

"No." Maggie struggles to sit up, then swings her legs over the edge of her bed.

"Oh, God. What if she doesn't wake up?" I sob, unable to control it.

She limps over and stands next to my bed. "Jo, try not to worry. The doctor explained this happens sometimes when oxygen is cut off from her brain."

"Oh, no, how long was it cut off?" I have no concept of time. The last twenty-four hours are a blur. Wincing from my pain, I swipe at the tears dribbling down my cheeks.

"Where's Roy?" I suddenly remember Mom's new male friend she refuses to call her boyfriend. I call him Roy the Rancher, since he has a big spread near Whitehall.

"He went back to get his boat that washed onshore at Goose Bay," replies Maggie. "He told your aunt he'll visit your mom when she's back in Butte."

"Oh." I feel alone without access to my tiny family.

Maggie sits on my bed. "Remember when we thought Sister Alex would expel us for what we did a few weeks ago? We got through it. We'll get through this too." Our school principal, also our eighth-grade teacher, is a force to be reckoned with.

"Nothing Sister Alex could do compares with what happens if Mom doesn't wake up."

"Don't think like that," admonishes Maggie. "I can't believe you got all three of us to shore. Jeez, Jo, how did you do that?"

"I couldn't have done it without you. I just kept praying we wouldn't die. Thank goodness for our life jackets...." I trail off, remembering how excited we were when Mom and her boyfriend drove us to Canyon Ferry Lake for our camping trip.

"We took swimming lessons because it seemed like fun way back when," I say in a small voice. "Never dreamed it would save our lives." I swipe away another tear. "Maggie, I'm scared."

"Move over." Maggie motions with her good hand for me to make room for her.

I ease myself over and the bed dips when Maggie crawls in beside me. Having her next to me calms me. My hand snakes over to her warm one, and I hang onto it like a lifeline. We both stay quiet, and my eyelids close. The distant beep of hospital monitors fades as my mind drifts to an unsettling event in my past that I wish I could forget.

Images come into focus: Mom's Pontiac Tempest careening along Route Ten, the two-lane highway between Butte and Anaconda. I can almost hear the screech of tires on the asphalt as she loses control—the sickening crunch of metal and glass shattering. In my mind's eye, the car lies on its side in the ditch, the tires still rolling.

I was only seven when Aunt Daisy told me about the crash, but it slammed me the same as when I fell off the cowboy swings at the Columbia Gardens and couldn't get my breath. I remember being terrified of losing my mother, and that same fear is now clawing my insides. The memory fades, but the fear doesn't.

I snap my eyes open to ground myself in the present. Needing a diversion, I tilt my head to study the cracks across the ceiling.

"Remember that book about the French girl who saw a rabbit on her ceiling? This one looks like a fox."

Maggie squints. "Not a fox. It's a cat."

"No, not a cat. Definitely a fox." I fail miserably to keep my voice from trembling. "What if she doesn't make it?"

"Let's wait to see what the doctor says." Maggie is my rock and has been ever since second grade. Her steady presence calms me, as it always has. Her unwavering support reminds me of what we've studied in literature class—friendship, loyalty, and trust—and who you turn to when times are tough.

Another random thought occurs to me. "Mags, remember that Shakespeare story Sister Alex assigned us to read, *The Tempest*? She gave me a 'C' on my test for listing betrayal and forgiveness as the main themes."

Maggie's expression turns quizzical. "Why are you bringing this up right now?"

"I was just thinking how I always miss the obvious," I say, recalling what Sister had scribbled in bright red across my test.

"Well, the main theme was love." Maggie is the brains of our friendship.

"That's what Sister wrote on my test, but how did I miss that?" My fingertips touch my dressing, and I wince. "The storm on the lake was also a tempest. My life feels like one big tempest after another. Do you remember in second grade when Aunt Daisy came to get me?"

"Yeah," says Maggie thoughtfully. "I remember."

"I've always known the real reason Mom rolled the Pontiac Tempest, and it had nothing to do with taking tranquilizers, her drinking, or why she didn't have insurance. It had everything to do with Dad abandoning us on Christmas Day."

"You mean when..." Maggie trails off.

"Yeah." I take a deep breath. "Remember Sister Meanie's class?"

Maggie chuckles. "How could I forget? She was unforgettable. And not in a good way."

"She was a..." I scan the open doorway to make sure no one hears. "A real bitch. There, I said it."

Maggie pretends to be shocked by my uttering the 'b' word. Then she chuckles. "I agree with you on that one."

"You have to admit, Mags, not every nun was nice. Not like Sister Alex."

"Why are you thinking about Sister Meanie right now? I remember some stuff, but what else did she do?"

"Okay, since we'll be here a while," I say.

Anything to keep my mind off my mother.

My words spill out in a torrent, a rush of memories taking us back to a different time in a simpler world. The sound of my voice blends with the images in my head.

Maggie listens, and as I talk, I realize how far we've come. We've weathered our own tempests, Maggie and I, and have emerged stronger for it. But this latest one—the boat accident and Mom's condition—is the biggest storm. When my throat tightens, Maggie squeezes my hand as I pray for the strength to face what lies ahead.

Whatever that may be.

Chapter 3
The Pagan Babies

December 1961, Seven years earlier in second grade

Our orange, four-story apartment house perched high on West Galena Street, directly across the alley from St. Michael's School, in uptown Butte. It loomed like a great pumpkin compared to the other normal-sized houses on our street. Lilac bushes encircled our home and every June their scent was so overpowering it felt like we lived inside of a grandmother's perfume factory.

Our backyard consisted of a narrow slab of concrete with five cement steps leading down to the cracked alley below. Our glassed-in back porch was the delivery spot for the milk man who delivered two bottles of milk twice a week. It was my job to bring them inside before they froze.

Whenever I stepped outside, my gaze was automatically drawn to the gigantic mountain, like a silent friend protecting our town. In the summer, it was green and blue. During winter, it put on a polar bear coat. Dad called it the East Ridge and said it was part of the Continental Divide. I never understood why continents were divided in half.

Last July, Dad couldn't wait to show us where they were filming for the *Route 66* TV show. He worked with a miner who owned the house up on Copper Street where they filmed. On our Sunday drives, Dad would drive up, hoping to glimpse the actors. One Sunday, a guy came out, and Dad was happy to get his autograph.

He always took our big, blue Buick to the same Texaco station on East Galena Street. From the back seat, I'd watch men in hats rush out to help us after the two bells ding when our front and back tires roll over the black hose. They'd wipe the windshield and put the nozzle in Dad's gas tank. After he handed money to the man in the green shirt with the star, we'd drive away singing the jingle: *You can trust your car to the man who wears the star... the big, bright Texaco star!*

Two memories of my dad stand above the rest. The first was when an earthquake shook our apartment house when I was five, and I was scared it would cave in on us. Dad had lifted me from my bed and carried me outside to the front porch. Along the way, Mom's pretty blue vase full of red and pink roses fell to the floor and shattered while the walls heaved around us.

The rumbling underground terrified me as we all stood on our long front porch. I clung to the railing and held my breath while Dad hung onto me. Our front windows rattled, and across the street, the Winston cigarettes billboard waved at us. Our tenants had rushed outside, and we watched blossoms drop from our rose bushes. I never liked the scent of roses after that.

The 1959 earthquake was centered near West Yellowstone, where a mountain slid down on top of the campers at the Hebgen Lake campground. Dad was surprised that we'd felt it in Butte, one hundred fifty miles away.

Another memory of my dad that stands above the rest is when I tried to save the pagan babies. It started on a chilly December day in Sister Anastasia's classroom and ended with an ass-whooping from Dad.

Sister Anastasia was crabby, so we named her Sister Meanie, because she was, well, mean. One day she made an important announcement.

"Children, we must save the pagan babies because they aren't baptized in the Catholic Church. Only a baptized baby can go to heaven. If not, they go to limbo." Her voice carried the weight of a holy mission. Sister Meanie told us we must sell Christmas seals at a dollar a book to earn money for the pagan babies. And didn't we want to outsell the other grades and save the most pagan babies?

Sister told us Christmas seals were stickers with the Holy Family that we'd lick and place on the back of our Christmas cards. She claimed without these seals, the envelopes would burst open and cards would escape, never reaching anyone. I pictured sad and lonely Christmas cards scattered around the post office, and people getting the empty envelopes.

A Christmas disaster!

THE NEXT DAY AT RECESS, I played with Mary Margaret Houlihan and Catherine Delaney on the big playground swings. The three of us got along so well I started inviting them over after school, and their moms said yes, since I lived right across the alley from St. Michael's. Playing at my house became routine—Mom liked having my friends around because she knew where I was and stayed out of her hair.

Maggie insisted on her nickname, not Mary Margaret, as the nuns called her. She was skinny, with shiny red hair and the bluest eyes I'd ever seen. She told anyone who would listen that her grandparents were from Galway, Ireland. Each day her mom French-braid her long hair, and Maggie chewed on her braids during reading and arithmetic. Sister said she'd get hair balls like a cat if she didn't stop. Maggie was really smart and told me things I didn't know.

Catherine Delaney, or "Cat" as we called her, was forever on the move, playing hopscotch, or threatening boys with fat lips if they bothered the girls. She was the playground cop because she had three brothers and took no guff. Cat's mom French-braided her golden hair tight to her head, leaving the rest of her hair hanging loose, like two wild horse tails. Maggie and I loved Cat's fun-loving, melodic laugh.

After recess, Sister held a shiny medal up to the class. "This is the Pagan Baby Medal. If you sell the most Christmas seals in the class, we will award you this medal!" Sister told us pagan babies even lived in Butte, and we all gasped. I thought they were on the other side of the world.

Breathless delight circulated the room, with oohs and ahs, as Sister displayed the medal to one side of the class, then the other. Oh, did I ever want that medal with the Pope on it, blessing the pagan babies! I exchanged glances with Maggie and Cat, as we wondered the same thing: how could pagan babies be living right here in Butte?

Sister didn't say, so I asked Dad that night after dinner. He laughed and told me the pagan babies were kept at the Anaconda Copper Mining Company. He always referred to it as "The Company."

"Oh, my goodness, do they put the pagan babies down in the mines?" I inquired in wide-eyed wonder.

"No, JoJo, The Company keeps them in the hoist rooms next to the gallus frames above ground." The twinkle in Dad's eye gave him away. What a relief! At least they'd have clean diapers and fresh milk.

"Who changes their diapers?" I persisted.

"The bosses at The Company," Dad's Irish lilt kicked in as he winked at Mom. That must mean someone took loving care of the pagan babies.

I got up bright and early the next morning, excited to go to school. I ran across the alley and bolted up the stairs to go to my classroom. After hurriedly removing my jacket and boots, I dashed to my desk and sat up straight, eager and willing.

After the bell rang and we said the Pledge of Allegiance, Sister announced, "For every five dollars you get for the Christmas seals, you may sponsor a pagan baby and choose a name. It must be a saint's name." She explained that the money and the names go to the priests in charge of baptizing pagan babies.

I raised my hand. "Sister, do we pick a girl's or a boy's name?" I glanced around the classroom, proud that I was asking a smart question.

"First, we will choose a boy's name—then a girl's name," explained Sister with a wave of dismissal.

I thought for a second, then raised my hand again.

"Yes, what?" Sister tapped her foot.

"Why can't we choose a girl's name first? Like, Bridget?"

Sister gave me a hard look. "Because there are more boy pagan babies than girl pagan babies."

"Oh." Puzzled, I pictured the boy pagan babies crawling around, pulling off each other's diapers and wreaking havoc at the Anaconda Copper Mining Company.

Sister gave each of us five booklets of Christmas seals with stern instructions. "When you knock on doors, you tell people each booklet is one dollar. Do not lose them, or you must pay for them yourself. Bring in the money after you sell them. And woe betide those who do not follow these instructions."

Sister Meanie's bushy brows pulled together into a fierce frown. Nuns instilled the fear of God in us right away, to set the tone for the rest of our student careers at St. Michael's School.

I tucked the five booklets carefully into my pencil case and zipped it closed. After school got out, I waited in the coatroom for Maggie and Cat, and we planned our strategy to get a pagan baby medal.

We were on a mission from God and Sister Meanie.

"Okay, let's go to my house so you can call your moms." I rushed to put on my snowsuit, boots, and mittens and the three of us hurried out into the cold and across the alley to my house. I was on a mission: save the pagan babies and prevent a post office catastrophe.

The weight of the world was on my shoulders.

Chapter 4
Score One For the Pagan Babies

December 1961

"Mom, we need to go sell our Christmas seals," I called out as we burst through the back door. "Sister says we must save the pagan babies. It's a buck a baby."

"Is that a fact?" Mom's mouth twitched as she lit an unfiltered Lucky Strike cigarette.

She exhaled her smoke in a long, smooth trail, then spat out pieces of tobacco. She plucked a stiff shirt from the grotesque tangle of petrified clothes she'd unpinned from the clothesline. A pile of wooden clothespins sat next to the frozen stack on the table.

"Can we go sell them now?" I figured Maggie and Cat would help convince her. I'd learned it was harder for Mom to say no when my friends were there to plead my case.

Mom glanced at the clock. It was three-thirty.

"You better get home on time or there will be hell to pay. That gives you kids two hours." Mom pointed her finger at me. "Got that?"

Why do grown-ups point like that? Don't they know we hear them without the finger?

Mom's Number One Rule was to *always* be home by five-thirty in the winter, when it gets dark, no matter what. If I showed up one second after, I'd get spanked with the yellow yardstick Dad had christened "Mr. Whackenstick."

Maggie and Cat called their moms for permission. We were already bundled up like Michelin men, but Mom wrapped crocheted scarves around our necks and faces for extra measure. She gave each of us a plastic bread bag to keep our precious Christmas seals dry.

"Put the money in these envelopes and keep them in your coat pockets. Don't lose the money." Mom handed us each a small white envelope. "Stay on Galena and don't go past Excelsior Street. Those are your boundaries."

"Okay, bye, Mom!" I was in gleeful anticipation of the pagan babies I'd save.

"Bye, Mrs. Wolohan!" yelled Maggie and Cat, as we gingerly stepped down the ice-covered concrete steps, clutching the black metal railing and venturing into the bleak light of the late afternoon.

"Let's start with our next-door neighbor," I suggested.

We stepped up onto the icy stoop and rang the doorbell. I peered through the frosted window on the side of the door, and a light flicked on. A figure moved toward us and opened the door.

"Hi, Mrs. McGuire. We're selling Christmas seals to save the pagan babies," I explained.

"Save the who?" Mrs. McGuire wrinkled her face.

"The pagan babies. If you buy a booklet of Christmas seals, it will save a pagan baby," I explained.

"What the hell are pagan babies?" Mrs. McGuire narrowed her eyes. "Is this for the nuns or the priests?"

"It's for the pagan babies," Maggie piped up earnestly.

"You kids shouldn't be out when a blizzard is on the way." Mrs. McGuire peered up at the darkening sky. "All right, I'll take two, since your mother mends my dresses," she said impatiently.

I handed her two booklets of seals, and she handed me two one-dollar bills. Dutifully, I stuffed the bills into my envelope and jammed it into my plastic bread sack.

"You'd better go back home. There's a storm coming." Mrs. McGuire waved us off her porch.

"Heavens to Murgatroyd! I saved two pagan babies!" I was elated.

"Uh-oh, look!" Cat pointed at a station wagon sliding sideways down the icy street. Cars were parked on both sides of the street with their fronts touching the sidewalk. I always thought it was 'angel' parking, but Dad said it was 'angle' parking.

Whatever it was, this station wagon was about to crash into the parked cars. We covered our mouths and watched as the car spun in a slow circle, then stopped at the bottom of the hill. By some miracle, it missed all the other cars.

"Wait, you guys. I have to see what time it is." I halted and stooped to set my plastic bag on the snow while I took off my mitten to check the princess watch Dad gave me last Christmas. The big hand was on the golden pumpkin carriage and the little hand pointed at the glass slipper.

I brushed away pesky snowflakes. "How can it still be three o'clock?" I tapped the face of the watch. "Oh no! My watch stopped!" I glanced up in horror at Maggie and Cat. "Do you guys know the time?"

"You always forget to wind your watch," lamented Cat, lifting her arms and dropping them to her sides.

"Let's ask someone what time it is." I itched to make more sales and motioned to a nearby house. "Hurry, ring the doorbell."

We rang three doorbells in a row with no answer. Giant flakes stuck to us as we trudged through deep powder piling high on the sidewalk.

The next few houses on Galena Street didn't have lights on, but we rang the doorbells anyway, without luck. We were halfway to Excelsior Street, and I'd only sold two booklets, with three left to sell!

Snowflakes stung our faces as we slogged through knee-high drifts to Excelsior Street. Church bells played a muffled five o'clock medley of Christmas carols.

Oh no, we only have thirty minutes to sell the rest of our Christmas seals and get home!

It was getting dark and harder to see where we were going.

"We have to hurry!" My voice wiggled as I pushed through the heavy drifts. Suddenly, my feet flew out from under me, and I landed flat on my back. I rubbed my eyes, trying to see.

"Hey, you guys! Help me!"

Cat and Maggie peered down at me, laughing as I peeked up from the snowdrift that had swallowed me whole. They each took an arm and helped me get to my feet. We looked like snowmen as stubborn flakes glued more layers onto us.

We continued knocking on doors, but no one bought anything. Defeated, I let out a dejected sigh and glanced at my two cohorts holding their plastic bags.

I took off my mitten when panic slammed me so hard I lost my breath.

"Where is my bag? Oh, no!" I was frantic. My plastic bread bag with the booklets and money envelope was gone. "My Christmas seals! I forgot to pick up my bag when I looked at my watch," I wailed in a panic, turning around to slog back the way we came.

"We can't go back! You'll never find it," yelled Cat.

I blindly slogged through piles of snow, but when you're only three and a half feet tall, the towering drifts may as well be a castle wall.

"If I don't find them, Sister Meanie will kill me deader than a doornail. I can't go to school without my Christmas seals or my money," I babbled hysterically, overcome with gut-wrenching sobs. The cold had seeped underneath my sopping wet coat when I stopped walking and wind-driven snow stung my face.

My friends stood there, watching me cry. Second graders weren't exactly experts in the consolation department. Cat and Maggie still had their plastic bags, but I didn't!

The streetlights had turned on, but we couldn't tell which street we were on because the signs were covered up. Blowing snow nipped our faces and walking seemed insurmountable. I prayed we wouldn't freeze to death.

As Charlie Brown always said, I was doomed. I'd lost everything. I was in big trouble.

A dark, snow-covered shape with dim lights moved slowly along the street. The driver's window was open, and I heard Dad's voice.

"Josephina Wolohan! Get in this car! Now!"

Mr. Delaney stepped out of the passenger's side in a long brown coat and moved toward us.

"Dad!" Cat cried out.

He escorted her to sit in the back seat, then motioned Maggie and me to get in beside Cat.

Our lips quivered from the cold, but mine trembled from fear, too. I blubbered about my lost Christmas seals and how much trouble I'd be in with Sister.

"You have more to worry about than Sister, young lady," Dad muttered, shifting into gear for the drive home.

After dropping off Cat and her dad, a car slid through a red light and Dad slammed on his brakes. Luckily, the car missed us. He drove Maggie home through the blinding snow to Copper Street and waited until she went into the house.

The only sound in the car on our way home was the wipers swishing sticky snow on the windshield. When Dad parked and set the brake, his silence was heavy. I climbed out numb and exhausted, trudging up the snowy steps into the house.

I was in for it.

"I told you five-thirty. You disobeyed me!" Mom was angry as she yanked off my snowsuit and boots, annoyed with my missing mitten. She snatched my wet clothes and stomped into the kitchen.

I stood next to the heat register in the front room, so I could stop shivering, but it only got worse when I saw Dad unbuckling his belt. He slid it from his belt loops and grasped it by the buckle, the leather dangling to the floor.

He steadied his gaze on me. "JoJo, do you understand why I'm doing this?"

I gave him a sad nod, since it did no good to say anything.

"Five whippings, because you were told to be home at five-thirty," he admonished.

I squeezed my eyes closed, biting my lip as Dad walloped me. Thank goodness I still wore my long pants. I couldn't understand how he could do this when he always said he loved me. Right then, it sure didn't feel like love.

"I'm sorry, Daddy!" I sobbed, tears blurring everything.

"I know, JoJo," he said quietly. "Now go to your room and think about what you did."

I ran to my room and flung myself onto my bed. Because of me, the Butte post office would face disaster, the pagan babies wouldn't be saved, and I wouldn't get a medal—all while facing Sister Meanie's dour-faced wrath.

I woke the next morning, not wanting to go to school, so I faked a stomachache. I told Mom I had a sore throat, too. I was too chicken to face Sister Meanie about my lost Christmas seals and money.

Mom didn't buy it. She made me get dressed and eat breakfast. I forced down my soft-boiled eggs and toast as best I could, but my stomach wanted to send them back up.

"Hurry, you'll be late." Mom held out my snowsuit that she'd dried. I put it on and tugged on my boots.

She handed me an envelope. "Give this to Sister. It's from your father. *Don't lose it.*" Mom straightened and tightened the belt on her pink chenille bathrobe, the 'L' displayed in cursive on one side of her chest.

I stared at the sealed envelope, dying to know what my parents had put in it. I thought about peeling it open to see when I got away from the house. The back door was hard to open in the tall snowdrifts, and I couldn't tell where the steps were. I edged to the first one and inched my way down, kicking snow off each step. The snow in the alley and on the playground was nearly as tall as I was, but I waded through it to the school door.

It was locked and I let out a howl after all the work it took to get here.

"Mary Josephina!" called out Sister Meanie, poking her square habit out of the back door of the convent. She motioned me over. "There's no school today, young lady." The nuns called all the girls in my class Mary because the pope declared 1954 The Marian Year, to honor the Blessed Virgin Mary. Didn't matter what our real names were, we were Mary at school.

"Okay." I pulled the envelope from the pocket of my snowsuit. "My mother told me to give you this." I hadn't peeked at the contents, so I had a tough time letting go as Sister's hand closed around it.

We had a slight tug of war until Sister frowned. "You can let go, now, Mary."

I let go and Sister opened it, lifting a five-dollar bill. "You sold all of your Christmas seals?"

I stood dumbfounded, nodding like a doofus at the miracle inside the envelope. Curious, I stood on my tiptoes to peer into it. "Is that all that's in there?"

"Yes." Sister's mouth inched up in approval. "You've saved five pagan babies! You just might win that medal."

"Yes, Sister." I was too stunned to say much else.

"Go home, and I'll see you tomorrow." She tucked the envelope into the recesses of her black skirt, then closed the door and left me standing there with my mouth open.

"Okay," I said to the closed door, baffled by what my parents did. I heaved a sigh of relief. I wasn't in trouble with Sister Meanie after all—she thought I sold all of my Christmas seals!

Not only that, five pagan babies were saved!

As I lumbered through the drifts toward my back door, the sun's glare reflected off the snow beneath a deep blue sky. I flopped onto my back to make a snow angel, thanking the guardian angel who'd spared me from today's potential nun catastrophe. I knew Mom and Dad couldn't afford what they did today. They always argued about paying bills and the school tuition at St. Michael School.

I would be sure to thank Dad for the Christmas seal money when he woke up after working the graveyard shift at the Mountain Con. I stepped inside our comfy house, stomping snow from my boots. With both parents asleep, I tiptoed to my room, undressed, and slipped into bed.

I dreamed I saved pagan babies by the hundreds with names like Teresa, Luke, and Bridget. Each pagan baby flew around, their feathery wings fluttering as they giggled in their downy-soft diapers. They gorged themselves on milk until it dribbled down their chins, and I was comforted they were safe and happy.

And just like Dad said... the pagan babies lived happily ever after at the Anaconda Copper Mining Company.

Chapter 5
Day Two of Lilly's Coma

May 26, 1968, afternoon, the day after the accident
The Townsend hospital releases us and Aunt Daisy drives Maggie and me back to Butte in her '57 Chevy. We follow the ambulance carrying my mother, and I watch it the entire way. I recall yesterday's nightmare in disbelief. I'm sure Maggie feels the same. Our shared traumatic experience will forever be seared into our memories.

We drop Maggie off at her house up on Copper Street, and Aunt Daisy takes me home to get my school uniform and some other clothes, my toothbrush, and other stuff. Next, Aunt Daisy drives us from Galena Street down the hill to the Silver Bow Homes. I'm staying at her place for the time being. Once I settle in, we drive to St. James Hospital.

Aunt Daisy leads the way to Mom's room and taps on the door. A nurse appears, and a doctor stands at the foot of Mom's bed, staring at a clipboard.

"Hello, Doctor Madison, remember me? Lilly Rose Wolohan's sister? And this is Josephina, Lilly's daughter," says Aunt Daisy, stepping into the sterile-smelling room. I nearly choke on the fusion of her Shalimar perfume mixed with disinfectant and bleach.

He lifts his gaze and beams at her. "Good evening, Daisy. How are you?"

A playful grin spreads across her face, increasing my curiosity. In Butte, everyone acts like they know each other even when they don't. Daisy seems already acquainted with every man she meets. When I ask how she knows them, she says the same thing with a dismissive wave. "From work, the store, or the Winter Garden Bowling Lanes." The men in Butte must go to all three places.

"Let's step out for a moment and I'll explain what's going on with Lilly," says Dr. Madison.

We follow him out to a barren hallway that reeks of antiseptic and pee. I wrinkle my nose. Down the hall, someone screams, which rattles me more than I already am.

The doctor sizes me up with a doubtful look, like I'm not old enough to hear the medical information.

"I'm fourteen years old," I tell him. "I can handle this."

He glances at Aunt Daisy, who nods. "We've x-rayed Lilly's skull to check for fractures and injected dye into the blood vessels to detect hemorrhages. We think Lilly suffers from a brain ischemia, a condition resulting from less blood flow because her oxygen supply was disrupted. Sometimes this happens with near-drowning victims. We have to wait and see how she responds to treatment."

"How do you mean—wait and see?" Daisy asks haltingly, a hand to her mouth.

He blows out air. "Medical technology improves day by day, but we don't know how severe her injuries are, given the procedures we currently have available."

I have trouble following his explanation. "What did you call it? A brain—"

"Ischemia," he finishes. "Your mother's brain was deprived of oxygen for a spell. How long was she underwater? Was it longer than five minutes?" he asks.

Panicked tears well up and spill over. "I—I don't know," I stammer, trying to remember. "Everything happened so fast. I can't remember how long it took to find her and get her face out of the water. Seemed like forever."

"I understand you and your friend are heroes." He removes his glasses and rubs the lenses with a hanky. "You swam your mother to shore. That was an amazing rescue in a storm like that." He hands me his hanky so I can wipe a tear from my cheek.

"Thanks. Well, Maggie and I had lifeguard training a few years back," I tell him, returning his handkerchief.

"Good thing," he says, taking it. "You saved your mother, and that is a huge deal."

"We're all proud of Jo," gushes Aunt Daisy, placing her hand on my shoulder.

"And Maggie," I add. "So what happens now?"

"We're doing everything we can for Lilly," Dr. Madison assures us. "We're waiting for signs of improvement. We suspect her brain tissue is swollen. We're giving her oxygen and monitoring her for changes in her level of consciousness. We're also sedating her with intravenous fluids, to reduce the swelling."

"Oh." I defer to my aunt, who focuses on the doctor.

"So, she's in a coma?" I detect a hint of hysteria in Aunt Daisy's voice and unease prickles my skin.

"I'm afraid so," replies Dr. Madison, stepping toward me. "Let's have a look at that contusion on your forehead."

I stand still while he works the dressing loose and examines it. "Quite a bump you have. Does it hurt?"

"Not unless I touch it," I tell him.

He chuckles. "So don't touch it. You had a mild concussion. Take it easy in the next few days. No swim meets or doing a fifty-yard dash, okay?" He takes a small bottle of Bayer aspirin from his jacket pocket and shakes out two tablets. "Take these, then two more at bedtime." He motions to a water fountain across the hall.

"Thanks." I pop the aspirin in my mouth and suck in water to wash them down.

"One thing, though," says Dr. Madison. "It does coma patients good when you sit and talk to them. Familiar voices can stimulate the brain, especially from loved ones."

"Good. We'll talk to her," says Aunt Daisy. "Thank you, Dr. Madison."

He disappears down the hall and we enter Mom's hospital room. She's so peaceful lying there with the oxygen mask over her nose and mouth. Her cheeks are pale, not the usual flush, and this worries me. Aunt Daisy moves up behind me and squeezes my shoulder.

"Be brave for her, Jo. Your mother needs you more than ever right now."

Tears threaten and I force them back. "I know."

Aunt Daisy pats my arm. "I'll leave you alone with your mom now while I go to the smoker's lounge."

"Thanks, Aunt Daisy." I wish I could hug away the worry on her face. Then, sudden panic smacks me at the thought of being alone with my mother. "What if Mom has problems breathing or something?"

Aunt Daisy dips her chin at a red button on the wall. "Press that and someone will be here in a flash. Be back in two shakes of a lamb's tail." My aunt ducks out of the room, her heels clicking down the hall.

I drag a chair over to sit next to Mom's bed. I don't know what to say to her, and the words stick in my throat. I wish Sister Alex were here. She'd know the perfect thing to say.

My feelings are a messy ball of twine. One minute I'm loathing my mother for things she did in the past, and the next I'm grinning at something funny she said before our boat capsized. I'm not sure what I should be feeling right now.

The rhythmic beeping of machines echo as I reach for Mom's hand. I give it a slight squeeze. It feels fragile, unlike the hand that skillfully rolls out dough for meat-and-potato pasties or resolutely presses a steaming iron onto stubborn wrinkles of clothes on an ironing board.

"Hi, Mom," I say timidly. "I hope you can hear me. The doctor said you might. Please know that I'm here, okay?" It felt weird talking to her like this.

I pause to gather my thoughts. "I know things weren't always easy for you and Dad," I begin, resisting the urge to break down in sobs. I take a moment to regain my composure. I don't want my mother thinking I'm a blubbering idiot.

"I'm sorry for the times I got mad at you. I didn't mean it." I pat her hand. "Mom, please wake up. I promise I'll be better. I'll help more around the house..."

A tap on the door interrupts me, and Maggie pokes her head in. "Hey Jo, is this a bad time?"

"No! Come sit with me," I say quickly, relieved she's here. "I planned to call you."

"My mother gave me a ride." Maggie has never referred to her mother as 'Mom.' It was always 'my mother.' With one arm in a sling, Maggie drags a metal chair across the floor, the loud, long squeak an assault to my ears. She sits next to me.

"Thanks for coming, Mags. I'm so glad you're here. How's your arm?"

"Have to keep the bandage on for a while." She attempts to lift it and grimaces. "It hurts when I do this."

"Then don't do that," I chide with a lopsided smile.

"Well, duh." She gives me her classic eyeroll and nudges her black-rimmed, Coke-bottle glasses higher on her nose. "How is she doing?"

"Dr. Madison says there's no change." I try my best to hold it together. Even if I can't, Maggie won't think less of me for it. We've been through everything together.

Maggie peers at Mom's face. "She looks a heckuva lot better than she did at the lake. Sister Alex called my mother when she heard what happened. She asked if you'll be at school tomorrow."

"Aunt Daisy thinks I should go, but I want to be here if Mom wakes up."

"Don't say if, say when," admonishes Maggie. She adjusts her glasses with the back of her hand. "There's only two weeks left of school. You have to finish out the year if you want to graduate. Where is your aunt?"

I tilt my head toward the door. "In the smoker's lounge having a cig." I flick my eyes up at the wall clock. "She'll be back when visiting hours are over. Stay and she'll give you a ride home."

"Okay. I'll tell my mother she doesn't have to come get me." Maggie moves to the black rotary phone and dials.

Her words fade while my attention stays on Mom. In my heart, I will my mother to wake up and ask me how my day was.

I don't want to be an orphan. I'm not grown up enough for that.

When Maggie replaces the receiver, she sits down and silence kicks around as we struggle for words.

I have to say it, or I'll burst. "I'm scared, Mags. What if she doesn't wake up?" Tears sting and threaten to fall, and I blink them back.

"We've shared lots of scary things that have happened, but we got through it together. We'll get through this too." I can always count on Maggie to cheer me up, no matter how bad things get.

"Yeah, but this is different." I manage a weak smile. "You've come a long way from the girl in second grade who lost her cool every ten minutes."

Maggie's mouth slides up. "Now I only lose it every *fifteen* minutes. That's progress." She pats my hand. "Jo, you're strong, like your mom. You'll both be okay. Blessed be the mothers in comas, for they probably hear everything we say." Ever since I'd known Maggie, she had a beatitude for everything.

"You think?" I chuckle at Maggie's pearls of wisdom. "Houlihan, you aren't too shabby for someone who claims the Beach Boys are better than the Beatles and who insists Ilya Kuryakin is cuter than Napoleon Solo in *The Man from U.N.C.L.E.*"

"I'm attracted to rock stars and actors with blond hair." Maggie holds up two Tootsie Pops and I choose the root beer one. "You always tell funny stories, so tell me about your mom and dad when you were little. Maybe it'll wake up your mom."

"You think?" I steady my gaze on Mom, lying peacefully while Maggie and I shoot the breeze. I drift back to my earliest memories, the days of raucous laughter and smiling faces.

I wish more than anything I could bring it all back.

Maybe this way I can.

Chapter 6
The Animal Bars

December 1961

My mother's favorite story to tell was how lucky of a gambler I was before I'd learned to walk. She loved bragging about this to anyone who would listen. Dad always joked that I was a lucky little ankle-biter.

Along with my parents, I became a regular at uptown beer joints, but not for the milk. Mom and Dad would perch me on the sticky wooden bar with my baby rattles, where they kept a close eye on me among the beer nuts and pints of Butte Beer dotting the long wooden bar. While other babies were mastering peek-a-boo, I'd developed a talent with punchboards.

According to Mom, I'd sit in my diaper stabbing at paper-filled holes with the metal pin, like a seasoned gambler. Most kids waited until kindergarten to develop vices. The regulars were tickled pink to see a little rug-rat racking up wins while clutching a rattle.

After I'd punch out five or ten little accordion papers with the big numbers on them, Dad would dig into his pants pocket for coins to pay for my punches. Sometimes he'd laugh. "Good Job, JoJo! You won! You Won!" and the bartender would give my dad money instead.

"Hey everybody! Our baby is a good luck charm!" Dad would happily boast.

Delighted by his reaction, I'd crawl along the shiny wood bar to the next punchboard and gleefully punch papers for other beer-guzzling gamblers. They'd grab their cans of beer so I wouldn't knock them over. People called me Lucky Punch Baby.

The bars had animal names: The Eagles, The Moose, and The Elks Club. The loud grown-up regulars were one big gulping, burping family who loved drinking lots of beer. I saw no real moose, elk, or eagles—just dead animal heads with pointy antlers that made creepy shadows on the walls.

Most of the time, my parents went to the Eagles bar. I didn't trust the scary stuffed eagle perched high on a tree branch above the shelves of Christian Brothers brandy, fiercely glaring as if it would swoop down and peck my eyes out.

By the time I was four, Mom and Dad had me wait in the car, and their friends would come out and check on me. When it was cold, they'd leave the engine running with the heater on full blast. The windows would frost over, and I'd draw pictures with my fingernail. I'd entertain myself singing songs with the radio while the 'F.O.E. Eagles' neon sign glowed through the frosted windows.

Whenever Aunt Daisy sat with me, she'd turn on the radio and we'd sing "Crazy," along with Patsy Cline and "All Shook Up" with Elvis Presley. I'd be fast asleep when Mom and Dad finally got in the car. I remember one snowy night I woke up as the car slipped and slid all the way down to Galena Street.

"Whee!" Mom would squeal whenever the car skidded sideways.

One time, we whizzed down a steep alley. By some Jesus-Mary-and-Joseph miracle, Dad didn't crash into the metal trash cans. He exhausted his guardian angel whenever he drove home from the animal bars.

When December rolled around, the animal bars had Christmas parties. The Eagles had the best ones in their backroom. Santa would come and he'd give each kid a red fishnet stocking full of candy, toys, and peanuts.

At age seven, I spent this year's Christmas party gleefully tossing peanut shells onto the floor, creating a crunchy carpet for the other kids and me to stomp on. I gorged on Dixie-cup ice cream and candy-cane taffy while the grown-ups danced to Curly McGillicuddy playing the "Beer Barrel Polka" on his accordion.

When Curly finished playing, Dad fed coins to the jukebox to play his favorite sing-along songs. The first was "Sixteen Tons" by Tennessee Ernie Ford, and the second was "Big Bad John" by Jimmy Dean. Dad and his miner buddies sang about one miner who got stuck underground during a cave-in and saved everyone but himself. It made me anxious whenever Dad and his friends sang it.

The party picked up speed when the grown-ups played "The Twist" by Chubby Checker on the jukebox and did the twist. I danced with them until my side ached. Then they danced the Jitterbug so hard it bounced the hardwood floor, and the gigantic Christmas tree fell over. Dad joked someone had poured whiskey into the Christmas tree stand as he and others lifted the drunken tree upright.

He held hands with me and Mom when we danced to "The Lion Sleeps Tonight." He then danced a slow dance with Mom to "Moon River" and "Can't Help Falling in Love" by Elvis. I loved watching my parents dance. You'd think they did it twenty-four hours a day with their feet moving exactly together. When things slowed down, I curled up and fell asleep on the peanut shells under the tables.

I woke up in my bed, the same mysterious way I've always done after a movie at the Motor-Vu Drive-in. Hollers from the kitchen woke me this time. It was still dark outside as I scrambled from my bed in my foot pajamas, clutching my stuffed dog, Sleepy, and peeked around the kitchen doorway.

Dad was holding Mom up by one arm while the rest of her drooped. "Lilly Rose, you're plastered! Let's get you to bed."

"I'm not going to bed," she slurred, in her full-length slip and nylons as Dad attempted to steady her. She flopped her arms. "Look at me, I'm Raggedy Ann!"

Dad chuckled, but when he let go, Mom slid down his leg and puddled to the floor. "I feel sick. Get me to the bathroom."

"It's too far." Dad eyed the back door. "We'll do it the old-fashioned Montana way." He grabbed Mom's wrists and dragged her over the linoleum and opened the back door. I tiptoed after them, careful to stay out of sight.

When he got Mom out to the porch, I slipped behind the metal hall tree to watch. Dad helped Mom sit on the single concrete step. The frigid air frosted their breath in the moonlight. Mom leaned forward, her body convulsing as she heaved, a guttural sound escaping her lips. Dad sat beside her, holding back her hair. I'd never seen my mother this way, and it frightened me.

"Feel better, Lilly?" Dad asked in a tender voice, smoothing back Mom's dark curls. He pulled a hanky from his pants pocket and gently dabbed the corners of her mouth. "You shouldn't have had that last boilermaker."

Mom placed her hands behind her on the cold concrete and leaned back, pointing her face to the sky. "Sing to me, Leo."

"All right," my dad relented. "But if I do, let me get you to bed."

"Okay. Sing 'Danny Boy,'" she said.

Mom closed her eyes in a dreamy expression as he serenaded her. A tear fell down her cheek. She'd always cried whenever Dad sang this Butte anthem.

"You're a wonderful singer," she purred. "You should be on *Lawrence Welk*."

People might say things about my parents, but one thing was for sure: Lilly and Leo loved each other. They showed it in quirky ways, like crooning to each other outside in the freezing December cold. I wondered if other parents did that.

Mom leaned into Dad, and he rubbed her shoulder as she gazed upward. "Aren't the stars pretty?"

I couldn't see the sky from my hiding spot, but if Mom said the stars were pretty, then they absolutely were. She always called things as she saw them.

"Come on, let's get you into the house." Dad attempted to lift her, but Mom protested.

"I want to stay and look at the stars!" The icy air hung heavy, capturing her breath and frosting it.

A frosty cloud escaped Dad's lips as he let out a weary sigh. "I sang for you, so you have to keep your end of the bargain."

"Just a minute." Mom lay back on the cold step, her gaze fixed on the twinkling stars as if they belonged solely to her. She fell asleep, which angered my father.

"Lilly Rose, get up! Come on, get up, dammit!" Dad yanked her arm to drag her back inside the porch.

My protective instinct kicked in, and I rushed forward. "Don't swear at Mom!"

He spun around and glared. "What are you doing out here? Get back to bed, you little shit!"

When he turned back to Mom, I stayed glued to the porch sobbing, his words still stinging. Dad never swore at me.

He stood looking down at my mother. "Wake *up* Lilly."

She didn't budge.

"All right, stay here, then. I'm going to bed," slurred Dad. He looked at me. "Maybe you can get her to bed." He marched inside the house, leaving the door open.

"Dad! Don't leave her here!" I threw myself over Mom's chest, crying with disbelief that he'd left her out in the frigid cold.

All was quiet, except for Mom's little snores. A dog barked a few houses away, and a car drove down the alley, brakes squeaking as it stopped at the corner. The world seemed normal everywhere else except here. Things were definitely out of whack at the Wolohan residence tonight.

The orange moon turned Mom magical as she lay across the doorway, her smudged lipstick and wild curls catching the starlight. She'd always been pretty, but now she looked heavenly, like she might sprout fairy wings and fly to her stars.

I didn't have the strength to get Mom into the house alone, so I rested my head on her chest and hugged her tight to keep her warm. Despite the chill, I was comforted by her gentle, rhythmic breathing when she put her arm around me.

A pair of hands lifted me off Mom and stood me up. Dad grunted as he lifted her into his arms. He glanced at me, nodding toward the house. "Come on, JoJo, let's get you inside." I followed him and he tucked me in after putting Mom to bed.

I woke up the next morning and wandered into the kitchen. Dad stood at the counter while the newspaper lay folded on the table. I slipped into my usual chair with Sleepy in my lap, while Dad opened the icebox for his buttermilk. While he dug around, I poured my Frosted Flakes, Tony the Tiger smiling at me from the box. I slid my hand inside, digging through the cereal for the prize. Triumphant, I pulled out a wind-up toy and held it up.

Dad's face brightened. "Good job, JoJo. Keep your eyes on the prize!" Dad had an uncanny ability to act as if everything was normal, even when Mom fell asleep outside in the dead of winter.

Dad busied himself with making his hair-of-the-dog concoction. He poured buttermilk into the glass, cracked a raw egg, added tomato juice, then topped it off with a generous sprinkle of pepper. He gave it a quick stir, then sat at the table with me and gulped the whole thing down. I marveled at how he could down that revolting mixture.

He sat back with a satisfied "Ahh," then grinned. "Never eat raw eggs. It's okay for me because I have an iron stomach. Do as I say, not as I do." Every grown-up said this like they all read from the same book, *How to Confuse Kids With Contradictions.*

Dad reached over and tousled my hair, then settled in his chair and snapped open the newspaper. As he disappeared behind the pages, I was content knowing things were back to normal in our quiet kitchen moment together.

That was Dad's special magic.

THREE DAYS LATER, ON Christmas morning, I awoke to the earsplitting sounds of Mom's panicked screams that turned my stomach to ice. I sprang from my bed and dashed to my parents' room to see my father in his PJs lying on the floor next to their bed.

He wasn't moving.

Mom sat with his head in her lap, rocking back and forth, sobbing, her face twisted and red, hair sticking to her wet cheeks. I wanted to run to her, but my feet wouldn't move.

"No! No! No!" she screamed over and over, her raw agony piercing my chest. Mom's gut-wrenching cries were unlike anything I'd ever heard—her primitive wailing terrified me.

Shocked tears flushed out, seeing Dad lying on the floor. Did he fall out of bed in his sleep? Was he drunk?

Then my world shifted into slow motion as Mr. Bloom, one of our tenants, appeared from nowhere. He scooped me into his arm and carried me away. I struggled for one last glimpse of my dad, but Mr. Bloom wouldn't let me see. I don't know where he took me because my memory blanked out after that.

My universe had buckled and folded in on itself as life became a harsh reality. Overnight, I'd changed from a carefree kid to a lost stranger whom I didn't recognize. My dad had vanished without warning, leaving behind a hollow void after his steady presence had anchored me ever since I could remember.

A bitter chill seized the once-warm places of my heart.

Chapter 7
The Christmas That Wasn't

December 1961

Christmas night, Mom appeared dazed and haggard in her oversized armchair, nursing her third can of Butte Beer. Aunt Daisy and Aunt Violet came over to cook our Christmas dinner, but no one had the appetite to eat it, and we only picked at our turkey. Mom said we'd offer the rest to anyone who happened by.

An endless stream of people stopped by our house that night, hugging us and sniffling into their pale hankies with fancy, embroidered initials. The ladies hugged me, while the men stood back, mumbling and shaking their heads.

Many brought casseroles, and others delivered pasties. One lady handed me a bowl of sweet potato salad, and another gave us a loaf of *povitica*, my favorite sweet bread with the yummy nut filling. My aunts busied themselves ferrying the food to the kitchen. Mom thanked everyone for taking time from their families to come over on Christmas.

When everyone had gone, Mom stood in front of the Christmas tree, staring at it as if its life was about to end, like Dad's had.

"What'll I bury Leo in?" she asked her two sisters, who sat on the davenport, dabbing at their eyes with monogrammed hankies. "His blue suit, or the gray? And he'll need a tie..." she trailed off, choking up.

"Blue was his favorite color, wasn't it?" Aunt Daisy responded, puffing her cigarette.

"Yes, the blue," echoed Aunt Violet, sniffling.

Their voices were a faraway dream as I sat cross-legged on our worn gray carpet, watching our black-and-white TV with wiggly lines waving down the screen. A man's voice announced, "Stand by, we lost our signal and have microwave fade."

"Josephina!" Aunt Violet's stern voice startled me from my dazed confusion. "Your mother is talking to you."

Chewing the side of my thumbnail, I glanced at my mother, who stood opening another can of beer. The TV blared with a commercial, a dancing tube of toothpaste singing, *You'll wonder where the yellow went when you brush your teeth with Pepsodent!*

I frowned at the stupid commercial that didn't care my dad had passed away.

"Jo, please get the Christmas gift you wrapped for your father." Mom's voice was especially quiet. She and I had walked over town to Hennessey's, where I'd picked out a blue tie for Dad's Christmas present. The store had wrapped it in silver and blue wrapping paper, and when we got home, Mom ran a butter knife along the skinny ribbon, turning it into curly spirals.

Our sparkling Christmas tree proudly perched before the living room window. The blue light bulbs glittered the long silver tinsel that Mom and I had carefully strung on each branch. I moved to the tree and inhaled the pine smell, picking up the gift my dad would never open.

As if lifting a candle in church, I placed the rectangular tie box in my mother's lap. She stared at it a long moment, holding her cig. Finally, she laid the cig on a glass ashtray and pulled one end of the curly ribbon to untie it. After she unwrapped the gift, a teardrop fell on the brilliant blue tie I'd gotten my father for Christmas.

"He'll wear this." Her voice was tight, and she stood and left the room, abandoning the new tie on her chair and her unspent cig smoking in the ashtray.

"Good choice, Lilly. The blue suit was his favorite," Aunt Daisy called after her, red-eyed and sniffling.

Aunt Violet signaled her approval with a subtle nod and blew her nose.

I couldn't cry. Was I supposed to? I floated on a rolling cloud I couldn't grasp. Dad was gone, but where did he go and for how long? Will he be back? My seven-year-old brain posed too many questions that no one was willing to answer.

The silky tie seemed forlorn in its box on Mom's chair. I stared at the pretty blue tie and felt sorry for it. Aunt Violet left to talk to Mom, and Aunt Daisy stayed still. She held a cig with a hand to her forehead, smoke rising from her long, elegant fingers. The ash got so long it fell to her lap, but she ignored it.

I kept my eye on it to make sure it didn't light her dress on fire. Suddenly, I was anxious about every little thing.

What if our house burns down? What if Mom gets a heart attack? Will I get a heart attack?

The doorbell rang once more, and I dutifully answered it. Monsignor Coyle stood in our doorway, larger than life. "Just a sec, I'll get my mom." I left him standing in the apartment hallway and ran back into our living room.

"Monsignor Coyle is here!" I announced. He was the head honcho in charge of St. Michael parish, that was kitty-corner from our house.

"What is *he* doing here? He doesn't make house calls," Mom grumbled, grinding her cig into the ashtray. "Tell him to come in." She waved away the smoke and heaved out a weary sigh, as if she was about to greet a bill collector.

I ran back to invite Monsignor in, his bumpy, bald head barely clearing the doorway. He took off his hat and held it in front of him with both hands as he approached Mom sitting in her armchair.

"Hello, Monsignor. Excuse me for not standing. I don't have the energy," said Mom.

"Mrs. Wolohan, on behalf of St. Michael Parish, I'm offering you our condolences." His Irish accent was so thick I barely understood him.

"Thank you, Monsignor." Mom motioned him to the other armchair. "Please have a seat. Something to drink?"

"I'll take a brandy." He set his black fedora on the armrest and sat, folding his hands in his lap. "I'm here to inform you of our services."

Mom flicked her eyes to signal Aunt Daisy, who left to pour his drink. Aunt Violet stayed, but she motioned me to leave the room. I pretended to head to the kitchen, then doubled back to assume a listening post in the dining room to hear the grown-ups' discussion. I tried to blend in with the pink-flowered wallpaper while cautiously peeking around the archway.

"I don't want a wake for Leo." Mom's tone was firm as she shredded her crumpled tissue into tiny strips.

Monsignor raised his chin. "A death during the holidays is never expected, Mrs. Wolohan, but the vigil for the deceased is never omitted. There must be a wake." His tone was firm, but kind, despite my mother's stubborn attitude.

Aunt Daisy set a small snifter on the table between the armchairs, then sat on the davenport, exchanging raised eyebrows with Aunt Violet.

"Thank you." Monsignor offered my aunt a curt nod, then picked up the snifter between his fingers, swirling the brandy. "We Irish Catholics hold a vigil and pray over the body of the deceased before the funeral. We did it in the old country and now we do it in Butte."

My gaze tracked to my mother, and I knew that look; it was Mom's *don't-you-dare-tell-me-what-to-do* glare. The same one she'd give my dad whenever he'd tell her to attend Mass with him. Then she'd go on about the way Monsignor Coyle ran things "across the street, nickel-and-diming his parishioners."

I held my breath to see if she'd chew him out. Aunt Violet elbowed Aunt Daisy, their glances darting back and forth between Monsignor and my mother like they expected fireworks.

My mother sat up straight. "I'm well acquainted with what a wake is, Monsignor. You may think I'm a shitty Catholic, but I *have* attended my share of Irish Catholic wakes." She fiddled with her shredded tissue. "I want to know what you'll do for Leo's funeral."

Normally, she'd be lighting up by now, but she probably didn't want to smoke in front of Monsignor on account of it was a sin and she didn't want to go to hell because Dad would be in heaven.

"Leo will have a requiem Mass to honor his soul. As you know, it's a Mass for the dead—"

Mom cut in. "I *know* what a requiem Mass is."

Monsignor continued swirling his brandy. "Mrs. Wolohan, your husband was a good man. We don't charge for this, but we'd appreciate whatever you can donate to the church."

Her mouth formed a straight line, and I could tell she wasn't pleased with him weaseling in the money bit. She gave him a direct look. "I'll agree to a Mass, but as I said, I don't want a wake."

My eyebrows winged up, right along with Monsignor's. No one sassed Monsignor. His word was gospel. No one, that is, except Lilly Rose the Rebel, as Dad used to call her.

Monsignor downed his drink. "I'm afraid without a wake, there will be no funeral." He put on his brimmed hat and stood to go.

Mom folded her arms, and I sensed she was bracing for a standoff. "So, it's an all-or-nothing deal, is it?"

"I'm afraid so." He lifted his chin with authority.

Mom's foot tap-tapped the floor like she was keeping time to a fast song. She crossed to a side table with Dad's photo on it. "What do you think, Leo?" She paused, then turned to face Monsignor.

My gaze tracked to my aunts sitting on the davenport, still as rocks. They appeared to be holding their breath, like me.

"Because Leo was a good Catholic, and out of respect for *him*—I'll allow a wake and a Requiem Mass." She said it with firm control, as if *she* were the one calling the shots.

My aunts let out air, and I did, too.

"Very well. The Church insists on having the funeral and interment as soon as possible after death. The rosary will be the day after tomorrow, after the wake." Monsignor cleared his throat. "I'd like to have things wrapped up by New Year's Eve so the living can welcome in the new year." He set his snifter on the table and offered my aunts a courteous nod.

My mother gave Monsignor a hard look. "I'm sorry my husband's death is such an inconvenience. We certainly wouldn't want to spoil the good people of St. Mike's celebration of the new year, would we?"

Monsignor glossed over her comment, buttoning his long wool coat. "Will you be holding the wake here or at Geraghty's on Park Street?"

"Geraghty's." Mom escorted Monsignor to the front door.

"I am so sorry for your loss, Mrs. Wolohan. Good night. May God bless you." He touched his fedora, then stepped outside into the snowy night.

Mom closed the door behind him and whirled around.

"That man burns me!" she fumed, racing to her pack of Lucky Strikes. She pulled out a cig and fumbled with Dad's metal lighter from one of the animal bars. It wouldn't produce a flame, so she tossed the lighter to a chair, and it clattered to the floor. Aunt Daisy picked it up and instead handed Mom a book of matches.

I darted from my covert listening post. "What did Monsignor mean by a wake? Does that mean Dad will wake up? So, Dad's death isn't a permanent thing?" My tone was hopeful.

Maybe heaven was a place Dad was only visiting. Then he could wake up and return to us!

Mom appeared flustered. "It's—it's—I don't know..." she trailed off and struck a match as if she were lighting a stick of dynamite, the way Dad used to do beneath the Mountain Con mine.

I waited patiently while she blew out a never-ending river of smoke.

"Mom, is a wake where Dad will wake up?" I persisted. "Can I go?"

I chewed my thumbnail, waiting while she took another puff and blew out the smoke. She looked ragged, her face shadowed with dark circles. "You'll go to the wake, but not the funeral. Now get to bed."

That must mean there's a chance Dad will wake up!

Once in bed, I recited as many Hail Marys as I could, so Dad would wake up at this awake thing. I desperately needed our lives to go back to normal, and everything would be the way it was before. Living my life without Dad was unimaginable.

I recited one more Hail Mary and threw in an Our Father to clinch the deal.

Chapter 8
Leo Has Left the Building

December 1961

After breakfast on the morning of the Awake, my aunts and I sat on the davenport in our living room. Mom breezed in wearing a black sheath and matching heels, and I caught a whiff of her Chanel No. 5 she saved for special occasions.

She held out a large flat box. "Open this, Josephina."

I stood to take the box, then squatted on the floor to tear off the gift wrap while Mom sat on the end of the davenport to watch. When I lifted the lid from Hennessey's and pulled the folded tissue away, my mouth fell open at a red velvet dress with a green satin bow and a white lace collar. A crinoline slip peeked out from underneath.

I ran my hand across the plush velvet. "This is so pretty. Thanks, Mom!"

"Your father picked it out weeks ago and asked me to wrap it for you for Christmas." Her voice was strained. "Now put it on and Aunt Daisy and Aunt Violet will take you to Geraghty's. I have to go early to do a few things."

Mom put on Grandma's beaver coat. When I was little, I'd wrap the luxurious fur around me and fall asleep on the floor of her closet.

"Remember, little girls are seen and not heard," Mom said to me, then she was out the door.

I never understood why I was supposed to stand around and not say anything.

My aunts and I bundled up in our winter coats, mittens, and boots. I pleaded with them to please take me to St. Mike's so I could say a prayer for Dad before we went to the funeral home. Snow fell as the three of us walked to church and climbed the wide concrete steps to the double bronze doors. Aunt Daisy opened one, and we ducked inside to the narrow vestibule.

"We'll wait here. Go say your prayers, JoJo," said Aunt Daisy through the black hat net that covered her face.

I gave her a sharp look. "Only Dad calls me JoJo." It came out meaner than I intended.

Aunt Daisy looked surprised, but she nodded. "You're right. I'm sorry."

I walked up the center aisle and lowered myself to a kneeler. Candles flickered in front of the statues of Mary and Jesus on either side of the grand altar, where giant white columns stretched to the ceiling. A colorful mosaic of Michael the Archangel guarded all of it, his sword raised, with wings spread wide.

Dad used to say if it was quiet enough, he could hear God breathing. I listened but heard nothing. I recited a Hail Mary and Our Father, pleading for Dad to wake up, then rose, genuflected, and walked to the back of the church. Aunt Daisy had stepped outside for a cig, so I dipped my hand in the marble font of holy water, crossed myself, and headed outside.

The three of us tramped uphill together in the falling snow. Uptown Butte was dressed for the holidays with wreaths, lights, and red-suited Santas ringing bells outside the liquor store on the corner of Montana and Park. Plastic bells dangled from lines strung across the streets between every intersection.

Constructed during Butte's copper boom, Geraghty's was one of the city's Victorian mansions. The white building had a gabled red roof, while two evergreen wreaths hung with broad scarlet ribbons on each double door. I squinted up at the steep roof, snowflakes catching on my eyelashes.

This must be where they wake the dead.

Groups of people clustered on the snowy sidewalk wearing their Sunday best, smoking cigarettes. People shivered, blowing out frosty smoke. Their conversation stopped as we approached; sad faces and silent nods said everything.

We stepped inside. Mr. Geraghty hung our coats, then guided us up the center aisle to the front row of folding chairs. As I approached Dad's shiny blue coffin, I felt like I was floating in someone else's dream. I stopped, thankful I was too short to see inside. Aunt Daisy put her hand on my back, encouraging me to step onto the kneeler. I squeezed my eyes closed and stepped up.

I opened them to my father resting on pale gray satin, wearing his blue suit with my royal blue tie. The top half of the coffin lid was propped open, and a red satin heart with "Beloved Father" hung on the inside of the open lid. Dad's eyes were closed, and I noticed his curly eyelashes. His hands held the red glittery rosary my godmother had made for him. He looked like he was sleeping.

Dad couldn't be in heaven like the grown-ups said because he was right here. How could he be in both places at once? I squinted at the ceiling for a trapdoor but only glimpsed a crystal chandelier. I waited for Dad to sit up and make faces at me.

Aunt Daisy tapped my elbow, then motioned at a folding chair in the first row. "Sit here."

I stepped back and sat down, with an empty chair beside me reserved for Mom. Aunt Daisy settled on my other side with Aunt Violet next to her. As people filled the rows of folding chairs, I craned my neck, taking in the red and white flowers blanketing the room. The sickening sweetness of carnations and roses made my stomach threaten to empty itself onto the wooden floor.

"Your father loved his gladiolus," murmured Aunt Daisy, nodding at the flowers on either side of the casket.

I busied myself looking for Mom and chewing my thumbnail.

Aunt Daisy brushed my hand away. "Stop that. Your thumb will be deformed."

"I wonder where they get all these flowers this time of year?" Aunt Daisy brushed snow from her petrified bubble-do where she'd unloaded a can of Aqua Net.

"Heated greenhouses," whispered Aunt Violet.

The pungent carnation smell, fused with hairspray and other stinky perfume, pounded my temples. A plump woman wearing a black pillbox hat with a matching fish net over her face played soft music on an organ, while Mom greeted people at the door.

The men stayed mostly quiet while women spoke in whispers and soft voices. "So sorry, Lilly...if there's anything I can do... is that Leo's poor daughter sitting in front? What a shame, and during the holidays..."

According to Aunt Daisy, most of the men had worked with Dad at the Mountain Con Mine. As more people streamed in, it seemed the entire city of Butte knew Leo Wolohan.

My godmother breezed in, her black hair in a Prince Valiant hairdo with ruby-red lipstick that popped off her mouth like *Betty Boop*. The same ruby red glossed her long fingernails, and her fake eyelashes reminded me of black furry spiders. I wondered if they'd leap from her eyelids and scurry away.

Godmother Mary specialized in dramatic entrances. She waltzed up to us, a red fox draped around her neck, ears forward, as if ready to lunge. If her eyelashes didn't attack me, this ravenous fox surely would. Bushy fox tails hung from her stole and waggled when she walked, as if insanely happy to be here.

She spread her arms to engulf me in a hug, and I jerked my head away so the fox wouldn't bite my nose. Her weighty perfume distorted my vision, the room twisting as she cloaked me with her fox-furry arms.

"You poor little dear! Godmother Mary is here to give you a hug." She'd always referred to herself as another person. "Mary is heartbroken about your poor father."

She grabbed my shoulders. "Oh sweetie, aren't you cute as a button? There, there. Don't cry. Mary doesn't like it when you cry." She took out a heavily scented hanky from her red-beaded purse and dabbed at my eyes. They were watering from the weighty perfume she must have bathed in. When she mashed her stinky hanky on my nose, I got dizzy.

"Blow! Now there's a good girl," she crooned, as I goggled at the fox's body parts.

Godmother Mary made rosaries with beautiful, glittery beads. She beaded everything, even her purses. People paid her lots for her glittery rosaries when she lived in Butte. But when her daughter had a baby, she moved to Spokane to be near her family.

More people filed into the Drawing Room wearing festive Christmas corsages on their coats. Each time the front door opened, cheerful Christmas bells rang from a nearby church, their festive tones clashing with the sad organ music inside.

A sudden ruckus sounded in the back, and I craned my neck to see what the fuss was about.

"Shh—be respectful and remove your hats," said Mr. Geraghty to the two men who'd just arrived.

My two uncles, Will and Ollie, staggered in, clutching their Stetsons to their chests. They were decked out in their cowboy best, their dark hair slicked back as if they'd emptied a tube of Brylcream on their heads (*we all knew a little dab would do ya*). They bounced off each other like two rodeo clowns as their lanky bow-legged bodies paraded up the center aisle.

"Christ on a bike! Our brothers are gutter-puking drunk," gasped Aunt Violet as her hand went to her nose and mouth in abject horror.

"Hell's bells, Lilly won't like that," breathed Aunt Daisy. I twisted to see if Mom had seen them, but she'd moved to another room.

Anyone could see they were sloshed. At the ripe old age of seven, I wasn't sure what death was, but I could tell when people were soused on their asses.

As Uncle Will staggered closer, the silver bull with glowing ruby eyes on his bolo tie caught my attention. My uncles wore scrawny black jeans secured by leather belts embossed with horses and lariats, their silver buckles etched with bucking broncs. Gold horseshoe rings—trophies from calf roping and bull riding competitions—glittered on their fingers.

They stumbled to Dad's coffin, holding each other up. When Uncle Ollie tripped on the kneeler, Uncle Will dog-piled on top of him, creating a jumbled heap that took some time to sort as they disentangled to kneel side-by-side. The intense blend of Old Spice, whiskey, and stinky perfume mixed with the overpowering flower scent had me begging my stomach to hang onto itself.

"What are we supposed to say?" Uncle Ollie whispered loudly to his brother.

"Say a damn Hail Mary for cripes' sakes." Uncle Will's belch echoed through the room, and he apologetically made the sign of the cross on himself.

"Hail Mary up in heaven, hallowed be her womb—" slurred Uncle Ollie.

"That ain't how she goes!" interrupted Uncle Will, shoving Ollie off his perch.

"It sure as hell is!" Ollie punctuated his proclamation with a musical belch as he crawled back onto the kneeler.

"Nah—it's Mary, Mary, full of grace—"

Will cut in. "Three little buffalo win the race!" His arm shot up in triumph as if he'd won a bucking bronc event.

Both uncles crumpled with laughter, then sobbed, followed by much throat clearing, sniffling, and hanky-blowing.

Mourners stilled to listen as the organ music continued playing.

Uncle Ollie's Stetson had somehow landed on Dad's chest. Stupefied, Ollie felt his head, then squinted at my dad.

"Leo! You stole my hat!" Uncle Ollie plucked his Stetson from Dad's chest and placed it on Dad's face. "There you go, partner. Have yourself a siesta."

"Aw Leo, why'd ja have to go 'n' die?" wailed Uncle Will, his lower lip distorted.

"Get outta that box, you sumbitch!" yelled Uncle Ollie, as if Dad was lying there just to piss him off. He yowled so loud and long, I expected every coyote in Silver Bow County to howl back.

I hoped Dad would sit up and say, "Shut up or you'll wake the dead!" But he was as unmoving as the Jesus, Mary and Joseph statues in St. Mike's church.

"Who's gonna make the Tom and Jerry's for New Year's?" blubbered Uncle Will, as he pulled a flask from his coat pocket, unscrewed the lid, and took a swig. He handed it to his brother, who did the same.

Uncle Will plucked the Stetson from Dad's face and held the flask under his nose.

"C'mon you Irish fucker, take a whiff and drink up!"

My jaw dropped. Gasps from the women mingled with chuckles from the men. I turned to see Father Murphy's reaction, but he wasn't in the room.

"William, behave yourself, dammit!" admonished Aunt Daisy.

Uncle Will tried prying Dad's mouth open with his thumb and forefinger. When that didn't work, he poured whiskey over Dad's mouth instead. Yellowish-brown liquid ran down the sides of his neck, staining Dad's starched white shirt Mom had sent to the cleaners.

"I said get up, sumbitch! We're goin' to the M&M!" Uncle Ollie grabbed hold of Dad's arm, shaking it as if he were trying to wake him.

The rosary flew from Dad's hand, sailed through the air, and plopped at my feet. I stared at it, knowing my godmother wouldn't approve of her rosary landing on the floor.

Sure enough, Godmother Mary was on her feet, foxtails wagging as she marched up to my uncles. "How *dare* you do that to the rosary I made for Leo! The pope blessed it!" She whirled to face me. "Josephina, fetch that damn rosary and give it to me. No one desecrates a holy rosary!" She acted like a heinous crime had been committed.

I rescued Dad's rosary and handed it to her.

"Both of you are a wretched disgrace!" shouted Godmother May as she shoved my uncles aside and arranged the rosary around Dad's hands the way it was before.

My uncles looked at my godmother as if they'd lost their last friend. "Sorry, Mary," Uncle Ollie mumbled.

By this time, people were standing to get a better view, like they were at the Friday night fights at the Civic Center.

Uncle Ollie grabbed Dad's hand and again tried yanking him from the coffin. "Come on, it's time to party!"

I wondered if Uncle Ollie really thought Dad would spring from his coffin and stroll out the door with them to the nearest bar. He wrestled Dad over to the side of the coffin, and I held my breath to see if he'd get my father out of it. But Uncle Ollie was too blitzed to pick him up. Instead, he shook Dad's hand as if making a business deal.

"Willy, don't be sad," hiccupped Ollie, with an arm around Uncle Will's shoulder. "Be happy Leo is partying with the angels."

"I'm so happy the crack of my ass is whistling a tune." Uncle Will broke into song. "*Mine eyes have seen the glory of the coming of the Lord, He is trampling out the vintage where the grapes of wrath are stored...*" He stood tall, marching in his cowboy boots, like a good soldier.

Uncle Ollie joined in. "*He hath loosed the fateful lightning of His terrible swift sword. His truth is marching on!*"

My uncles couldn't remember the words to the Hail Mary, but they didn't miss a word of the "Battle Hymn of the Republic."

Others joined in, and the organ picked up the melody. "*Glory, glory, hallelujah! Glory, glory, hallelujah! Glory, glory, hallelujah! His truth is marching on...*"

No one seemed to know the rest, but the organ kept playing, like a Cubs game on the radio.

"William! Oliver! What the hell are you doing?" bellowed my mother, marching up the center aisle. It was a miracle how fast Mom moved in her spiky high-heeled shoes. With cheeks that matched the smelly red carnations, she glared at her brothers, and I knew they were goners.

Everyone stayed standing, no doubt expecting another sing-along.

Mom was on her two brothers like a pissed-off mine boss. "Dammit, let go of Leo or *you'll* be the ones pushing up daisies!" Grabbing their collars, she hauled them down the center aisle like puppies who'd peed on the rug.

As Mom lugged her shit-faced brothers to the door, Father Murphy froze with a Christmas cookie halfway to his mouth. He didn't miss a beat as he swung the door open with his non-cookie hand. "Fair play to ya's, boys!" His cheery voice rang out as Mom tossed her brothers out onto the snowy city sidewalk.

"Get out and stay out until you sober up!" thundered Mom. She swiped her hands in a decisive motion, stepped inside, and slammed the door shut.

Mom smoothed her dress, patted her hair, and strode to Dad's coffin. She positioned him back into place, then tenderly smoothed back his hair and wrapped the rosary around his hands.

When she finished, Mom turned to face the room. "Well, doesn't that take the cake? Wait'll Ann Landers hears about this!" Mom liked to read the Ann Landers' advice column out loud to Dad and I every evening. Now, I was the only one left to laugh at it.

Mom's comment broke the tension, and laughter followed. My mother could always be counted on to crack a joke—even with a broken heart at her husband's wake.

When the laughter died down, she continued. "I apologize for my brothers' behavior. They're distraught, as we all are, over Leo's death. Thank you so much for coming today." Mom took the seat next to me and folded her hands in her lap while Father Murphy said some prayers.

When he finished, Godmother Mary rushed over with her furry foxes. "So good seeing all of you." She blew us air kisses, then pointed her scarlet spear-tipped finger at me. "Mind your P's and Q's so you don't wind up like your uncles when you grow up. Come visit me in Spokane. Bye now!"

I dutifully nodded, and she dashed away to talk to my mother. Despite her flouncy manner, I wished my godmother hadn't moved away. Her absence had always felt like a piece of me was missing.

"We have to get to the apartment house," said Aunt Daisy, putting on her long camel-hair coat with the dark fur collar and cuffs. "People will stop by. I made some cocktail pasties and must heat the casseroles and set out the salads people brought over."

At the mention of food, my stomach gurgled. For the first time since Dad's heart attack, I looked forward to eating.

The three of us bundled up and left the funeral home. Mom stayed behind to thank people for coming. Snow continued falling, and I faced upward to catch the flakes with my tongue.

Aunt Daisy stopped to light a cig, then blew out smoke. "Tipsy Sullivan's uncle climbed into the coffin with his wife at her wake," she said to Aunt Violet. "They couldn't get him out, so they threatened to close the coffin with him in it. Should have seen how fast he hightailed it out of there!"

"There's no excuse for what William and Ollie did," said Aunt Violet, shaking her head. "They're an embarrassment to the family. I'm sure they'll hear about it from Lilly."

"You got that right. Jo, when you grow up, don't drink." Aunt Daisy loved dispensing her wisdom. She took a puff, then exhaled fresh blue smoke. "What is your favorite memory of your dad?"

"Sitting in his lap, telling me stories about the war of the copper kings. Did you know they poured whiskey in the gutters to get votes?" I warmed at the memory. "I always pictured them wearing copper crowns and waving copper swords."

Both my aunts laughed, and the sound comforted me.

What I didn't tell them was that I'd miss Dad's Sunday Drives down Montana Street to the Bonanza Freeze for a banana split, or out to the A&W Root Beer Stand on Continental Drive for frosties and baby mugs of fresh root beer....our trips to the Columbia Gardens where I played inside the yellow and green playhouse, then got on the cowboy swings while Dad yelled, "Higher, JoJo!"

Aunt Daisy switched to a serious voice. "Jo, your mom thinks it's not a good idea to have you go to your dad's funeral and burial at St. Patrick's cemetery. What do you think?"

I hesitated, not used to being asked what I thought about *anything*.

It was traumatizing enough seeing Dad lying in the coffin, let alone what the burial would be like. "I don't want to see him go into the icy ground. He'll get so cold down there..." I burst into tears, unable to deal with that wretched thought.

Aunt Daisy squatted and hugged me tight to her chest. We stayed that way in the falling snow until my sobs calmed down. "It'll be okay, Josephina. I promise." She brushed back my snow-drenched bangs and wiped tears from my cheeks with her gloved thumb. "Come on, let's get you home."

I'd cried so hard my breathing came in ragged hitches, wrenching my body and aching my chest, leaving me gasping for air.

Aunt Daisy let go of me and stood and dropped her cig to the snowy sidewalk. She squeezed my hand. "You have the crying jags. Don't worry, they'll eventually stop."

My hope that Dad would wake up was gone... I finally understood death was permanent. Mom wouldn't be making his lunches with liverwurst sandwiches wrapped in wax paper, then tucking them inside his black metal lunch pail with two hard-boiled eggs. I wouldn't be bringing him newspapers and glasses of buttermilk. No more sitting in his lap listening to stories about Butte's copper kings.

From now on, I'd have to learn how to grow up and live without him.

For the rest of my life.

Chapter 9
Day Three of Lilly's Coma

May 27, 1968, in the present

Going back to school today gets my mind off my mother. At lunchtime, Maggie, Cat, and I cross the alley to eat at my house. Aunt Daisy had given me the key to get into our apartment, where I make chicken noodle soup and baloney sandwiches for lunch.

Maggie and I are glad to take a break from school. We're tired of answering questions about the boat accident, and we don't want to relive it every ten seconds. Cat ran interference for us like a referee at this morning's recess, shooing kids away so we could get some peace.

"I was thinking about last night when you talked about the tough time you had when your dad died," says Maggie. "I don't know why I wasn't tuned into that back then."

"Not your fault. We were just getting to be friends after selling our Christmas seals for the pagan babies." Saying this so matter-of-factly all these years later strikes me funny and I laugh.

"Oh, my God, those gosh darn pagan babies." Cat chortles along with me. "We thought the world would end if we didn't sell those doggone things." She becomes serious. "Maggie told me you shared all that with her last night. I'm so sorry, Jo."

"It actually feels better to talk about it now, since so much time has gone by," I say with a dismissive wave, not wanting to burden my friends with guilt. "We were only second graders."

We finish our lunch, then head back across the alley to school, where I spend the afternoon fidgeting. Hard to concentrate when all I can think about is Mom.

After school, Aunt Daisy picks me up and drives us to the hospital, where we eat dinner in the cafeteria. I get creamed tuna on toast with green beans and Aunt Daisy gets a bowl of chili, which we eat before going up to see my mother. As my aunt points out, we need to keep up our strength.

"I stopped by the apartment house while you were in school today to see if the tenants needed anything," says Aunt Daisy. "The lady in Apartment Three had a plugged-up toilet, so I attacked it with a plunger and fixed it."

"Oh, that's Miss Hackman," I tell her. "She works at the Woolworth's lunch counter."

"Nice lady. She said for us to stop by for French fries and gravy, and it'll be her treat."

"I love French fries and gravy," I say, before stuffing a forkful of drippy tuna into my mouth.

"I'm also taking care of your mom's bills and finances," says Aunt Daisy. "She put me on her checking account after your dad passed away. If you need money for anything with graduation coming up, just let me know, okay?"

I move my head up and down, wishing this wasn't happening and Mom would magically get better. We finish our meal and take the elevator up to the third floor. I inhale the sanitized smell as we push open the door to Mom's room.

"I'll leave you alone with her." Aunt Daisy excuses herself to visit the smoker's lounge with her *Valley of the Dolls* book, and I take up my post in the chair at Mom's bedside. I wish more than anything that Mom would wake up and sing "Beautiful Dreamer" and "Good Night, Irene," like she used to when I was little.

A few minutes later, there is a tap on the open door and Sister Alex peeks around it. Today at school, she said she'd stop by to see how Mom was doing.

"Hi Sister!" I get to my feet like I always do when a nun enters a room, then I scurry across the floor to drag another metal chair over next to mine.

"How is she doing?" Sister gathers her full black skirt and sits, the ever-present crucifix hanging at the end of a black beaded belt circling her waist.

"No change, but otherwise, Dr. Madison says she's fine," I reply.

"More to the point, how are *you* doing?" Sister's tender tone pings my heartstrings—a rare softness I've seldom heard. At school she uses her principal voice, the kind that makes you sit up straight and feel guilty about things you didn't even do.

"How about we say a rosary for your mom?" she suggests.

"That would be great." I blush. After all the nefarious things I've done that have been frowned upon by the nuns, a tiny bit of shame knocks at my chest when Sister volunteers to pray with me.

"I brought this for you." Sister hands me a small white plastic box with a clear lid. A plain blue rosary is coiled inside.

"Thank you, Sister." I take it out, and we pray the rosary. I finger the beads, glad to have something to do with my hands. I've never prayed alone with just me and Sister Alex. I stiffen because it feels awkward, but after the first ten Hail Marys, I relax a little.

When we finish saying the rosary, I hope it'll help Mom wake up. As time passes, clinging to hope feels like holding onto a snowflake. But it's all I have right now.

"The congregation at St. Michael's is praying for your mother." Sister Alex rests a caring hand on my shoulder. "Monsignor asked the parish to pray for her during Sunday Mass."

A torrent of emotion overwhelms me for not having been an obedient daughter, a good student, a good friend...a good person. I let out a long, remorseful sigh. I'm not sure why I'm beating myself up; maybe because I'm suffocating with regret.

"Josephina, this must be hard since you lost your father—" starts Sister.

"Seven years ago." I don't mean to interrupt, but the loss is still so real for me.

"That must have been hard," says Sister. "Having the burden of grief at such a young age."

I'm reminded of what my mother said to me in the fifth grade. "Mom says grief never goes away. It hides in your soul, then jumps out and wrecks any happiness you've scratched out for yourself." Her wisdom hits home as soon as the words leave my mouth.

That's exactly what's been happening to Mom and me in the years since Dad's passing.

"Would it help to talk about what happened after you lost your dad?" Sister suggests quietly.

I let it hang there while I try to decide. If I tell her what it was like after losing my father, will I disintegrate into a pile of sobbing hysterics, or... will it help in some way?

I stare at the rosary in my lap. "I guess I can talk about it." I flick my eyes to hers. "Well, I got into some fights."

Sister's brows lift. "Really? Tell me about it."

"Did you know Sister Anastasia?" I ask tentatively, with a sideways glance.

"She left before I came to St. Michaels," replied Sister Alex. "But I've heard mention of her."

"I can tell you what she was like, but you probably won't like it." I fiddle with my fingers, wondering if I should tell her.

Sister's brows furrow. "Why is that?"

"Because she was nothing like you," I blurt. Boy, was that ever the truth.

Sister gives me a quizzical look. "Is that a compliment?" She cocks a brow, a smile twitching the corners of her mouth. I've always thought she was too pretty to be a nun.

"Yes, I guess so." I blush a little. I can't lie to Sister Alex. It's like she has a spell on me or something. Her opinion matters—I want her to like me.

What do I have to lose by spilling my guts? Graduation is only a week away, and after that, I'll be moving on to high school, leaving St. Mike's in the dust.

The gates swing open and out rush words I haven't said to anyone in a long time...a really long time.

I tell her everything.

Chapter 10
The Fallout

February 1962, Second grade

Without Dad, Mom grew distant, and I felt exiled in my own house. I didn't know which end was up. I went from being the center of Dad's universe to becoming an insignificant quark in everyone else's.

There was no one to call me JoJo anymore.

Mr. Bloom in Apartment Five helped Mom get the apartments ready to rent out. He also rounded up the renters for Mom by word of mouth since she didn't have money for a want ad in *The Montana Standard*. So, she rented the remaining five studio apartments to copper miners.

My entire world had crashed and burned after Dad died. I was mad all the time. When one kid made fun of me, I pushed him into the drinking fountain. Another day, Sister Meanie made me erase my drawing of the mountains because I used a black crayon instead of blue for the sky. Then, when I scribbled all over my masterpiece, she sent me to the principal.

The next day when Sister yelled at me for getting my subtraction problem wrong on the chalkboard, I threw my eraser, bonking a kid in the head. He called me a stupid idiot, so I kicked his desk, knocking his arithmetic book to the floor. Another trip to the principal.

At night I hid under the covers and cried, sopping my pillow. When I threw Dad's framed photo onto the floor and broke the glass, Mom spanked me with Mr. Whackenstick. She didn't understand that seeing his photo made my chest hurt so badly I couldn't breathe. The hurt wouldn't go away. I was out of control and didn't know how to fix myself. It felt like a seething monster lived inside of me.

Mom was off in a world of her own, grieving and crying about how she missed Dad. She didn't get that I missed him, too. Aunt Daisy and Aunt

Violet would try to cheer her up, but Mom was determined to stay sad. Aunt Daisy called Dr. Madison one afternoon when Mom refused to get out of bed and he prescribed her a bunch of pills.

During school, Cat, Maggie, and I entertained each with our nun imitations. When she thought no one was looking, Sister Meanie would take a sandwich out of her desk drawer and take bites, her mouth chewing fast. Cat would imitate her by puffing out her cheeks and stuffing her face with pretend food, which cracked us up.

Cat was as tough as she was funny. She cussed swear words we never knew existed and flipped the bird to anyone who gave her any guff. If a bully got in her face, she'd smack the kid with her braids until the kid backed off. Those things were deadly.

Mrs. Delaney French-braided Cat's hair so tight to her scalp, Cat swore her eyes would stay stretched out. She'd exaggerate it even more with her fingers, yelling in a Munchkin voice, "Mommy, Mommy, my braids are too tight!" She always cracked us up.

One day after school while playing Barbies in our living room, Mom overheard Cat swear. Maggie and I were used to it, so we thought nothing of it. After Cat and Maggie went home, Mom said Cat's mouth should be washed out with soap. I visualized Mrs. Delaney trying to cram a bar of Lifebuoy into Cat's mouth. Her mouth wasn't *that* big, even though some kids called her a big mouth.

A new kid named Butch McKnight had just transferred to our school from Centerville, higher on the Butte hill. He targeted me the first week at recess, making rock-hard snowballs and pitching them into my back, like he was tagging me out at home plate.

I spun around and yelled, "Knock it off! I'm not a baseball bat!"

"Hey dummy, ever have a hurts donut?" McKnight followed his question with another ice-ball that socked me square on the forehead.

"Ow!" The unexpected blow made me dizzy, and I stumbled back, holding my head.

"Hurts, don't it?" His wicked laugh made my neck hairs stand on end.

Where was a doggone nun when you needed one?

"Stop throwing snowballs at me!" I yelped, rubbing my throbbing forehead.

McKnight snorted another laugh, his freckles popping off his face like Tiddly Winks.

Cat moved next to me, with her hands on her waist. "You're in big trouble, McKnight! I'm telling Sister!" she shouted so Sister Meanie could hear.

The nun snapped her gaze to McKnight's freckled face, giving him the stink-eye. When he blinked innocently at her, she turned away.

"I hear you don't have a father," he persisted, like he took joy in it. "That makes you the daughter of a floozy!" His words cut like glass.

Maggie moved close. She and Cat stood on either side of me, creating a solid kid wall.

"What's a floozy?" I whispered to Maggie out of the side of my mouth. She'd gotten a new pair of glasses with lenses so thick they were like the bottoms of two coke bottles. They made her eyeballs look gigantic, like Elsie the Cow.

"Uh—you know—a lady of the evening," she whispered back.

"No one says that about my mother!" I snarled. "Take it back, you puny little pea-brain... and take back what you said about my dad!" I was fed up with feeling broken because I no longer had a father. This stupid little smart-aleck was pushing me over the edge, and I refused to let him get away with it.

McKnight copy-catted me in a baby voice. Then he stepped back with a satisfied grin.

"I said take back what you said!" I clenched my jaw so hard it hurt.

"Yeah, take it back, you pus-eating fart sniffer!" echoed Cat, flipping him the bird.

"Make me," he sneered.

"Give me the recipe and I will," hissed Cat in her snottiest voice. "You stink like snake-infested hot dog water, you square weenie!"

Maggie pointed to his nose. "Well, look at that, will ya?"

His eyes crossed, looking at his nose. "What?"

"Your face is so ugly you could make ugly cookies!" Leave it to Maggie to make a slam dunk that made everyone laugh.

McKnight stepped toward me. "I bet you killed your dad and buried his body in your basement." His words dripped with venom.

"You're a scab licker!" Cat lobbed back. "Only a moron would say that!"

Another boy yelled, "Hey Wolohan, did you really kill your dad?" The words fell on me like a bucket of ice, and I sucked in a gasping breath.

"How can you even say that, you dirt-eating worm?" I choked out through gritted teeth.

McKnight smirked, his mouthful of metal glinting. "See? The butt sniffer admits it!"

"Shut your fat mouth or you'll get a knuckle sandwich!" I'd never punched anyone, but there was a first time for everything. My entire body was an undersea volcano, ready to spew lava.

"Ooh, I'm really scared," scoffed McKnight, snickering.

"You should be!" I struggled to keep my voice from quivering. Jamming my hand into my pocket, my mind spun into overdrive as I scrambled for a way to make good on my threat.

My fingers discovered a forgotten pencil in my pocket: a method of defense. Fury poured out of me like a broken dam, as I lunged forward in a blind rage, screaming every cuss word I knew while stabbing the little creep's puffy jacket with my tiny weapon.

McKnight backed up. "Ha, what an idiot. You're not hurting me."

"Stab the creep's balls!" yelled Cat, like a heckler at a Butte hockey game.

I wasn't sure where a boy's balls were exactly, so I shot a *where-the-heck-are-his-balls* look at Cat. If anyone knew, Cat would.

"Under his coat!" she hollered, pointing.

"Wanna bet I can't hurt you?" I charged forward, aiming my pencil where I thought his balls were.

McKnight's ensuing howl surely woke the dead in the cemeteries down on The Flats. Everyone in town must have heard it. I pictured people muttering about the riff-raff getting rowdy again up on the hill.

The boys groaned in empathy and the girls grimaced.

"Hurts, donut, McKnight?" I hollered as he curled into a moaning ball on the hard-packed snow.

Sister Meanie barreled through the crowd of kids, parting them like the Red Sea. She snatched the pencil from my hand, her face bulging around her habit like a swollen marshmallow. Her double chins quivered in holy outrage as she squeezed my neck, steering me toward the principal's office.

I was in big trouble, but I wasn't sorry. I wanted to hurt the mean little creep—because Dad left me when I needed him the most. He'd abandoned me, and I was infuriated.

I wanted him back!

McKnight's insults had dug into a deeper wound. Tears rushed out, my shoulders heaved, and sobs racked my body. The nuns declared that age seven was the age of reason. So now I was expected to tell right from wrong and therefore be responsible for my actions. I wondered which commandment I'd broken. Didn't matter. I'd have to confess it to Monsignor on Saturday, anyway.

Then I'd *really* be in trouble.

Cat and Maggie tried sticking up for me, but no one would listen. It was nuns ten, kids zero, as usual. Not long after the principal called my house, Mom's furious footsteps echoed in the hallway as she stormed in, her face dark as a thundercloud.

"I haven't raised you to get into fights!" hissed my mother as she swung the door open to the principal's office, then slammed the door behind her.

I gnawed on my thumbnail, unable to hear the conversation until the door opened.

"Damn right she'll be punished!" Mom snatched my arm and yanked me from the chair. "Get a move on!" She dragged me out of school across the trampled snow, then up the icy steps to our back door.

Once inside, tears welled. "Please don't be mad at me, Mom. The new kid kept saying I killed Dad and hid his body in the basement!" I blubbered.

"Damn kids. Why do they have to be so mean?" Mom dug into her purse and lifted her hanky with the big 'L' looped on it. "Here, wipe your nose."

I blew my nose and wiped my cheeks.

"He probably deserved it." She flicked her gaze to me and pointed her finger. "Don't you dare tell the nuns I said that. But in *no way* does that mean stabbing a kid's balls is okay to do."

"I know," I heaved out relief that I wouldn't get Mr. Whackenstick.

"Cat and Maggie stuck up for me," I said, returning Mom's hanky. "They told the kid to take back what he said."

Mom filled a glass with water and handed it to me. "You're lucky to have friends like that. Hang onto them for life. Now go to your room while I make dinner. And never do that again."

"Okay." Thankful that Mr. Whackenstick hadn't visited my backside, I shuffled to my room.

Mom shocked me by saying Butch McKnight probably deserved what I did. I realized Dad's death not only crushed me, but it had also devastated my mother. I ached for both of us all over again. Mom said sorrow was born from a sense of bliss and a burst of happiness that never lasted.

I understood why I had rammed that pencil into dear sweet Butch.

Because our hearts were still broken.

Chapter 11
Purple Fuzzy

March 1962

Second grade dragged on like the liver and onions I always shoveled into the kitchen table drawer when Mom wasn't looking.

After the Christmas holidays, Sister Meanie said I couldn't keep up with the class, so she labeled me 'retarded' and made me sit with Tommy Laurent in the back of the class. I couldn't figure out why I was being punished. I thought something was wrong with me... or I was being punished for stabbing Butch McKnight. Hard to tell with Sister Meanie, who held onto grudges like a baby with a blankie.

One dreary afternoon, Sister Meanie caught me making funny faces at Cat, who'd turned around in her seat. Storming to the back of the room, Sister grabbed my cheek, stretching it like a rubber band. It felt like she'd pull it right off my face.

"Stop that nonsense! You retarded children must stay busy," she snapped.

"You're not supposed to say that word!" I shouted, defiance oozing out every pore. "My mom says we shouldn't call people that!"

The entire class stilled. The only sound was Cat and Maggie's fast intake of breath because no one talks back to a nun. *Ever.*

"How dare you sass me!" Sister Meanie raised her hand like she was going to strike me. I cringed, lifting my arm to protect myself and squeezed my eyes shut, waiting.

When nothing happened, I inched one eye open to see Sister Meanie's chubby, red face. To my relief, she lowered her hand, snorted, and strode to the front of the room.

I wasn't slow; I didn't care about spelling or arithmetic. At least I hadn't fallen off a gallus frame, or headframe, like Tommy Laurent had.

Last summer he climbed one on a dare. When he got stuck near the top, his dad had climbed up to get him. Something went wrong, and they both fell off. His dad died, but Tommy survived with a brain injury. Sister Meanie made him sit in the back corner of the room at a small table, and now she made me sit there, too.

Tommy had a hard time staying quiet, and his favorite thing was to sing "The Monster Mash" until kids torpedoed him with spit wads.

"Motherfuckers!" Tommy would holler, then Sister would grab him by the cheek and tug him out to the hall. I figured our cheeks would be dragging on the ground by the time we hit the eighth grade.

I shuddered to think about what she did to Tommy out in the hall. Judging by his distressed yells, I figured she shoved him into the empty coat hooks to stab his neck and back, same as she did with other kids. Tommy was the cutest boy in our class, and I always felt bad for him.

Sister Meanie seemed to enjoy humiliating and hurting kids. The next day, she did another thing that lived up to her name.

Dad had gotten me a purple mohair sweater for Christmas and placed it under the tree. When no one wanted to open Christmas gifts, Mom stashed Dad's gift in the cedar chest. She let me open it for Valentine's Day, so I took an instant liking to the soft sweater and named it Purple Fuzzy. I wore it everywhere because it made me feel close to my dad. At night, I cuddled with it under the covers.

The next day at school, Sister Meanie made me take off Purple Fuzzy because it didn't match my green plaid uniform. She balled up my sweater and stuffed it inside her desk drawer.

Stunned, I stood there staring. "When can I have it back?" My voice cracked as a lump formed in my throat.

"At the end of the school year," snapped Sister.

After school, I ran home and begged Mom to please get my sweater back. I burst into tears and spilled my guts on all the things Sister Meanie had done since the beginning of the year. I told Mom Sister said I was slow, like Tommy Laurent and made me sit with him in the back of the room.

"That does it! She's getting a piece of my mind!" Mom's expression could boil copper as she sprang off the davenport and stubbed out her cig. "Hang on while I put on my face."

Mom rushed to her closet to put on a dress, nylons, and her high-heeled kickerino ankle boots. She ratted her hair into a round bubble-do and put on her makeup, topping it off with ruby red lipstick.

Mom slid into Grandma's long beaver coat. "You're coming with me."

"Can't I stay home?" The last thing I wanted was to spend another agonizing second in Sister Meanie's presence.

"Nope! Bundle up. Let's go." Mom breezed out the back door, practically dragging me across the icy alley back to school.

Sister Meanie sat at her desk, correcting papers. She didn't bother to look up as the sharp click of Mom's heels echoed in the quiet classroom, with me trailing behind her.

"Sister Mean—I mean Sister Anastasia, I'd like to have a word," Mom said firmly, standing in front of Sister's desk.

I stifled a giggle at Mom's slip of the tongue.

Sister looked up and set down her red pen. She folded her chubby hands and rested them on her desk in a typical nun pose. "What can I do for you, Mrs. Wolohan?" Her voice dripped with icicles.

I fixed my gaze on my mother because she was a wild card (Dad's words). He'd explained how Mom flipped the bird to a police officer when he shook his finger at her for speeding down Montana Street. When he pulled her over, she fluttered her eyelashes. "I can't waste all these green lights, now, can I?" The policeman had let her off with a stiff warning.

I wondered if Mom's charm would work with Sister Meanie.

"I'm here for Josephina's sweater." The tapping of her foot and the grim set of her jaw made it clear that Mom meant business.

"You mean Mary's sweater," corrected Sister.

Mom lifted a brow. "No. *Josephina's* sweater."

Sister frowned back. "Mrs. Wolohan, Pope Pius declared 1954 The Marian Year, to honor the Blessed Virgin Mary. Monsignor Coyle therefore christened all baby girls baptized in that year with the first name of Mary."

My mother held up her hand in a stop motion. "Yes, I *know* all about the Marian Year, Sister. Her birth certificate says Josephina Irene Wolohan."

"Nonetheless." Sister Meanie sat upright in her too-small-for-her-big-butt chair. "St. Michael's students may not wear sweaters over their uniforms unless they are white or forest green."

"We wouldn't want to ruin the look of the gaudy green plaid jumper and fashionable *Howdy-Doody* bowtie, now, would we?" Mom smiled sweetly. Even though school uniforms saved money, she thought they lacked style. "Sister, I'm not here to debate fashion. Please return Jo's sweater. It was one of her father's last Christmas gifts." Mom lifted her chin, her lips a thin, straight line.

"As you wish. But she cannot wear it to school." Sister opened her drawer, handed Mom the balled-up sweater in one fluid movement, then returned to her folded-hands nun pose.

"You should know how difficult Josephina is in the classroom." Sister opened her grade book and rotated it so Mom could see. "Her grades are low because she is slow and lacks discipline. She doesn't follow directions and doesn't do as she's told. You'll notice she has an unsatisfactory mark in Deportment."

I wasn't sure what discipline and deportment meant, but it wasn't good if Sister Meanie said I lacked it.

Mom leaned forward and placed her hands on Sister's desk, glaring at her the way a lion sizes up a zebra before pouncing on it. "Where do you get off saying Josephina is slow? Let me refresh your memory. My daughter lost her father at Christmas. She's having a hard time at school because she's grieving her loss."

My mother rose and looked down at Sister Meanie. "Starting on Monday, you will seat Josephina at her regular desk. You'll stop treating her like she's mentally deficient, because I can assure you she is very capable. I'm sure Monsignor wouldn't appreciate it if I were to stop making my hefty tuition payments because of this."

"Well, I'm sure that—" started Sister.

Mom interrupted, lifting her chin. "Josephina is one of the smartest kids I know, and she has a heart of gold. Good day, Sister." She jerked her head toward the door, my cue to scram. I scrambled from my seat and followed Mom out the door, her heels clicking on the hallway's faded linoleum.

As we left school and waded through the slush across the alley, I filled Mom in on other things—like when Sister Meanie slapped a boy who'd giggled during catechism, and made a kid stand in the wastepaper basket for throwing a wad of paper into it from across the room.

"Unbelievable! That woman needs a comeuppance," she said in an irritated voice. "Why can't these nuns call you by your real name? Honestly!"

"I know, Mom," I happily agreed. "I'm one of a million Marys."

Mom snorted. "What happens when a nun calls on you in class?"

I shrugged. "All the girls raise their hands."

"Oh, for heaven's sake, that's ridiculous. Your second-grade teacher has an edge to her I don't like. Watch yourself," warned Mom, climbing the icy concrete steps to our back door.

"Thanks for sticking up for me with Sister," I said, following her. "And thanks for saying I'm smart."

She shot me a startled glance. "Of course—I'm your mother. And you *are* smart."

Once inside the house, she handed me Purple Fuzzy, and I let out a tremendous sigh of relief. "Only wear this at home." Mom dug into her purse for a Camel. She lit it, took a long drag, and exhaled a stream of smoke. "I'll buy you a white cardigan for school."

Saturday morning, we walked over town to Burr's Department Store on Park Street, where Mom used her grocery money to buy me a white sweater. I hadn't been there since I sat in Santa Claus' lap the day before Dad died. The same day he told me the Burrs' escalator took people up to heaven if Santa decided they weren't on the naughty list.

We walked another block to the dime store, where Mom let me get penny candy. I got some dots I ate off the paper and a candy necklace I put around my neck and bit off pieces at my leisure. I also picked up a skinny box of candy Winston cigs.

Mom snatched the box and returned it to the shelf. "You're too young for those. It'll lead to real cigarettes."

"They're fake, Mom! It's candy. Besides, you smoke the real ones," I pointed out.

"Do as I say, not as I do," she said with finality. Mom's warnings mostly went in one ear and out the other. Like when she'd say I'd get worms eating raw cookie dough and cake batter. I couldn't bear the thought of not stealing dollops of cookie dough.

So far, I hadn't come across any worms. Knock on wood.

Chapter 12

Yellow River

May 1962

Toward the end of second grade, I got the flu with a high fever. Mom told me afterward I was delirious and babbled about little blue men running up and down the walls.

I missed a few days of school, so at recess my first day back, Maggie, Cat, and I were chatterboxes as they caught me up on what I'd missed: Sister Meanie had slapped Tommy Laurent's face when he once again yelled "Motherfuckers!" and she also made another kid stand in the wastepaper basket for hawking spitballs at Cat.

Thirsty after my high fever, I drank a ton of water and juice before school. After we said "The Pledge of Allegiance," I asked for permission to use the lavatory, and Sister said I must wait until recess. I couldn't concentrate on my spelling test because the more I tried to hold it in, the more my stomach cramped. I chewed the side of my thumbnail, desperate to relieve myself.

Cat leaned across the aisle while Sister wrote on the chalkboard. "What's wrong?" she whispered.

My face twisted. "I have to pee, really, really bad!"

"Ask Sister," whispered Cat.

"I did, but she said wait until recess." I raised my hand and kept it there, waiting for Sister to turn around. Rocking back and forth, I tried with all my might to hold it in. Desperate for recess, I watched the clock, but it was an eternity. I broke out in a sweat as I squeezed my legs together.

Sister finally turned around. "Yes, Mary?"

"Sister, may I please go to the lavatory?"

Her flat gray eyes peered at me over her glasses. "I told you to wait until recess."

"But this is an emergency!"

"Don't talk back to me, little missy. Now work on your subtraction." She continued writing on the board.

Despite all attempts to hold it in, an uncontrolled stream whizzed out of me like a fire hose, dripping to the floor. A yellow river snaked its way between the wooden desk runners, puddling at the feet of the kids sitting ahead of me. The pungent urine smell gave me away.

Maggie and Cat were the first to spot my accident. Cat let out an involuntary gasp, and everyone turned to stare—tracking her horrified gaze to me. The steady drip-drip to the floor was mortifying.

I wanted to die.

"Eew!" One kid shrieked, flying out of his seat. Two more kids jumped up and screamed, pointing at me.

Sister Meanie waddled back to me, red faced. "Mary Josephina, clean up this disgusting mess this instant! Go to the lavatory and get paper towels to wipe it up!"

Now she tells me to go to the lavatory?

Humiliated, I choked back a sob and hurried out the door. When I got inside the bathroom stall, tears fell on my hands as I took off my soaked undies and stuffed them in the garbage bin. The back of my uniform was sopped. I grabbed a handful of brown paper towels to dry myself and another handful to take with me.

My feet dragged with each dreaded step back to my classroom. I got on all fours to wipe up the mess while the entire class watched. The smell was revolting, and kids held their noses, whispering to each other. I wished I were anywhere but here. When the bell finally rang and everyone left for recess, Cat and Maggie stayed behind.

Sister Meanie also left the classroom, so my friends squatted to help. Each grabbed a paper towel to wipe the floor.

"Thanks, you guys," I sobbed. Mom said I must hang onto good friends for life. Now I understood what she meant. Maggie and Cat were more precious to me than anything. I promised myself I would hang onto them forever.

Maggie patted my shoulder. "It's okay, Jo. Sometimes I can't wait for recess either."

Sister Meanie breezed back into the classroom. "Get outside, girls!" she barked at Maggie and Cat. "This is Mary's mess, not yours. She must scrub the floor to wash away her sins."

My two friends sat back with sympathetic looks. "But Sister—" Cat protested.

"I said go!" Sister glared at Cat and Maggie, her hands planted on her hips.

Maggie was terrified of Sister Meanie and jumped up and backed away, sadly staring at me.

"See you at lunch," whispered Cat, and they scurried out the door.

Sister pointed to my mess. "Clean up every disgusting drop! When you go home for lunch, be sure to tell your mother what a sinful thing you did." Sister tsked, then left me alone in the classroom. My humiliation was unbearable, and I couldn't stop crying.

Mr. Kearney, the janitor, stepped into the room with a bucket and mop in hand. "Josephina, what's wrong? What are you doing on the floor?"

"Hi, Mr. Kearney. Oh, I spilled something." I didn't care if I went to hell for lying. I would rather die than tell him what I did.

But he knew when his gaze fixed on the remnants of my yellow river. "Step aside, little Jo. I'll get the rest of this."

He swished his mop, rinsed it in the bucket and squeezed, then swished it some more. "There you go, good as new. Accidents happen." He pulled a hanky from his pocket. "Dry your tears. I'd better go before your teacher returns." He winked, then hurried from the classroom.

Sister Meanie came in, munching a sandwich. "You have a week of detention for creating this putrid mess," she said with her mouth full. "Go home for lunch and clean yourself up. And be on time after lunch or you'll get another week of detention."

My chest clenched at the thought of spending more agonizing time with Sister Meanie after school for a whole week. I hurried out of school and ran across the alley. Mom was on the phone when I came in, so I tiptoed to my room to change into my other uniform. Thank goodness Mom had bought a used one from the mother of a former student.

I put on a fresh pair of undies and dry socks, then rushed to the bathroom to rinse the wet ones in the sink. I wrung them out and dashed to my room. I hid my wet shoes in the closet, and as I hung my undies and socks on a wire coat hanger, I thought this wasn't the first time Mr. Kearney had come to my rescue.

When I was a toddler, I'd wandered from our yard all the way down to St. Mike's Church. Mr. Kearney told Mom he found me tottering up the center aisle during Sunday Mass with nothing on but a diaper. He said it was a miracle I didn't get run over crossing Galena and Washington streets. The doors had been propped open, so when I'd toddled up to the communion rail babbling baby talk, Mr. Kearney lifted me and carried me home. He told Dad it was a wee bit early for my first communion.

Dad had invited him in for a highball and they became good friends. Mr. Kearney understood what a hard time I was having after Dad died. "God bless ya, Miss Jo," he'd say whenever he saw me at school.

On the last day of second grade, Sister Meanie made an announcement. "I won't be returning to St. Mike's for the next school year. I'm transferring to a Catholic school in Boston." She glanced around like she expected our class to dissolve into tears.

Most of us sat still while a handful of teacher-pet-brown-nosers put on sad-sack faces and whispered, "Oh, no!"

I swallowed a smile along with the urge to jump up and yell, "Hurray!"

After school, Maggie, Cat and I skipped across the alley to my house, singing, "Ding dong, the witch is leaving!" We sat on the front steps of our long, covered porch.

"Do you think Sister Meanie ever confessed the awful things she did to us?" asked Maggie.

"Probably not." A devious glint sparkled in Cat's eyes. "Do you think Monsignor Coyle fired her?"

"Hope so. Good riddance, like my dad would say." God, I missed him.

"Those poor kids in Boston." Maggie shook her head. "I wish we could warn them."

"Me, too," Cat chimed in. "Too bad she didn't leave before she was our teacher. I don't care where she goes, as long as it's far away from here!"

"Me, three!" I raised my hand in jubilation, and we all whooped for joy.

I was so relieved when school was out for the summer. My second-grade year had been the worst. But without Maggie and Cat, life would have been awful.

I'll always remember them helping me clean up my embarrassing yellow river.

Chapter 13
Playing Checkers

September 1962 – June 1963, third grade

Nine months after Dad had passed away, Mom and I had reluctantly settled into life without him. She was getting back to her old self, though we both missed him terribly. She wasn't spending as much time in bed, and she was joking and laughing with my aunts again.

Dad's monthly social security checks finally arrived, so we could abandon our never-ending diet of eggs and toast. Mom figured bread was the biggest bang for the buck at twenty-three cents a loaf, and eggs were fifty-five cents a dozen. Eating meat had been a rarity because Mom said it was too spendy. When the first check rolled in, she bought roasts, pork chops, and burger. I thought I'd died and gone to heaven because we ate pasties with meat again!

When third grade started, Mom treated me to a new pair of Hush Puppies at Newman's Bootery on East Park Street. She enjoyed going there because the shoe salesman, Barney, had been Dad's friend. While Barney measured my foot on the silver and black shoe-sizer, I watched two monkeys playing in a glass cage on the back wall. After trying several pairs, Barney made sure my toes didn't touch the tips of the ones I wanted.

Mom called them my blue suede shoes and that night she played Elvis Presley's record, "Blue Suede Shoes." We danced for the first time since last year's Christmas party, when Dad was alive.

Third grade brought us a nice teacher. Sister Beatrice took the time to help me learn cursive using my *Palmer Method* booklet. She taught me to form my letters correctly, but she wasn't mean about it the way Sister Meanie had been. Sister Beatrice had us copy the cursive letters that ran along the top of our green chalkboard. She passed out paper with dotted lines on it so we knew how big to write our letters. I liked to make mine loopy.

"Jo will catch up, eventually. She just needs extra help," Sister Beatrice told Mom in the first parent-teacher meeting. Mom explained to her how Dad's death had affected my grades.

When I told Maggie about it, she said, "Blessed are the friendly teachers, for their students shall always like them."

Although Sister Beatrice was a pleasant teacher, Maggie dubbed her Sister Mary Boring because she droned on in the same tone of voice, always repeating herself. We didn't mean any disrespect, as she was super nice. Not the way we'd poked fun at Sister Meanie.

Tommy Laurent was upset that I no longer sat with him at the table in the back. He didn't have anyone to play checkers with. We'd be in the middle of an arithmetic test and he'd yell, "JoJo! Checkers! JoJo, checkers! Now!" Tommy pounded on his little table and screamed so loud that kids jumped in their seats. At least he'd stopped yelling "Motherfuckers!"

I asked Sister if it would be okay to stay in class during recess to play checkers with Tommy. She said okay, so that was what I did. It bugged Maggie and Cat that I stayed in, but they understood. Tommy and I had become buddies ever since second grade, and I wanted to keep him company when no one else would. He didn't poke fun or bully me like some of the other boys did.

When October rolled around, the grown-ups became nervous because Walter Cronkite said America was close to a nuclear war after President Kennedy discovered Soviet missiles in Cuba. He called it the "Cuban Missile Crisis" and said we had to prepare for nuclear attacks under the Civil Defense program. Mom was annoyed by the news bulletins because they cut into her soap operas.

Butte's Cold War air raid sirens were originally used for mining accidents, but now they blared for nuclear bomb drills. At school, Sister Mary Boring made us hide under our desks or squat against hallway walls until the sirens stopped. When the sirens sounded on weekends, Mom and I crawled into our claw-foot bathtub with my old mattress over us. The drills ended right before Halloween when the president announced the crisis was over.

Since Mom was in a better mood, she hosted chili lunches and sleepovers for my friends. I also invited other girls from our class. Mom thought a couple of them seemed skinny and malnourished after the long miner's strike, so she took it upon herself to fatten them up with cheesy hamburgers and juicy hot dogs.

Mom enjoyed having my friends over because she missed entertaining like when Dad was alive. Our apartment house had been a gathering place, especially on the holidays. Dad was famous all over town for his Tom & Jerry drinks, and family friends crowded around our kitchen table every New Year's Day. People held out their Tom and Jerry cups spiked with whiskey or rum for Dad to spoon dollops of Tom & Jerry batter into them. I used to love smelling the nutmeg and cloves he'd sprinkle on top.

Besides sleepovers, TV became my part-time babysitter. During the week, Mom let me watch TV while I did my homework.

That way, she could drink her brandy ditches upstairs with Mr. Bloom. She'd graduated from Butte Beer to ditches, made with brandy and water. Whenever Mom went upstairs, it took her a long time to come back down. When she finally showed up, flushed and in a good mood, I'd watched *Rocky & Bullwinkle, The Flintstones,* and *The Beverly Hillbillies.* I wondered what she did up there. Whatever it was, it put her in a better mood, so I hoped she'd keep doing it.

On the weekends, Maggie and Cat came over to watch TV at our house, since Mom bought a new Zenith color TV with Dad's leftover insurance money. We'd watch *Beany and Cecil* and *The Jetsons* cartoons on Saturday mornings, and Ed Sullivan and Walt Disney on Sunday evenings.

When we tired of watching TV, we strapped on metal roller skates to our shoes, tightening them with our metal skate keys. I kept crashing into fences when I got going on a steep sidewalk because I didn't want to zoom into an intersection. One day Cat did, and a Thunderbird swerved around her and almost crashed into some parked cars.

The summer after third grade, we traded in our roller skates for bikes. Bikes were freedom, and we milked every second until the streetlights came on in the evening and we had to go home. We clothes-pinned playing cards to our spokes and Maggie, Cat, and I were cool everywhere we rode. Our favorite destination was our neighborhood store, Bauman's Corner Grocery, on Jackson Street because they had the best penny candy. The yummiest were the flat sugar-coated watermelon wedges, the wax coke bottles with juice inside, licorice sticks, *Double Bubble* gum, and cinnamon bears. Maggie liked *SweeTarts*, but my face twisted and my eyes crossed every time I ate one. We thought we were oh-so-grown-up, pretending to smoke the candy Winstons. Summers were never long enough, and we didn't want this one to end.

Chapter 14
Day Four of Lilly's Coma

May 28, 1968, the present at St. James Hospital
I'm sure I blew Sister Alex's nun socks off last evening with my recollection of second and third grades. She seems to understand me better now. Too bad I'm leaving St. Mike's... I could have used her tender understanding earlier this year when I got into all the trouble.

With less than two weeks to go before graduation, Monsignor called an after-school meeting with students and parents in St. Mike's gymnasium to review the graduation schedule. Earlier this afternoon, our eighth-grade class had set up the rows of folding chairs for the meeting.

Since Mom can't attend, Aunt Daisy comes in her place. She tells me Aunt Violet is on her way from Seattle. While I'm glad she'll be here to visit Mom, I have mixed feelings. It's been four years since we've seen Aunt Violet, and she only wrote two letters in all that time. Not wanting to make a big deal about it, I keep my thoughts to myself.

I hear a whistle and Cat waves us over. I avoid the curious stares of other parents who know about Mom. While I appreciate their well wishes, I get overwhelmed by all the "How's your mother" questions. I always respond the same: "She's good. Doing better."

No one can say whether Mom is improving, and it's frustrating. Dr. Madison explains they continue to monitor her brain swelling, so we all wait. And hope. And pray.

As my aunt and I scoot along the third row of chairs, Cat pats the seat next to her and I sit, leaning across her to say hi to Mrs. Delaney. Aunt Daisy sits on my other side. I spot Maggie hurrying in with her mother, and they sit in the last row.

Monsignor Coyle clears his throat to begin the meeting as Father Murphy hands out the graduation day schedule. I sniff the mimeographed paper; its fuzzy purple ink will always remind me of St. Mike's. Monsignor explains how we'll line up for the graduation Mass and receive our diplomas afterward.

Father Murphy and Sister Alex throw in their two cents, and Sister reminds us not to forget our new gold-gilded prayer books and our white mantilla veils. When the meeting ends, we rise from our chairs.

"Mom, can Cat and Maggie come to our house for dinner tonight, since the boys will be gone?" Cat springs this on her mother without warning.

"That's a great idea." Mrs. Delaney looks at my aunt. They've become acquainted after all the pickups and drop-offs at Cat's house. "How about it, Daisy?"

"I have a fondue Tupperware party to attend, but I can drop Jo off after we visit Lilly in the hospital. You never know when you need to burp a lid to seal in freshness." Daisy smiles, and Mrs. Delaney gets a kick out of that and laughs.

"Oh, I love fondue! You're welcome to come just the same," says Mrs. Delaney.

Maggie rushes up. "Hey, everybody, what's the scoop?"

Cat gives Maggie's mother a pleading look. "Can you and Maggie come to dinner at our house? Mom is cooking a pot roast, and my brothers have baseball games, so they'll be gone."

Maggie checks her mother, who shrugs. "I suppose that would be okay. Sure, why not?"

"Good, then it's settled," says Cat. I am confident Cat will have her own country to rule someday.

"Is everyone good with two hours from now?" Mrs. Delaney glances at her watch. "Say, around six?"

"You got it," I say happily. This will be fun, although I sense Maggie's unease at her mother agreeing to come. I don't think she expected her to agree.

AUNT DAISY AND I SPEND an hour with Mom, and I feel guilty about having to leave early for dinner at Cat's house. I lean over my mother's bed and kiss her warm cheek. Guilt squeezes my chest because I hate myself for leaving her so soon.

"Sorry, Mom. I promise to spend more time with you tomorrow." My heart rips in half when I walk out the door and we hurry to Aunt Daisy's Chevy.

She drops me off at Cat's house, then goes inside to chat with Cat's mom before taking off for her fondue Tupperware party. I love going to Cat's house. It's such a cheerful place, and I like her family.

The two women chat until Aunt Daisy says, "I'd better get going. Don't want to be late."

"You go on ahead and enjoy your evening." Mrs. Delaney pats my aunt's arm. "Get the multi-colored bowl set with the avocado green, mustard yellow, and pumpkin orange bowls with burping lids."

"You betcha," says Aunt Daisy. "Wish I could stay." As she turns to go, Maggie and her mother arrive.

Aunt Daisy and Mrs. Houlihan exchange an icy stare for a moment, but their hostile encounter isn't lost on me.

I break the scratchy tension. "Mrs. Houlihan, have you met my Aunt Daisy?"

Maggie's mom dips into a terse nod. "We know each other from a long time ago."

"Yes, we do at that," adds Aunt Daisy as she turns to go. "See you kids later. Bye, all!" She gives us a quick wave and hurries out the door, closing it behind her.

Maggie shrugs with a quizzical glance in my direction.

Now, I'm curious. "Mrs. Houlihan, how do you know my aunt?"

"We were in the same class at Butte High School. We ran around together for a while." Her response sounds final, so I don't pursue it, though I'm still curious.

Everyone helps Mrs. Delaney to get the food on the long mahogany dining table, and we all sit to eat. I inhale pot roast and potatoes like it's my last meal.

Afterwards, Mrs. Delaney serves us lime sherbet, chatting with Mrs. Houlihan about current events.

"Have you heard of those demonstrators in Washington, D.C., demanding human rights and housing for the poor in this country? They're protesting like they do for the Vietnam War." Mrs. Delaney leans forward, her face serious. "Americans shouldn't have to protest to have food and lodging. It's inexcusable."

Cat speaks up. "Walter Cronkite talks about protests every night on the evening news. He says the war is ending, but it keeps going. Have you seen the sit-ins where college kids stay for days at a time?"

Maggie pipes up. "Yeah, and they carry signs and chant 'ban the bomb and make love, not war.' They're even doing it in Butte at the army recruiter's office."

I look at my friends in surprise. "How do you guys know all this stuff?" After the words leave my mouth, it occurs to me my evenings have been consumed with hospital visits instead of watching TV.

Maggie shrugs. "I watch the news while eating dinner on the TV trays my mother bought with S&H Green Stamps."

"I hate the way people disagree about everything," says Mrs. Houlihan. "The younger generation disrespects people our age. I hate this damn war, the race riots, and the burning of the draft cards." She gives Maggie a hard look and I sense they've argued about these things.

Mrs. Delaney leans back in her chair. "When our young men return from the war, they're treated miserably. People shouldn't shame our sons and nephews for going to Vietnam when they didn't have a choice!" Mrs. Delaney's voice tremors.

"Can I tell them?" Cat puts her hand on her mother's shoulder.

Mrs. Delaney slowly blinks her approval.

Cat turns to us. "My cousin Daniel was drafted and got sent to Vietnam. His helicopter was shot down a month ago. He's in a veteran's hospital." Cat's words fall on us like bricks.

"Why haven't you said anything?" I ask, stunned. I remember meeting her handsome cousin when he came to Cat's house last year.

Cat gives her mother a tentative look. "Mom thinks I shouldn't, so our family won't be dragged through the mud by those against the war."

"It's unfortunate it has come to this." Mrs. Houlihan shakes her head, fingers tapping the table. "This division in our country pits the old against the young and the ones who want peace with the ones who fight. What's the world coming to? Martin Luther King gets assassinated not even a month ago, and the whole country is on edge."

"The King assassination is like President Kennedy getting shot all over again," says Mrs. Delaney, biting her lip. Her expression turned to indignation. "And their killers shot them both in broad daylight!"

"These are worrisome times," agrees Mrs. Houlihan. "Horrible. Simply horrible."

Both women shake their heads while we three friends exchange edgy glances. Since the adults had spiraled into gloom and doom, Cat changes the subject to a different day of despair.

"Remember back in the fourth grade when you repeated what your mom said?" She shoots me a lopsided grin.

"How could I forget?" I murmur back.

Mrs. Delaney turns to us. "I seem to remember having to see the principal because the nuns wanted to expel Catherine. Imagine that, expelling a little fourth grader."

"Yes, imagine that." Cat winks at me and makes a face.

"They wanted to expel a bunch of us," I say wryly.

"Let's see…" Cat looks up to remember. "What was it your mom said about the president?"

Mrs. Delaney leans back in her chair, folding her arms. "Yes, do tell how all that happened. When your mom talks about it, she has us in stitches. I've not heard you tell it from your side."

I hesitate, and Cat elbows my ribs.

"Come on, Wolohan. Enlighten us." The twinkle in her eyes is fiendish. She reminds me of a devil in disguise, but a fun-loving devil. Cat is full of "piss and vinegar," as Mom always says.

Everyone waits expectantly.

"Okay," I say finally, loving an opportunity to tell a tall tale. After all, I learned it from one of Butte's best: Lilly Rose Wolohan, the teller of tall tales. These next stories I'm pretty sure no one else can tell.

Especially how I got the crap beat out of me.

Chapter 15
The Cockeyed Octopus

September 1963

When fourth grade rolled around, I was back to feeling like a normal kid, thanks to Maggie and Cat. We'd become inseparable. I still missed Dad something awful, but my friends kept me in stitches with their whacky nun imitations and knock-knock jokes. No one bullied me after the pencil-in-the-balls incident. The boys kept a safe distance, and that was fine by me.

My buddy Tommy Laurent didn't return this year, because his mom put him in a special school forty miles away in Boulder, where there were other kids like him. I would miss playing checkers with him.

Things were hunky-dory until the fourth-grade nun showed me her own agenda. Sister Monica was older than God. On the first day of school, Cat nicknamed her Sister Appleface because her face wrinkled like an apple doll that had baked in the sun for a hundred years. She looked older than Montana. At first, she was all smiles, and I was hopeful for a good year.

"Josephina Wolohan! See me in the hall," announced Sister, right before recess.

I obediently stood and followed her out to the hall, and she closed the classroom door behind us. Never saw it coming. Sister Appleface's bony hand slapped my cheek so hard that my head spun to the side. So much for hoping for a good year.

"You're the troublemaker who lives across the alley from our convent," she machine-gunned, with a steely glare that could melt copper at the Anaconda smelter. "Sister Anastasia told me about you and your friends. This is a warning to behave in my class. Understand?"

"Y-yes Sister," I squeaked.

She pointed a blue-veined, skeleton finger at my nose. It smelled like Vicks Vaporub and skunks. I couldn't help crossing my eyes to look at it. "Don't think for one minute you can misbehave in *my* classroom, or woe-betide you."

I didn't know what woe-betide meant, but the nuns said this when they wanted to scare us. I figured it had something to do with laundry detergent. I uncrossed my eyes and automatically moved my head up and down.

"Yes, Sister."

She lifted her chin from the too-tight white nun's habit and opened the door to the classroom.

When I ambled back into class rubbing my cheek, every student gaped at the red finger marks on it. Even with the closed door, I was sure everyone heard Sister Appleface and her dire warning. There was only one problem.

I didn't know why.

NOVEMBER 22, 1963

On a gloomy Friday morning when I got to school, Sister Appleface announced to the class that President John Fitzgerald Kennedy had been assassinated. Someone shot him while he sat next to his wife, Jackie, as they rode in a convertible in Dallas, Texas.

My mind raced back to last year, when Sister Mary Boring taught us about President Kennedy, since he was an Irish Catholic President. She talked about him as if he were the greatest man that ever lived...next to Jesus, of course. She'd roll out the clunky film projector with the two giant film reels, and we'd watch newsreels of his speeches. Then she'd quiz us on his words.

The one I remembered was, "Ask not what your country can do for you, but what you can do for your country." I remembered it because Aunt Violet's husband had been killed in the Korean War in the 1950s. She'd cussed President Kennedy and threw a beer can at the TV. Mom had to wipe Walter Cronkite's face with a kitchen towel.

Class activity stopped when Sister Appleface rolled a black-and-white TV into our classroom. The 5th graders filed in, and we were told to share our seats with them. All the nuns were crying, including Sister Appleface, as she turned the channel knob to catch the news bulletins. Walter Cronkite filled the screen with sadness, saying President Kennedy had passed away. He wiped his face as his own tears fell.

My nine-year-old brain couldn't comprehend how a president could be shot in this day and age. Abraham Lincoln's assassination happened in 'the olden days.' Didn't we have an army of people protecting the President now? Why would anyone want to hurt a man that Sister claimed was like Jesus?

Then again, look what happened to *Him*.

When the bell rang to end the school day, I ran home and burst through the door with my news. "Mom, President Kennedy got shot!"

"I'm following it on TV." Mom had placed our portable black-and-white TV at one end of the wooden kitchen table while she made our pasties. Two large bowls full of salt-and-peppered cubed beef and cubed potatoes with chopped onions sat next to the TV.

She'd pinned her hair in small tight spirals to create curls, pinning them with crisscrossed bobby pins. A red scarf held it all in place, tied at her forehead, matching the blouse she'd knotted at her waist.

Mom set down the rolling pin and retrieved her spent cig from the glass octagon ashtray, tapping a long droopy ash into it. She took a strong pull on her cig, then let out a river of smoke that curled up to our paint-chipped ceiling.

"Oh, for Pete's sake. How could this Oswald character do such a thing?" Her brow furrowed as she straightened with one arm folded and the other holding her cig.

"Search me. Who's Oswald?" I asked.

"They're saying he shot Kennedy." Mom took a puff from her cig, inhaling so forcefully the paper crackled as her cigarette devoured itself.

"How could anyone not like the president?" I shook my head. I just didn't get it.

Smoke trickled out with her words. "Kennedy was nothing but a cock-eyed octopus!" Mom slammed the rolling pin down, attacking the helpless pasty dough. She had a way of summing things up with swear words, the way miners used to cuss in the animal bars. I hoped she wouldn't wind up in purgatory, or worse—where devils waited with pitchforks and jagged tails.

My brows winged up. "Why would you say that about President Kennedy?"

"Because he was an idealist, thinking he could save this country from going to hell in a handbasket." She thumped her rolling pin on her pasty dough again, so I figured she meant it.

I gave her a blank look. What does a president have to do with an octopus? Is that like a squid? Last year Sister Mary Boring read us a Jules Verne book, *Twenty Thousand Leagues Under the Sea*, where a giant squid they called a *kraken* attacked Captain Nemo's Nautilus submarine. Thank goodness Butte wasn't near the ocean, but I still had nightmares about squids coming to get me.

"Why are you talking about squids?" Mom gave me a funny look, lit another cig, and impatiently blew out smoke. "Go do your homework until dinner is ready. Sister said you're behind in arithmetic."

"But why is Kennedy an octopus?" I persisted.

Mom gave me a dark look, and I eyed Mr. Whackenstick sitting upright in his usual corner. Rather than incur Mom's wrath, I stopped asking for fear she would think I was picking an argument. No one argued successfully with my mother; she bullied her challengers into submission whenever they tried.

"I said get started on your homework!" Mom waved her cigarette, dismissing me. I could tell Kennedy's assassination really bothered her.

I trudged to the living room and sat on the floor to do my homework on the coffee table as the smell of baking pasties filled our apartment. Mom brought me a pasty covered with brown gravy and ketchup, then I took a bath and went to bed.

For the rest of the weekend, Mom and I were glued to the TV. We watched as military pallbearers carried the president's flag-draped coffin into the East Room of the White House, where he lay in repose. Jackie Kennedy stood next to him, holding young John-John and Caroline's hands. The next day, horses pulled the caisson as it carried President Kennedy's casket to the Capitol.

Walter Cronkite said Jackie refused to change out of her pink suit with President Kennedy's bloodstains on it, even when Lyndon Johnson was sworn in as the next president. She told him, "I want to let them see what they've done."

THE FOLLOWING MONDAY, we watched the president's funeral on TV. At recess, I marched up to the three smartest girls in our class. Cat had nicknamed them the Einsteins after her older brother told us about Albert Einstein. The three of them established their territory on the school steps to sprinkle us with their wisdom. Some kids hung onto every word they uttered, like they were the three Jesuses on the Mount.

Not me. I was tired of their taunts that we weren't as smart as they were. Their parents were lawyers and doctors, where ours were miners or those who worked for the lawyers and doctors. Not a recess went by without them bragging about their dads. I thought of this as I stood before them, preparing to deliver my newfound knowledge. I couldn't have predicted the consequences of what an Irish-Catholic girl in a predominantly Catholic town would say about the Catholic President of the United States.

As they discussed JFK's funeral, I parroted my mother. "Kennedy was a cockeyed octopus!" I harrumphed, proud that I possessed information no one else was privy to.

Apparently, I didn't understand the gravity of what I'd said until Einstein One flew off her perch and connected her fist with my nose. It happened so fast, it was like time traveling in the *Twilight Zone.*

I staggered backwards, holding my nose, my pink mitten rapidly turning red.

"Ow, goddamit!" I sputtered. "Why did you do that?" I'd only repeated what Mom said. Moms were never wrong—Moms knew everything.

"How dare you say that about President Kennedy!" Einstein One shrieked, shoving me. "It's disrespectful!" she hollered.

"You can't call President Kennedy names." Einstein Two piped up behind her.

"And you took the name of the Lord in vain. We're telling!" Einstein Three chimed in.

"My mother said he was an octopus," I insisted in a nasal voice, holding my nose.

"Your old lady is a lunatic!" sneered Einstein One.

"My mom says your mother is a dingbat," Einstein Two taunted.

Cat rushed to my side, her middle finger lifting off like a rocket. "Jo's mom is not a lunatic!"

"And she's not a dingbat either," added Maggie. She stood on my other side, and it was three to three.

That did it. *No one trashes my mother.*

A volcano vibrated my insides as I seized Einstein One's long, dark hair with both hands and swung her in a half circle, like Crack-the-Whip.

"Let go of me, you idiot!" she screamed.

My temper jumped the tracks and charged down a dirt road as I invoked the worst insult I could think of. "Your mother wears army boots to bed!"

Kids from all corners of the playground rushed over to get in on the action. Maggie's and Cat's eyes grew wide, as if I'd turned into the Tasmanian Devil.

"Let go or you're dead!" threatened Einstein One.

"*You're* the one who's dead!" So what if I got detention and the wrath of Mr. Whackenstick?

It would be worth it.

I pushed Einstein One onto the icy playground and sat on top of her. Adrenaline fueled me as I mashed mittens of snow into her face.

"Wolohan, I hope your nose is broken!" yelled Einstein Two.

Cat moved close, displaying her middle finger. "Sit on this and rotate, motherfucker!" For a second, I thought she'd shove her bird finger up Einstein Two's nose.

A collective gasp circulated at the 'F' word, and I knew all hell was about to break loose.

And it did.

Einstein Two slapped Cat, who yanked her ponytail. Einstein Three stepped in and shoved Cat, who pushed Einstein Three down and pinned her arms to the icy asphalt, spitting on her face.

We'd become the Friday Night Fights, with one squirming mass of five entangled bodies.

Maggie cheered from the sidelines. "Pound 'em, Jo and Cat!" she hollered, punching her hand with her fist.

The boys yelled their tired pun. "Cat fight, cat fight! It's three against two!"

I said every swear word I could think of and even stole some of Cat's cuss words when a blur of black and white flashed as a swarm of nuns swooped in to break up the melee.

"Stop this at once!" Sister Mary Boring moved in to separate us, while Sister Appleface frantically clapped to stop the fracas.

The rest was a nightmare—getting dragged to the principal's office, waiting for the ax to fall, waiting for my mother to show up and wash my mouth out with soap. I hadn't been in a fight since the pencil incident two years ago. This time was even worse: I'd called the President a cockeyed octopus, used the son of God's name in vain, and topped it off with an F word... all mortal sins.

I cringed in a chair next to Cat, going to town on my thumbnail while waiting for the nun-parent hurricane to blow in. I thanked Cat and Maggie for sticking up for me. "You guys are the best friends anyone could ever have."

"You, too," smiled Cat.

Maggie answered with a firm nod, and we linked pinkies to seal our steadfast friendship. "We will always stay together and watch out for one another."

I whizzed through the commandments, ticking off which ones I'd broken. When Mom arrived, she gave me her stink-eye, then marched into the principal's office. The words 'suspension' and 'expulsion' echoed through the closed door. I shuddered at the thought of going back to Sister Appleface's classroom after her dire warning on the first day of school. I did the very thing she'd warned me not to do.

We each got a week's detention, but Sister Appleface didn't slap me again. I wasn't expelled because the school needed our tuition. What terrified me the most was walking back to the apartment house, my heart wanting to leap from my chest and run away. And I wanted to run away with it. All I could think of was Mom wielding Mr. Whackenstick like an angry leprechaun. I had heard leprechauns could be downright mean on occasion.

I walked inside, my shoulders tense and stomach knotting as Mom whirled on me with a bemused look on her face. "You thought I said President Kennedy was a cockeyed octopus?"

"But that's what you said!" I countered, somewhat dazed.

"I said he was a cockeyed *optimist!*" Mom burst out laughing. She cackled so hard tears fell down her cheeks. She finally caught her breath, wiping her eyes with her hanky. "Just the same, for someone to punch you for saying that was ridiculous."

"What's an optimist, anyway?" I asked, relieved Mom thought this was funny and I could sit down without an assault from Mr. Whackenstick.

She thought for a minute. "An optimist is someone who is always hopeful about the future, and believes that good triumphs over evil."

"But evil won in his case, didn't it? I don't get it because JFK was so popular." I shook my head, bewildered.

Mom lit an unfiltered Camel. "He was a person who was idolized for his positivity. Butte liked him because he was an Irish Catholic, when others despised him because of it. I believe JFK fought for the people in our country, though not everyone obviously agreed."

"I guess not," I said.

My mother pointed her cig at me. "No more cussing, Josephina. Do as I say, not as I do." She spit a piece of tobacco out the side of her mouth, chuckling. "Your father would have gotten a kick out of this. He'd be proud of you for sticking up for yourself, but not for losing your temper." She tapped her ash into an ashtray.

"Dad would be proud?" I asked shyly, my insides warming at the sticking up for myself part.

Mom shook her finger. "From now on, settle things peacefully. You can't get into a fight whenever you disagree with someone."

"Okay. But the other girl started it." No way would I tell Mom the Einsteins had called her names. I'll never tell Mom the real reason I lost my temper. Some things are better left unsaid.

"The nuns said you kids left fistfuls of hair on the playground." Mom's mouth twitched, and I sensed she was stifling more laughter. I said nothing, only smiled.

LATER ON, I THOUGHT about little John-John saluting when his dad's caisson passed by. Should I have saluted my father when I stood next to his coffin two years ago? He hadn't gone to war, and that's why the American flag hadn't covered his coffin. Maybe I should have saluted him, anyway. As long as I live, I'll never forget seeing the lone riderless horse on TV, with boots reversed in the stirrups, plodding down the street in Washington, D.C.

A few weeks later, the entire school was ushered into the gymnasium, where the nuns had set up the film projector and a large screen stood on the stage. They played the movie, *PT-109*, about JFK in the Navy before he ran for president.

As the black-and-white images flickered across the screen, it seemed impossible that only weeks ago, this brave man with the toothy smile had been our president. How could someone who'd survived a crash with a Japanese destroyer and swum for miles towing an injured sailor be killed by a single bullet? I thought of how quickly Dad had died and a nun saying, "only the good die young." If that was the case, I didn't want to die young, and I'm sure Cat and Maggie didn't want to, either.

When the movie ended, I thought about Mom's comment about JFK being an optimist. He had us believe if we did what was right, and we worked together, anything was possible. His idealism had inspired several generations and was why so many were distraught. He didn't even get to finish his first term as president.

I knew I'd forever remember where I was and what I was doing when I heard the news. It was seared into my memory like images etched into stone. As kids, we'd been robbed of our innocence, facing the harsh reality the world was a dangerous place, where people thought nothing of harming others.

After the terror of nuclear bomb drills, and now the death of a president, so much was out of my control. Anxiously, I prayed I would make it to my teen years.

Only time would tell.

Chapter 16
Farm Out

June 1964, fourth grade summer

While working as a waitress at Harrington's Café near the Bus Depot, Aunt Violet met a guy and fell for him. About two months later, she informed Aunt Daisy she was moving out of their shared apartment at the Silver Bow Homes. She was moving to Seattle with her new boyfriend, Chuck.

We all watched as Aunt Violet stuffed a suitcase. Mom let her younger sister know in no uncertain terms that she wasn't pleased. As Aunt Violet closed her suitcase and headed out to her boyfriend's idling blue Chevy, Mom said, "Chuck's a bum. He's an Idaho spud-muncher and hasn't worked a day in his life. You'll regret this!"

"Well, it's better than being an old maid, like you!" retorted Aunt Violet, tossing her suitcase in the back seat of the car. She hopped in front with Chuck the Bum, and away she went.

Aunt Violet's old maid comment had done a number on my mother. Mom started dressing like a teenager in miniskirts and scoop-necked tops. She bought a pair of green fishnet stockings, and knee-high white go-go boots with platform heels. She topped it off with hoop earrings big enough to stick my hand through.

I overheard her tell Aunt Daisy, "I'm not an old maid, but I'm not getting any younger. I have to get another man while I can!"

When she suggested I would stay at other people's houses to give her more freedom on weekends, I resisted. Loudly.

"Mom, how can you do this?" I blurted, after she hung up the phone from talking to one of her friends. "You're not being loyal to Dad!"

Mom threw her arms up, seemingly exasperated. "Jo, have you any idea what it's like for me, trying to make ends meet? Since your father died, it's been a struggle for me to make sure we've had enough to eat and to keep this apartment house going. Not only that, but I get lonely. I want to share my life with someone."

"But I'm here and Aunt Daisy is here. You can share your life with us!" I countered.

"I want male companionship. Is that too much to ask?" Mom popped a cig between her lips, her hands shaking as she lit it with a metal lighter and flipped it closed.

"It's so weird you would do that," I muttered, pouting. "Can I at least stay with Aunt Daisy in the Silver Bow Homes?"

Mom gave me a sharp look. "She no longer lives there. When your Aunt Violet left, Daisy couldn't afford the rent, so she moved out."

"What do you mean? Moved where?" I burst out like she'd stabbed me in the heart. I couldn't believe she hadn't told me. "Where did she go?"

"She moved to a—to a—house on East Mercury," she said dismissively, lighting a cig.

"Well then, let me stay there."

"No, Jo. It's only for adults. No kids allowed." Mom gave me an impatient wave.

I couldn't believe Aunt Daisy would live somewhere I wasn't allowed to go. It didn't make sense to me. "Which house? Can I at least go visit her?"

The only houses I knew about on East Mercury were the Dumas and the Windsor.

"No, Josephina. That's all there is to it!"

"But—"

"I said no!" Mom held her hand up in a stop motion, signaling me to shut up about it. Why was Aunt Daisy living in a place that didn't allow kids? It made no sense.

"I'd rather not stay at someone else's house," I whined.

"Too bad! That's what you will do until I—until I—" she seemed flustered and her face turned red. For a second, I thought she'd burst into tears. Instead, she ground out her cig in an ashtray and stomped out of the living room, like I'd robbed the Metals Bank.

Suddenly I felt all alone. Unable to see Aunt Daisy, Aunt Violet was gone, and Mom was off in her own grown-up world of "gotta get a man."

I'll never understand grown-ups as long as I live.

THE FOLLOWING WEEKEND, Mom had a bowling tournament in Great Falls, so she arranged for me to stay with the Jones family, who lived in an old run-down house way down on The Flats. She'd become acquainted with Mrs. Jones from another bowling team. I wasn't crazy about staying so far away from Maggie and Cat. We'd become like sisters.

The Joneses were nice enough, but their house was absolute chaos. The parents worked on the weekends, leaving their oldest daughter, Susan, in charge. She was a senior in high school. Mr. Jones worked in the mines while Mrs. Jones cleaned houses.

I couldn't talk on the phone because someone was always hogging it. Whenever I picked up the receiver to dial Maggie or Cat's number, someone would snatch it to make their own phone call. To make things worse, the Joneses shared their phone with other families on the same party-line. If anyone wanted to use the phone, it was survival of the quickest.

I had a tough time figuring out how many kids were in this family because they were never home at the same time. Their house was a three-ring circus: kids coming and going, basketballs bouncing, and non-stop hollering. Boys and girls of all ages wandered in and out, and I couldn't tell who lived there and who didn't. Dogs sometimes loped in with them, grazing on spilled Cheerios or licking up Frosted Flakes, which seemed to be everywhere.

The first Friday I stayed at the Jones house, Susan fed me a bowl of Hamburger Helper, and I curled up on their davenport to watch *The Wizard of Oz* on TV. A loud engine revved outside, and I peeked out the window at a high school kid in black leather sitting on his motorcycle. I pressed my forehead to the glass for a better look.

I hollered at Susan in the kitchen. "Is this Evel Knievel? The guy that does those motorcycle stunts at the racetrack?"

"No, just someone who thinks he's Evel Knievel!" Susan rushed from the kitchen, her bell-bottom jeans with the paisley flares hanging off her hips, showing her belly button. Good thing her wide white belt held them up. She flung open the front door, brandishing a wooden spoon like a sword.

"Michael Wallawander, I've told you a thousand times! Don't ride your bike up our sidewalk to the front door! Were you born in a barn?"

The long-haired guy snatched the spoon and licked the chocolate chip cookie dough sticking to it. "Susan, you're such a fox. Hop on and take a ride with me."

Susan snatched the spoon. "Sorry, flattery won't work. Scram or I'll stick you in the oven with my cookie dough!"

He winked at her, smiling. "Maybe next time."

"In your dreams!" she hollered as he turned his bike around, revved his motor, and zoomed down the street.

Susan closed the door and walked over to me. "Don't mind him. He's a dope with the manners of a caveman. Want a cookie fresh from the oven?"

"Sure." I studied her electric-blue eyeshadow and blonde hair parted in the middle, held in place by a rainbow headband with long tails. My gaze dropped to her Ban the Bomb t-shirt with 'Weed is Good For You' under the peace sign.

Susan darted into the kitchen, and I went back to my spot on the couch. She returned with a saucer of warm cookies, their delightful aroma making my mouth water. I chose the one with the most chocolate chips. I munched more cookies, trying not to show my terror of the flying monkeys and the wicked witch on television.

Susan plopped onto the davenport, deftly avoiding the spring sticking out of it. "What's your story? Why are you staying here?"

I thought for a minute. "My mother started dating men. She's forgotten my dad," I blurted, sounding like what Mom was doing was the scourge of the earth. Well, to me it was. Forgetting Dad was a horrible thing to do, but I hadn't the guts to tell her.

"What happened to your dad?" asked Susan.

"He died three years ago, when I was seven."

Susan's expression turned sympathetic. "That's a royal bummer. I bet your mom hasn't forgotten him, though. She probably just wants to move on with her life."

While I tried not to blame my mother for wanting to move on, I didn't like hearing it, so I changed the subject. "What's high school like?"

Susan twirled the tail of her long headscarf around her fingers. "Mostly cool, but sometimes it's heavy."

My blank look caused her to explain. "Heavy—as in it gets intense when we argue with teachers—about the Vietnam war and all the protesting."

"What do you do when you aren't in school?" I wanted to know what I had to look forward to.

"Hang out with my friends, mostly," she said, biting a cookie. "And I work at the Donna Belle Drive-in for extra bread when I don't have to babysit."

"The Donna Belle gives out loaves of bread?"

Susan laughed. "Bread means cash. Hey, want to go with me to get a cheeseburger? I'll get my brother Robbie to watch the kids since we won't be gone long."

I lit up. "Really? Neat-o!"

After Susan hollered upstairs to let her brother know he was in charge, we went out the back door to a dirt driveway. She pointed to a Volkswagen bug.

"Meet Beetle," she said.

The tiny car was covered with stickers of blue peace signs and large pink flowers. We got in and she turned onto Harrison Avenue. She turned up the radio and sang along with Bob Dylan to "Blowin' In the Wind."

Then she shoved an 8-Track tape into her player. "We'll groove to this psychedelic rock while we cruise the drag." She reached into the jockey box and took out a plastic daisy, then pulled it off the stem and tucked it behind my ear. "Now you're a flower child."

Susan pulled an unfiltered cig from her pocket and tucked it between her lips. She struck a match to it, then took a long drag and held in the smoke. When she let it out, a pungent smell hit my nostrils.

"I'd offer you a hit, but you're not old enough," she said, taking another pull on the stinky cig. "Crack your window," she choked out, blowing out smoke. She rolled down her window part-way, and I cranked my window down.

She shot me a sideways glance. "Haven't you ever seen someone smoke a joint?"

"Oh, sure," I lied, with an over-exaggerated wave of my hand.

Susan pointed at me. "When you're old enough, trust me, you'll dig pot." Cars were stacking up behind us because she'd slowed down. A lot.

"My cousin lives in Laurel Canyon and is part of the happening music scene. Next month when I turn eighteen, me and a friend are driving Beetle to San Francisco to get in on the outta sight hippie scene at Haight-Ashbury. Then we'll head to Laurel Canyon."

"What goes on in all those places?" I asked as several cars honked behind us.

Susan's arm shot out the window, flipping them the bird, but they only honked louder.

"Haight Ashbury is a hippie scene. Laurel Canyon is where Joni Mitchell, Buffalo Springfield, and others write folk music, rock ballads, and protest songs. That's totally my bag. My cousin lives in a commune, and she said I can move in, too."

"That sounds neat-o," I said, trying to sound mature.

What the heck is a commune? I didn't want to let on I didn't know anything about anything.

Susan punched my shoulder. "Hey, get with the program, man. No one says 'neat-o' anymore. Are you hungry?" She abruptly turned into the Donna Belle Drive-in parking lot and lurched Beetle to a stop. We both shot forward, and my hands flew to the dash to avoid smashing my face.

"Wait here. I'll leave the radio on." Susan pulled out the 8-Track tape, left the engine running, and hustled inside.

While I waited, I listened to "She Loves You" playing on the radio. Back in February, Maggie, Cat, and I watched the Beatles' first appearance in America on the *Ed Sullivan Show* at my house. We couldn't get over the screaming girls when the Beatles sang "All My Loving."

Susan returned to Beetle with two paper sacks. "Here you go. Dig in." A cheeseburger and French fries and gravy replaced the pot smell, making my stomach growl. I lifted out the food, my mouth watering.

Susan settled into the driver's seat and dove into her sack. "Ah, the Fab Four. Turn them up."

I turned up the volume just as "I Get Around" played by the Beach Boys. I peeled back the cheeseburger wrapping and took a mouthwatering bite. I closed my eyes, enjoying it. I plunged my white plastic fork into the French fries, and stabbed one, dripping with brown gravy.

After inhaling our food, Susan said she was tired and needed to crash, so she drove us back to the house. As I slept in one of the empty beds that night, I thought about all the stuff I'd learned: heavy, psychedelic, main drag, flower child, joint, and pot... these words had different meanings from what I knew. I couldn't wait to impress Cat and Maggie by laying all this on them. If not for Susan, I wouldn't have learned any of it. I loved spending time with her.

She was like the big sister I never had and I couldn't wait for next weekend.

Chapter 17
Day Four of Lilly's Coma (continued)

In the present. Dinnertime at Cat's house

Aunt Daisy thinks I need time away from the hospital, so she gives Mikey Ann and me a ride to the Delaney's house, since Mikey Ann's dad has a Knights of Columbus meeting. She tells us to have fun and speeds off to her fondue Tupperware party.

The four of us girls, along with Cat and Maggie's mothers, all group around the dining room table after eating pasties and coleslaw. We sip our bottles of pop, and mine is a Pepsi.

"Your cockeyed octopus story is funny, although I can see why your classmates didn't appreciate your remark," Mrs. Houlihan says drily.

"They had issues, all right." Maggie shakes her head. "Fourth graders can be brutal." Her arm is still in a sling, so she eats and drinks with one hand.

"You're telling me," adds Cat.

"I'm sorry you couldn't stay with us when Cat's dad lost his job at the power company," says Mrs. Delaney. "We were having a rough time financially and were forced to cut back. And then you know what happened later, with Mr. Delaney."

"Yeah. That was a royal bummer." I flick my eyes to Cat, who trains her gaze on the table.

"Whatever happened to Susan? Did you see her again?" asks Mrs. Delaney.

I shake my head. "*The Montana Standard* reported that Mr. Jones had been arrested for drunk driving, so Mom wouldn't let me stay there anymore. Mrs. Jones left him and the kids, and they wound up in the state orphanage in Twin Bridges." My heart tugs a little. "I heard Susan went to California, but I don't know if she ever returned to Butte."

Maggie speaks up. "You said she was like the big sister you never had."

Cat nods. "Yeah, I remember. Susan introduced you to lots of cool things."

"Yeah, she was the first teenager I got to know, so I didn't dread becoming one after that." I take a sip from my bottle of Pepsi, wishing I knew what happened to my long-lost friend.

"So, your mother dumped you on other people so she could party down at the White Swan?" Mrs. Houlihan asks, then leans toward Cat's mom with a know-it-all look. "My friend saw her there on weekends, partying like there was no tomorrow." She sips her coffee from a dainty china cup.

Maggie's eyes dart to my red face. "Mom, please! Gossiping is uncool!"

"I stay with my Aunt Daisy now." Backed into a corner, I defend my mother. "Mom only left me at the Jones's house for a couple of weekends that summer until Aunt Daisy moved back to the Silver Bow homes." I want to wipe that smug smile off Mrs. Houlihan's face. "And my mother doesn't go out anymore, now that she has a boyfriend."

Mrs. Houlihan's next comment pokes needles into my chest. "Jo, everyone knows your Aunt Daisy worked on Mercury Street. It's not exactly a secret."

Her words hang in the air, and I'm not sure what to say. I glance at Cat and Mikey Ann's wide eyes, round as their ice cream bowls. No wonder Maggie doesn't talk about her mother or invite us to her house.

Maggie looks horrified. "Mom, stop it! Let it go! What happened between you two, anyway?"

Mrs. Houlihan only shakes her head, but I want to know, too. Since Maggie's mom won't divulge the reason, I'll ask Aunt Daisy.

I realize my mistake of talking about Aunt Daisy. But if I hadn't, how else would I know that her side occupation at the Dumas was no secret? If others knew, then it wasn't entirely my fault for letting Aunt Daisy's skeleton out of the closet.

Just then, the doorbell rings to break the uneasy tension. Mrs. Delaney rises to open it.

Aunt Daisy pokes her head in. "Hello, everyone! Jo, are you ready? Mikey Ann, do you need a ride?" she says in a cheerful voice.

"My dad's picking me up," replies Mikey Ann.

"Alrighty, then. Hope you all enjoyed your evening. Come on, Jo. Bye, all!" Aunt Daisy waves and turns to go.

"Bye, Aunt Daisy!" my friends say in unison. I love them for it, after Mrs. Houlihan's cutting remarks.

"Thanks for dinner, Mrs. Delaney." I hurry to put on my sweater, avoiding Mrs. Houlihan's gaze.

On my way to the door, I overhear her say, "I'll bet she burped more than those Tupperware lids." I restrain myself from turning around to give her a piece of my mind, but I would never do that to Maggie. To her credit, Mrs. Delaney says nothing. I love Maggie, but her mom is not a nice person. I dart outside, closing the door behind me.

As Aunt Daisy pulls away from the curb, guilt and regret stab me. I had no business talking about my aunt's private life and would never do anything to hurt her. The most I can hope for is that no one will tell her what I said—or what Mrs. Houlihan said. My ears burn at the thought of it.

As I lay on the davenport, I'm unable to sleep. All I can think about is what Mrs. Houlihan said. Restless, I get up and go to the kitchen to get a glass of milk. Aunt Daisy is sitting at her small metal table, wrapped in her blue chenille bathrobe, fiddling with her new Tupperware bowls and burping the lids. She burps an avocado-colored one and looks up, cold cream on her face.

"Jo, why aren't you asleep? You have school tomorrow." Daisy puts a bottle of fizzing Fresca to her lips and swallows.

"I keep thinking about Mom." I shuffle to the icebox and pour a glass of milk.

"Oh, honey, I know. I'm so glad you have such good friends to help you through this. All three are diamonds in the rough." Aunt Daisy reaches across and places her hand on mine. "Those are the kind of friends you must hang onto for the rest of your life."

"Mom said the same thing when I was in fourth grade," I recall with a half-smile. "I don't know what I'd do without them. They've gotten me through everything since Dad died."

"I'm sorry life dealt you that shitty poker hand. No kid should lose a dad, especially when you were so young." Aunt Daisy burps an orange lid and holds up the bowl. "Isn't this the cat's pajamas?"

I chuckle, pulling out a chair and sliding into it. "Since Mom has been in the hospital, I've done a lot of thinking. She's had a tough time with Dad being gone. I mean, he was her husband."

"Yes, she's had a very rough time." Aunt Daisy shakes her head. "I'm glad you're seeing things from your mom's point of view."

"I could kick myself for not realizing this before." I pick up a mustard-yellow Tupperware bowl and burp the matching lid.

"Honey, don't beat yourself up. You and your mom each grieved differently. We get caught up in our own grief and don't see how others are dealing with theirs," says Aunt Daisy, lighting a Winston. "Anyhow, those friends of yours will steer you straight."

"Yeah, Mikey Ann says her Italian family eats their way through grief. They have lasagna, cannoli, and all the other noodles at their funeral receptions," I point out.

Aunt Daisy leans back, like she's evaluating what I said. "You're right. They do. When Luigi's mother died, we had a feast."

I finish my milk and rinse my glass in the rectangular sink. I hesitate, gnawing my thumbnail as I summon the courage to ask her—I have to know.

"Aunt Daisy?"

"Hm?"

I turn and lean against the sink. "Do you care if people know that you were a—that you—um, that you lived and worked on Mercury Street?"

She hesitates. "Why do you ask?"

"Mom mentioned it back when I wanted to stay with you. She said you moved there after Aunt Violet left."

Aunt Daisy hesitates. "I lived there a few months until I got back on my feet. My sister left me high and dry with rent and utility bills. I had to make money fast and had little choice. And I didn't want to be a burden to your mother."

"Oh." I'm ashamed now.

She heaves out a long sigh. "Jo, I guess you're old enough to understand. I still work there once in a while, when I'm strapped for cash." She looks me in the eye. "It's no secret. I just don't blab about it. I still have my bookkeeping job at The Company, but I have to make ends meet, just like everyone else. They won't let women work in the mines, where it pays more."

"I think you'd look amazing in a miner's hardhat with a headlamp on it." I pause. "Is that why you and Mrs. Houlihan don't get along? Because you work on Mercury Street? Or is it something else?"

She lets out a long sigh. "That, plus I stole her boyfriend our senior year. I didn't mean to, it just happened when we did the musical, *Brigadoon*. He played Tommy Albright, and I played Fiona Campbell. We sort of continued our onstage romance offstage."

"Oh, wow! I didn't know you acted and sang onstage. Mom never mentioned it." I gave her a devilish look. "Didn't know you were a boyfriend stealer, either."

"That was short-lived. We never saw each other after graduation, but Maggie's mom never forgave me for it." Aunt Daisy wrinkled her nose. "Regarding your mother, there may have been a bit of jealousy when I landed the lead in the musical, so I'm not surprised she never told you. I had fun doing it, though."

"Aunt Daisy, can I ask you one more thing?" I ask shyly. "What was Dad like? I mean, I remember him and all, but when I was seven, I didn't stop to think what kind of person he was."

"Well," she thinks for a moment. "He was gentle and kind, loved a good joke, and was a super good Catholic. Never missed Sunday Mass. He had a solemn manner, except with you he was all smiles. He loved watching you waltz along with the bubble dancers on the Lawrence Welk Show and made everyone giggle with his Jack Benny and Red Skelton imitations. He was a fun-loving guy and everybody loved him." Aunt Daisy looks off as if she sees him standing in her kitchen.

"I remember how everyone gathered around him at the animal bars," I say, digging into my memories.

Aunt Daisy chortles. "Is that what you called the Eagles and the Moose?"

"I was a little kid, you know?" I give her an I-don't-know shrug. "I really miss him. The saddest thing is he won't see me graduate. For that matter, Mom might not, either." With a shake of my head, I blink back tears.

"Oh, honey, your father loved you so much. And he loved your mom, too." Aunt Daisy squeezes my shoulder. "Don't worry, he'll see you graduate. He'll be with you in spirit. He loved St. Michael's church. He used to say he heard God breathing when it was quiet."

My head snaps up. "I heard him say that, too!" I gaze at my attractive dark-haired aunt, who's been my rock ever since I could remember. "I love you, Aunt Daisy. I don't care what kind of job you have or whose boyfriend you stole."

She chuckles. "Thanks, Hon. You can always count on me, no matter what. I promise you that. Love ya, kid." She closes the distance and hugs me hard.

Not knowing what would happen with my mother, I needed to hear this right now. Aunt Daisy is my lifeline, and I would fiercely protect that with all my heart. Never again will I betray her trust.

We say goodnight and I crawl onto the davenport with my transistor radio while Aunt Daisy shuts off the lights and closes the door to her bedroom.

I turn the volume down low, listening to Creedence Clearwater Revival sing about the bayou. I wish I could see one. CCR made bayous sound like amazing places, but I'm stuck way up here in the toolies of Butte, Montana.

My mind wanders to Aunt Daisy as I stare into the darkness. I'm thankful for her, thinking of what she said about my friends being keepers. Images and events roll through my mind like a filmstrip. I pause one of my favorite memories...how the Clover Girls came into being.

It happened on the scariest day of my life, when I thought I was going to die.

Chapter 18
The Clover Girls

October 1964

Fifth grade brought a new kid to our friend's circle. Mikala Ann Quinn barreled into our class like a buffalo eager for her first day in a brand-new pasture. The first thing out of her mouth to Maggie, Cat, and me was, "Call me Mikey Ann. What sports do you play?"

Mikey Ann's dad drove her to school each day from Walkerville, on his way to work. Her brothers caused so much trouble at their old school, Mr. and Mrs. Quinn transferred their kids to St. Mike's. Since Cat, Maggie, and I hadn't been to Walkerville, we figured Mikey Ann was from a wild and exotic place after hearing all the wild stories about the little town north of Butte.

And that made her a neat kid in our book.

Mikey Ann taught us how to Chinese jump rope, because she needed three girls to make it an even four. Two of us positioned the elastic around our ankles, and the other two hopped in and out with fancy cross-steps. Mikey Ann was a head taller than us three, with muscular arms and legs compared to our scrawny ones. She had a wildness about her, like she was always ready for action. Her reddish-brown ponytail looked like it hadn't been brushed since dinosaurs roamed the earth. When she laughed, she snorted, making everyone else laugh, too. Unlike Maggie and me, she was like Cat—she never worried about anything.

Mr. Quinn picked Mikey Ann up each day after school, when he got off work from the Terminal Meat Shop on Park Street. He was a butcher, and Mikey Ann told us never to piss off her dad because he'd come after us with a meat cleaver. We took great pains to be polite around Mr. Quinn.

After Mikey Ann came to a few sleepovers at our house, Mom decided she liked her because Mrs. Quinn was on her bowling team at the Winter

Garden Bowling Lanes over on Montana Street. Mom suggested I stay with the Quinns for the weekend.

I asked her why I couldn't stay at Cat's house, but Mr. Delaney had lost his job at the Montana Power Company, and Mom didn't want Cat's parents to worry about an extra mouth to feed. She didn't want me staying there anymore.

Friday after school, Aunt Daisy and Mom showed up in a brand-new blue Chevy, with my aunt at the wheel. She drove us up to Daly Street in Walkerville, and Mom pointed her cig at the gray and blue building on the way to the Quinns. "There's Pisser's Palace. We had some crazy times in *there*."

"You got that right." Aunt Daisy laughed, puffing out smoke from her cig.

Curious, I stared at the building as we drove past. "What is it?"

"Just a bar." Mom took a drag on her cig and exhaled a blue stream with a big grin. She sipped a can of Butte Beer she'd nestled between her thighs.

By the time we pulled up to Mikey Ann's house, Cat and Maggie were there. Mikey Ann had mentioned she'd invited them up for the day.

"'Bout time you showed up, Wolohan," said Cat, offering everyone a Pez candy from her Sylvester the Cat dispenser.

We held out our hands, then popped the Pez in our mouths.

"Mikala, your dad and I have to run some errands," said Mrs. Quinn, coming out the front door. "Your big brother will keep an eye on you kids." She gave each of us a "mom look" as a warning to behave, then got into the car with Mikey Ann's dad, and they drove off.

Mikey Ann led us inside the house. "So, what do you guys want to do?"

Cat sauntered over to the black phone on a side table. "Let's call the 'It Club' in Rocker."

"Why?" I asked.

"Listen." Cat picked up the receiver and dialed. She motioned us close so we could hear.

"This is It!" answered a woman's voice.

"This is what?" asked Cat, grinning.

"This is It," the woman repeated. "The It Club."

"*What* is It?" Cat's smirk widened.

"All right, you smart-assed kids, stop playing on the phone!" yelled the woman, slamming down her receiver.

We cracked up, and I suggested another prank. "Let's call someone and ask them if their fridge is running."

"If it's running, then run after it!" laughed Mikey Ann. "That one's outdated. No one falls for that anymore. Hey, let's go play tether ball." She motioned to the back door and led the way out.

Maggie pointed to a pile of old furniture next to a shed. "Hey, let's put those lampshades on our heads and pretend we're astronauts, like *Lost in Space*. Now *that's* funny."

Mikey Ann looked at Maggie like the lampshades were sticking out of her ears. "You're a trip, Houlihan."

"Did you watch the first episode? It's set in the future, all the way into nineteen ninety-seven!" justified Maggie.

"That's so far in the future it's not even funny," I said, and everyone nodded in agreement.

"Hey, I'll get us some popsicles." Mikey Ann went inside and returned with banana and root beer flavors.

I bit off a chunk of my root beer popsicle and talked with my mouth full. "The 'It Club' gave me an idea," I said, chewing and swallowing. "We should name ourselves the Butte Girls' Club."

"Yeah, I like that." Maggie waved her banana popsicle. "I like Butte Girls' Club for our official name, but we need a code name."

"She's right," said Mikey Ann. "We need a secret code name."

Another idea hit me. "There are four of us, so our code name can be The Clover Girls. Since there's four leaves on a clover!" I was proud of my explosion of creativity and glanced around for unanimous agreement.

Mikey Ann tilted her head. "Not bad."

"I like Butte Girls' Club better." Cat bit into her banana popsicle, then gave us a noncommittal shrug. "But I can live with Clover Girls."

"Then it's settled!" agreed Maggie, clapping her hands. "Clover Girls is our code name, like on *Get Smart*. No one but us will know what it is."

"Yeah!" I held out my pinky. "From now on, we'll be friends forever. Shake and swear!"

We wrapped our little fingers together, then raised our joined hands up and hollered, "Friends forever!"

"We need to prick our fingers and rub our blood together, so we're blood sisters. Mikey Ann, go get a knife," ordered Cat.

"I hate blood," grimaced Maggie, pushing her thick glasses higher on her nose.

Mikey Ann ran inside and returned with a sewing needle. "Who wants to be the stabber?"

"I will." Cat took it and held it up. "Okay sports fans, hold out your bird fingers. It won't hurt as much."

Cat expertly pricked each of our middle fingers. "Now squeeze some blood out."

We slid our thumbs along our middle fingers to force blood to our fingertips.

Maggie made a face and squeezed her eyes shut. "This is gross. Just do it already!"

We each coaxed our droplets out, then rubbed them with each other's fingers.

"Now the Clover Girls are officially blood sisters," announced Cat.

We cheered, and Mikey Ann turned on the hose. We rinsed our fingers, then she handed out tiny adhesive bandages with roadrunners and coyotes on them.

I raised my face to the sky with crossed fingers, hoping our friendship would last. None of us knew what life had in store. I shook the thought from my head as a nearby black headframe caught my eye. The ominous monstrosity seemed to follow us around.

"What's the name of that mine?" I asked Mikey Ann.

"The Lexington. Dad calls it the Lex. It hasn't operated for years. He tells us to stay away from it. The taller the headframe, the deeper the mine shaft. They used cages to lift miners in and out of the mine. My uncle was a cage operator."

We craned our necks, gazing up at the imposing headframe.

"Holy cow! This one is really tall," breathed Maggie.

Later that afternoon, I regretted having asked about the Lexington Mine.

Chapter 19
Climbing Mount Everest

Octorber 1964

Mikey Ann motioned us into a tight circle. "Don't you dare tell anyone what I'm about to tell you, or I'll have to kill you. Cross your heart and hope to die?"

"Yes," we all chorused, anticipating her breathless revelation.

"Me and my two brothers have climbed the Lex gallus frame." Mikey Ann waited for us to be amazed.

Cat didn't disappoint when her eyes grew the size of a pizza. "How high did you go?"

Mikey gave us a wicked grin. "All the way to the top!" She laughed at our collective intake of breath.

We were severely impressed, but every Butte kid knew the golden rule: *never, ever climb a gallus frame because if you fall, it's the kiss of death!*

"My dad warned me and my brothers about Tommy Laurent's accident. He said Tommy was the poster child for falling off a gallus frame," said Cat, knowingly.

"Thought it was called a headframe," said Maggie, shoving her glasses higher on her nose.

"Same thing. Depends who you talk to," said Mikey Ann.

Cat was the first to verbalize the forbidden suggestion. She jerked her head toward the house with a gleam in her eye that spelled trouble.

"When will your mom and dad be back?" She took off her elastic headband and wrapped it around both her ponytails as if she were preparing for a softball game.

"Not for a while. Why?" asked Mikey Ann.

"You aren't thinking what I think you're thinking," I said to Cat, eyeing the looming tower of black steel.

Mikey Ann gave us a playful grin. "She sure is. We'll be up and back before my parents get home."

Maggie's eyes popped out of her head. "No way, it's too dangerous! We'll get into so much trouble. I refuse to be grounded. And I'll have to confess it on Saturday!" She acted like the headframe was a monster that would come alive and eat us.

"Come on, Fraidy-Cat. It's a cinch to climb," chirped Mikey. "Don't be such a goody two-shoes."

"Mikey Ann, take it back and apologize," I breathed, giving Maggie a cautious glance. I knew better than to call Maggie a Fraidy Cat. Last year, when a boy called her a Fraidy Cat for hesitating to do a somersault on the trampoline, Maggie climbed down and flattened him with a bloody nose. Then she burst into tears and apologized, afraid she'd killed him.

Maggie bristled, gritting her teeth. "I have to be a goody two-shoes, as you call it. Sorry to break it to you, but I plan to go to heaven!" Of the four of us, Maggie wore a genuine halo. Like most of us, she didn't want to wind up down in that scary place with all the flames.

Mikey Ann raised her hands in a stop motion. "Jeez, Louise, cool your jets, okay? Sorry, I didn't mean to call you Fraidy Cat." Her face brightened. "Come on, let's pretend we're climbing Mt. Everest!" She skittered to the backyard gate that opened onto an alley.

Cat bolted after her while Maggie and I stared after them.

"It'll be fun." I gulped, trying to convince both of us.

"Yeah," grumped Maggie as we followed Mikey Ann and Cat.

Maggie had reminded me of a little old lady ever since I've known her, with her black horn-rimmed glasses with lenses so thick her eyes took up half her face. She'd always had a mature wisdom, as if she'd experienced all there was in her first decade of life.

We strolled over to the mine, its black tower stretching to the sky behind a tall wood fence. Run-down, abandoned buildings sat next to it, the paint long peeled off their walls.

Mikey Ann led us to the end of the fence, then pushed in two boards on the bottom. "Go through here."

I crawled through, and Cat and Maggie followed. Mounds of dirt and orange rocks were piled everywhere around the headframe. Mikey Ann explained this was where they used to lower miners and equipment thirty-two hundred feet underground to mine silver in the 1940s.

"Come on, let's climb to the top." Mikey Ann started toward a narrow flight of metal stairs at the base of the frame.

"The top?" I echoed, noting the never-ending stairs. Some things you don't tell your friends. Admitting you're scared is one of them.

Maggie hesitated. "How tall is this thing?" She squinted at the American flag waving from the tall pole at the top.

"A hundred feet," Mikey Ann called over her shoulder.

"Wow!" chirped Cat, as we all gazed up at it.

It may as well be a million feet tall, as far as I was concerned. I put on a fake brave front for Maggie's benefit. She feared heights; that was why she wasn't a fan of the trampoline.

"Come on, Maggie, this'll be fun. It's our first Butte Girls' Club—I mean Clover Girls adventure!" I stepped up the first set of metal stairs. By the time I got up to the second, Mikey Ann and Cat were on the fourth flight. I twisted to see Maggie reluctantly plodding up after me. A tinge of guilt poked me for talking her into this.

Mikey Ann's and Cat's heads appeared over the railing. "You guys coming?"

"Yeah!" I shouted back, trying to sound tough. I stopped to rest before the last set of stairs, noting the weathered wood planks crossways on the deck platforms and the spaces in between that made me dizzy when I glanced through them.

I took a moment to take in the view. The surrounding mountains had always been a source of constant comfort—the East Ridge, the snow-capped Highlands to the south, and Mount Fleecer to the west. I spotted our orange apartment house down on Galena, like a giant pumpkin hunkered in the middle of uptown.

"I'm going back down," Maggie hollered up.

No argument from me. "Okay!"

I looked up at Mikey, clinging to a tall metal column with large holes spaced a foot apart. She climbed the angled column and swung herself around to climb onto the next angled beam. Cat clambered after her like a nimble monkey.

"No way. You've got to be kidding," I muttered under my breath, eyeing the slanted bar of steel.

"What are you waiting for? Pretend you're climbing Mount Everest!" Mikey Ann hollered down to me. "Get a move on!"

Not wanting to be a Fraidy Cat, I pretended my heart wasn't knocking around in my chest. I sized up the rest of the black steel column, making sure there were spaces for my footholds.

Mikey Ann peered down at me from the top platform. "What's taking so long?"

Cat stood next to her, hanging over the railing with a triumphant grin. "Come on up, it's really cool up here!"

I knew kids who'd bragged about climbing headframes without falling. It was a badge of honor. I visualized Tommy Laurent back in second and third grades, sitting in the corner playing checkers. I bet he thought the same thing when he climbed it. I tried not to think about it as I tackled what was left of the climb, my red-dot Keds finding footholds as I made my way up the steel bar. I slowly climbed around it, then clung to it for dear life. If I didn't look down, I wouldn't get dizzy.

It was a sunny, windless afternoon. A small airplane flew over and I tipped my head back, wondering if the pilot saw me climbing up the headframe. I was distracted when I lifted my foot and shoved it hard into the wrong hole. When I went to lift my foot for the next foothold, I couldn't move it.

I'd wedged my tennis shoe into the tiny space so tight I couldn't dislodge it. No matter what I did, my foot wouldn't budge. I feverishly stole a glance at the ground—a big mistake—everything around me spun in circles. I squeezed my eyes closed, clinging to the cold steel.

"What are you doing down there? Hurry up!" hollered Mikey Ann.

"I can't move!" I shouted back.

"What do you mean, you can't move? Get up here," she yelled.

"I can't! My foot is stuck!"

"Pull it out!" hollered Cat.

I tried with all my might to wriggle my tennis shoe loose, but it was glued to the steel. The headframe clutched me in its claws like a monster.

"I can't!" I screamed, bile rising in my throat.

Holy Mother of God, don't let me throw up. I'll fall off!

"Cat, go help her," ordered Mikey Ann from her perch on top.

Cat swung herself over the railing to the steel bar below to work her way down to me. She got even with me on the other side of the angled steel pole. She bent to loosen my foot, but she couldn't budge it, either.

"She's really stuck!" Cat hollered up to Mikey Ann.

"Shizzle sticks! All right, let me try," she muttered, easily lowering herself.

Cat climbed down to the stairs so Mikey Ann could position herself to help me. No matter how hard she tried, she couldn't budge my shoe.

"Holy smokes, this is a problem." She said it with all the gravity of someone about to perform brain surgery.

"Oh, no!" Her somber tone scared the jeepers out of me, and my tears rushed to the surface. I had to keep it together. I couldn't panic and lose my cool a hundred feet in the air because my stupid Ked was stuck in a hole tighter than a spider's butt.

"Now what do we do?" I fought to keep the tremor from my voice. My leg and arm muscles shook from clinging so tight to the beam.

Cat hollered up at us from the stair platform. "Should I go get help?"

Frightened tears rolled down my cheeks as Mikey Ann considered this option. "We don't have a choice. I'll go. You and Maggie stay here with Jo." She lowered herself to the slanted steel beams, jumped to the stair platform, and sped down the stairs.

My cheek pressed firmly against the steel as I glimpsed Mikey like a little ant, running back to her house. Terrified, my heart knocked against my chest. I wanted off this hundred-foot steel monster I'd been stupid enough to climb. My entire world had squeezed into this tight space between me and the cold steel.

Panicked despair grabbed hold of me, and I wept against the steel with jagged breaths.

Hail Mary, full of grace…

Chapter 20
Just Like Rescue 8

October 1964

"Jo! Are you okay?" hollered Cat.

"Yeah, are you okay?" echoed Maggie, standing next to her.

"No! I'm scared." My voice broke as I fought sobs.

"Don't cry. I'll keep talking to you, okay? Okay, knock-knock," said Cat.

"Who's there?" My eyes squeezed so tight it felt like they turned inside out.

"Duane."

"Duane who?" I choked out.

"Duane the bathtub, I'm d-wowning," Cat's Porky Pig imitation made things lighter for a split second.

I dared not laugh, fearing I'd lose my grip.

"What time do ducks get up?" yelled Maggie.

I let out a shuddering breath. "I don't know. When?"

"The quack of dawn," she bellowed, as Cat's loud chortle drifted up to me.

Too scared to laugh, I stole a peek toward the Quinn house. What was taking so darn long?

"Hold your horses," shouted Cat. "Here comes Mikey Ann and her big brother!"

I heaved a sigh of relief. Surely, he'd help me get off this steel monstrosity.

"My brother Bryan is here to help!" Mikey Ann hollered up, standing with Maggie and Cat.

Bryan bolted up the stairs two at a time and soon he was next to me. "Hey, you almost made it to the top!" He was a cute seventh grader, but right now I didn't care what he looked like—I only cared about getting off this thing without killing my body.

"Let me see if I can get your foot out." Bryan tried, but couldn't budge it, either. "Mikey, go call the fire department. They're the only ones who can help."

"No!" I yelled in a panic, knowing the trouble I'd be in.

"Mom and dad will kill me!" protested Mikey Ann.

"I don't care. Go call them right now!" Bryan peeked through the hole at me. "I'll stay with you until they get here. You'll be okay, don't worry."

"Okay," I said in a feeble voice, fixating on Bryan's sky-blue eyes through the peephole as Mikey Ann sped to her house.

Bryan made idle chatter, talking about stuff like wanting to race a beat-up car for the demolition derby, but his words bounced off me; all I could focus on was hanging on for dear life. A distant siren grew louder as a fire engine rushed up the hill. Peeking down, I saw flashing red lights nearing the headframe.

I sobbed in humiliation that the Butte Fire Department had to rescue me, but I was super relieved they were here.

"Are you hurt?" A man's voice hollered up at me.

"No!" I called back.

"Don't worry, we'll get you down!" he shouted.

Bryan patted my hand. "You'll be fine. I'm going back down."

"Thanks," I said, blinking back tears of relief.

I trained my gaze downward to see several firemen pile out of the truck with their silver helmets. They looked like miniatures as they sawed the lock off the double gates and swung them open. The fire engine drove through and parked.

A long aluminum ladder lifted from the engine, then swung toward the headframe and extended up to my level. A fireman rode the tiny platform up to me and climbed onto the steel beam I was clinging to.

He peeked through the beam. "What's your name?"

"Josephina," I squeaked out in a shaky voice.

"All right, Josephina, I'm going to get you down. Can you move your foot?"

"No."

He squinted. "Hang on while I try to get your foot out, okay?"

"Okay." I tried to sound brave.

He swung around the beam to wriggle my foot but couldn't budge it. "She's in there pretty good," he said grimly. "Josephina, what school do you go to?"

"Um, St. Mike's," I rasped, my voice hoarse from breathing so hard.

"That's where our family goes to church," he said calmly. "Okay, Josephina, here's what I want you to do. You must stay as still as St. Mike's statue while I cut your shoe. Don't worry, I'll be careful."

I didn't know how he planned to do that, and anyway, I was too scared to look. "Okay."

"Stay still as a deer," he ordered.

I held my breath as he slid something inside the back of my shoe, then tugged at it.

"Pull your foot out," he instructed.

To my surprise, my foot backed out of my tennis shoe, which stayed wedged in the tight space.

"Climb around to my side. Nice and easy. Make sure you put your feet in the bigger holes, not the small ones. Then I'll help you onto the ladder. Got it?"

"Yes." My stomach jumped up to my throat. I took a steadying breath as his hands clamped onto my waist and hefted me onto the small, round ladder platform.

"They'll lower the ladder, so it won't be as steep when we walk down." The fireman stood behind me as I gripped the sides of the ladder for dear life and fixed my gaze on the Highland Mountains south of town. I swear I was as high as they were. The ladder swayed slightly and moved away from the headframe, and my grip tightened as the ladder lowered, then stopped.

"Take one step at a time and hang tight to the sides," instructed the fireman.

I stepped down slowly, and when I reached the fire engine, two firemen helped me to the ground. I thanked my lucky stars I was off that stupid gallus frame and hadn't fallen into the deep mine shaft.

"McCaffrey, how'd you get her foot out of the shoe?" one of them asked.

The fireman lifted a long metal shoehorn and grinned. "I keep this handy to help my grandmother put on her shoes. I slid this in back of her heel to protect her foot, then cut her tennis shoe with metal snips, and got her foot out with the shoehorn."

He pulled a cherry Tootsie Pop from his pocket. "This is for being brave. But never climb these headframes again. These abandoned mines are dangerous. Stay away from them. Understand?"

"Yes, sir." I gratefully accepted the Tootsie Pop.

"Wow, that was just like that *Rescue 8* TV show my dad used to watch," said Maggie. "Only in real life!"

"How about you don't see another one in real life?" said the fireman, heading to the fire engine. "Goodbye, girls. Stay out of trouble, okay?"

"We will!" we all chorused.

As the fire engine drove back down the hill, it passed Mrs. Quinn, stomping toward us.

"Mikey Ann, what the hell were you thinking?" demanded her mother. "You know you're forbidden to go near the Lex. Do you realize what could have happened?"

Mikey Ann pointed at me. "I know, but nothing did. Jo is okay."

"Only because of the fire department. Make sure it doesn't happen again." Mrs. Quinn put her arm around my shoulder to help me hobble back to her house, since I was minus one Ked.

On the way back to the Quinn's house, I asked her if she planned to tell my mother.

She cast me a side glance. "Do you want me to?"

"Not really. But I promise never to do it again."

"I'll leave it up to you whether to tell your mother, but she'll ask you what happened to your shoe," she said at last. "I hope you learned your lesson." She gave me a squeeze.

I turned to Cat and Maggie, walking on either side of me. "Thanks, you guys. Your jokes kept me from freaking out."

Cat bumped my hip. "You're such a klutz, Wolohan. You almost made it to the top of Mt. Everest. I was nervous you'd laugh at our jokes and fall off. Didn't want you winding up like Tommy."

"I don't care that I never got to the top. Not after getting stuck like that," I said, shaking my head.

Maggie hugged me. "I'm so glad you got down safely. Blessed be the firemen, for they are the fearless ones."

I hugged her back. "And blessed be the headframe climbers, for they have learned their lesson!"

Chapter 21
Day Five of Lilly's Coma

May 29, 1968, in the present

The day after our graduation meeting, Aunt Daisy picks me up after school. Aunt Violet is in the car after Aunt Daisy picked her up at the Greyhound bus station. We greet each other politely and the three of us go to the hospital to resume our vigil at Mom's bedside.

While I'm glad Aunt Violet has returned to Butte, I hold my tongue about not having heard from her very much in the last four years. Aunt Violet will stay with Aunt Daisy and me at the Silver Bow Homes.

Unlike my outgoing Aunt Daisy, Aunt Violet was reserved, and the youngest of the three "flower sisters," as Dad used to call them. While Aunt Daisy was a second mother to me growing up, Aunt Violet had more important things to do than spend time with me. Whenever her standoffishness hurt my feelings, Mom would say she loved me—she just wasn't affectionate like her sisters.

The smell of antiseptic and talcum powder hits me as we enter the hospital room. A nurse finishes Mom's sponge bath, offering us a supportive smile as she gathers her supplies and slips out. Mom's chest rises and falls in a steady rhythm, the only sign she's still with us.

Aunt Daisy lifts the clipboard hanging on the foot of Mom's bed, her fingers trembling slightly as she flips through the pages of medical information. The fluorescent lights cast harsh shadows across her furrowed brow.

Aunt Violet stands frozen in the doorway, her knuckles white as she clutches her purse. When she steps inside, tears pool seeing Mom's motionless form. She sinks into a chair across the room as if Mom's proximity makes this nightmare even more real.

I move to Mom's side, picking up a brush from the nightstand. The plastic handle is cool against my palm as I run it through her hair, careful not to tug on it. Her hair seems thinner.

"Nothing has changed." Aunt Daisy's voice cracks as she returns the clipboard to its hook, the chart rattling against the metal bed frame. "This could go on for months. Maybe even years."

I gasp at this terrifying possibility, and a quiet panic clutches my chest.

Aunt Violet's sharp intake of breath cuts through the room and she covers her nose and mouth with a handkerchief. "You shouldn't say those things. What if Lilly hears you?"

"You're right." Aunt Daisy moves to my mother and smooths her hair back, exposing her sharp widow's peak. "Sorry, Lil, I didn't mean that. You'll be up and at 'em in no time."

Her gaze locks onto mine, and I sense my aunt wanting forgiveness for saying what I've been fearing but couldn't say out loud. "You know I didn't mean that. I'm sure your mother will wake up anytime now. She's too stubborn to stay down for long."

A nurse pokes her head in to say she needs to check Mom's vitals. When she finishes, the scratching of her pen on the clipboard seems unnaturally loud. She checks the IV drip, then looks up. "Her vital signs remain stable. Dr. Madison will make his rounds in an hour if you'd like to speak with him."

"Thanks," Aunt Daisy and I both say automatically as she leaves.

We watch Mom's chest rise and fall, like almost counting each breath as if keeping track keeps her tethered to this world.

The machines beep rhythmically as I adjust Mom's blanket, smoothing out the wrinkles, fighting back tears. I guess I hadn't thought about how long people could stay in a coma. I've been so focused on waking Mom up by telling her stories, I avoided thinking about it. The possibility of weeks or months stretches before us like a forbidding tunnel with no guarantee of light at the end.

Aunt Violet blows her nose, then looks at me. "Jo, tell me what happened in the years I was gone from Butte." Her voice is tentative. "Daisy mentioned you nearly burned down the apartment house. Then your mom hired live-in babysitters? I also heard our brother Ollie took care of you for a while. I'd like to hear all about it."

I'm surprised by Aunt Violet's sudden interest after seldom hearing from her for so long. Her eyes, so much like Mom's, watch me expectantly. Four years of absence hang between us, but that distance seems insignificant now.

"Oh, right." I chuckle, tracing the pattern on Mom's hospital blanket with my fingertip, feeling the rough texture.

Instead of going to the smoker's lounge as she usually does, Aunt Daisy pulls up a chair and sits. "I wouldn't mind hearing this, too."

Aunt Violet leans forward. "Your mother always had a temper, but she never could stay mad for long." A smile plays at the corners of her mouth. "Remember when we were kids, Daisy? Lilly stuck that garter snake inside Mrs. Reed's mailbox because she thought the old lady was mean to the neighborhood cats."

Aunt Daisy snorts. "She felt so guilty she baked Mrs. Reed cookies every Sunday for a month."

"She did that?" I asked, surprised I'd not heard this story.

Aunt Daisy leans over and pats Mom's leg. "She did, indeed." My aunt glances at me. "Tell us about the babysitters you had when your mom wanted to sow some wild oats... and what happened in Apartment Three? Also, the celebrity you shook hands with. Lilly told us about it, but it'll be more entertaining when you tell it."

Welcoming the respite from focusing on my mother and the steady beep of machines, I think back to the sixth grade, and the weird time when it seemed like all Mom and I did was argue.

Outside Mom's sterile room, the hallway bustles with activity. Away from its medicinal smells and mechanical sounds, time is suspended as I talk about the past—hoping that somewhere in the darkness where my mother drifts, she'll grab hold of it and find her way back to us.

Chapter 22
A Winter's Flame

January 1966, sixth grade

Mom came up with the brilliant idea that the apartment house tenants would get a reduced rent for babysitting me. Between her sewing job, spending time with her new bowling buddies, and hanging out at the Elks animal bar, she was gone most evenings and weekends. I didn't mind so much since I spent most of my time with the Clover Girls.

I could tell the tenants from the sounds they made walking in and out of our building. My favorite was Gracie White, who rented Apartment Two and babysat me sometimes in the evenings. She had a don't-mess-with-me high-heel walk. Now and then she caught her spiky heel in a tiny square of the heat vent on the hallway floor.

"Dammit-to-hell, not again!" she'd cuss, extracting her heel from the metal shoe-trap and up the stairs she would go.

Gracie worked in women's lingerie at Hennessy's department store. When Mom and I went shopping one day, Gracie helped her select a new girdle—or a "merry widow" as she called it. What a weird name for a girdle. Mom sure wasn't merry when she became a widow.

"This new merry widow design has lace cups, a satin rear-end panel, and six garter straps." Gracie swept her hand over it like a game show host. "See how this garment extends over the hips? Do you want black or white?"

The wretched contraption had hundreds of hooks-and-eyes down the front that would take Mom so long to fasten, she'd surely grow cobwebs before she finished. Gracie held it up as if to show everyone in the store.

When Mom bought one, Gracie rewarded me with a sweet-smelling sachet to put in my undie drawer. She insisted the big girls did it, and it was part of becoming a lady.

Another tenant, PeeWee, watched me on weekends. Mom said everyone called him PeeWee because he was the runt of an eight-kid litter. His light footsteps tapped a rhythm coming down the stairs: Ta-tap, ta-tap, ta-tap, as if he was warming up to dance with Fred Astaire. He was a bookkeeper for The Company at the Mountain Con Mine, where Dad used to work. He wore clean, white shirts with rolled-up sleeves. Mom liked him and said he was a good kid. Mom called everyone a kid, even eighty-year-olds.

Mr. Bloom still lived in Apartment Five. He's the tall guy who'd carried me from the room when Dad died. Mom would prop the door open to our main floor apartment to lure prospective babysitters in with a beer or a highball. This was how she talked him into watching me after school on her bowling days. She still visited him in his room occasionally, returning in a much happier mood than when she went up. Mr. Bloom drove a uke, the humongous orange trucks that hauled ore from the Berkeley Pit.

The babysitting routines worked for a while until Mom's arrangement went up in smoke. Gracie announced she was moving to Helena over Thanksgiving. PeeWee switched to a swing shift at the mine after Christmas, and on New Year's Eve, Mr. Bloom married a lady from Deer Lodge and moved there for a job as a prison guard at the state penitentiary. We were sad to see him go, since he was Dad's last remaining tenant. He'd been with us for six years.

Mom's bowling friend, Netta Willingham, told her about students who attended the Butte Business College a few blocks from us on Galena Street, so Mom distributed fliers at the college for live-in babysitters. She figured the out-of-town students might want to babysit in exchange for rent.

Mom interviewed several and chose a pale skinny girl named Patricia Pounds. Cat called her 'Pixie' after the Pixie and Dixie mouse cartoon because of her oversized ears and pointy nose. Maggie called her the Holy Ghost because she floated around the house without a sound and didn't clomp up and down the stairs like other renters. She had a constant astonished expression, as if everything she encountered amazed her. She had a boyfriend that sometimes came around.

One day I asked Patricia if Maggie, Cat, Mikey Ann and I could play in Apartment Three, the empty studio apartment next door to hers. She said sure, so we hauled all my dolls and doll clothes inside, and I shoved the doll clothes inside the stove oven, pretending it was a closet. Patricia popped in now and then to make sure we were okay.

The four of us kids were playing house when Mom came home with Netta one late afternoon. She was from Dublin and her husband was a boss at the Montana Power Company. Mom hollered for me to go downstairs to meet her daughter, Helen. Cat and Maggie came with me to the kitchen, where Mom told us to play with Helen while she and Netta visited. Mom had invited PeeWee to join them for highballs since he had the day off.

As the five of us headed back upstairs, we heard the three of them laughing while they listened to the stack of records on the hi-fi: Jim Reeves, Nat King Cole, and the Righteous Brothers.

I let Helen play with my dolls while I set the table for our pretend dinner. I set out miniature doll plates and plastic chocolate chip cookies and a doll-sized cookie sheet that came with my old, broken Easy Bake oven.

"I'll bake the cookies!" announced Helen, snatching the plastic cookies and arranging them on the cookie sheet.

While Helen was busy playing house, the rest of us switched to playing Candyland and Mr. Potato Head. I had to go to the bathroom, so I went into the tiny bathroom and closed the door. As I finished up, my friends pounded on it.

"Jo, get out here! Helen started a fire!" yelled Mikey Ann.

"Hurry up, Jo!" shouted Cat, beating the door. "Your house is gonna burn down!"

"What?" I flung the door open to find smoke billowing from the oven, creeping along the ceiling and curling back on itself.

"Holy crap! What did you do?" I screamed at Helen.

"All I did was turn on the oven to make my cookies!" sobbed Helen, backing away.

In disbelief, I rushed to the gas stove to see the oven knob turned to the highest setting.

"My doll clothes!" I screamed, yanking open the oven door despite its hot handle. Flames leaped out as the door bounced on its hinges. I pin-balled around the smoke-filled room, desperately running my fingers along the wall to find the window—only to discover it was painted shut.

"Help me, you guys!" I ordered. "Get the fire out before my mother finds out!"

Cat and Maggie grabbed bowls from the kitchen cupboard, filled them with water, and threw it at the stove. It only sizzled, making a worse mess.

"What happened?" Patricia stood in her white bra and panties, her boyfriend peering over her shoulder in his underwear.

I was in a blind panic. "Helen started a fire and we can't get it out!"

"I did not! I did not!" shrieked Helen, and she ran out the door.

"Go get your mother!" Patricia and her boyfriend rushed to her apartment to get dressed as smoke billowed out into the upstairs hallway.

Helen had alerted Mom, Netta, and PeeWee, and they were already on the landing as we thundered down the stairs.

"There's a fire!" I sobbed, pointing up the stairs.

"Dammit, Jo! What did you do?" Mom grabbed the pink receiver off the princess phone from the hall table and called the fire department. PeeWee sprinted upstairs with a fire extinguisher he'd pulled from the downstairs hallway. The deafening roar of the extinguisher scared us as much as the fire.

"Grab your coats and get out of the house!" ordered Mom.

We snatched our jackets and scurried out the front door and down the icy steps, then stood on the shoveled sidewalk, shivering. Patricia and her boyfriend stood outside with us, zipping up their jackets.

When the fire engine arrived, the firemen ran to the corner with flat hoses, shoveled the snow away, and screwed them into the fire hydrant. They snaked the fat hoses through the front door, along the hallway, and up the stairs.

"Is everyone out?" one fireman asked, his breath puffing frost in the wintry air.

"Yes, sir," said PeeWee. "Luckily, most tenants aren't home from work yet."

The fireman peered at me as I gnawed on my thumb.

"Hey, I know you. You're Josephina." He removed his helmet. "Remember me? I'm Fireman McCaffrey, the one who helped you off the gallus frame." He smiled at Mom. "You and your husband have a brave little girl."

"Oh, I'm a widow, but thank you." She offered him her broadest smile.

His smile widened at this news. "She was a real trooper. Did what I told her to do so we could get her down." His gaze lingered on Mom.

"I'm grateful to you for helping her. I gave her a stern talking to," she gushed.

I was mortified Mom was flirting with him while he was putting out our fire.

He winked at both of us, then hurried inside our smoking house.

We waited and watched as dark smoke swirled out of the upstairs hallway window. Neighbors stood in their front yards, watching. The firemen finally extinguished the fire and rolled up their hose.

McCaffrey walked down the front steps and held out a gloved hand with the incriminating evidence: blackened snaps, zippers, and melted doll shoes.

Mom glared at me. "Dammit, Jo! I've told you not to turn the stoves on when you play in the empty apartments. Now I have to pay to fix all of this!" she thundered.

"But Helen was the one who turned on the stove!" I protested in defense.

"You shouldn't have put your doll clothes in the oven!" countered my mother, striding up the steps and into the house.

Maggie wrung her hands. "So sorry, Jo. This is awful."

Cat stood on my other side, shaking her head. "This is the pits. Sorry, Jo."

"You guys, it wasn't your fault. Helen was the one who turned on the oven." I glanced around to see where Helen was, but she was gone, and so was her mother.

THE NEXT MORNING, I was sure I'd be on the receiving end of Mr. Whackenstick as I watched Mom remove the sheets and covers off the bed in the damaged apartment. While not much had burned outside of the stove, everything else had smoke damage.

I stood in the doorway, fidgeting. "I'm sorry, Mom. But Helen turned on the oven."

"But you were the one who put the doll clothes inside it." Mom yanked a corner of a sheet off the bed as Patricia appeared next to me.

Mom pointed a finger at her. "You were supposed to watch the girls. Pack your things. I want you to move out."

Patricia backed away with a hand over her mouth.

"Mom, it wasn't Patricia's fault!" I rushed to explain. "It was mine and Helen's."

Mom ignored me and glared at Patricia. "It was your responsibility to watch Jo. Go, Patricia. Now." Mom balled up the sheets and blankets and tossed them to the floor.

Patricia scurried out the door, and her boyfriend showed up that afternoon to help move her out. They carried boxes down the stairs and out to his blue Ford Thunderbird.

I explained to Mom what happened, how the unused oven would be a good place to store the doll clothes, and how Helen turned the oven to the highest setting.

"Patricia was supposed to keep a close eye on you. If she had, this wouldn't have happened," Mom said sternly.

I felt terrible and wanted to tell Patricia how sorry I was, that it wasn't entirely her fault.

But I never got the chance.

Chapter 23
The Porno Nanny

January 1966

After the fire, Mom dated Mike McCaffrey, the fireman who had helped us. When she got the insurance money after the holidays, Mike helped her replace the smoke damage in the upstairs apartment. With the leftover money, she paid a company to remodel ours on the main floor. She installed slippery white linoleum with gold and black specks in the living room and hired carpenters to rip out the wall to her bedroom, to make it one big front room.

Mom dubbed our house "The Lilly Apartments," so Mike made a sign and mounted it next to the front door. She moved her personal things into Apartment One across the hall so she could use it for her bedroom. She bought blue kidney-shaped davenports and chairs, and white kidney-shaped end tables. Our living room resembled *The Jetsons*, and I expected George and his boy Elroy to float by any second in their space car.

Mom found another babysitter from the business college to watch me in exchange for rent. Pepper Brady was heavier than Patricia, with chin-length jet black hair parted on the side, and black pointy-rimmed glasses like Maggie's. She was from Havre, up by the Canadian border.

Pepper was always busy typing while Maggie, Cat, Mikey Ann, and I played Barbies after school in her apartment. I paid little attention to what Pepper typed, until one day when she was downstairs talking to Mom, I stuck my nose where it didn't belong.

I picked up a page that was face-down on Pepper's desk and read about a girl and a boy who swam in the ocean. The girl got sand inside of her, and the boy helped her get the sand out. They kissed, and he climbed on top of her and stuck his... I blushed at the 'P' word.

"You guys, come read this!" I waved Maggie, Mikey Ann, and Cat over and handed them each a page to read. Their eyes grew to the size of frisbees.

Maggie's face contorted in disgust. "How does sand get inside a person?"

I shrugged, returning a clueless stare.

"Eew, that's gross!" Mikey Ann wrinkled her face. "And he put his mouth on her...her...I can't even say it!" She shoved the page at me, her eyeballs popping out of her head.

"Nipples? Criminy! Her *nipples*? Only babies do that!" I was horrified. "I don't get how sand can get inside a girl, either. And why is this boy on top of her?"

"You don't know?" Mikey Ann sounded incredulous. "Anyone who has brothers knows this stuff!"

"I don't have brothers," I sputtered. "So, fill me in, Miss Know-it-All!"

"I can't believe you don't know why boys get on top of girls!" shrieked Mikey Ann. "You're a fifth grader and you don't know how babies are made?"

"Why are they making babies?" exclaimed Maggie. "They aren't even married!"

I stared at Mikey Ann. "Okay, Smarty Pants, since you're the expert, explain this." I pointed to the penis word on the page, seriously agitated that everyone but me magically knew this stuff.

Cat let out a cackle. "Jeez, Louise, Jo! That's a boy's wiener and a girl's—" Cat leaned in and whispered. "Oosie."

I choked on my spit. "A *what?*"

Cat straightened with a serious expression. "My mother calls a girl's private part an oosie."

Maggie guffawed. "No way, shut up!"

"An oosie?" I echoed. "That's just—that's just..." I shook my head in denial, running out of words.

We all dissolved into peals of laughter until tears ran. Mikey Ann was the first to recover. "I'm amazed you've never seen a penis." She howled again, holding her stomach.

"That word by itself is gross," I retorted. "I gather you've seen one in person?"

Cat spoke up. "I see them all the time when I walk in on my brothers peeing in the bathroom. Funny-looking things, like stubby garden hoses. Glad I don't have one."

"That's disgusting!" hollered Maggie, covering her mouth.

"They look like those Vienna sausages in a can." Mikey Ann shrugged.

Cat laughed and Mikey Ann snorted while Maggie and I shrieked with incredulity.

"I'm never eating another Vienna sausage!" Maggie pawed at her tongue while Cat fell back onto Pepper's bed, laughing so hard she clutched her stomach.

"How can I see a penis if I don't have a brother?" I asked, just as Pepper swung the door open. Her face became murderous at seeing the pages in our hands.

"What are you doing? Give me those!" Pepper strode over, yanked the paper from her typewriter, and snatched the papers from each of our hands. "You kids shouldn't be reading this!"

Cat's brows shot up. "Why not?"

"For one thing, it's against the law!" She shoved the stack of typewritten pages into a binder. "You can't read stuff like this until you're twenty-one!"

"They were just sitting there," I attempted, my face warming. "So, what does 'pop a cherry' mean?"

"Oh, my land!" Pepper lowered her horn-rimmed glasses, peering over them. "Don't those nuns teach you the facts of life at that Catholic school?"

"We have to wait until the eighth grade," I grumbled. "You didn't answer my question."

Pepper let out a heavy sigh. "A cherry is slang for a hymen."

Maggie placed a hand on her hip. "So, what's a hymen?"

"Those things are on a need-to-know basis, and you don't need to know." Pepper seemed exasperated, waving her hand dismissively.

"I know what a hymen is!" blurted Cat. "My cousin busted hers riding a ten-speed bike on the railroad tracks." She nodded emphatically.

"Oh, no, did she get a plaster cast?" asked Maggie, tapping her glasses.

"It's not like breaking an arm," Cat said matter-of-factly. "It's on the inside. Where the man puts his, you know—wiener."

Maggie threw her arms up. "How in God's name does he do that?"

"All right, all right. Good grief!" Pepper shook her head and pulled out a thick text from her bookcase, *Gray's Anatomy*. "Eighth grade is too late for learning the facts of life, for crying out loud," she grumbled, flipping through the thick text. She opened to a page and held up the book for our viewing pleasure.

"Does this answer your question?"

Right there for God and everyone on planet Earth to see was a gargantuan wiener that took up the whole page. It stuck up like a rocket on a launch pad at Cape Canaveral, only with a knobby thing on the end and a tiny hole in the middle.

"That doesn't look like a Vienna sausage," I observed, squinting. I pointed to the bulging things hanging beneath it, like flesh-colored ping-pong balls. "What are those things?"

"Testicles. Scrotum." Pepper rolled her eyes. "Most guys call them balls."

Cat rolled around on Pepper's bed, laughing. "I've seen those, too!"

A light bulb clicked on, recalling Cat telling me to stab Butch McKnight in the balls back in second grade. She knew what these things were even way back *then*.

"Delaney, you're a traitor! You've been holding out on me!" I shouted, crowding in for a close-up of the wiener. "Boy, that thing is *huge!*"

"They're not normally as big as this one." Pepper tilted her head in a critical assessment. "Well, maybe sometimes..."

"They change sizes," Mikey Ann reported matter-of-factly, popping a lime Lifesaver into her mouth. She offered one to us, but we were still fascinated with the giant wiener.

"They do?" Maggie's face twisted as she leaned closer. "How the heck do they do that?"

"Okay girls, that's enough." Pepper snatched the *Gray's Anatomy* text and returned it to the bookshelf. "You'll get the gory details in the eighth grade."

"That's a million years from now!" I whined, as I was reminded of something. "I saw one of those Vienna sausage things in person when I was five. A kid named Shawn chased me into the alley and told me to pull down my pants."

Maggie's eyes widened into two moons. "Did you?"

"No, but he unzipped his and pulled it out. I screamed it was a monster, so he stuffed it back in and ran away."

"What a little pervert!" Pepper wrinkled her nose. "Hey, I'm not the one to give you the birds-and-bees talk because I don't want the wrath of your parents. And don't you dare tell anyone you read my story!"

She grabbed a black book from her bookshelf and held it out. "Put one hand on this Bible, raise the other, and swear."

"I swear." We each took turns placing our hands on the Bible, like we were witnesses in a *Perry Mason* trial.

After my friends went home, while "Walk Like a Man" played on the radio, I took out my Barbie and Ken dolls. I lowered Ken's pants to see if he had one of those wiener things. Nope, only a smooth bulge. Not anything like the one in the book. So real guys had them, but men dolls didn't? I made a mental note to write a letter to Mattel to tell them they got Ken's private parts wrong, and they'd better fix them.

The following weekend, the Clover Girls came over, and we sat on Pepper's bed with Barbie, Ken, Midge, Allen, and Skipper. Pepper loaded a stack of 45 records on her portable stereo, and we listened to "Big Girls Don't Cry" and "Sherry" by The Four Seasons. We took turns singing into a hairbrush.

Pepper walked out with several bottles of Coke she set on a table. "I'm celebrating because I sold a story to a magazine. I'm a published author!"

Mikey Ann's jaw dropped. "Really?"

"Which story?"

"That beach story you guys read. They paid me for it and said I have potential. I've been submitting stories for the past few years and finally got one published," Pepper said with a proud smile.

I exchanged crazed looks with Maggie while Cat covered her mouth to hide her laughter.

"Someone actually paid you for that?" I was incredulous.

"They sure did." I could tell Pepper was delighted about the whole thing.

"Wow." My mind spun in curious circles as I drank my pop, the carbonation nipping my nose.

When Mom got home, I walked the Clover Girls to our front door, and we congregated on the porch.

"I can't believe Pepper sold the story with that nasty stuff!" exclaimed Cat, wide-eyed.

"Blessed be the porno nanny for teaching us about girl-and-boy parts," deadpanned Maggie, arms spread like a priest giving a sermon. "Like Paul Harvey says, guess we'll have to wait for the rest of the story."

Cat's eyes gleamed. "Unless we ask the nuns to fill us in on the gory details?"

Mikey Ann snorted. "Yeah, like that'll happen."

AT THE END OF HER SEMESTER, Pepper moved out and returned to Havre. She told Mom and me she had to go help with the family ranch. We Clover Girls had grown used to spending time with her, and she'd read us her other stories... carefully skipping the sex parts.

After she left, I missed her terribly. She wrote me a couple of letters, but eventually they stopped. Her last letter informed me she was authoring articles for magazines and writing books under a different name.

"They're paying me enormous advances for my love stories," she'd written.

When I told Mom, she said, "Good for Pepper! What stories does she write?"

"Uh, love stories. Like the ones in *Redbook* and *Good Housekeeping* magazines." I figured a little white lie wouldn't hurt anything.

"I'll have to get one and read it next time I go to the store."

"Pepper writes under another name," I blurted.

"What is it?" Mom asked, staring at me. "Did she tell you?"

"Uh, no," I lied, feigning ignorance. Pepper had told me her pen name, but I didn't want Mom to find out what she wrote. That would open a huge can of worms I wasn't willing to deal with.

I made a mental note to be on the lookout for an author named Tiffany Desire, so I could read Pepper's books the second I turned twenty-one.

Chapter 24
Cowboys and Naked Women

July 1966, sixth grade summer

Uncle Will and Uncle Ollie were dyed-in-the-wool cowboys stuck in the olden times. They left the ranch for steadier work in the Butte mines. They called themselves cowpunchers. I pictured them standing on the prairie, punching cows. Both lamented about being 'busted up' after a lifetime of riding horses.

Before Dad died, my uncles were at the house so often it was like they lived with us. But after Mom had thrown them out of Geraghty's Funeral Home at Dad's wake, they were gun-shy about showing their faces at the apartment house.

One sunny day when Maggie and I walked over town to the Woolworth lunch counter for French fries and gravy, we spotted Uncle Ollie in the chewing tobacco section. After we shared a bear hug, I pleaded with him to come to our house and make peace with Mom. Four years had passed since he and Uncle Will tried hauling Dad out of his casket at Geraghty's funeral home. I told him how much we missed them.

He stuffed a mouthful of chew inside his bottom lip and winked at me. "I'll give it a think."

A week later, both uncles showed up at our door. I let them in, hoping Mom wouldn't have a conniption fit. To my relief, she hugged each of them and welcomed them inside. After that, Uncle Will and Uncle Ollie stopped by regularly, like they used to. Mom frequently invited them over for pasty dinners with homemade coleslaw and sweet potato salad.

Mom and her brothers loved spinning yarns about the Lone Creek Ranch in northwest Montana. Will and Ollie boasted that the ranch once employed Charlie Russell (the famous western painter), Calamity Jane, and

Bertrand Sinclair, known as the Fiddleback Kid. Mom's stories captivated everyone with her ornamental cuss words and colorful language, painting scenes as vividly as Russell painted bucking broncs. The more highballs and brandy ditches she consumed, the more entertaining the tales became.

I watched my mother, transfixed, when she animated her stories. She'd tilt her head and waggle her brows, her dark curls flopping back and forth. I'd lose myself in the cadence of her words, until she'd hit the grand finale, always with a funny punchline. She reveled in the laughter that followed. I loved how Mom came alive in these moments.

One Friday night, Cat, Maggie, and Mikey Ann came to our house for a sleepover. After a pasty dinner with my uncles, we all gathered in the living room where Uncle Ollie and Uncle Will parked themselves in their usual spots on the davenport. The four of us sat on the floor, playing Monopoly.

I rolled the dice and moved my silver racecar to pass 'Go' and collect my $200.

"Hey, Mom, tell the Zack story!" I called out to her in her armchair. This one was my favorite.

Mom grinned. "That's Uncle Ollie's story. He should tell it."

"Heaven help us," teased Uncle Will with a hand to his forehead.

"Poor Zack. He was a cantankerous old geezer." Uncle Ollie slurped his beer. "Zack was the 'bean master' on our ranch." Ollie looked at us kids. "The ranch cook."

"Oh." We all nodded.

Cat shook the dice as Ollie continued. "Zack came to Montana from Chicago along about the 1930s, during The Great Depression. You've heard of that, right?" He gave us a direct look.

"Just say yes," I whispered out the side of my mouth to my friends.

"Yes," they dutifully chorused.

Cat moved her old shoe to Boardwalk and bought it. I counted out her change.

"One day, Zack cooked his last biscuit and moseyed up to that stovetop in the sky," said Ollie, shaking his head.

"A cryin' shame." Uncle Will grimaced, then burped. "His ticker gave out."

Maggie giggled, and he winked at her.

"After a day of herding slow elk, we hit the bunkhouse and Zack was sprawled on his cot," said Uncle Ollie.

Mikey Ann scrunched her face. "What's a slow elk?"

"Rancher talk for a cow," I filled in.

Uncle Ollie continued. "No one believed Zack was dead. Hell, we thought he'd only fallen asleep. We'd been in town celebrating getting hay up for the winter and were pretty much shitfaced. Dunno how we made it back to the ranch. Good thing the horses knew the way, or we'd still be out there somewheres."

"Horses are smart," said Maggie.

"Yes, they are," agreed Uncle Ollie. "Anyways, we thought Zack was only sleeping, so Will propped him up in a rocking chair and ladled whiskey down his throat."

"You fed whiskey to a *dead person*?" Maggie's face scrunched up.

"We thought he was sleeping." Uncle Will acted like this happened every day of the week. "Hell, we were trying to wake him up."

Uncle Ollie chuckled. "I said here's to mud in yer eye, and Will opened Zack's mouth and fed him a drink from my flask."

"Then we told Zack we was taking him to town," explained Uncle Ollie. "We saddled up and propped him in front of me on my old buckskin quarter-horse, named Buck. Someone left the door open to the Mint Bar, so I rode Buck inside. He clomped up to the bartender and whinnied, like he knew Old Zack needed a drink."

"You rode your horse inside of the bar?" Mikey Ann snorted an incredulous laugh.

"Yep. The barkeep lined up a couple shots, so Will and me wrangled Zack off my horse and set him in a chair at a table." Ollie stopped talking to sip his beer.

"Then what happened?" asked Cat.

"The barkeep said Old Zack was dead, and the undertaker was there and said yep, he'd kicked the bucket, so they hauled him away." Uncle Ollie pointed at his brother. "Seems to me you sniveled and raised a ruckus."

"And *you* blubbered all the way back to the Lone Crick spread." Will shook his head, lost in the past. "Never mind that we were three sheets to the wind."

"Didn't you get into trouble for riding horses inside the bar?" asked Maggie.

"Nah, everyone did it back then," snorted Uncle Ollie. "Then there was the time when Calamity Jane and Charlie Russell—"

Mom cut him off. "Okay, that's enough tall tales. These kids have to go to bed."

"Calamity who? Who's Charlie Russell?" asked Mikey Ann.

"A famous Montana artist," said Uncle Ollie, popping open another Butte Beer. "Good night, you kids. See you in the funny papers."

Once we'd settled into bed, my friends were stunned by my family's stories. I loved watching their jaws hang open. Maggie had reacted with disbelief, but it normally took a lot to surprise Cat and Mikey Ann—and they were completely amazed.

AFTER PEPPER HAD GONE, Mom asked Uncle Ollie if he would babysit me. Uncle Will had found a girlfriend from Butte's Fourth of July parade. She rode horses with the Petticoat Patrol and was a barrel racer. This tickled Uncle Will down to his cowboy boots. She moved back to her ranch near Bozeman, and Uncle Will had gone with her a few weeks after our sleepover.

Mom and I missed him, but his leaving was harder on Uncle Ollie. Since Pepper had returned to Havre, Mom offered him an apartment in exchange for babysitting me when she went out of town for bowling tournaments. Uncle Ollie moved into Apartment Five at the far end of the second-floor hallway.

The other Clover Girls liked to come over when Uncle Ollie was in charge because he let us do stuff our moms wouldn't let us do.

Mom had firmly instructed him, "No drinking when you're around Jo and her friends!"

He didn't, except one Saturday in late July, when Mom gave Uncle Ollie money to take Maggie, Cat, and me to the Rialto Theater on East Park Street to see *The Man Who Shot Liberty Valance* at a matinee. Mikey Ann couldn't go because she was out of town, vacationing with her family.

Once we got our popcorn and settled into our seats, the lights dimmed, and the movie started. Uncle Ollie whipped out a can of beer and pierced a hole in the can with his metal opener. The sound brought an usher with a flashlight, who shined it in our faces. Uncle Ollie slid the beer to me, and I stuck it under my t-shirt while he stared straight ahead, still as a post.

"Do you have canned beverages in here?" the usher demanded, his cap tilted to the side.

"Nope, just popcorn," Uncle Ollie drawled, reaching into my cardboard box and popping a kernel into his mouth.

"Just so you know, no canned beverages are allowed." The usher switched off his flashlight and pranced back up the aisle.

Uncle Ollie and I exchanged 'oops' looks, and Maggie elbowed me in the ribs. We giggled, holding our red-and-white striped boxes of buttered popcorn. I could tell Uncle Ollie was smiling as he sipped his beer.

Each day for lunch, my uncle fed me a glass of milk with a ham and cheese sandwich or stinky sardines from a flat tin, with the top curled back. We'd eat our lunch on his chipped-paint table and he'd turn on his black-and-white TV. We'd watch *Days of Our Lives* or game shows like *Password*, *The Match Game*, or *I've Got A Secret*, with Garry Moore. It was fun yelling our guesses out before the stars did. This was our routine, and we grew comfortable with it.

One day after school, I saw my first naked woman in Uncle Ollie's apartment. While rummaging through a desk drawer for a pen and paper, I spotted a pin-up calendar. It had fuzzy felt on the top of the transparent lift-up piece that was the woman's swimsuit, and underneath was a bare-naked lady. Her upper parts were bare, but her lower part stayed covered—not that I wanted to see that part since I had one of my own—and knew what it looked like. I didn't want Uncle Ollie to get in trouble with my mother, so I kept my mouth shut. I would never rat out my uncle; he was the closest thing to a father I had.

Near the end of August, I came home from Cat's house and asked Mom if I could go watch "Let's Make a Deal" with Uncle Ollie.

She didn't look up from her magazine. "No, he's gone."

I thought I was hearing things. "What do you mean, gone? Where did he go?"

"He moved back up to Lone Crick." Mom took a drag on her cig and blew out a trail of smoke. "He won't be back."

"No!" I cried out, rushing upstairs to Apartment Five. I threw the door open. The furniture was still there, so I yanked a dresser drawer open, and it was empty. His cases of beer were gone, too.

Mom followed, and pulled down his horse and ranch calendars, tearing them up and taking them downstairs to throw in the garbage. I wanted them as a remembrance of our fun times together, but she didn't give me the chance to keep anything.

When she left, I crumpled to the floor and cried.

Uncle Ollie's leaving left a hole so big it ached my chest. What was it with people who waltzed into our lives, then vanished like the Holy Ghost? It felt like I'd lost Dad all over again. Every time I cared for someone, they vanished from my life. It felt like I was cursed and I fought back paranoia about something happening to Mom or Aunt Daisy.

A few months later, I overheard Mom talking with Aunt Daisy about Uncle Ollie. She said his liver had finally conked out after a lifetime of drinking. Mom and Aunt Daisy drove to the ranch for his funeral, but since I had school, I couldn't go. I stayed with Mikey Ann and her dad drove us to school until Mom and my aunt returned. Cat and Maggie tried to cheer me up at school, reminding me of his fun stories.

Mom explained to me when he found out about his liver cancer he didn't want to die in Butte—and he didn't want us to watch him die. I did my best to understand, but we could have taken care of him. A huge chunk of my heart fell out of me after he'd gone.

At least I still had my mother, Aunt Daisy, and the Clover Girls.

I would always have the Clover Girls.

Chapter 25
Hope For The Future

September 1966

"Robert Francis Kennedy is visiting Butte next month!" announced Sister Roberta Marie on the first day of seventh grade. We called her Sister Bertie for short. "He'll be here to campaign for his political party. School will let out early that day in honor of his arrival."

Yay! No school!

A shocked gasp circulated around our class. We remembered the JFK assassination, and watching the president's brother Bobby, walking behind the president's casket on TV with Jackie Kennedy, and Caroline and little John John.

Our eyes bugged out of our heads as Cat, Maggie, and I exchanged glances. We mouthed words at each other, thinking the same thing: someone famous is coming to Butte, and we have to go see him!

Sister Bertie bowed her head whenever she invoked the name Kennedy, like Jesus Christ himself was coming to Butte. I had heard about Robert Kennedy from TV and stories in *The Christian Science Monitor*.

"You must learn about your government." Sister Bertie rolled out the Bell and Howell movie projector and showed us film clips about the Kennedys. Afterwards, she grabbed chalk and wrote in cursive on the green chalkboard:

Write a one-thousand-word essay about Robert F. Kennedy. Due two weeks from today.

The entire class groaned.

One-thousand words? In TWO weeks?

Sister turned around. "You may work in groups of four for this assignment and you are each responsible for writing two hundred fifty words." That eased our pain a little. But to a sixth grader, writing two hundred fifty words was like a prison sentence.

After school, I cornered Mikey Ann, Maggie, and Cat. "Okay, let's be a group. Good grief, how are we going to do this?"

Cat brushed back blonde tendrils that escaped her half-braided ponytails. "One thousand words? I've never written that many words in my whole life!"

"Me neither," said Mikey Ann and Maggie in unison.

"Who has encyclopedias? We don't." Maggie shrugged.

Cat made a face. "We do, but our husky chewed up the 'K' volume, so Dad tossed it."

Mikey Ann snorted and rolled her eyes. "Well, we have a set, but you guys will have to come up to Walkerville to work on it."

"That's a million miles from here." I had an idea. "Let's go to the library before anyone else beats us to it."

We ran most of the five blocks to the Butte Public Library on Broadway. The librarian let us use her phone to tell our moms we were working on our new assignment.

"You better be telling me the truth and you're not up to no good," warned Mom. "Be home by five-thirty, or..."

"Or I'll get Mr. Whackenstick, I know." In Mom's book, tough love was the way to keep me in line. She'd only used her yardstick on me a couple of times, but she acted like she whacked me every five minutes.

The librarian wouldn't let us check out the encyclopedias, so we spread the massive "J-K" volume of *The World Book Encyclopedia* on a square table. We each took a different section and scribbled our valuable information. I wrote:

Robert Francis "Bobby" Kennedy is an American politician from Massachusetts. He is John Fitzgerald Kennedy's younger brother and was the United States Attorney General from 1961 to 1964. He left that post to run for election to the United States Senate.

"There!" I sat back, proud of myself for my forty-nine words.

I leaned over and peeked at Cat's writing. She had the neatest penmanship in the class and the gold stars on her forehead to prove it.

Her letters fit perfectly between the lines in our *Palmer Method* booklets. I practiced until my hand fell off, but my cursive was never as good as Cat's.

Cat put down her pencil. "Okay, listen to mine. Robert Francis Kennedy was born on November 20, 1925, in Brookline, Massachusetts. He is the seventh child of Rose and Joseph P. Kennedy. That's twenty-three words," she proudly announced.

"Listen to mine!" Maggie cut in, lifting her paper in front of her coke-bottle glasses. "He graduated from Harvard in 1948 and earned a law degree from the University of Virginia Law School. Upon graduating from Harvard, Kennedy sailed on the *Queen Mary* with a college friend for a tour of Europe and the Middle East." Not to be outdone, she lifted her chin in triumph. "Forty-one words!"

"Neato! We'll have a thousand words in no time." I squeezed my tongue between my teeth as we each worked to write our sections. Before we knew it, the librarian told us it was five o'clock.

"Time to split. My stomach is growling." Mikey Ann zipped her pencil inside her transparent pencil case.

"Mine is, too." I gathered my pencils and tablets and hurried home, making it before five-thirty. Once again, I'd avoided Mr. Whackenstick and took that as a win.

We handed in our essays by the due date, and we all got A's and *Very Goods* marked in bright red ink on our papers. I crossed off the days with a giant 'X' on our large ACM Company calendar as the days ticked by.

I couldn't wait.

ON OCTOBER 25, SCHOOL was released at lunch so the St. Mike's students could go see Bobby Kennedy give his speech outside the Miners' Union Hall, up on Granite Street.

Bursting with excitement, Cat, Maggie, Mikey Ann, and I hoofed up to Granite Street with the crowds. I was surprised seeing so many people already crowding the street.

"How will we see him all the way back here?" I fretted.

"Let's worm our way through," suggested Maggie. "Follow me."

"Easy for you to say. You're the smallest," mumbled Mikey Ann, who was often mistaken for a high schooler because of her height.

We did our best to wedge through the hundreds of people crowding both sides of Granite Street. Rope barriers prevented people from spilling into the street. Police cars were parked at each intersection, lights flashing.

I glanced around, realizing I'd lost sight of my three friends, and the throngs of people made it impossible to find them. I squeezed through the crowd until I was directly in front of the Miner's Union Hall.

People stood on rooftops and hung out of second and third-story windows of nearby buildings. Whoops and hollers sounded at one end of Granite Street as the motorcade turned onto it. Girls screamed like Bobby Kennedy was Paul McCartney on *The Ed Sullivan Show*.

"We love you, Bobby!" They squealed repeatedly. "Butte loves you!"

The crowd went crazy, with everyone cheering and screaming like he was a movie star. By this time, I'd squirmed around a big lady to find myself at the rope barrier. I'd reached the front row and spotted a blue convertible with Bobby Kennedy standing and waving as it slowly came toward us.

This was so exciting!

The car rolled to a stop at the Miners' Union Hall on West Granite, next to a wooden platform that was built for the occasion. I glimpsed Mrs. Kennedy's blonde hair in the back seat.

Bobby stood for a moment among the cheering crowd, smiling and shaking hands, as he stepped from the car. He helped his wife out of the car, and they walked up the steps to the platform that was trimmed in half-flags of red, white, and blue.

People carried on like Bobby was a rockstar, jumping up and down, yelling and screaming. I half-expected the teenagers to faint like in the movie *Bye Bye Birdie*, where Conrad Birdie appeared and the whole town swooned on the spot.

Senator Metcalfe spoke first, then Bobby talked about the stops he'd be making in Missoula, Bozeman, and Billings. What mesmerized me was his radiant smile and his big, pearly white teeth. This was the first famous person I'd seen in the flesh, besides Evel Knievel and his motorcycle stunts out on The Flats.

Everyone quieted for his speech. He talked about supporting those in his political party that were running for office for the November elections. Then he talked about the youth of Butte, and how young Americans have an independent spirit and possess a profound sense of idealism and the importance of unity, compassion, and understanding of our fellow Americans.

He said, "Only those who dare to fail greatly can ever achieve greatly, and the youth in this country are the best hope for mankind and should be encouraged to reach their maximum potential."

He didn't talk for long, but I didn't care. He said things in a way I understood, and it felt like he was talking to people my age. I had an urge to holler at Bobby that I was sorry Mom and I had called his brother a cock-eyed octopus back in the fourth grade. I also wanted to ask him to please keep us safe from nuclear bombs.

Bobby ended his speech, and Monsignor Coyle stepped onto the platform to say a prayer and give the Kennedy family a blessing. Then the family waved and stepped back into the blue convertible. Bobby stood on the floor of the car, waving and shaking hands. People jostled me as they pushed toward the convertible with outstretched arms. I was determined as anyone to shake Bobby's hand.

The crowd surged forward, knocking down the rope barrier posts, everyone wanting to touch him. The police stepped forward, hollering at people to get back onto the sidewalks.

People shouted, "We love you, Bobby!" while a band played, "You're A Grand Old Flag." As the car inched away from the Miners Union Hall, it was now or never; my one and only chance to shake Bobby's hand.

I weaseled my short, sinewy body around taller people, ducking under elbows and winding my way to the head of the pack. I put my head down, thrust myself forward, and suddenly there I was, next to the blue convertible!

I stretched both arms out like a *Night of the Living Dead* zombie, reaching like everyone else. I stayed alongside the car as it crept through the throngs while Bobby bent to shake hands.

"Bobby! Bobby! Over here! Over here!" I screamed at the top of my lungs.

He looked straight at me and smiled. Ecstatic, I grasped his hand and hung on for all I was worth, jogging alongside the blue convertible.

"Hello, young lady!" Kennedy laughed, holding my hand until the moving car pulled my hand from his grasp.

The moment happened quickly, but it would stick with me…maybe for eternity. People emptied the street, pushing and shoving in their haste to keep up with the convertible, but I no longer cared.

He said hello to me and held my hand!

Dazed, I stood in the middle of Granite Street, watching the blue convertible as it turned left and disappeared down Montana Street.

"Omigosh! Did you *see* that?" I shrieked to no one, clamping my wrist as if the hand that touched Kennedy's might detach and scurry away, like Thing from *The Addams Family*.

A car honked, and I spun around to see an agitated driver pointing his thumb toward the sidewalk.

"Josephina! Get out of the street!" Cat ran up, grabbed my elbow, and led me to the sidewalk. "You look like you saw the Holy Ghost."

"Bobby Kennedy held my hand! He *held* my hand! I touched him, Cat, I touched him!" I floated along, fixated on the hand he'd touched.

My eyes darted around in a panic. "Quick! Give me a tissue!"

Mikey Ann rushed up. "What's wrong? Did you hurt your hand?"

"Don't touch it!" I shrieked, jumping backwards. "This hand touched Bobby's hand. I have to save his *touch*. Quick! Who has a tissue?"

Maggie fumbled a wrinkled pink tissue from her pocket and offered it to me. "Don't worry, there's no snot on it."

"That helps. Thanks, Mags." I snatched it and wiped Kennedy's touch onto the tissue. I carefully folded it and put it in my pocket. Now his touch was on the tissue, forever preserved.

We stopped at S&L Ice Cream for ice cream cones, and as we inhaled them on the way home, I clutched my Kennedy-touch hand as if it were made of gold. When I got home, I found a blue stationery envelope and hurried upstairs to my room. Carefully retrieving the tissue, I eased it into the envelope, then gingerly tucked it inside my musical jewelry box with the pirouetting ballerina.

I did the dishes that night with one hand, for fear of washing off my Kennedy touch from the other. I also delayed taking a bath for several days until Mom wrinkled her nose in disgust. "For the love of God, take a shower!"

The day after Bobby's visit, Sister Bertie read *The Montana Standard* newspaper article out loud to our class. "Kennedy spoke to over thirty-five hundred people in front of the Butte Miners Union Hall. Fifteen hundred people lined the motorcade route from the airport to Granite Street, and seven hundred fifty gathered to see Bobby Kennedy as his plane lifted off from the Silver Bow County Airport."

A few days later, an eighth grader was selling black-and-white headshot photos of Bobby. I bought one for fifty cents, framed it, and hung it on the wall above my jewelry box with the Kennedy Touch Tissue safe inside.

My heart was filled with hope for the future, and I couldn't wait to get started.

Chapter 26
Day Six of Lilly's Coma

May 30, 1968, the present at St. James Hospital
I keep thinking if I bring in more cheerful voices than both of my aunts' fearful ones, Mom might wake up. When Aunt Daisy and Aunt Violet leave, the Clover Girls gather round Mom's bedside.

We settle into our chairs, and Dr. Madison arrives as part of his evening rounds. "Hello, young ladies. How are we doing today?" he says in an upbeat tone.

"Good," we all say.

"I'm sure your mother appreciates you girls spending time with her," he says, lifting the clipboard and scribbling notes on it.

"I'm hoping if she hears us talking, it might wake up her brain," I reply. "We'll be graduating soon, so we want to fill Mom in on what's going on."

"Great idea," he says in his jovial manner. "It sure couldn't hurt." He turns to Maggie. "How's that arm? Do you mind if I take a look at it?"

"Not at all." Maggie pushes up the long sleeve of her blouse and lets Dr. Madison unwrap her bandage to inspect her stitches.

"It's healing nicely," assures Dr. Madison. "It'll be good as new in no time, though you'll have a scar. All right, ladies, carry on." Dr. Madison winks at me as he leaves. "And don't forget the laughter."

"Coming right up," says Mikey Ann. "I have a joke. Why was six afraid of seven?"

We all shrug.

"Because seven eight nine. Get it?" She waits expectantly, grinning.

We collectively groan.

"Why is the math book so sad?" Cat pipes up. "Because it has too many problems."

We groan louder.

"My turn," says Maggie. "What did the ocean say to the beach? Nothing, it just waved."

"Not to change the subject," Cat says, "but do you guys have your graduation dresses?"

Everyone nods except Maggie. "Mrs. H. says I must get mine at the Jack and Jill shop. She won't let me go to Diana Hughes or Hennessey's, but the Jack and Jill dresses are for little kids. I'll look like a kindergartner." Maggie had taken to calling her mother Mrs. H after her lewd comments during dinner at Cat's house.

I don't blame her. All Maggie talks about is when she can move out of the house after high school graduation, while the rest of us are just hoping to make it out of eighth grade.

"Why Jack and Jill's?" asks Cat.

"A friend of Mrs. H. works there and lets her put things on layaway. The other stores won't let her do that because she doesn't make payments on time."

Cat glances up. "Jeez, Mags, I can loan you some cash from my babysitting money."

"Mrs. H. made me whittle my choice down to two dresses, and they're on hold until tomorrow." Maggie waves dismissively. "Thanks, you guys, but that's okay. I'll only wear it for one day. You know how I love wearing fancy dresses." She gives us an eyeroll.

"I can't remember when you last wore a dress besides your uniform," I tease.

"Seventh grade Confirmation," Cat points out. "You always complain dresses squish your boobs and you can't breathe."

Maggie tucks her chin, peeking at her sizeable chest. "Who knew these things would fluff up like balloons?" She lifts them up and lets them fall into place, and we all laugh.

"Hey Jo, I'm glad you reminded your mom how funny your uncles were, and when Robert Kennedy visited Butte," says Mikey Ann.

"You need to tell her about our spooky letters," adds Cat, grinning.

I smile at the recollections. "And how mad you got at the spelling bee?" I razz Maggie.

"Tell her your side of the story about the Fizzies," suggests Maggie, her face serious.

"She knows most of it. Ever since Dad died, it feels like Mom and I have lived in separate worlds. Except for times like when she got my purple fuzzy sweater back and after my fight about the cockeyed octopus."

Now that I think about it, I wonder whose fault it is, hers or mine? Maybe both.

"Now is a good time to fill your mom in," says Cat.

Mikey Ann tosses me a devilish grin. "Lilly will wake up shocked that her innocent little daughter was a worse troublemaker than she ever could have imagined."

"Ha, she already knows that. Okay, what the heck. What else is there to talk about except graduation?" I guess it's time Mom knows the rest of my sordid activities.

"Go ahead, Jo. Tell her everything," urges Maggie, tilting her chin at my mother's peaceful form. "What can it hurt? You can even tell her what happened with my parents. I don't mind."

"You sure, Mags? Okay, here goes. Buckle in, Lilly," I say, preparing to launch into the stories of my checkered past. I recall the events like movies playing in my mind.

Anything is worth trying to wake my mother.

Chapter 27

Even Rocks Have Heartbreak

January 1967, seventh grade

As snow swirled outside and ice encased everything in a subzero chill, I listened to my transistor radio at night, sneaking it under the covers and falling asleep to the Turtles singing "Happy Together." Mom got me one for Christmas, and I thought it was the coolest thing since the invention of color TV. I listened to Butte's radio station, KXLF, where they played "Light My Fire" and "Puff the Magic Dragon."

Our seventh-grade teacher, Sister Bertie, was a fanatic when it came to classical music. She brought in a small record player and had us listen to Beethoven, Mozart, Chopin, Bach, and Debussy. She explained each composer's unique style, then she'd quiz us by playing snippets, and had us identify who composed it.

We liked it, but after a while, we begged her to play modern music. She turned down our requests to play the Beatles or the Beach Boys, so she played Simon and Garfunkel songs instead. One afternoon she played "I Am a Rock," and we discussed the meaning of the lyrics.

A bunch of kids raised their hands. Maggie's hand was usually the first to shoot up, but this time she folded her arms, staring straight ahead.

Sister Bertie appeared to notice this, so she called on her. "What do you think the song means, Maggie?"

Maggie let out an impatient sigh. "I guess they're singing about people who are hard as rocks inside, and they don't want other people around them anymore."

"Why do you suppose that is?" asked Sister Bertie.

"Because someone hurt them really bad." Maggie stared at her lap.

I knew why, and my heart went out to her. I wished Sister would let it go, but she persisted.

"It's hard when those we care about hurt us," she said slowly.

My eyes flicked to Maggie's, and they'd filled with tears. She sprang from her seat and ran out of the classroom. I rose from my seat to go after her, but Sister Bertie held up her hand in a stop motion and excused herself from the class.

Cat, Mikey Ann, and I exchanged grim looks. Maggie told us after school yesterday that her dad had divorced her mom and moved in with another woman. Maggie didn't give details and refused to say anything more about it. We did our best to cheer her up, knowing the divorce had shattered her.

Sister Bertie returned to the room, but Maggie hadn't. Sister Bertie asked us three to stay after school, so when everyone left, she closed the door. "Mary Margaret is having a hard time right now. I know the four of you are close friends. You need to be there for her. She needs all of you very much for support."

"Sister, Maggie won't talk about it," I confided.

"She needs time," cautioned Sister Bertie. "She's distressed about her parents splitting up and sees it as her fault. She was too upset to return to class, so I sent her home."

I wasn't sure home was where Maggie wanted to be right now. I sure wouldn't.

"Sister, it's not Maggie's fault. Her parents have always demanded good grades. In the fifth grade, her dad took his belt to her when she came home with B's and C's. After that, she pressured herself for straight A's." I didn't care if Maggie got mad at me for outing her.

Cat and Mikey Ann looked daggers at me for revealing such a thing outside of our trusted friends' circle, but I trusted Sister Bertie. She wasn't like the other nuns—she cared for her students. Besides, she was already aware of Maggie's situation.

"I'll help her however I can," said Sister Bertie. "But each of you must help her as well. Talk to her, let her know you are there for her."

"Yes, Sister," we chorused.

We stood around talking about it outside after school.

"I felt terrible when Maggie told us yesterday." Cat paused. "I didn't know what to say."

"Me neither," added Mikey Ann.

"It's horrible when the dad leaves." I knew that firsthand. "I'll call her to see if she wants to come over and watch TV."

"I'll see if she'll come with us to the Saturday matinee at the Montana Theater tomorrow," volunteered Cat.

"Yeah, *The Ugly Dachshund* is playing. It's supposed to be funny," said Mikey Ann.

"Maybe that would help." My gut told me nothing would help as my heart broke for Maggie.

She wouldn't come to the phone when I called. Mrs. Houlihan tersely said Maggie wasn't feeling well and hung up before I could say anything.

I didn't want my best friend to feel like a rock or an island. I also knew she needed time, the way I had after Dad died. The passage of time hadn't mattered all that much. I still missed him terribly. He'd missed out on most of my life.

He would never see me grow up, get married, or have kids. Losing Dad was like one horrific, painful nightmare that I couldn't wake up from. Now Maggie was going through losing her dad, too, but at least he was alive.

None of it was fair.

Chapter 28
Dear Mrs. Freakface

S*eventh grade*

We bombarded Maggie with phone calls until Mrs. Houlihan told us to stop. Maggie didn't want to talk about the divorce, so we didn't press. But she knew we were all there for her if she needed us. We made sure of it.

We followed Sister Bertie's advice and did whatever we could to get Maggie to laugh. It mostly worked—Maggie stopped turning down our invitations to go to Trethewey's Music to drool over record albums, get hot dogs, fries and gravy at Ben Franklin's, and come over for a sleepover.

We had a super snowy winter and entertained ourselves by bonking cars with snowballs. Mikey Ann was especially good with her aim because of her softball pitcher's arm. When we tired of snowballs, Cat brought along eggs to throw at cars, but when one splattered and froze on the mayor's windshield and he stopped his car to chase us, we abandoned that action, too.

We took up hooky-bobbing, gripping the back bumpers of cars at stoplights for a fun slick ride on icy streets. It was fun until Maggie let go and nearly got run over by a court judge, who hollered and shook his fist at us in his black robe. That freaked Maggie out, plus we were tired of choking from car exhaust. Maggie finally got back to her old self again, thanks to our mission to keep her occupied.

Ice skating was next on our agenda at the Cinders skating rink. We'd all gotten figure skates for Christmas, except Mikey Ann, who got speed skates. We spent hours on the ice, playing Crack the Whip and showing off for each other. We oo'ed and ah'ed while Maggie skated arabesque on one leg and did slow spins like the Olympic skaters on TV. I spent most of my time falling on my butt. On Saturdays we walked to the Shoetorium on Park Street to get our skates sharpened.

Mikey Ann was a flash on the ice, and she began entering speed skating events at the Civic Center, and it wasn't long before she won blue ribbons. We cheered her on from the sidelines. She had instant popularity at the Cinders rink and at school. The boys fawned over her like she was a world champion speed skater.

When we weren't on the ice rink, we got into the secret agent shows on TV, like *Get Smart, The Man from U.N.C.L.E, Secret Agent, The Avengers, and Mission Impossible.* We went to a birthday costume party at the firehouse wearing spy raincoats with fedoras we bought from Tony the Trader's thrift store. Cat got her brother's squirt guns so we would look like real secret agents. Maggie was Agent 99, I was Agent 86, Cat was Emma Peele and Mikey Ann was *The Girl from U.N.C.L.E.*

Our mission—should we decide to accept it—was to stay in secret agent mode at school. We passed highly classified notes to each other, printing the alphabet backwards in a secret code. We wrote about how we'd torture our bullies and poked fun at the nuns. Thankfully, when Sister Bertie caught me with a note, she couldn't break our code. She asked me to explain what the 'gobbledygook' meant. I made my eyes as big and round as I could, telling her someone must have put it on my desk as a prank.

She must have bought it because she wadded the paper and tossed it into the wastepaper basket. Mission accomplished.

One Friday night at a sleepover at Cat's house, we watched *The Screaming Skull* on *Frightmare Theater*. When it ended at midnight, "The Star-Spangled Banner" played, and Cat came up with the idea for us to write Dracula blood letters to each other, inspired by the *Addams Family and The Munsters.* We talked excitedly about it until we fell asleep staring at the TV test pattern.

We got to work over the weekend, writing in red ink to simulate blood so we could gross each other out. We didn't use our real names and agreed to pair off and trade the letters. Here was my letter to Cat:

Dear Mrs. Freakface,

I used my blood this time to write you this letter with my sharpest fountain pen. Cousin Herman fell off the ladder and bounced on his head, but Lily says he'll be fine with another steel plate inserted. Fang's plant, Cleopatra, is feverish with a temperature of 1,000, and she isn't eating as many rodents today. She's only eating two instead of her usual ten. Fang is worried and is thinking of calling the Venus Fly-trap doctor. Did Baby Dracula get the giant tarantula I sent for his birthday? And did your husband like the birthday coffin we delivered to your mansion? I'm thinking of getting my werewolf cousins a new mattress made of dried grasshoppers and ants. Would you like to have a picnic in the graveyard? I'll bring lunch. How do spider legs souffle and dissected toad surprise sound? I have a secret sauce that makes them scrumptious! Write back and fill me in on your bite adventures!

Your Friend, *Henrietta Frankenstiltzken, Monsterville, USA*

P.S. Remember no real names!!

On Monday morning during English, Cat had written her reply on the other side of my letter and sneaked it to me when Sister Bertie's back was turned.

Dear Mrs. Frankenstiltzken,

Thank you so much for sending Baby Dracula the giant tarantula! He loved it and played with it for hours, feeding it tiny mice. He named it Blacky, and it sleeps in my dead plants. Did I tell you my husband Clyde was so hungry he bit me last night? I'll tell you, I don't know what this world is coming to when you can't get enough blood to drink. In the middle of the night, he snuck downstairs and ate our son Charlie's octopus right out of the aquarium. I adored the bloody red-ink letter you wrote to me. (I want a pen like that! Did you get that at Ben Franklin's?) I would love to have a graveyard picnic. We'll make enough noise to wake the dead (har har) I dyed my hair purple and green and styled it in cobra snake curls. Baby Henry ran away again, and I found him in the graveyard talking to the spirits. How precious! Today is Friday the 13th and as you know, it's a holiday for our families! Well, gotta run. There are necks to bite.

Eternally Yours,

Vampira

Cat's cleverness made me giggle. A paper airplane sailed across the classroom and landed on my desk. This one was from Mikey Ann. Good thing Sister had left the room to talk to someone. I unfolded the paper airplane and read:

Dear Cousin Googly Eyes,

My husband, Mr. Snot Rat, isn't feeling well today. He killed and ate too many monsters last night and now he can't stop burping. So, for dinner tonight, we're having toad skin, pig eyes, roasted spider legs, and chocolate-covered toads for dessert. Ichabod, our son, dove off our roof and broke his neck. He looks handsome with his head hanging to the side, especially with his new fangs that are coming in nicely. Our stupid dog ate twenty cats today, and he is sick to his guts. He likes to chase our new pet bat around. Well, I must track down what happened to Foot. He crawled out of his box and has been tiptoeing around the house, stepping on our pet insects. We think he's in love with Thing. See you soon!

Sincerely, Flubber-Butt Addams

I guffawed loud. Cat, Maggie, and Mikey Ann all sprang from their desks at the same time to exchange letters just as Sister walked into the room. She looked at all four of us as I jammed Mikey Ann's letter inside my desk.

I must have looked the guiltiest because Sister Bertie came straight toward me, holding out her hand. "I'd like to see that sheet of paper you were so interested in."

My heart jumped to my throat. I stalled. "What paper?"

She snapped her fingers. "Give it to me. Now." Sister Bertie was mostly nice, but when she meant business, we didn't mess with her.

Reluctantly, I pulled out Mikey Ann's letter and across from me, Mikey's hands flew to her face, and she dropped her head to her desk.

Sister snatched the letter and read it. Her eyes bulged. "Open your desk."

"But—but..." I slowly lifted the top of my desk and Sister spotted the other Dracula blood letters written with red ink.

"Hand them over," commanded Sister.

She scanned the other letters and had seen my three friends rushing to their seats as she entered the room. "Miss Delaney, Miss Quinn, and Miss Houlihan, front and center. All of you are going to see the principal." She waggled her finger for me to follow.

The class was deathly quiet as we rose to follow Sister Bertie. She went into the principal's office first to talk with Sister Clare, the oldest nun in the school. Sister Clare had trouble staying awake and would nod off in mid-sentence. Ending a conversation with her was tricky. She was also hard of hearing.

Sister Bertie placed our Dracula blood letters on Sister Clare's desk and left the office. We assembled in front of Sister's desk, while she squinted through her round spectacles, reading each letter—an agonizing wait that took forever.

We nervously busied ourselves while we waited: Maggie picked the lint off her skirt, Cat studied the ceiling like God was giving her a thumbs-up, and Mikey Ann quietly whistled "Kill The Wabbit" from *Bugs Bunny*, knowing Sister couldn't hear.

I was trying hard not to laugh.

Sister lowered the letters to her desk and folded her hands on them. She scowled at each of us, then rested her gaze on me. I shot a sidelong glance to Maggie, who'd sidled away from us next to the statue of the Blessed Virgin Mary as if the statue would save Maggie from a fate worse than death.

"What is the meaning of this nonsense?" demanded Sister Clare.

"Meaning?" I echoed. When in doubt, play dumb, a stalling tactic every kid used.

"Yes! Which of you wrote this disgusting diatribe about biting people in the neck and drinking blood? And this malarkey about a bulldog eating cats? Explain yourselves!" The side of her fist hit the desk, and we jumped.

"We, um...we, uh, didn't actually write these," lied Cat in her earnest voice. "Someone put these on our desks."

"Yes, Sister," seconded Maggie, to my amazement. "Somebody stuck one on my desk, too. I have no idea who did it." She offered a winning shrug with her innocent cow-eyes, worthy of a standing ovation. *Good girl.*

Sister grimaced with a wrinkly hand cupping her ear. "What? Repeat that."

Cat and Maggie loudly repeated what they'd said.

Mikey Ann let out a quiet, descending whistle through her teeth, and I choked back a laugh.

Sister glared at me. "Miss Wolohan, you think this is funny?"

"No, Sister." I gave her my guiltless-as-a-baby expression.

Cat's foot kicked my shin in a don't-aggravate-the-principal warning.

Sister Clare sat back in her chair. "If none of you wrote this drivel, then who did?"

We vigorously shrugged, hoping she'd notice the halos over our heads.

Maggie spoke in a loud voice. "Sister, the eighth graders did it. We heard they put the letters on our desks while we were outside at recess."

Sister's gaze pierced Maggie. "Mary Margaret, how do I know you aren't lying?"

"Maggie doesn't lie, Sister," yelled Cat. "That would be breaking the seventh commandment."

Sister drew back as if Cat had thrown mud on her face. "That is the *eighth* commandment, young lady! And just for that, all of you get detention." She pointed to Cat. "And *you* will write the eighth commandment on the chalkboard fifty times."

Cat's jaw dropped. "What if I run out of space?"

Sister's face scrunched. "Say again?"

Cat repeated it loud and slow.

"Don't get smart with me!" growled Sister. "If the eighth graders wrote these satanic atrocities, they are the spawn of the devil and should hang their heads in shame! But you will be punished for reading these vile words."

We were astounded she'd bought our lie. "Yes, Sister."

"What's to become of your generation?" She plucked a black rosary from her desk drawer. "Go home and tell your parents what you did, and I'll pray for your wicked little souls," she mumbled, nodding off and snoring with the rosary wrapped around her knobby fingers.

"I guess we can go?" I whispered, making a what-should-we-do face.

We tiptoed out to the hallway, where we busted up laughing.

When school ended, we crossed the snowy alley to my house and tramped inside, removing our boots. Mom had left a note saying she'd gone shopping. Now that I was a seventh grader, she left me home alone while she ran her errands.

The four of us sat at our kitchen table talking and laughing about the Dracula letters. I made us chocolate milk with Nestle's Quik and dropped brown-sugar-cinnamon Pop-Tarts into the toaster. When they toasted, I served my friends and sat down.

"Since we'll be on detention, I guess we'd better tell our parents," muttered Cat.

Maggie tapped her glasses. "And tell them we wrote about graveyard picnics and eating spider-legs souffle?"

I grimaced. "We just tell our moms we got caught passing notes. We don't tell them what the notes said." I was proud of my flawed logic.

"You wrote the best letters, Jo. You ought to be a writer when you grow up." Maggie bit into her Pop-Tart.

"Well, Mom says I have a wild imagination. But Cat wrote the funniest ones." I pointed at her.

"Then both of you should be writers." Maggie lowered her glasses and peered over them. "I was thinking of running for president. We need a woman president."

"You'd make a good one," said Mikey Ann, stirring her milk. "But you can't freak out when bad things happen."

"She's right," said Cat, slurping her milk. "On second thought, don't run for president. They tend to get shot, like Lincoln and Kennedy."

"Good point." Maggie thought for a minute. "Then my backup plan is to be an astronaut. They need women astronauts, too."

"You said you're afraid of flying. Remember that Chuck Yeager guy Sister told us who broke the sound barrier? You'd have to go faster than him."

Maggie gave us an assured look. "I could handle that."

"When was the last time you broke the sound barrier?" I quipped.

"I haven't yet, but I will," said Maggie, her voice firm and resolute.

"Save me a ride in your rocket ship, then." I had no doubt Maggie could someday work for NASA. She was the smartest kid in our class; she just didn't brag about it.

"I will. Pinky promise." Maggie held out her little finger, and I hooked mine around it.

"Blessed be the astronauts," I said. "For they shall land on the moon someday."

"Sister Bertie says they're working on it. That would be neat to see people on the moon," said Maggie, polishing off her chocolate milk.

A few days later, the news reported the Apollo One spacecraft had a fire during a preflight test at Cape Canaveral that killed all three of the astronauts, Gus Grissom, Ed White, and Roger Chaffee.

We were as shocked as everyone else. Once again, our nation felt gutted because such things weren't supposed to happen. Astronauts were invincible, like presidents and the pope. *Weren't they?*

This didn't bode well for Maggie's plans. I told her being an astronaut was too dangerous, and suggested she choose a safer profession, like being a rocket scientist. Or a brain surgeon.

Maggie said she'd think about it.

Chapter 29
How To Lose a Friend in Ten Days

March 1967, seventh grade

Early on Monday, Sister Bertie announced we had ten days to prepare for the Montana Statewide Spelling Bee. She gave us a week to study words from past tests, then distributed a packet containing the official words list. The following Monday, she lined us up along the walls of our seventh-grade classroom for our class spelling bee.

During the first round, the words were easy, and no one was eliminated. Then Sister gave us harder words in the second round and kids began dropping out. The next round were words from our spelling tests, which eliminated the students who hadn't studied. When school ended for the day, nine girls were left.

Tomorrow would be the deciding factor.

After school, Maggie, Cat, and Mikey Ann came to my house so we could study our words. Since Mikey Ann had been eliminated, and the rest of us were still standing, she read us our words. This was serious business. Mom fed us cheeseburgers and French frics while we spelled words like walking dictionaries.

Mikey Ann glanced at each of us. "Who do you think will last the longest?"

We all shrugged, sensing the tension.

"You guys, I have to win this spelling bee!" blurted Maggie. "Both my parents said if I do, they'll each give me twenty-five dollars! They said I must make straight A's to land a scholarship for college."

Mikey Ann let out a descending whistle. "Gee, Mags, that's forever from now."

"Yeah, like five years," added Cat.

My competitive nature tugged at me. I wanted to win, too, because spelling was one of the few things I was good at and always got A's. Otherwise, I had B's and C's on my report cards, but Mom didn't pressure me for grades like Maggie's parents did.

"Maggie will be the last one standing," I declared definitively, not wanting her to know my nagging desire to win. "She'll get her scholarship, and we'll get jobs as monks, rewriting the old dead sea scrolls," I joked.

Everyone laughed, and it was getting late, so Mom sent everyone home. I hardly slept that night. When morning arrived, I woke up with a knot in my stomach, nervous as a nun on East Mercury Street.

After we said "The Pledge of Allegiance," Sister Bertie had the nine of us line up in front of the class. Four more were eliminated. Then it was down to five of us: Cat, Maggie, Rosa, one of the Einsteins, and me. Round after round, we nailed our words. The line grew shorter and my eye twitched as I silently spelled every word. I rocked on my heels, wiping sweaty palms on my uniform skirt.

"Pandemonium," Sister called out to the Einstein.

"Pandemonium. P-A-N-D..." She paused, staring at the floor. "Please say it again?"

"Pandemonium," Sister repeated.

"P-A-N-D-I-M-O-N-I-U-M."

"Incorrect."

A gasp circulated around the room.

"Congratulations to the four finalists from the seventh grade. You will compete in the school spelling bee," announced Sister Agatha.

Everyone broke out with applause.

Now I had to compete with two of my best friends.

THE FOLLOWING MONDAY, the entire school convened in the gymnasium. We four seventh-graders, along with four students from the sixth and eighth grades, sat in two rows of folding chairs.

Sister Agatha, the new second-grade teacher, announced words like senatorial, spontaneity, and felonious. We each stepped up to the microphone at center stage and survived each of those words.

Rosa tripped on 'recommend,' spelling it with two C's. Maggie spelled it correctly, and Rosa gave her a thumbs-up as she left the stage. I liked Rosa. She'd turned out to be a pretty good friend, and she was a good sport. Plus, she was an excellent speller.

After two more rounds, six of us were left standing: Cat, Maggie, me, and three eighth graders. I couldn't believe we three were the last seventh graders remaining.

Maggie stumbled on 'coincidence' and I spelled it correctly. She leveled a death stare at me as I mouthed, I'm sorry! She burst into tears and fled the stage. I was horrified that she missed her word, and I had to be the one to correct it.

"I'm sorry, Mags!" I called out as she stumbled down the side stairs into Sister Bertie's arms, where Sister consoled her.

I let out a moan, knowing how badly Maggie wanted to win. I should have misspelled the word. I was a selfish monster for putting myself first, but I couldn't help it... I needed to win! Everyone loves a winner, so I couldn't help wanting this.

After another round, it was down to Cat, me, and an eighth-grade boy. I avoided Cat's gaze on the other side of the stage. I rubbed my clammy palms over my uniform to dry them as my stomach roiled and twisted.

The eighth-grade boy stood at the microphone.

"Subterranean," announced Sister Agatha.

"Subterranean. S-U-B-T-E-R-A-N-E-A-N?" He spelled it as a question, with a hopeful look at Sister Agatha.

"Incorrect. Miss Delaney, spell subterranean."

Cat stepped to the microphone. "Please repeat the word, Sister?"

I crossed my fingers. I wasn't sure what to hope for—me to win or Cat to win. Selfishly, I hoped I would, but I didn't want Cat mad at me, like Maggie surely was. I was a bundle of nerves and nibbled on my trembling thumb.

When Cat looked at me, I vigorously moved my head up and down in a you-can-do-this gesture. She spelled the word correctly and my heart skipped a thousand beats as Cat collapsed into her seat. How could this come down to one of my best friends and me? I never dreamed this would happen, but here we were.

Cat and I each spelled five more words correctly. It was Cat's turn, and she stepped to the microphone. Was I seeing things, or was she totally calm and composed? She didn't seem nervous, unlike me, who quaked like a chicken at becoming a Sunday dinner.

"Assassin," announced Sister Agatha.

Cat winked at me, and I knew she had it in the bag. She hesitated for what seemed forever. It took her longer to spell the word than it took for the earth to form.

"A-S-S-A-S-S-A-N," spelled Cat, stepping back from the microphone.

"Cat, no!" I burst out. "You *know* this one!"

Sister Agatha's bushy eyebrows knitted together like two caterpillars. "Quiet, Miss Wolohan!" She turned toward Cat. "Incorrect, Miss Delaney."

As Cat left the stage, my mouth fell open. I couldn't believe Cat missed this word! When we'd practiced last night, I'd misspelled it. Cat was the one who explained how we'd remember it: "There's two asses in a row!" We'd crumpled in laughter, and I joked the nuns wouldn't put a word in the spelling bee with two asses in it.

Sister Agatha peered at me over her glasses. "Miss Wolohan, spell assassin."

In that instant, I realized Cat had missed this word on purpose, tossing me a slow pitch for the win. Her selflessness caused my selfish guilt to slam me like a truck. I stayed in my seat, flummoxed, while the entire school stared.

Should I say Cat misspelled her word on purpose? Will she get into trouble if I do?

"Miss Wolohan! To the microphone, please." Sister Agatha's voice snapped me back to the present.

Cat moved her head up and down, with an urgent spell-it-right expression. Maggie glared at me, shaking her head. She pointed to Cat, hinting for me to be a stool-pigeon and rat on Cat. I felt like King Soloman, faced with an impossible decision.

What if Cat doesn't want me to say she deliberately missed the word? Maggie was motioning me to do it. What to do, what to do…

Growing up as an only child, selflessness wasn't second nature to me. Sister Bertie's words floated in to put my neighbor before myself and I considered this for all of two seconds—but when I saw Rosa shaking her fist in a get-this-done motion, I thought, baloney!

I want to win this spelling bee!

Alone on the cavernous stage, I was the last kid standing. I stole a glance at Cat and Maggie, standing next to Sister Bertie, along the wall on the gym floor. Cat smiled, while Maggie still scowled. Everything turned to slow motion as I rose and stepped to center stage. I adjusted the microphone, Sister Agatha repeated the word, and I pronounced it.

"Assassin. A-S-S-A-S-S-I-N." Spelling ass twice was awkward in front of the little kids and the nuns after the four of us had joked about it last night.

"Correct! Congratulations, Miss Wolohan. You're the winner of the St. Michael School Spelling Bee. You'll represent us in the 1967 Treasure State Spelling Bee in Dillon, Montana."

Stunned, I darted a wild-eyed glance at Sister Bertie, leaning against the wall, clapping and nodding her approval. My seventh-grade class hollered and whistled.

Rosa and Mikey Ann cheered along with everyone else. "Seventh grade beat the eighth graders, woohoo!"

I was ecstatic, but it was hard to be happy with my stomach twisting about Cat and Maggie.

AFTER SCHOOL, I WAITED on the Park Street sidewalk for my three friends. Younger kids congratulated me as they spilled out of St. Mike's, grouping around me like I was a movie star.

Mikey Ann swaggered up and patted me on the back. "Way to go, Jo!"

"Thanks." As I opened my mouth to say more, Maggie rushed up and fixed me with a penetrating stare. "That was a horrible thing you did to Cat! You knew she could spell assassin correctly. We all did, after last night. I can't believe you didn't tell Sister that Cat missed her word on purpose!"

I'd never seen Maggie so angry, and it unnerved me.

Mikey Ann came to my defense. "Cat obviously had a reason for doing it."

Cat moved up behind Maggie. "I wanted at least one of you to win."

"Winning meant more to me than it did to all three of you put together!" Maggie threw up her hands, then whirled on me. "Why didn't you hand me the win? Instead, you hoarded it for yourself!" she accused, as if I'd drowned a litter of puppies.

"I hoarded nothing!" I shouted. "I won fair and square!"

Maggie pointed her forefinger at me. "You should have told Sister that Cat missed the word on purpose!"

"Okay, smarty-pants, tell me how I should have done that? 'Sister Agatha, Mary Catherine spelled her word wrong on purpose. Give her another chance to spell it correctly, pretty please with sugar on top?'" My cheeks were so hot they burned my face. "What do you think she would have said?"

Cat intervened. "Come on, you guys, stop arguing. I misspelled the word deliberately because I wanted to!"

"But why would you do that?" I was incredulous. It didn't make sense.

Cat's lower lip trembled. "I couldn't go to Dillon, anyway. My dad is dying of cancer. I have to stay with my mom right now." She teared up and her chin dropped to her chest.

We all quieted in the awkward moment.

"Oh, no, Cat," empathized Mikey Ann. "That's awful."

"I'm so sorry about your dad, Cat, but Dillon isn't that far away," I protested. "You could have taken the bus."

Cat shook her head. "No. When I told Mom I was a finalist for the spelling bee, she told me I couldn't go. And when it got down to you and me, I wanted you to win. I didn't have a choice."

I fought back tears as I hugged Cat. "I'm sorry, I feel like a dope."

Cat squeezed me so hard I felt her pain. "Promise me you'll spell your words correctly for the state spelling bee."

Maggie rushed forward to hug Cat. "I'm so sorry. I just thought Jo should have told Sister you did it on purpose. I didn't know."

"No one did," said Cat, patting Maggie's shoulder. "My mom didn't want me telling people about my dad."

"I'm still mad at Jo for not speaking up." Maggie glared at me with folded arms.

"What was I supposed to do? Everyone expected me to spell the word correctly!" I argued.

"It's the principle of the thing," sniffed Maggie with a hard look.

Exasperated, I whirled on her. "Alright, I'll tell Sister Agatha! I'll go to confession and tell Father I was selfish and wanted to win the stupid spelling bee. There! Satisfied? Will that make you happy?" Hands on my hips, I drilled my stare into her.

"It's too late, the damage is done," scoffed Maggie. "I'm not sure I want to stay friends with someone who is only out for herself. Cat is losing her dad! I lost my dad in the divorce! How do you think that feels, Jo? Way to abandon your friends in our time of need!" She spun on her heel and ran up the hill toward home, leaving me staring after her.

"Like I haven't lost my own father?" The words tore from my throat as I yelled at my best friend, my whole body shaking.

Maggie didn't even turn around, and it ripped my heart out. She must have ripped Cat's out too because tears fell down her cheeks. In all the years I've known Catherine Delaney, I have never seen her cry. Ever.

Granted, my loss was five years ago, but that didn't mean the pain was any less. According to Maggie, I guess losing my dad didn't count. I turned to my two friends. "You guys, I didn't mean for any of this to happen. This whole thing is a royal bummer."

"I'm sorry, too. I didn't mean to upset Maggie," said Cat with a rueful expression. "Sure, I wanted to win. It would have been fun. I probably would've missed the next word, anyway!" She wiped her eyes with the hanky Mikey Ann offered her.

"Maggie is still upset because of her parents' divorce," I said glumly.

"I think so, too," said Mikey Ann, taking the hanky Cat handed her. "And she took it out on you."

"Well, you guys, I've got to get home," said Cat. "See you at school tomorrow."

"I have to get going, too," added Mikey Ann. "Don't worry about Maggie. She'll come around." Mikey Ann always put our worries to rest, though not mine. Not this time.

"Okay, see ya, Cat. I'm so sorry about your dad." I stepped in to give her a hug.

"Me, too. Mom keeps crying that she is going to lose her best friend. I can't console her," said Cat, hugging me back.

I'd not seen Cat emotional like this and an uneasiness took hold, knocking my world off kilter. Cat was my rock, like Maggie had always been. I wanted them both to be happy, as I'd always known them to be. And now Cat was sad, and Maggie was mad. I couldn't win for trying.

I trudged across the alley to the apartment house, surprised by what my selfless friend did. Cat was my new role model. I'd always admired her, but now my respect and admiration for her had grown even stronger.

Shame rocked me as I realized I'd been too selfish to make the same choice Cat had—maybe I would have had if my father had been lying in a hospital, fighting for his life. But my dad was gone. He never got to meet the Clover Girls. He'd missed everything, including my proudest moment winning the school spelling bee to qualify for the state competition.

To me, that was punishment enough, and it was hard for me not to blame God for it. That, and losing my best friend for my selfishness in wanting to win. Guilt cemented my soul, and I was desperate to win Maggie back. There was no way I would break up the Clover Girls. No way could I lose one of my best friends.

Cat and Mikey Ann were my pillars of support, but Maggie was my Rock of Gibraltar. I sure didn't want to be an island, like the Simon and Garfunkel song. The thought horrified me. And I hated death. It only robbed, it only stole.

And there was nothing any of us could do about it.

Chapter 30
Day Seven of Lilly's Coma

May 31, 1968, in the present

The hospital hallway seems even longer tonight as I follow Aunt Daisy out to the car after our hospital visit. The weight of the day settles on my shoulders, and I ask Aunt Daisy if we can stop at St. Michael's church to light a candle for Mom.

The evening air has a bite to it as we step outside, the spring chill clinging to Butte like it never wants to leave. The streetlights cast yellow pools on the pavement, and the giant 'M' on the mountain glows white against the darkening sky.

Aunt Daisy's Chevy hums along the streets past storefronts now closed for the night. Neither of us speaks. What is there to say? The doctors don't know whether Mom will wake up. All the stories I've been telling her—about our Clover Girl adventures and all the trouble we got into—might never reach her consciousness.

The towering orange brick church looms before me, its stained-glass windows dark except for the faint lights from inside. The church is eerily empty, and an incense smell lingers in the air, mingling with the mustiness of old wood and prayer books. My footsteps echo when I walk down the center aisle, genuflect before the altar, and slide into a pew near the front.

The rack of votive candles flickers to my right, dozens of flames dancing inside tall red and cobalt glass. I dig into my pocket for the quarter Aunt Daisy gave me and drop it into the donation slot. Selecting a fresh candle, I pick up a lighting stick and dip it into a flame, then watch as the flame catches and steadies itself inside the blue glass. Blue is Mom's favorite color.

"This is for my mother, Lilly Rose," I whisper to God. "Please wake her up."

I return to the pew and kneel, trying to say the prayers I've recited my whole life. But the words don't come. Instead, they jumble in my head, so I talk to God like He's sitting next to me.

"I'm not the best Catholic in the world," I begin. "I'm sure You know the trouble I've gotten into—of course You do—You know everything because you're everywhere all at once. Wish I knew how You could do that... I would *love* to do that! I told Mom about wanting to win the spelling bee, our Dracula blood letters, and shaking Bobby Kennedy's hand and what it meant to me.

I shift uncomfortably on the kneeler. "There's something else. Instead of telling Sister that Cat knew how to spell 'assassin,' I said nothing because I wanted to win the spelling bee. Cat knew how to spell it because she'd joked about assassin having two asses in it!" I swallow a laugh. "You have to admit, two asses in one word *is* funny."

My smile fades as I recalled Maggie's face after the spelling bee. "I wanted to win so badly I let my best friend down. Please forgive me for being selfish. I haven't told my mother so many things because I'm always afraid of disappointing her."

The church is so quiet I hear the candle flames sputter, but I don't hear God breathing like I thought I did when I was little. A tear escapes, and I brush it away.

"I can't lose my mother, God. Not after Dad. Please don't let her die." The word catches in my throat. "I need more time with Mom. I have so much more to say."

I reach for the words. "I haven't told her how I worry the Clover Girls will drift apart in high school. She doesn't know I still cry over Dad before I go to sleep at night. I want to say I'm sorry for making her life harder—for the detention slips she signed, the trips to the principal's office, and the calls from Sister Alex." I sniff and wipe a tear from my cheek.

The candle I lit flickers violently, as if God heard what I said.

"I'll make You a deal," I bargain. "If You let Mom wake up, I'll be a better person. I'll help more around the house. And if Mom wakes up, I promise to tell her everything. No more secrets. No more hiding the truth. She deserves that much."

Standing, I make the sign of the cross and genuflect toward the tabernacle. As I walk to the back of the church, the weight on my shoulders seems lighter.

"Ready, kiddo?" Aunt Daisy asks, rising from the last pew.

"Yes," I say, giving the altar one last look. "I think so."

As we step outside into the spring evening, the stars shine brightly above Butte, crisp and clear in the big mountain sky. I take a deep breath, letting the fresh air fill my lungs. Tomorrow is another day. And when I visit Mom, I'll tell her about the mean pony at summer camp, how the Fizzies disaster happened, the spats with the new kids at the beginning of the year, and the communion hosts in Sacristy—and I'll figure out how to tell her what I did to Sister Alex's goldfish.

I can't know what tomorrow will bring, but tonight, in the sacred silence of St. Michael's church, I've found something I thought I'd lost.

Hope.

Chapter 31
Twinkles the Evil One

July 1967, seventh grade summer

Before school ended for the summer, I'd been eliminated in the final round of the state spelling bee. At least I'd won for my school—or rather, Cat and I *both* won, as far as I was concerned. I had added Cat's name to my spelling bee certificate and showed it to her before putting it in my scrapbook.

June was a tough month. Mr. Delaney had passed away shortly after school was out. Cat stayed close to home because her mother depended on her. They were a close family, and his death was hard, especially for Cat's brothers. I missed Mr. Delaney making us popcorn and taking us to the A&W root beer stand out on Continental Drive for 'Frosties' or he'd take us to the Bonanza Freeze, where we shared banana splits. It wasn't much consolation, but I told Cat she was lucky to have a father for as long as she did.

Mom thought it would be a meaningful gesture for Maggie, Mikey Ann, and me to go to Mr. Delaney's funeral mass at St. Michael's Church. We sat near the back, and it was tough hearing Mrs. Delaney cry. It was even harder seeing Cat cry while she tried consoling her mother.

Afterward, I hugged Cat hard, and we both cried on each other's shoulders. My heart broke in half for my happy-go-lucky friend and her delightful family. Despite Maggie's dad leaving Maggie and her mom, at least she and Mikey Ann still had their dads.

Maggie stayed mad and didn't speak to me at the funeral. And for a week after that, whenever I called her, she'd slam down the receiver. Frustrated, I grabbed my scrapbook and marched up the hill to the pink house on Copper Street and pounded on Maggie's door.

Mrs. Houlihan opened it. She didn't smile, but then she rarely did. "Hello, Jo. Come in."

"Hi, Mrs. Houlihan."

She hollered behind her. "Maggie, Jo is here." She turned and disappeared into the kitchen.

Maggie appeared at the door.

"I've called you like twelve thousand times. Why do you keep hanging up on me?" I demanded.

Maggie folded her arms. "I'm still mad at you."

"Mags, I told you I was sorry. I really mean it; I want to stay friends. Please don't be mad—Cat couldn't have gone to Dillon, anyway!" I held up my right hand. "I promise I won't do anything like that again, so help me, God." I opened my scrapbook to show her the spelling bee certificate. "See, Cat's name is on this, too."

Maggie studied it for a moment. "How can I stay mad at you when you put it like that?"

"Besides, I miss hanging out with you and doing things together. It's not the same without you around," I added.

"In that case, ask your mom to get you a YMCA membership so we can take swim lessons," replied Maggie, cracking a smile.

"Okay. Sounds like fun." I breathed relief Maggie had accepted my peace offering. I wanted us to get back to normal and don't know what I would have done if she hadn't taken my olive branch.

Later that afternoon, Maggie helped me convince my mother to get me a 'Y' membership. We reasoned it would keep us out of trouble and would be an excellent influence. Mom agreed to pay part of it since she had money from the apartment house rentals and doing seamstress alterations for an uptown dress shop. She made it clear I had to earn the rest.

Maggie explained the 'Y' awarded membership scholarships, and the Red Cross would certify us if we trained to be lifeguards and we could earn money on the weekends. I told Mom I would apply for a scholarship and take lifeguard training as part of our agreement.

We both signed up for swimming lessons and in no time, we'd bypassed Sinkers, Floaters, and Minnows to land at the Fish level. Our goal was to get into Flying Fish, so we could try out for the junior swim team.

When we got promoted to Flying Fish, we celebrated by riding the city bus up to the Columbia Gardens for Nickel Day. We hopped on the merry-go-round, the roller coaster, and the flying airplanes until we got dizzy. Those Thursdays were special for Maggie and me. Cat couldn't go because she was still needed at home, and Mikey Ann's life revolved around softball practice.

To take a break from our routine, one day Maggie and I rode our bikes a half mile west of town to Green Pond to go swimming. Mikey Ann told us about it, and she came along since softball practice was canceled. She told us we'd glow in the dark after swimming in it. That night at my house, Maggie and Mikey Ann slept over and we all positioned ourselves in front of the bathroom mirror with the lights off to see if we were glowing.

My jaw dropped. "Criminy, Mikey Ann! Look at you!"

She was the only one who glowed. I glanced down at myself, then at Maggie, but we weren't glowing.

"Ha, fooled you, suckers!" Mikey Ann laughed so hard I swore she'd split a gut. She'd worn a new t-shirt, so when I switched off the light, it glowed a fluorescent green.

"You think you're so smart, Mikala Ann Quinn!" Maggie pretended to be annoyed, but she burst out laughing and so did I.

"Green Pond is full of mining waste, so people think you glow after swimming in it," said Mikey Ann authoritatively, like she was a science expert.

"Well, that sounds safe, doesn't it?" teased Maggie. "Think I'll stick to swimming at the 'Y' pool."

"Yeah, me, too," I added. "I've heard people say Butte's water is polluted from the mines. I have no desire to turn into the creature from the green lagoon."

Mikey Ann spread her arms and made a scary monster noise. She even looked like one in the dark with the whites of her eyes and her eerily glowing t-shirt.

THE NEXT DAY, MAGGIE called. "Hey! Do you want to go to a summer camp? We can take our lifeguard classes and get our Red Cross certification there."

"Wow, really? Where at?" I asked.

"Camp Elkhorn, up by Helena. The YMCA runs it, and members get discounts. It would be more fun than sneaking around the neighborhood during tent sleepovers or watching high school kids make out on the balcony of the Montana Theater." Maggie had a point.

"Sure. I'd be up for that." I hesitated, wondering why she was trying so hard to convince me. "Is everything okay, Mags?"

She paused. "I need to get away from my house. When my dad comes over, all my parents do is yell at each other." She grabbed my hands and put on her begging-puppy-dog face. "Please say you'll go. We'll ride horses and try out for the junior swim team."

"Wow, horses and swimming? Okay, I'll ask." That sounded way more exciting than staying in town all summer.

A week later, Aunt Daisy and Mom drove us up to Camp Elkhorn, which sat in the middle of the Helena National Forest. It was two hours from Butte, and when we arrived, we checked in at the main lodge, a giant log building that was more like a barn. A tall, straight-backed lady with "Miss Hazel" on her name tag checked us in without cracking a smile. She assigned us to Cabin Six and handed us a mimeographed sheet with a hand-drawn map of the camp.

Mom and Aunt Daisy helped us haul our duffels, sleeping bags and pillows to Cabin Six. As we said our goodbyes and hugged, I unexpectedly teared up when it occurred to me we'd be away from home for two whole weeks.

We were the first campers in Cabin Six, so we had dibs on the two upper bunks end to end. As we unrolled our sleeping bags, our cabin counselor, Beth, told us we had to take a swim test in the lake before we could go boating. Maggie and I changed into our red-and-white striped 'Y' swimsuits and easily passed, swimming several laps without stopping. We thought we were hot stuff because we were in Flying Fish and were now eligible to try out for the junior swim team and take lifeguard classes.

On our first evening after dinner, we hiked a well-worn trail to the big campfire Wampum Ring, where the entire camp gathered for together time. Afterward the counselors did some skits and led a sing-along with "This Land is Our Land," and "If I Had a Hammer." The songs had already been burned into my brain from Mom playing the Christy Minstrels and "Sing Along With Mitch Miller" records.

Bright and early the next morning, all campers gathered for breakfast in the main lodge. Beth distributed our schedules, which Maggie and I had worked out in advance to make sure we'd be in the same activities together.

Maggie pointed to the schedule. "Look! We ride horses first, then crafts, then lunch, and swimming in the afternoon! Perfect!"

We giggled with excitement. "Let's hurry and finish so we can be the first to choose our horses," I said as I shoveled eggs and bacon into my mouth as fast as I could.

We finished up and raced to the horse barn. We checked out their stalls, noting names like Cinnamon, Silver, and Twinkles. Outside, we stood next to a gray rail fence, petting the horses who stuck their heads out for food. We were instructed not to feed them, but I fed the little one a handful of grass on the sly.

I didn't have cowboy boots, so I wore my red-dot canvas Keds. I thought I was cool, wearing pedal-pushers that hit me just below my knees. Everyone else wore long stretch pants, but they weren't nearly as fashionable.

A guy with a cowboy hat named Jason welcomed us and said he was a high school senior who lived on a nearby ranch.

"Here's what we'll do," he explained. "You'll draw straws to see who gets first pick and so on until the six of you have been assigned your horse. Longest gets first pick. Shortest gets last." He held out a handful of straws and we each plucked one, then raised them to compare.

Jason took Maggie's longest straw. "You have first pick."

Maggie walked up to a spirited chestnut mare and rubbed her nose. "I want Cinnamon."

I drew the shortest straw, so I got the last pick—the pint-sized Shetland pony named Twinkles, who I'd been slipping hay to between the fence rails.

"This little guy is an excellent choice for someone your size," said Jason, smiling.

I figured it was a compliment in a cowboy sort of way.

Jason helped us mount our horses, though some girls already knew how. Twinkles stayed still while Jason showed me how to mount him, then handed me the reins.

"I hope this is a calm horse. I haven't ridden in a while," I lied. The closest I'd come to riding was sitting in the saddle of Uncle Will's girlfriend's horse after the Fourth of July parade last summer. I figured that counted.

"And you're a Montana girl? Let this pony know you're the one in charge, and you'll be fine," he drawled. Jason led Twinkles by his bridle to the end of the line, next to Maggie's horse. "Line up in pairs, so each of you has a riding partner," he instructed.

"Maggie, have you ridden?" I tried to keep the tremor from my voice.

"I've ridden quarter horses at my cousins' ranch in Wise River," she replied.

"How come I never knew that?" My friend was full of surprises.

She offered me a dismissive wave. "It was a long time ago."

"Everyone ready? Move out." Jason clicked giddy-up, urging his chestnut bay forward. The other horses followed. All except Twinkles, who stilled, like he was waiting for a bus.

Maggie rode on ahead, motioning me to catch up. "Come on, Jo!"

I clicked a giddy-up, prodding Twinkles with my stirrups. He stayed glued to the ground. I tried reasoning with him. "Twinkles, if you go, I'll give you some oats."

Twinkles twitched his ears and heaved out a sigh. He shifted his weight but wouldn't move. The others had trotted ahead and disappeared around a bend.

"Twinkles! Get your butt in gear!" I dug my heels hard into horse flesh.

Twinkles didn't like that. He laid his ears back and bolted toward a group of Douglas Fir trees. Sharp pine needles assaulted me, and I let go of the reins to shield my face. The branches swept me from the saddle, and I plummeted down to the dirt. The devious pony galloped off to catch up with the rest.

"Twinkles! Come back here!" I pushed to my feet, brushing off pine needles. Wincing at my sore bottom, I gimped after the stubborn little shit.

Jason was heading toward me, leading Twinkles by the reins. "You fall off?"

"He deliberately ran under the trees to brush me off!" I said, exasperated.

"You need to show him who's boss." He hooked a finger around the bridle and turned Twinkles in a half circle to follow the others. "Doesn't she, boy?"

The pony nuzzled him, which stuck in my craw. Twinkles wore his horsey halo whenever Jason was around, but with me he was like Sylvester the cat, torturing Tweety the minute Granny's back was turned.

"I *did* show him who's boss, but he ignores me," I complained, mounting the pony once more. I clicked him to giddy up.

Jason's chestnut bay patiently waited for him to swing back into the saddle. Everyone else had stopped, and when we caught up, they resumed their ride. Jason trotted up to the front, leaving me and Twinkles at the back of the line.

Things were okay until Twinkles aimed for a wood rail fence and ran next to it, trying to knock me off. I pulled my foot from the stirrup and swung my leg to ride sidesaddle to keep from being squished against the slivery wood. Twinkles jerked away from the fence, and I lost my balance and went flying.

Jason trotted back, looking displeased. "What happened this time?"

"He knocked me off again!" I eyed Twinkles, blinking innocently and swishing his tail like he hadn't a care in the world.

Jason waited while I mounted a third time and grasped the reins. As I opened my mouth to say giddy up, Twinkles spun around and tore off like a racehorse with a burr inside its butt—all the way to the stables.

"Hang on!" Jason hollered after me.

By some miracle, I stayed in the saddle as Twinkles galloped back to the horse corral. He bolted through the gate, then suddenly halted, somersaulting me over his head. I thudded to the dirt, wondering what I'd broken. Twinkles had the nerve to nicker and nuzzle me as I lay there, staring at the clouds. One looked like an elephant, which I wished I'd ridden instead of this holy terror.

Jason and the others soon showed up at the stables after I peeled myself off the ground. My dignity was as bruised as my backside as I grabbed the reins of my pint-sized nemesis to tie them to the fence. I swore the little turd smirked as I silently renamed his breed from "Shetland" to "Shitland."

"Here you go, you poor excuse for a horse," I grumbled, rubbing my sore hip.

Twinkles innocently munched hay, then nuzzled me like I was his best friend.

It was solidly against the Montana code to hate a horse, but I detested Twinkles with all my heart. He was pure evil. Twinkles had it out for me, and that was all there was to it. My cowboy uncles would be forever disappointed if they knew, so I vowed never to tell them.

Hopefully, I'd never see that crabby-assed little horse ever again.

AFTER LUNCH, WE LEARNED how to paddle a canoe. The green dot on our name tags meant we had passed our swim test, so our canoe instructor showed us no mercy. Greg made us swamp our canoes, then made us rescue ourselves. When he checked us off on his trusty clipboard, we paddled out to the floating dock in the middle of Bear Lake, which wasn't big. After learning the "J" stroke and how to rudder, we were confident enough to circle around the dock and return.

Maggie and I were the cat's meow with our canoe skills—that is, until two girls wearing Anaconda t-shirts pushed the side of our canoe down with their paddles and flipped us over in *Parent Trap* style, whooping and hollering in triumph.

"Hey! That wasn't nice, you Anaconda creeps!" spluttered Maggie, grabbing our overturned silver canoe. She spit out water, and I thought she'd blow a gasket.

The girls laughed and paddled away, while Maggie and I struggled to right our swamped canoe. Now I was glad Greg made us practice swamping one. I swam to get our paddles, and it took a fair amount of time to get our water-laden canoe back to shore.

Greg was not pleased. He greeted us with folded arms and a scowl.

I pointed to where we'd overturned. "Did you see that? Those girls flipped us over!"

He rolled his eyes. "Yeah, right."

Maggie was incredulous. "You honest to God didn't see that?"

I couldn't believe it when he shook his head, and then I remembered he'd been flirting with two of the counselors when we paddled away from shore.

We tilted the canoe to dump the water, then Maggie and I rolled it upside down and heaved the dripping thing up onto the rack.

Maggie and I swore we'd get back at the Anaconda girls. We found out they were in Cabin Five, right next to us. *How convenient.*

As we fell asleep plotting our revenge, I thought of the song, "Camp Grenada: Hello Muddah, Hello Fadduh," that Allan Sherman sang on TV and on the radio.

I sure felt like him in that song right now, as a twinge of homesickness sliced into me.

Maybe tomorrow will be better.

Chapter 32
Of Frogs and Fizzies

July 1967, seventh grade summer

The morning after the fiasco with Twinkles, I asked to ride Silver, the gray mellow horse. Jason must have taken pity on me because he let me ride him, leading us along a trail through the woods. We picked our way down a gentle slope, the horses stepping between downed trees. Silver was a vast improvement over Twinkles because he was older and slower, absolutely perfect—until he skidded on the dirt and rolled onto his side—with me still in the saddle.

"Help! This horse is squishing me!" I yelled, trying in vain to get him off me. Oblivious, Silver lay there like a slug, lazily munching grass. I couldn't feel my leg.

Jason appeared and grabbed Silver's bridle, easing him off of me. "Roll out of the way so he doesn't stand on you when he gets up," he instructed.

Grunting like an old man, I rolled over and belly-crawled away from the lazy gray horse.

Jason coaxed Silver to his feet. The feeling returned to my leg, and it was mostly okay, except for a scrape and a bruise that was sure to stick around for a good while.

"Guess I'm horse jinxed," I said, defeated.

"Well, don't take it personal, cowgirl," drawled Jason, handing me the reins, and I mounted Silver and rode back to the stables.

Despite my cowboy heritage, becoming a Montana cowgirl wasn't in the cards. I repeated my vow never to tell Uncle Ollie or Uncle Will. The next day I walked like a bowlegged bronc buster, so I chose archery. Beth let me change my activity schedule after I filled her in on my equine misadventures.

Maggie, on the other hand, had a talent for horseback riding. I told her she should ride horseback in the next Butte Fourth of July parade, while I'd follow in a pink convertible, decked out in a ball gown and tiara, waving to the crowd and tossing taffy and bubble gum. That was more my style.

By the end of our first week of camp, we'd settled into our routines. One night, after everyone gathered at the Wampum Ring for songs and stories, I whispered to Maggie, "Let's check out that other trail at the fork!"

Armed with our trusty flashlights, we casually slowed to let everyone go ahead of us. When no one was watching, we ducked onto the overgrown path, blazing a trail like Lewis and Clark.

"Doesn't look like anyone uses this trail," I commented as we made our way between tall grass and elderberry bushes. I cast furtive glances into the pine forest, hoping no bears, wolves, or sasquatch would pop out and eat us. The camp counselors loved terrifying us with stories of yetis or sasquatch kidnapping young girls from their sleeping bags.

"Check out these cattails and pussy willows!" Maggie pointed out as we came upon a cute little pond with more frogs than we could count, leaping from lily pads into the water. There were so many frogs, the whole pond seemed to move. It was a froggy baby boom.

A worn, crooked sign was jammed into the dirt: "Pollywog Pond."

I stood for a moment, taking in the laid-back beauty of this tranquil setting, when an idea occurred. "Are you thinking what I'm thinking?" I asked Maggie with a vicious grin.

She gave me a solemn nod. "The Anaconda girls."

"Great minds think alike." I laughed. "Mags, that's why someday you'll be President of the United States."

On our way back from the Wampum Ring the next evening, we sneaked onto the old trail and returned to the pond with dixie cups. We each caught five little frogs and hurried back to Cabin Five, where the Anaconda girls bunked. We hid in the bushes and waited until everyone headed to the bathhouse to brush their teeth. Then we scurried inside and planted the frogs inside the bottom of their sleeping bags. It was easy to tell which bunks they were, with the Anaconda t-shirts hanging off them.

We gleefully skedaddled back to our cabin and jumped into our own bags. Giggling, we waited for the screams once everyone settled in for the night. Right on cue, shrieks pierced the darkness, warming our evil little hearts.

Ah, paybacks. Revenge was sweet.

I high-fived Maggie in the bunk next to mine. "That'll teach Anaconda to mess with Butte."

THE CABINS ROTATED dish duty each night after dinner. We'd taken our turn the first week, and our turn came around again during the second week. When the dining hall cleared, the eight of us gathered the dishes and stacked them in the kitchen to be hand-washed. Beth assigned our tasks. She assigned Maggie and me to dry the dishes and put them away.

I swung the other cupboard doors open in the room next to the kitchen and gazed in awe at the top shelves. "Get a load of the Chips Ahoy, Cocoa Puffs, and Frosted Flakes!" But what caught my eye on the lower shelves were the endless boxes of Fizzies!

Maggie appeared next to me. "Wow! Someone in this camp sure likes Fizzies."

We gaped at the seemingly endless stacks of boxes containing eight-packs of Fizzies. We loved creating carbonated soft drinks with them when we popped them into a glass of water and watched them bubble and fizz. Every flavor was there: grape, orange, lemon-lime, strawberry, including my favorites, which were cherry, root beer, and cola. I'd never seen so many.

"Watch the magic begin, the second you drop a Fizzie in!" Maggie and I chorused, singing the jingle from the TV commercials.

"Let's take some. No one'll know," I whispered longingly.

"It would be stealing," said my Pollyanna goody-two-shoes friend.

"Not exactly," I reasoned. "Look at it this way: our moms paid for us to come to this camp, so technically, they paid for these Fizzies." I was proud of my twisted logic.

Maggie wrinkled her nose. "You sound like my dad when he does his taxes."

"Are you with me?" I fastened my gaze to the Fizzies, visualizing all that fizz on my tongue.

"I want cherry ones!" Maggie snatched a handful of red aluminum packs, stashed them down the back of her jeans, and pulled her t-shirt over them. She twirled with her arms spread. "Can you tell?"

"Nope. Way to kype Fizzies, you're a genius!" Inspired by Maggie's ingenuity, I did the same. For once, we were grateful our moms had bought our jeans a size too big.

On impulse, I covertly shoved another bunch of Fizzie packs down the front of my crowded jeans. We were like the *Pink Panther* on a jewelry heist.

"Act normal and don't freak out," I hissed as our cabin finished the dishes and left the kitchen.

Trying our best to look casual, we moseyed to our cabin to unload our contraband, hearts beating a mile a minute. Anxious as all get out, we waited impatiently for the last girl to leave our cabin so we could hide our loot. Finally, the cabin was empty.

"Mags, stick yours in my duffel," I instructed, lifting a small key. "Mom gave me this tiny padlock to lock my zipper." We stashed our Fizzies, locked the padlock, and I hid the key under my pillow.

The next day we were obsessed with getting more Fizzies. Having discovered all those boxes was like finding *The Treasure of the Sierra Madre*—we simply had to have more. Unfortunately, we weren't on dish duty. Over dinner, we hatched a plan.

"After Cabin Four finishes the dishes, we'll sneak in through the back door and get some more," said Maggie, between forkfuls of mashed potatoes. Sometimes she surprised me: her devious side popped out now and then, like a regular Jekyll and Hyde.

We were regular ninjas as we carried out Maggie's plan with expert sneakiness. The next night, we snatched even more Fizzies and crept back to our cabin. Along the way, we popped them into our mouths to ride the wild carbonation rush. I stuffed two in at once and it felt like miniature fireworks exploding in my mouth. I considered a triple header but didn't want my face to fall off.

One thing was evident: we'd become Fizzie addicts.

And we couldn't stop.

THE DAY BEFORE THE last day of camp, I wanted to make it a memorable one and came up with what I thought was a cool idea.

"Maggie, let's put Fizzies in Pollywog Pond to see what happens!"

Maggie shoved her glasses higher on her nose. "The frogs will go nuts and hop all over the place, that's what'll happen."

"But it would be cool to watch," I persuaded.

"I don't know..." hedged Maggie. "What if they die or something?"

"Nah, they won't," I said convincingly. "Fizzies are harmless. After all, humans eat them."

After dinner, Maggie and I rushed to our cabin, where we armed ourselves with Fizzies. The setting sun dappled the lodgepole pines as we made our way along the trail to Pollywog Pond. Squirrels chattered, and we chattered back. Falcons and golden eagles glided overhead, scouting for easy meals.

When we reached the pond and pulled back the tin foils covering the Fizzies, we filled our hands with as many as we could hold. "One... two...three!" we hollered, flinging them as high as we could.

We watched Fizzies pelt the water like a colorful hailstorm. When they hit, there was dead silence, except for the fizz. Then all at once, a cacophony of croaks erupted as frogs leaped frantically between the lily pads, some catapulting onto the trail, desperate to escape.

"Oh, no, don't go on the trail!" I shouted, like the frogs would obey me.

Maggie and I stood frozen at the sight of the frog frenzy. We'd tossed in all the colors, but the pond was blood-red, as if the frogs had detonated instead of escaping at supersonic speed.

"Holy crap!" I shrieked. "The frogs are heading toward camp!"

"If they get to the fork in the trail, the campers will trample them on their way to the Wampum Ring!" yelled Maggie.

We frantically waved our arms to shoo the freaked-out frogs back to the pond. "Miss Hazel will kill us! We'd better get out of here!" I was in fight-or-flight mode.

"What about the frogs?" Maggie sounded as desperate as I felt.

"I don't know... they'll get out of the way, maybe." I said it mostly to convince myself.

Beating ourselves up for our lack of foresight, we sprinted toward camp, aiming our jiggling flashlight beams on the root-strewn path—all the while praying we wouldn't step on tiny, unsuspecting frogs. Our flashlight beams bobbed and weaved as we stumbled along the uneven trail. At last, we broke free of the woods and beelined for Cabin Six.

When we rounded the corner of our cabin, my flashlight suddenly illuminated a spooky face, and I skidded to a stop. Maggie crashed into me, and we both screamed.

"Hey, girls, it's me!" said Beth, eyeing us suspiciously while we panted like wild dogs. "Where were you two?"

"Hi Beth, we were just—we just—" Words weren't landing in my mouth. Maggie stepped around me. "We just saw a grizzly bear!"

"What? Where?" Beth flicked her flashlight behind us as if a bear was bearing down on us.

"Back in the woods on the opposite side of camp from the Wampum Circle," I seconded Maggie's lie, hoping my nose wouldn't sprout a twig and grow. When someone else invented a lie, it was easy to piggyback onto it.

Beth gave us a dubious look. "Why were you all the way over there?"

"We uh…" I started.

"We did an exploratory walk for our last night at camp," finished Maggie.

"Yeah, an exploratory walk," I echoed, my head bobbing. I sent a silent air hug to Maggie for being quick on her feet.

"Well, don't go there again. We don't want bears in camp," cautioned Beth. "Time to go to our last Wampum Circle. Bears don't bother us there with all the noise."

Thank goodness Beth bought our story. As our cabin mates strolled toward the Wampum Circle talking and laughing, Maggie and I joined them, hoping the frogs had settled down and wouldn't be near the main trail. We listened carefully once we were close to the pond—no croaks or ribbits, just campers' voices. So far, so good. Maggie and I heaved out sighs of relief.

I dreaded the light of day, fearing what we'd see. I said a quick prayer for the poor little frogs of Pollywog Pond. No way around it…we'd have to confess this one. And it wasn't just a venial sin.

It was a bona fide Frogicide.

Chapter 33
Amphibious Redemption

*J*uly 1967, seventh grade summer

The next morning at breakfast, Maggie and I quietly filled each waffle hole with syrup, trying our best not to look guilty. Miss Hazel and the counselors each made speeches and handed out cabin activity awards. We rolled our eyes when the Anaconda girls in Cabin Five got the best canoeing award. Cabin Six got the best swimmer's award, which made us happy.

As we filed up to get our award certificates, I avoided looking at Miss Hazel for fear she'd sense our guilt. Everyone said their goodbyes, and Maggie and I bolted to Cabin Six to pack up and wait for Mom and Aunt Daisy to come get us. Once inside the cabin, I grabbed an empty coffee can I'd retrieved from the kitchen trash.

"I'm going to save what frogs that I can. I'll catch some and take them home, where I can take care of them."

"Not a good idea, Jo." Maggie was nearly in hysterics, jamming clothes into her duffel. "What if there're no frogs left?"

"Don't worry. I'll be back in a minute." I grabbed my coffee can and ran as fast as I could to the pond. Breaking through the trees to reach the pond, I didn't see signs of frog life.

Oh, no, where are they?

I hiked to the Wampum Campfire ring, stepping around frog corpses, searching for survivors. I found ten baby frogs and put them in my coffee can with a bunch of grass, then put the plastic lid on and made a mental note to punch holes in it.

I wanted to redeem myself by saving these little guys. I'd have to confess this as a mortal sin, since so many deaths were involved. Except this was too horrendous to confess to anyone, let alone a priest. I'd probably go to cruelty-to-animals jail.

When I returned to Cabin Six, I quickly stashed the Folger's coffee can in some bushes before going inside. Beth was waiting with Maggie. "Miss Hazel wants to talk to the campers one more time before you all go. And she wants everyone to bring their award certificates."

"Why does she want us to bring those?" Maggie's face fell.

"I guess we'll see," I said with some unease.

Maggie and I walked up to the lodge with Beth and stepped inside. Everyone sat at the dining room tables with somber faces, staring at us as we took our seats.

Miss Hazel crossed her arms, her mouth in a firm, straight line. "We've had a series of unfortunate occurrences. First off, Fizzies are missing from the pantry. Second, there are dead frogs on the trail to Wampum Ring and, by some strange coincidence, Pollywog Pond has turned red." Red-faced, she scanned the room, searching for the guilty party.

Stark terror seized my soul and hot shame waved through me as Maggie and I glanced nervously around the room at the wide-eyed campers exchanging astonished looks.

"Who would do something like that?" piped up an Anaconda girl, giving Maggie and me a side-eye. Why was she assuming we were the guilty party?

I stuck my tongue out at her, then wore my halo of innocence as I returned my gaze to Miss Hazel.

"No one leaves this room until the guilty ones come forward. Your parents must wait until you're all released." Miss Hazel's expression was grim and forbidding.

Everyone groaned as Maggie and I froze in our seats, guilt plastered on our faces like clown masks. Maggie leaned sideways and whispered, "We have to tell her!"

"No way," I whispered back, louder than I intended.

Miss Hazel homed in on us. "Something you want to say, ladies?"

Maggie's eyes filled up, and she cracked. "We took the Fizzies!"

A collective gasp arose from the campers as Miss Hazel announced, "The rest of you girls are free to go." She pointed at us. "You two remain here."

The Anaconda girls smirked as they filed outside with the others. I sat on my hands so as not to flip them off, as Cat surely would have done.

Miss Hazel moved to our table, snatched our award certificates, and ripped them in half. "What do you have to say for yourselves?"

Maggie choked out between sobs. "It wasn't our fault! We couldn't help it!"

Her outright confession stunned me, and I didn't know whether to laugh or cry.

Miss Hazel's face was stormy with disapproval. "It's one thing to take one or two packets of Fizzies—but eight boxes? What's worse is that you dumped them into Pollywog Pond and killed those poor frogs. I'm disappointed in you girls."

Maggie cried even harder, while I beat myself up with an imaginary Mr. Whackenstick.

"We're so sorry. We'll never do it again," I mumbled through my hot cheeks.

"You're darn right you won't! You're both banned from Camp Elkhorn. Neither of you will be welcome here in the future, either as a camper or a counselor. And you'll reimburse us for what you stole, plus more for the environmental disaster you caused with Pollywog Pond and the frogs. I'll figure the dollar amount and will let your parents know." She swept her hand toward the door.

A cloud of doom descended as Maggie and I left the Main Lodge and trudged to Cabin Six. Beth had already gone, so we gathered our duffels, sleeping bags, and my coffee can of baby frogs. We shuffled to the parking lot, and the bottom fell out of me when I saw Miss Hazel talking to my mother, both with thundercloud expressions. I stopped short, unable to make my feet move.

"I'll be grounded for ten years," groaned Maggie, bumping into me.

"I'll be grounded for twenty," I echoed glumly as Miss Hazel marched from the parking lot, leaving Mom staring at a sheet of paper in her hands.

As we timidly approached, Aunt Daisy leaned on her Chevy, smoking a cig, while Mom stood with legs spread and a hand on each hip.

"What is the meaning of this?" Mom waved the paper, glaring at me. "Why would you do that?"

I gave her an apologetic shrug. "We wanted the Fizzies."

"So, you stole them? And then threw them into a pond, killing the wildlife?" Mom threw her arms up. "Heavens to mother-loving Betsy! Don't they teach you anything at that damn Catholic school?"

"Obviously not the ninth commandment," murmured Aunt Daisy, dropping her spent cig and extinguishing it with her foot.

"The ninth commandment is 'thou shalt not lie,'" corrected Maggie. "Thou shalt not steal is the eighth."

"Looks like you kids broke both. You stole, then you lied about it, according to your camp director." Aunt Daisy opened her trunk, picked up our duffels and tossed them both in, along with our sleeping bags.

"But we told the truth to Miss Hazel," I countered. "I mean, Maggie did," I corrected.

"Now I have to pay for those stolen Fizzies, plus the environmental damage Miss Hazel said you did!" Mom lit a cig and pointed it at Maggie. "And you owe me for half, Little Missy."

"Yes, Mrs. Wolohan," chirped Maggie. "Please don't tell my mother."

"We'll see about that. You two, get in the car!" Mom jerked her head toward the back seat, her mouth in a straight line.

We scrambled into the back seat, quiet as church mice. I set my frog can on the floor between my feet and couldn't wait to get out of here.

Aunt Daisy pulled onto the highway to Butte, and an occasional ribbit floated up. Maggie and I pretended not to hear it.

"What is that noise?" Mom glanced around, lighting another cig.

"Sounds like frogs." Aunt Daisy winked at me in the rearview mirror.

"For cripes' sakes! You brought those things with you?" My mother hand-cranked her window down to let out the smoke. "They aren't allowed in the house when we get home!"

Every time a frog thumped inside the coffee can, my heart tugged a little. Never mind the ones we'd decimated with our Fizzies. It'll take me a lifetime to do penance for that one.

Maggie leaned over and whispered, "Blessed be the froggies, for they shall go to froggy heaven."

I let out a sullen sigh, patting the plastic lid of my frog hotel. I was determined to make it up to these survivors for fizzying their relatives.

We dropped off Maggie and when we got home, Mom made me leave the frogs outside, so I set the coffee can next to the back step. I put in fresh grass, small bugs, and a water dish to make the frogs comfortable. Just so they could get more air, I even punched holes in the plastic lid.

The next morning, I found the can on its side with the lid off. To my horror, flattened frog bodies stuck to the alley next to our house. Somehow, they'd escaped and hopped down and got run over. With a sinking heart, I dug a hole in our front garden to bury what frogs I could find.

I asked the patron saint of all living creatures to forgive me. "St. Francis of Assisi, please forgive me for the Frogicide," I prayed. "I'm gonna need your help to stay out of hell for this one. Amen."

I promised to save every living thing I came into contact with from now on: I wouldn't step on ants, and I'd return worms to the dirt when rain washed them onto the sidewalk. I even vowed to spare the lives of spiders. Mosquitoes would be a stretch.

"Oh, and one last thing," I whispered to St. Francis. "Please forgive me for eating that bumblebee when I was two. I don't remember doing it, but Mom reminds me whenever she sees a bee. She said it was a miracle it didn't sting me on the way to my stomach."

Maybe if St. Francis knew I was sorry, I wouldn't go to hell. Maybe he'd go easy on me with a fast tour through purgatory instead. I needed a get-into-heaven free card and would jump on the first available opportunity to get one.

Chapter 34
The Fighting Irish

September 1967, beginning of eighth grade

We were too young to experience the Summer of Love, so instead, we crushed on rock stars like the Beach Boys or the Beatles. We had endless arguments over who was cuter—until we watched Jim Morrison sing "Light My Fire" on *The Ed Sullivan Show.* Then we were goners.

For most of the summer, I listened to music on my transistor radio. I laid awake at night under the covers, fidgeting with the tuner. My favorite radio station was Wolfman Jack, who howled like a wolf and played the Top 40. I had to turn the volume all the way up because it was way down in California. On Saturdays, I watched *American Bandstand* on TV with groups singing "Chewy Chewy," "Yummy Yummy Yummy," "Sugar Sugar," "Mony Mony," and "Woman Woman." Whoever wrote these songs sure liked to repeat themselves.

The evening news showed flower children and hippies in San Francisco, and college kids protesting Vietnam, carrying "Ban the Bomb" signs. I didn't quite get the "tune in, turn on, and drop out" thing older kids talked about. But we Clover Girls loved the psychedelic colors that were everywhere—neon greens and blues on posters, clothes, and billboards. Older kids wore peace sign necklaces and love beads, and girls wore flowers in their hair with colorful headbands. We watched women on TV burning their bras in the streets.

They must have really hated those bras.

In mid-August, the Butte miners went on strike. During the last strike in 1959, I was only five, but I remember Dad being home every day, reading *Golden Books* to me. We hadn't been able to take our Sunday drives because Dad couldn't afford gas, and we ate Spam and egg sandwiches. Mom would rush to the courthouse for potatoes delivered from a nearby farm, so we ate hash browns and gravy with our Spam.

The current miners' strike was hard on families whose dads worked for The Company and for Mom and me, who relied on income from miners paying rent. Since the copper miners weren't working, everyone was on edge.

To make things worse, the post-war baby boom in the 1950s had created a surge of students, and with fewer women entering religious life, there weren't enough nuns to teach all of us. Some schools closed on Butte's east side in Meaderville and McQueen, so The Company could mine beneath them.

The remaining Catholic schools took in students from the school closures and some parents sent their kids to the public schools because they could no longer afford the tuition. I begged Mom to let me stay at St. Mike's, so she worked out a deal with Monsignor Coyle to pay part of my tuition until the strike ended. Maggie, Cat, and Mikey Ann's parents did the same. I was relieved, as I couldn't bear the thought of being separated from the Clover Girls.

A bunch of kids transferred into our class from Holy Rosary School that had closed over the summer. Our eighth-grade class was a sudden madhouse with sixty-six kids. Our new principal was also our eighth-grade teacher, Sister Alexandria. We called her Sister Alex. On the first day of class, there weren't enough desks, so the nuns brought in small tables, until Mr. Kearney could have desks hauled across town from Holy Rosary. There was so much tension in our overcrowded classroom, you could slice it with Mr. Quinn's meat cleaver. The St. Mike's kids sat on one side and the Holy Rosary kids sat on the other.

The new kids didn't wear uniforms, and Sister told them they didn't have to until the miner's strike was settled. I was downright jealous that some kids got to wear regular clothes. Our tacky dark green bow ties, white shirts, and green-plaid skirts suddenly made us feel like we were stuck in *Howdy Doody's* closet back in the caveman era.

During the first week, I'd sneak peeks across the room at the Holy Rosary girls with their don't-mess-with-us expressions. The boys smiled at us occasionally, and they were friendlier and kind of cute. An older-looking, red-haired kid wore a Rolling Stones t-shirt and Sister Alex told him it wasn't appropriate and not to wear it to school.

When I glanced at him, he winked, and my face heated. St. Mike's boys never winked at us girls. They were too busy impressing each other with who was the funniest, the grossest, and the coolest.

When Sister left the room, a spitball smacked Cat, who sat in front of me.

"Ow, gross!" she yelped. Two months after losing her dad, Cat was still hurting but fighting her way back to normal. We admired her resilience, doing our part to make her laugh with our dumb jokes.

I swiveled my head to see the red-headed kid a few rows over, grinning at us. He pointed to the boy in front of him. "He shot the spit ball!"

"Nuh-uh, you did, you creep!" hissed Cat, peeling the slimy wad from her hair. She flicked it to the floor. "Eew, disgusting!" Felt good to have Cat back to her sassy, smart-alecky self.

I leaned forward and whispered to Cat. "What's that kid's name?"

"Thomas MacGregor. They call him Mack," she whispered back.

I sized him up from across the room. He towered over most of us with actual sideburns, unlike the other boys. His curly hair and dimpled smile stood out, and he seemed experienced beyond his years. He caught me staring, and I snapped my attention to Sister, who'd returned with a stack of papers.

She passed out mimeographed sheets with the intoxicating purple ink we couldn't resist sniffing, listing the chore assignments. Maggie and I landed on the canned food drive list, and Mikey Ann and Cat on the clothing drive list. The boys were assigned to clean the blackboards, erasers, and the tiny supply closet in the back corner. Everyone took turns feeding the goldfish and cleaning the aquarium, which Sister Alex had informed us was her pride and joy.

Maggie sat behind me and tapped my shoulder. "Don't look now, but the new girls keep staring at us," she whispered.

I sneaked a peek and was met by several none-too-friendly faces.

"Gee, I can't wait for recess," I said under my breath.

Sure enough, when our class hit the playground, it was an us-and-them deal. Four distinct groups clustered like four sports teams: the new Holy

Rosary kids and the old St. Mike's kids, with two groups of girls and two groups of boys.

Sister Alex stepped over to us St. Mike's girls. "It's important that you welcome our new students to St. Michael's and make them feel accepted. Imagine if you had to leave your school and the neighborhood where you grew up. All of this would seem strange to you."

Sister directed her remarks to us Clover Girls like *we* were the ones in charge of the eighth-grade class welcome wagon, peacemaking mission.

"Yes, Sister," we mumbled as she moved off to talk with the boys.

I heaved out a sigh and waggled my finger at Maggie, Mikey Ann, and Cat. "Come on, you guys. Let's go talk to them." When our group approached the new girls, they banded together like a hostile street gang. Not a good sign.

Maggie was the first to extend her hand. "Hi, I'm Mary Margaret Houlihan. Everyone calls me Maggie."

The girls only stared at her with folded arms.

I strolled up to the pretty tall girl with short, brown hair cut in a trendy bob. "Hi, I'm Jo Wolohan."

More icy stares.

Cat stepped forward. "I'm Catherine Delaney. Call me Cat."

"And I'm Mikey Ann Quinn." Mikey Ann rested her hands at her sides, waiting expectantly.

The tall girl sized up Maggie, Cat, and me, then settled her gaze on Mikey Ann. "I'm Danica Radovich and I can kick anybody's ass in this school." She locked stares with Mikey Ann, like a gunfighter on *Gunsmoke*.

Mikey Ann straightened to her full height; matching Radovich's as they sized each other up. The air crackled with enough electric tension to light up the Big "M."

I gulped, hoping nothing would spark fisticuffs.

"Well. Alrighty then," quipped our perky little Maggie, pasting on a smile. Ever the peacemaker, she held out a Chinese jump rope. "Want to jump rope with us?"

"Aren't you a little old for that?" Another girl stepped forward with folded arms, her brown eyes narrowing. "So, what are you all into in this school? Shamrocks and wee little leprechauns?" She yanked Maggie's green clip-on bowtie, then glanced back at her friends, who laughed.

"Yeah, the little wee people!" The one with long, black hair pressed her thumb and forefinger together to illustrate her point.

A girl with dark hair held back by a blue plastic headband laughed. "Good one, Nuna." She turned to us. "I'm Rosa Garcia. And I'm not Irish."

"Okay, well...not everyone at St. Mike's is Irish." I motioned at the other green plaid uniforms on the playground.

"Doesn't matter. My Blackfoot tribe from Browning wouldn't be welcome here." Nuna whipped her hair behind her shoulder.

"Why not?" challenged Cat. "Every person is welcome here."

"No, we aren't. Because we don't look like you." Nuna motioned to Rosa and the other girls. "Even if we wore those ugly uniforms and lame bow ties."

Mikey Ann pointed to the other kids on the playground. "Look around. Cecilia and Louise are from the Philippines, Carlos over there came from Mexico, and Jillian's parents moved here from the Crow Reservation." She shrugged. "We all get along just fine."

"That doesn't mean squat." Nuna tossed her hair over her shoulder, her silver feather earrings glinting in the sun.

"Neat earrings," Cat said quickly. "But don't let the nuns see you wearing them. Sister Bertie says pierced ears are barbaric and the work of the devil."

Nuna took a step forward, nose to nose with Cat. "Are you saying I'm the devil?"

Cat stood her ground, folding her arms. "Well, I don't know. *Are* you?"

Nuna lifted her chin. "No. But I know what *you* are." She shoved Cat so hard Cat stumbled back and her butt hit the asphalt. "You are on the ground, down for the count!" She motioned like a referee when a boxer hits the floor.

I winced at what Cat's tailbone must have experienced.

The new girls laughed while everyone else gasped.

"That wasn't nice!" hissed Cat, glowering at her.

"Tough bounce, weirdo." Rosa leaned over Cat, her smile dripping with venom. "What are you gonna do about it?"

Cat sprang up and flipped Rosa off so fast her finger could have smoked. "Rotate on this!"

"Ooh, I'm scared!" laughed Rosa, along with the other Holy Rosary girls. By this time, others on the playground had floated over to get in on the action.

"Oh, Lordy, here we go," murmured Maggie, stiffening.

"Yep, here we go," I echoed. Apparently, we hadn't left our playground kerfuffles back in the second and fourth grades. Except this time, we were older. And bigger. And punchier. This confrontation had the potential to make our previous ones seem like a kindergarten cupcake party.

Rosa lunged at Cat, shoving her.

"Leave her alone!" Mikey Ann towered over Rosa and shoved her into the new girls standing behind her.

"Drop dead, bitch!" hollered Rosa to everyone's gasps at the 'B' word.

"Pipe down, or we'll all get detention!" I glanced at Sister Alex, busy talking to the boys, who were having their own hostile soiree.

Skyscraper Radovich looked down her nose at me. "Who are you, Michael the Archangel?" Her arrogant tone sped hot marbles through my veins.

I should have left it alone.

"Hey Radovich, what's the weather like up there?" I shot back in a snotty voice.

She leaned over and spit on my head. "It's raining."

As laughter broke out, I stood there in disbelief that this Miss Priss baptized me with her spit.

Maggie grimaced. "Get that grody slime ball out of your hair, Jo. It's gross!"

My fingers found the revolting spittle in my hair, then my hand balled into a fist. I had a decision to make, so I made it. I swung at Radovich, but she leaped aside, and my fist punched Quiet Girl's chest.

Rosa lunged for Cat and swung. Cat ducked, and Rosa's fist connected with Mikey Ann's eye instead. Mikey Ann returned the favor by punching Rosa's boob. Hard.

"Ow! You'll pay for that!" Rosa tackled Mikey Ann, and they fell to the ground, tussling.

Cat slapped Nuna's face. Nuna grabbed Cat's braids and yanked them up and down as if driving a team of horses. Howling in pain, Cat twisted around and bulldozed her head into Nuna's stomach.

Quiet Girl lit into me with the ferocity of a cougar, scratching and clawing. Insults flew like rocks as we grappled with our opponents, hurling obscenities that would make miners blush. Cat's inventive profanity made the rest of us sound like babbling toddlers by comparison.

The boys ran over, with shouts of "Cat fight, cat fight!"

"Shut up, dipshits!" I yelled, exasperated at their tired, pathetic pun whenever Cat had got into it with someone.

The Holy Rosary boys cheered for the new girls, and St. Mike's boys cheered for us old girls—like Bulldogs vs. Maroons at Butte High's Naranche Stadium. It reminded me of "The Troubles" our parents used to talk about with Catholics fighting Protestants in Ireland, except here, Catholics were duking it out with each other, which made no sense. Then the boys jumped into the fray, and it became girls against girls, boys against boys. The entire eighth grade class had erupted into a full-blown barnyard brawl.

I whirled to confront the last person who'd shoved me when Sister Alex grabbed my elbow, yanking me away. "What in the Billy-blue-blazes is going on here?" Sister's face was the color of beets.

Other nuns intervened to break up the prize fight, and Sister Alex blew her whistle. "Everyone, stop this immediately! RIGHT NOW!"

I'd never heard a nun yell so loud and was sure everyone down on The Flats heard her. Swarms of nuns came out of nowhere, clapping hands and pulling kids apart. We all stumbled back and stood there, panting like a pack of wild dogs. I surveyed my Clover Girls: Mikey Ann's eye was swollen, Cat's lips were bleeding, and Maggie's bowtie hung crooked and one of her braids had come loose. We all had scratches on our arms and cheeks.

Sister Alex pointed toward the door. "Single file and get back inside!" I'd never seen Sister so angry—angry enough to blow a gasket.

The nuns ordered everyone into two lines: new kids in one, and us old students in the other. We tramped back into school, knowing that you-know-what was about to hit the fan.

"We're in for it now!" sputtered Cat behind me. "We are SO dead!"

"We're beyond dead," I muttered back. "*Way* beyond dead."

Chapter 35
Can't We All Just Get Along?

We shuffled into the classroom; Holy Rosary kids on one side, St. Mike's kids on the other. Sister Alex informed us not only was she canceling the afternoon recess, but we were all in detention. She stood in front of the class with folded arms and a face-load of fury, while Sister Bertie handed out moist paper towels to those who needed them. There were two bloody noses that Sister Alex sent to the school nurse.

Cat held her sweater to her lip, and Sister Bertie handed her a moist towel. "Press this to your lip to stop the bleeding."

Without warning, Cat burst into tears and covered her face with her hands. We hadn't seen Cat cry since her dad's funeral. "I want my dad!" she choked out.

It seemed several of us were having our own personal emotional crisis as Sister Bertie helped Cat from her seat and escorted her out to the hall. I know I was, but I'd learned how to bury my emotions after years of heartache from loss.

Mikey Ann and I exchanged astonished looks while Sister Alex circulated with a tissue box. "Who else needs one?"

Several hands shot up, but most of us only had bumps and bruises. Sister Alex returned to the front of the class with folded arms. Her ominous silence lasted forever: an ant could have sneezed, and we would have heard it.

The door opened and Sister Bertie and Cat filed in. Cat blew her nose into a tissue as she took her seat. Her eyes met mine as a corner of her mouth lifted, letting me know she was okay.

Sister Alex broke the silence. "I'll only ask this once. Who started the fight?"

Arguments erupted like molten lava as we picked up where we had left off outside, hurling insults at each other with much finger pointing.

"Enough!" Sister Alex raised her hands in a stop motion. "One person at a time. Raise your hand to speak."

Everyone's hands shot up. "Mikey Ann, you go first."

"Sister, Rosa called me a bitch!" Mikey Ann twisted to look at her.

"You *are* a bitch!" hollered Rosa from the back of the room.

Mikey Ann jumped from her seat. "I am not!"

Sister Alex clapped her hands. "I said enough! Sit down, Miss Quinn. That is not lady-like behavior. Do not say that word again." She glared at our side of the room. "I am extremely disappointed in each and every one of you, especially our old St. Michael's students. Name calling and insults shall not be tolerated in this school. You each had better figure out how to get along with one another or you'll face severe consequences. Do I make myself clear?" she boomed in her outside voice, eyes blazing.

I glanced at Radovich and the other girls, searching for glimmers of remorse. Instead, I saw defiant faces.

"I expect each one of you to apologize to whomever you insulted today." Sister directed her piercing gaze at those of us in green uniforms.

Rosa raised her hand, and Sister called on her. "Sorry, I called you a bitch," she called out to Mikey Ann. "But stop treating us like we're aliens from outer space. We didn't ask to come to this school."

"Please introduce yourself," replied Sister.

"Sorry, Sister. My name is Rosa Garcia."

"Miss Quinn, do you have something to share with the rest of us?" Sister turned toward her with a hard look.

All eyes went to our side of the room as Mikey Ann twisted in her seat. "Sorry I pushed you," she mumbled.

"Apologize like you mean it. And please introduce yourself properly," ordered Sister.

Mikey Ann sat up straight and cleared her throat. "I'm Mikey Ann Quinn, and I'm sorry I shoved you." She glanced in Rosa's direction, then Sister's, checking to see if her sorry was good enough.

The quiet girl raised her hand. "My name is Sarah Brandenberger. Sorry I scratched you." She pointed at me.

"Josephina Wolohan. Me too," I mumbled, looking at the ceiling.

"Me, too, *what?*" Sister's sharp voice sliced through the tension; her glare could melt a hundred gallus frames.

I swallowed. "I'm sorry I decked you." Some kids snickered at my word choice.

Sister sighed and gave me an I-guess-that-will-do-look.

The girl with the feather earrings spoke up. "I'm Nuna Redfox. Sorry I pulled your hair," she said to Cat.

Cat was back in control. "As I said at recess, my name is Catherine Delaney. Sorry I slapped you."

"That's better. Anyone else?" Sister glanced around at the boys, waiting for them to speak up. "Recess will not be a boxing match or a push-and-shove contest. This will *not* happen again. Am I making myself clear?"

The class mumbled responses of "Yes, Sister," their 'S' sounds making a soft hiss that filled the room.

"Now spend the rest of the hour in silence thinking about what you did." Sister sat at her desk and busied herself with grading papers.

After our class was dismissed from detention, we Clover Girls stood outside, licking our wounds about what happened. Rosa came up to us. "I really am sorry. It's just that none of us wants to be here and we took it out on all of you."

"We're sorry, too," I said. "Want to hang out with us?"

A slow smile spread across Rosa's face. "Sure."

Thomas "Mack" MacGregor tapped down the front steps, brushing his long bangs back in that cool way the older teenagers did. "Guess we shouldn't mess with you St. Mike's chicks, huh?" He grinned and offered us a lifesaver.

I popped a red one in my mouth and rolled it around, savoring the cherry flavor.

"None of us want to be here." Mack exchanged looks with Rosa, who nodded.

"We liked our smaller school, where everyone wasn't so uptight," said Rosa. "Everyone got along, and our parents were good friends. How would you like it if you had to change schools your last year of grade school?"

"I would hate it," I admitted, understanding how they must feel. "Sorry you had to do that."

"Long as you treat us like humans, we'll get along fine. Or we'll sick Mack on you." Rosa elbowed him and grinned.

"Where'd you get that accent, Thomas?" Maggie asked shyly.

"Just call me Mack. I'm from Dundee. My family moved here for the mining jobs." His lopsided grin sent heat creeping up my neck.

We all gave him a blank look. "Where is Dundee?" I ventured.

"Don't they teach geography at this school?" Mack shook his head. "It's a coastal city in eastern Scotland."

Maggie gave him a wide smile. "Well, Mack, you have a cool Scottish accent."

He thickened his brogue. "Glad I ken be of service to all of you bonnie lasses."

We laughed, and I liked how he rolled his 'R's. No one talked the way he did. He was far more worldly than we were, that was for darn sure.

Mikey Ann motioned to Rosa. "Did you grow up in Butte?"

"Mostly in Southern California. Came here when I was ten so my dad could work in the mines," explained Rosa. "We had to move from our East side house down to West Silver Street, away from my friends."

"Yeah, that's a bummer. The Berkeley Pit is gobbling up the town. There's a rumor it might take over the Columbia Gardens." We all groaned, and Cat shook her head. "Sorry you lost your house."

"Being from California, I'll bet you miss the sunny weather," gushed Maggie, glancing up at the pale winter light threatening to dump snow on us any second.

"I do miss it sometimes. Hey, there's my dad. See you all tomorrow." Rosa climbed into a car that had pulled up to the curb. Her dad waved at us, and we all waved back as he pulled away.

"I gotta get going, too. See ya's tomorrow," said Mikey Ann, heading toward home.

I was fascinated by Mack. "You seem older. Were you held back a grade?" He was a head taller, like Mikey Ann.

A corner of his mouth turned up. "Two grades."

Cat's jaw dropped. "What are you, like fourteen?"

"Fifteen."

"No way!" I said, incredulous. "You're almost legal and everything!"

"Three more years." Once again, he tossed his long bangs. "I live down on Park Street. Anyone walking this way?"

"No, but we'll walk a block or two with you," I found myself saying, avoiding sly looks from Cat and Maggie.

"Far out," said Mack, ducking into an alleyway.

We followed him like little ducklings. He pulled a pack of Marlboros from his coat pocket, shook the pack, then pulled one out with his mouth. He passed the pack around. "Help yourself."

"Sure!" we chorused, wanting to be the cool, hip 'with-it' girls.

We formed a circle holding our cigs in that elegant way the adults did at their 'groovy' fondue parties. Once Mack lit our cigs and we took our first drag, Maggie and I coughed out a lung. I eyed Cat suspiciously as she puffed on her cig and exhaled like an old pro.

"Delaney, you've been holding out on us!" I accused between coughing fits.

"First time, eh?" Mack grinned, his bangs falling forward. He flipped them back with a quick head toss that hitched my breath.

Maggie held up her cig and stuck her tongue out at it. "How can you smoke these vile things?"

"I breathe my mom's smoke, so I'm used to it," I bragged, hoping I sounded sophisticated as I coughed out another lung. "Just out of practice."

Maggie and Cat rolled their eyes at my white lie.

Mack exhaled an expert stream that made my mother seem like a beginner. He unleashed more of his Scottish accent, puddling my heart to the pavement. "You bonnie lasses held your own today. I'll tell the boys not to tangle with you."

"They listen to you?" asked Cat.

"I'm older and wiser, so I'm their fearless leader." His infectious grin skittered my insides. "The nuns call me a juvenile delinquent."

Cat expertly blew out a smoke stream like a movie star. "So, you're a bad boy. In that case, we'll make a list of demands for you to tell the other boys. They don't listen to us."

Mack chuckled. "Sure, I can do that. They'll listen to *me*."

I seized the opportunity to brag about the Clover Girls. "Mikey Ann and Cat are one of the toughest girls in class. They go nose-to-nose with anyone who ticks them off. Mikey Ann wins speed skating, volleyball, and softball games, and Maggie is the smartest, but she doesn't brag about it. Cat and I are class clowns and play off each other like Tommy and Dickie Smothers."

When Mack's brows rose like he was impressed, my friends broke out with appreciative smiles.

I was curious about him. "When did your family move here? What do you think of Butte?" I acted casual, flicking my ash like a hip kid.

"Two years ago. What do I think?" He took a drag from his cig and let it out in a smooth stream. "This place gets so cold I defrost my toothpaste with a blowtorch."

Maggie and Cat cracked up while I choked out a laugh on another inhale attempt.

We filled Mack in on our past triumphs over the boy bullies, and Mikey Ann's searing revenge one hot summer day when she pressed a kid's wrist against the scorching metal of the swing set for calling her a sissy.

"She did it to another kid who called me Wolly No-Boobs." I puffed my cig, imitating my cool buddy, Cat, but when the smoke hit my lungs, I spluttered.

Mack's gaze lowered to my chest, and I instantly regretted my boobs remark. I was suddenly self-conscious that not much had blossomed there yet.

His brogue morphed into John Wayne. "Whoa, easy there, pilgrim. Remind me not to mess with you, ladies."

"Spread the word," instructed Cat, pointing at him with her two cigarette fingers.

"Right on. You got it." Mack expertly flicked the ash from his cig.

Strange things were going on inside of me: a rush of heat fluttered my stomach and a giddiness I couldn't explain whenever Mack looked my way.

I took a shaky breath and turned to Maggie. "Geez Louise, what time is it?"

Maggie checked her watch with the famous mouse with big black ears and white gloves on the hands. "Quarter after five."

"I gotta make like a tree and leave," I said, trying to sound like a cool chick. "Thanks for the cigs, Mack."

"Gimme some skin, Wolly." Mack held out his palm.

The boys called us girls by our last names, as if saying our first names would mean they liked us. The boys called me Wolly all the time, but the way Mack said it made me feel tingly. I brushed his palm and flipped my hand over so he could brush mine. When he did, heat shot up my neck, and I wanted to escape before anyone noticed.

"See you guys tomorrow." I bolted down the alley and took a shortcut to my house, coughing up more disgusting smoke.

Mack was far more mature than the other boys in my class, and I liked how he listened to me, treating me as if I mattered. Plus, he was two years older.

I didn't dare share my secret crush with the Clover Girls. Some things you did not tell your friends.

They would tease me forever beyond eternity.

Chapter 36
Get Into Heaven Free Card

September 1967, eighth grade

Sister Alex gave the girls a choice: sign up for the Legion of Mary or Church Sacristy. The Legion of Mary met after school on Tuesdays, where discussion centered on the Blessed Virgin Mary. Sacristy was twice a week, and we didn't have to discuss anything. When Maggie said we'd be closer to having get-into-heaven-free cards if we did Sacristy, we signed up for Mondays and Wednesdays after school.

We needed all the help we could get.

The following Monday after school, the four of us reported to the church Sacristy, which was restricted to priests, sacristans, altar boys, and Mr. Kearney. We knocked on the narrow door at the front of the church, left of the St. Michael the Archangel statue. Father Murphy let us in because we weren't allowed to have keys.

Once inside, Father instructed us how to arrange the silk and satin vestments on the countertop for the priests. Then he explained how to dress the altar and how to count out and prepare the unblessed, unconsecrated hosts and sacramental wine for Mass. I breathed in the incense smell that lingered on the altar from the weekly benediction.

How could we possibly remember these tasks? To our relief, Father Murphy pointed to a typed list on the wall. We clustered together, reading it:

Lay the vestments out on the counter. Pour wine into the decanter. Put sixty wafers into the gold chalice. Place the wine cruets and two altar candles on the table next to the Sacristy door. Don't forget the matches. Set the water cruet, finger bowl, and finger towel on the side altar table. Make sure the gold communion chalice is also on the side table. When you finish, thank the Lord for being able to do this for Him, and go in peace.

Easy enough, I thought to myself.

A few weeks later, we four were on Sacristy duty when Cat put us into hysterics. She was bouncy and giggly after one of the cute new boys had flirted with her in class. She slipped a white altar boy surplice over her uniform—we called it a holy nightgown—and danced the Jerk and the Twist while counting out communion hosts. Cat had a way of turning the most serious tasks into comedy scenes, like on *The Carol Burnett Show*. One time during Novena, she dropped a marble, and it rolled under the pews all the way up to clink against the marble step at the communion rail. The nuns had no clue while we quietly shook with laughter.

Today, Cat had bobby-pinned a blue tissue on top of her hair and it hung off the side of her head. Annoyed, she jerked it back into place. "Why do we have to keep our heads covered in Sacristy? This is so Middle Ages."

"Because the pope says we have to, even in Sacristy," replied Maggie with an air of authority. As the Sergeant-at-Arms for our class, she knew all the rules and kept us in line like a stern Mother Superior.

"You guys, I don't understand why you don't keep your mantillas inside your desks. That's what I do," chided Maggie, pinning her white triangle-shaped chapel veil to her head, the lacy sides hanging to her shoulders. Sister Alex had instructed all of us girls to purchase them at the beginning of the year.

"I keep forgetting mine," I grumbled, accepting an unused blue tissue from Maggie from the packet she kept in her coat pocket. She handed me a bobby pin. "That's my last one."

Maggie handed Mikey Ann a tissue. "You'll have to improvise since I have no more bobby pins."

Mikey took a paper clip from her pencil case and paper-clipped the tissue to her hair. "Done!" she quipped.

"Looks like the wind blew road litter onto your head," said Cat.

"Well, yours looks like you expect a pigeon to drop one on your head!" retorted Mikey Ann, sticking out her tongue.

Cat stepped to a cupboard and took out a gallon bottle of Mogan David wine. She sniffed, quirked one eye closed, and grimaced. "Phew, this stinks! How do the priests drink this stuff?" Cat stared at it, then hauled the bottle to her mouth like a pirate and took a swig.

"Good grief, Cat! You can't do that!" Maggie waved her hands back and forth. "Father Murphy will notice some of the wine is gone."

"Like the priests measure it?" Mikey Ann scoffed. "They're too busy taking their own swigs."

Cat shrugged. "We'll add water to it, and they'll never know. My brothers do it all the time with my mother's brandy."

"That's genius! Okay then, hand it over," I instructed, with an impatient hand motion.

Cat offered me the bottle, and I gulped, my face puckering. "It tastes like sour grape juice."

"Sour grape juice on acid. Hot diggity-dog, I'm buzzed!" Cat motioned for the bottle. "Stop bogarting the wine, Wolohan."

"You learn that from your brothers, too?" I smirked at her. "Jeez, it tastes like vinegar mixed with Kool-Aid."

A warmth rushed through me as I passed the wine back to Cat. "Have another swig. I feel lighter." The truth was, I tingled all over.

"Cripes, we'll all get fired!" shrieked Maggie.

"Fired from what? We're not paid to do this. And don't say hell in Sacristy," I added, glancing upward. "Besides, the wine isn't blessed. Technically, it's not the blood of Christ until the priest consecrates it during Mass."

Maggie busied herself laying out the vestments instead of swigging wine like an alkie. "We're doing this to get into heaven, remember? Get busy!"

Cat put a forefinger on her lips. "Put a lid on it or every priest within a fifty-mile radius will stampede in here."

The wine made us giddy, and when Cat let out a long, vulgar burp, Mikey Ann snorted a laugh that sent the three of us into uproarious ripples of hilarity. Even Maggie laughed.

"You guys, no more wine!" Maggie reached for the bottle and filled a glass cruet. She tossed me a flannel cloth. "Wipe the inside of that chalice. And be respectful. It's a sacred vessel."

"Aye-aye, Sergeant." I stared into the glittery insides. "Wow, this must be genuine gold."

Mikey Ann lifted a stack of paper-thin communion wafers from a narrow carton, a devious smile on her lips. "Five bucks for anyone who can fit fifty of these in your mouth."

The wine emboldened me. "All at once?"

Mikey Ann nodded emphatically. "Yep, all at once. I triple-dog dare ya."

"You're on!" I said, without thinking what I was getting myself into. A triple dog was serious business.

Mikey Ann upped the ante. "If you fit over fifty hosts in your mouth, we'll each pony up two bucks. Right, girls?"

"Whoa!" laughed Cat, while Maggie's eyes became frisbees.

"Okay, then," I said decisively. "Hand them over."

"This I gotta see." Cat grinned, selecting the first ten wafers resembling vanilla Neccos in their tidy white box. She handed them to me, and I stuffed them into my mouth.

Maggie snatched the box from Cat. "We'll be excommunicated and thrown in jail if anyone finds out."

"Don't be a worrywart. It's not a sin until the hosts are consecrated during Mass, remember?" Cat retorted, snatching the box from Maggie. She counted another ten wafers and held them up like a stack of poker chips. "This makes twenty."

"Hurry, before someone comes," urged Mikey Ann.

I darted a nervous look at the big oak door leading into the hallway to the rectory, then popped the next ten wafers into my mouth. Even though they weren't the bodies of You-Know-Who yet, I still didn't chew them.

Cat counted out another ten and waved them in my face. "Here you go, my lovely. Open for a total of thirty." She tossed them into my gaping mouth like a robin feeding her chicks.

"This is a mortal sin!" fretted Maggie, wringing the flannel polishing cloth.

"Jeez, Mags, relax already!" I said around the glom in my mouth.

Maggie crossed her arms. "Don't come crying to me when you all go to hell."

"It'll be too darn hot to cry down there, Mags." Mikey Ann counted out another ten and held them out. "Here comes forty. Stuff 'em, Wolohan."

I wedged them into my already full mouth, my cheeks ready to explode.

"Ha, you look like a squirrel. How does a squirrel scratch his nuts? Like this!" Cat scratched my bulging cheeks. I dared not laugh, or I'd choke to death. Felt like I had bowling balls in each cheek.

Cat's joke drew a giggle from Maggie, who forgot herself for a split second.

Mikey Ann snorted a laugh, then counted out the last ten and held them out. "A grand total of fifty! Open wide for Chunky!" she sang like the TV commercial.

My mouth was so full I couldn't swallow my spit. By the time I crammed the last of the wafers, a door slammed, and we came off the floor like startled cats. Each of us sprang into action.

"Oh-no-oh-no-oh-no!" Maggie ping-ponged around the room, waving her arms like the *Lost in Space* robot.

I tried to talk, but the hosts had glommed together in my mouth.

The priest voices grew louder.

Mikey Ann shoved me toward a narrow door in the corner. "Get your butt inside that closet or you'll be in a world of hurt!" she hissed.

"Mm! Mm!" I sounded like Lurch on *The Addams Family*.

Wide-eyed with fright, I yanked open the door to the tiny utility closet—tossed a mop at Cat, then pitched a broom to Mikey Ann, who caught it like a right-fielder. I ducked inside, tugged the door closed, and waited in the dark.

My right foot landed inside a metal pail, its metallic clang echoing like Luigi's one-man band. Something attached itself to my hair, and I muffled a scream, saliva dribbling down my chin. I took out some of the gummed-up hosts from my mouth and squished them into my fist. I chewed the rest, gulping them as fast as I could.

"Good afternoon, girls. Aren't there normally four of you?" asked Monsignor Coyle. He sounded way too close for comfort, and my stomach dropped to my penny loafers as I stood quaking in the noisy metal pail.

Maggie rushed to explain. "Usually there's four of us, but Josephina got sick and went home. We're getting everything done, though." Her voice resonated with confidence—heck, I even believed her acting. On second thought, maybe Maggie *should* go to Hollywood.

"Good to hear." Father Murphy sounded jovial. "Where's my prayer book? Thought I left it in here. We're going up to Immaculate Conception church for a prayer meeting."

Drawers opened, and I heard people shuffling around. "Here's your prayer book, Father Murphy!" babbled Maggie.

"Excellent," responded Father in his usual cheery voice.

Please, God, don't let Father or Monsignor open the door to this closet!

I probably shouldn't pray to the Big Guy after gobbling all those communion hosts.

Finally, Monsignor and Father wished my friends a good afternoon, and then their voices faded when they left the room.

The door flew open, and Cat peeked in. "Jo, are you okay? Oh my God! I can't believe they came in just now!"

My friends gaped at the drool dribbling from my mouth, then their gazes drifted down to my white uniform blouse, where my saliva had dripped.

"You look like a zombie from *Night of the Living Dead!*" howled Cat, and everyone but me collapsed into laughter. I wasn't amused.

Maggie's stare drilled into me. "Did you swallow all those wafers?"

I lifted my fistful of slimy ones. "All except these."

Tears of laughter streamed down my friends' cheeks as they plucked Brillo pads from my hair. Even Maggie cracked up. Gasping for breath, they all bolted from the room, sprinting down the hallway to a tiny bathroom, their cackling echoing behind them.

I prayed lightning wouldn't strike me as I separated myself from the stupid metal pail. I tore off a paper towel from a roll on the shelf, wrapped it around the glommy mess in my hand, and crammed it into the pocket of my shaggy pink jacket. No way would I leave any damning evidence behind.

My partners in crime returned, wiping their eyes with toilet paper.

"We'd better finish up and split before anyone else comes," said Maggie.

We hurried to finish arranging the altar, then fled the scene, giggling all the way to the apartment house. One by one we collapsed on the front steps, jabbering about what might have happened had the priests discovered me in the closet with the hosts.

"You should be in the *Guinness Book of World Records* for how many hosts you crammed into your mouth." Mikey Ann teased a confused black ant with a leaf as it scurried on the step.

"How would you confess that? Let me see..." Maggie wrinkled her face. "Bless me, Father, for I have sinned. I ate over fifty Sons-of-God since my last confession?"

Cat burst out laughing. "Yeah, that'll get you brownie points with the Big Guy upstairs."

"But seriously, if anyone finds out, you'll be expelled," Cat pointed out. "No way can you tell anyone. Not a single soul, or someone will nark on you."

"No one will know but us," I assured them. "By the way, I won the bet so pony up the dough. Six bucks, by my reckoning."

"Gotta hand it to you. You stuffed in all fifty and then some. Here, catch!" Cat tossed me four quarters, one at a time. "I'll give you the other dollar later."

"Same here," Mikey Ann and Maggie chorused.

Maggie leaned back. "How many hosts did you actually swallow?"

"I don't know. A lot." I had lost count in all the excitement.

Maggie tilted her head, scrutinizing me. "I have a feeling you're about to suffer for what you did."

"What do you mean?" I asked cautiously.

"After swallowing all those hosts, you'll be in the bathroom for quite a while." Maggie lowered her glasses and peered over them. "When the Son of God makes His grand exit, that'll be punishment enough. Get my drift?" She waited for her words to sink in.

A stunned silence knocked around as we all realized what I was about to go through.

"Oh, man..." Mikey Ann and Cat winced, pursing their lips.

Everyone offered empathetic looks as I swiveled my head toward Maggie. "Holy crap. I hadn't thought of that."

Cat stood and patted my shoulder. "Technically, it won't be Holy Crap, since the hosts weren't blessed."

"Cat's right." Mikey Ann got to her feet. "It'll be more like Unholy Crap."

My friends all laughed as Maggie pushed to stand. "We'd better split since you have business to take care of. See you tomorrow." She flashed me a cheesy grin, as they took off down the street, laughing.

I sat there like an idiot, fearing my unavoidable doom. Leave it to Maggie to make sure the scales of right-and-wrong were evenly balanced.

Maybe she should become a lawyer.

Chapter 37
The Fishpocalypse

October 1967, eighth grade

Sister Alex had set up a twenty-gallon aquarium filled with dime-store goldfish. It sat on the counter underneath the windows on the side of the classroom. Each Friday, everyone took turns to change the water and clean the aquarium. Sister was strict about us following her list of directions she kept in the top drawer of her desk.

There was a new kid, Andy O'Neil, who showed up in our class a month after school started. I had an instant crush on him. He'd whip his blond bangs back with a snap of his head, just like the high school kids. He was witty and made everyone laugh. I was smitten.

When Friday rolled around, Andy's partner was absent, so I volunteered to replace him. We stayed in during afternoon recess to clean the fish tank. Sister Alex had left the classroom along with everyone else, but when I opened her desk drawer to get the instruction sheet, it was gone.

"Hey, Andy, I can't find the cleaning instructions," I said, opening the other drawers.

"We don't need instructions," he said with confidence and authority. "I know how to clean an aquarium." Since I had a tiny crush on him, I trusted his know-how.

"Get the pitcher and six Dixie cups from the utility closet," he instructed, motioning his head toward the back corner of our classroom.

I gathered the supplies, thinking how fun it was doing this with a boy I had a crush on.

"Okay, hand me the net," he ordered.

Once we had three fish in each cup, we emptied the aquarium water into buckets, then dumped it down the utility sink. We took out the gravel to rinse it.

"Are we supposed to scrub the aquarium with a cleaner?" I asked.

"My mom uses Dutch cleanser and Mr. Clean for everything. See if there's any in the closet," he replied, rinsing the gravel.

The shelves in the tiny closet at the back of the room were crowded with cleaning bottles. Not seeing Mr. Clean, I grabbed the powdered Dutch cleanser and headed back to help Andy.

We both sprinkled the gritty powder onto wet paper towels, then scrubbed the inside of the glass, the sharp smell watering my eyes. I glanced up at the wall clock. "Recess is almost over. We'd better hurry." I grabbed the plastic pail and scurried to the supply closet to fill it with fresh water, then hurried back to our cleaning operation.

We wiped the cleanser off the glass, then put fresh water in the tank. We placed the plastic seaweed and the pirate's treasure chest on the bottom, then dumped in the goldfish.

As kids straggled in from recess, they took advantage of Sister not being in the classroom yet. Boys threw erasers to chalk-bomb the girls. Laughter erupted when erasers hit their targets, exploding white powder on hair and clothes.

Mack and his friends came in, laughing their heads off about something. He eased into his seat, his shoulders shaking from laughing so hard. Maggie and Cat always teased him about being a sex maniac because he told dirty jokes to the boys, who passed them on to the girls. We thought they were disgusting.

"Hey, Mack, what's your problem?" Cat hollered across the room.

I'm not sure why I said the next thing. But once it was out, I couldn't take it back. "Yeah, Mack, what's your deal? You're such a loser!" I was showing off for Andy.

The wounded expression when Mack looked my way had me instantly regretting my words. He suddenly flew from his seat and ran red-faced into the hallway, holding a book below his belt. The boys cracked up, hooting and pointing.

"What's so funny?" I called across the room.

Andy O'Neil hollered back. "Mack has a boner!"

Cat rolled her eyes. "So what?"

I'd heard that word before but wasn't clear on what it was exactly. Apparently, the entire class knew what it was, except for me. I envied Cat and Mikey Ann for having brothers and magically knowing all this stuff.

I leaned across the aisle and whispered to Cat, "What's a boner?"

"For crying out loud, you don't know?" Cat whispered out the side of her mouth. "It's a hard-on. You know—that guys get?" She held up her forefinger, which caused Mikey Ann to snort a laugh.

"Sister Alex is coming!" warned Maggie.

The entire class hushed. It was so quiet I could have heard a flea sneak around the room. We waited to see what would happen when Mack came back to class. Sister breezed in and everyone grabbed geography books covered with brown paper sacks, pretending to read.

Mack sauntered through the open door, red-faced.

Sister's brows rose. "Mr. MacGregor, thank you for joining us. Recess ended ten minutes ago." She glanced at the wall clock. "Make that thirteen minutes ago. What's your excuse?"

Mack sat at his desk and opened his book, which was upside down. I stifled a laugh, despite feeling terrible about my loser comment.

Sister cleared her throat. "Thomas, I asked you a question?"

Andy O'Neil's face was red from laughing and he put his head down on his desk.

"Mister O'Neil, is there something you'd like to share with us?"

His head shot up. "No, Sister."

"Very well, then." She walked over to Mack's desk and stared down at him. "Thomas?"

"I had a—I had an upset stomach," said Mack. "I didn't want to get sick in class, so I went to the lavatory."

Andy and the other boys snickered as Sister cast suspicious glances around the class.

"All right, enough nonsense. Let's get to work." She lifted a book from her desk and flipped through it. "Open your geography books to chapter five." Her gaze drifted to the aquarium, and her eyes widened as if she saw a killer shark zipping around the tank. "What in Sam Hill happened to my fish?"

She hurried over, staring at the dead goldfish floating on their sides. Some were upside down, drifting around the tank.

I homed in on the lifeless fish, then shot a horrified glance at Andy O'Neil. He stared back at me, then at Sister.

"Miss Wolohan and Mister O'Neil, I demand an explanation. On the double!"

A flashback of last summer's Frogicide sped my pulse. Now I had a Fishpocalypse on my hands, along with my crush-of-the-moment, who pointed at me accusingly, the traitor.

"Sister, Jo Wolohan did it!" His betrayal stung like a hornet.

What a turncoat. That's what I get for trying to impress Andy at Mack's expense.

"You can't blame it all on me!" I cried out. "We both cleaned the tank! You told me you knew how to do it." And just like that, my boy-crush vanished like Samantha on *Bewitched*.

"These fish would be alive if you would have followed my instructions." Sister moved to her desk and opened a drawer, then slammed it closed. "Where are they? Did someone take them out of my drawer?"

We all looked at each other, but no one raised their hand.

"Sister, I couldn't find the instructions. You were gone, and I searched everywhere," I sputtered.

Sister stood firm with her hands on her hips, glaring at us. "What did you use to clean the fish tank?"

The entire class hushed. Everyone knew how Sister Alex loved her goldfish.

"Dutch cleanser," I squeaked out.

Sister pinched the bridge of her nose. "Please say you didn't do that. Never use cleaning solvents to clean a fish tank."

"Sister, we were going to use Mr. Clean, but—"

She interrupted. "Here is what you'll both do. Eighteen fish, so nine apiece. Each of you will bring in the money to replace nine goldfish." Sister's disappointment made me wince. "Detention for both of you. Class, let's begin."

After school, Sister made Andy and me scoop up the dead fish and flush them down the toilet. I watched their blurry little bodies swirl around the bowl and disappear down to the sewers, never to swim again. Remorse gutted me.

I'd learned my lesson—just because a boy is cute doesn't mean you should do what he says. I was officially un-smitten. What bothered me most was that I'd wrecked my friendship with Mack, showing off for Andy.

Mack wasn't the loser...I was.

Chapter 38
Orbiting Saturn

November 1967, eighth grade

It took a few months for the new and old kids to become friends or at least be civil with one another. We all shared one thing in common: we couldn't wait for eighth grade to end, so we could graduate.

Rosa hung around with us during school, and Danica sometimes came with us to the movies or hung out with us at Woolworth's. Rosa and Danica still displayed their don't-mess-with-us death stares whenever older kids bullied us.

The miners' strike had ended, and people were in a happier mood. Everyone now had to pay the full tuition to St. Michael's School. Mom was buying good food again and made her pasties with meat instead of only potatoes and onions.

Once a week, we piled onto a school bus and went to the Webster Garfield school down on Front Street, for home economics for the girls and shop class for the boys. Away from the nuns, we were wild hellions.

The Clover Girls got detention when our Home Ec teacher told Sister Alex we had pie dough fights—like snowball fights—where we made marble-sized dough balls and bonked each other. Unfortunately, one stuck to the ceiling, then fell onto the Home Ec teacher's wig. She walked around like that all day until another teacher plucked it off.

She wasn't a happy camper.

I sewed my dingle balls upside down on my poncho and had to tear it out and do it over. Cat sewed her sleeve to hers, and Mikey Ann glued her dingle balls to her poncho because she hated using the sewing machine. Sister Alex was also not a happy camper receiving reports of our goof-ups and unacceptable behavior, so she put us on a week of detention.

We were also navigating the treacherous waters of the popularity contest, where the cool kids decided on everyone's social standing. Surfing popularity was like orbiting Saturn, trying to figure out which ring to grab onto. We weren't in high school yet, and already cliques had formed for jocks, brainiacs, troublemakers, and stoners. We didn't count the holy rollers who'd been talked into becoming nuns.

I wasn't sure which category the four of us Clover Girls fit into—but like it or not, we were swept into it when Danica and Rosa informed us our popularity would set the stage for freshman year next fall. If we didn't rise in the ranks now, we'd be trampled in the popularity stampede in high school. We weren't worried because the Clover Girls had a solid popularity resume, priding ourselves with the funniest, smartest, and toughest girls in the eighth-grade class.

One day, Mack announced the boys would award a Miss Class Clown trophy to the funniest girl in our class. The four of us took the competition seriously and figured at least one of us would land the trophy. Mikey Ann prided herself on her knock-knock jokes, Cat's one-liners got the loudest laughs, and Maggie was funny with her cow-eyes under her coke-bottle glasses. All I could come up with were imitations of *Bugs Bunny* and the munchkins from *The Wizard of Oz*.

Our all-time favorite was to imitate the nuns for the boy votes. Cat mimicked Sister Alex floating around the classroom like the Holy Ghost. Mikey Ann spoofed a hilarious imitation of Sister Clare with her blinky eyes and falling asleep in mid-sentence. I mimicked Sister Bertie, who always folded her hands on her Dolly Parton chest like it was a shelf. Her chest invariably entered the room before she did.

Cat flirted with the boys in a shameless attempt to get votes, and it paid off. While we all got laughs, the boys voted for Cat as the funniest girl. I was perfectly fine with Cat winning the paper crown Mack made for the Miss Class Clown trophy. He also awarded her a miniature troll with long purple hair to stick on her pencil. I didn't mind riding my bestie's coattails to edge higher on the popularity scale.

When the contest ended, I overheard Sister Bertie grumble to Sister Alex, "Here we go with the raging hormones."

AFTER SCHOOL, WE SAT on the apartment house's front steps when I relayed what I'd overheard Sister Bertie say about raging hormones. I asked my besties if theirs were raging.

"Oh, my God! Sister Bertie said that?" Maggie waved her arms. "How would she know about hormones? Nuns are celibate."

"They're what?" I gave her a curious side-eye.

"Celibate—you know, when people refrain from having sex," explained Maggie, our walking dictionary.

"Hm, nuns can't have sex. They're too holy," I reasoned.

"They can't have sex because they're married to Christ." Mikey Ann said it like she was delivering a baseball score.

Cat guffawed. "No one can have sex with someone who's dead."

"Christ isn't dead," sniffed Maggie. "He's up there, zipping around the clouds."

"Well, He isn't exactly alive, either." I rolled my eyes. "Houlihan, you think you're so smart with your big words."

"If you read more, you too, would have a large vocabulary," Maggie shot back.

"Ouch. I am a reader," I retorted. "For your information, I read *Nancy Drew,* the *Hardy Boys, Bobbsey Twins,* and *Trixie Belden.* Why are you so grouchy?"

"I started my monthly!" snapped Maggie, pushing to her feet. She folded her arms, pacing back and forth on our cracked sidewalk.

That shut us up real quick. The dreaded puberty curse was striking close to home.

Cat was the first to venture a response. "Since you're the first, you can clue the rest of us in on the wide, wonderful world of becoming a woman."

The way she said it made us all laugh, but I didn't know whether to offer Maggie sympathy or congratulations. How do you congratulate someone for starting a monthly, where blood loss was involved? The whole thing grossed me out.

"Yeah, Mags, you're breaking ground for the Clover Girls." I shot her a confidence boosting smile that at least got her to laugh.

"You guys, I don't want to grow up," grumbled Maggie. "I was crying in the bathroom, thinking I was dying of cancer, when Rosa came in. She explained I'd started my monthly and gave me a quarter to buy a sanitary napkin from the dispenser in the corner."

"Oh, always wondered what that thing was. Never paid attention," I shrugged. "That was nice of Rosa."

"I don't want any part of that monthly nonsense." Mikey Ann made a dismissive gesture.

"You won't have a choice. We're all sitting ducks." Cat hummed an ominous death march like it was the end of something instead of the beginning.

Growing up meant change, and none of us wanted things to change. We liked things how they were. Besides, I'd had enough upheaval in my life. There wasn't much we could do about the fact that no matter what, our bodies were moving on, even if our minds didn't want to keep up with them.

And so... we all went kicking and screaming into puberty.

Chapter 39
Day Eight of Lilly's Coma

June 1, 1968, in the present

Determined to say extra prayers for my mother, I get up extra early to attend Mass before school, since I have to walk to St. Mike's Church from the Silver Bow Homes. I didn't want Aunt Daisy to have to get up to drive me.

When I get there, I'm secretly delighted to see Mack as one of the two altar boys at today's Mass. When I walk up to receive communion, and he holds the gold platter under my chin, Mack winks at me as Father Murphy sets the host on my tongue. Heat shoots up my neck and I hope Mack doesn't notice.

After Mass, I hurry outside so I wouldn't be late for school. To my surprise, Aunt Daisy climbs the concrete steps toward me, looking grim.

As I wait for her to reach the top, my throat tightens. "Aunt Daisy, what is it?"

She rests her hand on my shoulder. "Dr. Madison called. Your mom's blood pressure has dropped, and she has an irregular heartbeat. They're monitoring her, but..." she trails off, glancing at people coming out of the church.

I swallow. "But what? Is she okay?"

"Josephina, Doctor Madison said he isn't sure your mom will come out of her coma."

The words land on me like pitchforks piercing my soul, and I pepper her with questions.

"What? Why? Why did he say that?" My biggest fear all along has been losing my mother...I'm still not ready to be an orphan.

Aunt Daisy speaks slowly. "Dr. Madison says they're doing the best they can. They may send her to a brain injury center in Seattle."

"No!" I yell, and heads turn in our direction as I inwardly panic at the news.

Just then Mack comes out of church with his altar boy clothes draped over his arm and a sack lunch in his hand. He notices my stunned expression and stops. "Hey, Wolly, everything okay?"

"Jo's mother has taken a turn for the worst," says Aunt Daisy. She turns to me and takes a shaky breath. "I need to talk to Monsignor about—about last rites if we need them."

"Extreme Unction? But that's for people who are..." I trail off, a lump in my throat as tears pool. How did we get to where Mom needed last rites? I can't wrap my head around this.

"Jo, you better get to school." She gives Mack a weak smile. "Do me a favor and walk with my niece? I have things to take care of."

"Sure," says Mack, glancing at me.

"Thanks. We'll talk later, Jo." Aunt Daisy hurries off and I stand there, frozen and numb. My breath comes fast. I'm lightheaded and stumble backwards.

Mack grabs my elbow. "Wolly, let's sit down for a sec. Sister will understand." He steers me back inside the now empty church, and we sit in the last pew.

So many emotions spin inside me—fear, anxiety, and despair—but I also don't want to embarrass myself by coming unglued in front of a boy like Mack.

"The doctor says my mom might not wake up," I choke out. "They want to send her to Seattle." I stare at my lap, fiddling with my fingers.

"Jeez, sorry to hear that," he says quietly.

Air unexpectedly catches in my throat. When I open my mouth to take a breath, my lungs refuse to fill. My hands fly to my chest as I fight to breathe. "I can't. I can't—"

"Breathe slow or you'll pass out." Mack empties his lunch onto the pew and holds the small brown paper sack over my nose and mouth. "Take slow breaths. That's the way. Nice and easy."

I force myself to slow my breathing, and the dizziness subsides.

He lowers the sack. "Feel better?"

I nod, staring at him.

"You just had a shock, and you were hyperventilating. Try not to worry," he says, stuffing his sandwich and potato chips back into the sack. "Just remember, miracles really do happen. I know from experience." He sounds like an adult, and his mature sincerity reassures me.

"How did you know how to do that?" I ask, my curiosity growing.

"I took a First Aid course at the 'Y.' I have younger brothers and sisters who've had the air knocked out of them playing sports." He held up his sack lunch. "Works every time."

"From now on, I'm calling you Doctor McGregor," I gush with a stab of guilt for flirting with him after hearing about my mother.

Aunt Daisy finishes talking with Monsignor and comes toward us. "Jo, you're still here? Okay, never mind school. I'll take you to the hospital instead." She glances at Mack. "Can you please tell your teacher that Jo will be late for school today?"

"Sure," he says. "Sister Alex will understand."

"Thanks for helping," says Aunt Daisy. "What's your name?"

Mack rises and extends his hand. "Thomas McGregor. I'm in Jo's class."

Aunt Daisy shakes his hand with lifted eyebrows. "You seem older."

"Long story," says Mack, smiling.

Aunt Daisy returns his smile, and that's when I realize he's an expert at charming the ladies.

"Well, thank you, Thomas. It's good to know Jo has a friend like you. Come on, honey, let's get to the hospital." Aunt Daisy turns and walks toward the enormous bronze doors.

Mack gets out of the pew, and I follow. "Thanks for what you did," I say shyly.

"Anytime. See you at school." He follows behind me as we leave the church. "Don't stress, Wolly. Your mom will be okay. Check you later." He taps down the steps.

"Bye, Doctor Mack!" I holler after him.

He turns to wave, then hurries off to school. Pangs of regret wave through me. How could I not have seen what a good person he was until now? My heart actually fluttered when he winked at me when I received communion. I'm ashamed of having called him a loser.

Why do I realize these things when it's too late?

Aunt Daisy and I head to her blue Chevy and slide into the seats. "I talked with Monsignor Coyle about last rites in case they take Lilly to Seattle. That is, if her condition worsens," says Aunt Daisy.

This sends daggers into my chest. "Is Mom going to die?"

"I hope not." My aunt lights a cig, and I sense her nervousness as she pushes out a fast smoke stream.

I don't remember the drive to the hospital, getting out of the car, or taking the elevator to Mom's floor. I dread what I'll see when I walk into her room. I can scarcely breathe.

When we enter Mom's room, Dr. Madison and two nurses are fiddling with monitors, tubes, and an oxygen mask over Mom's nose and mouth. Aunt Daisy and I make ourselves invisible in the corner chairs, the beep-beep of the monitor a false comfort.

When the nurses leave the room, Dr. Madison turns to Aunt Daisy. "Did you tell her?" He says it as if I'm not there.

"Yes, I've explained it." My aunt gives me a sidelong glance.

"Why do you have to send my mother to Seattle? How will I see her?" I hear the despair in my voice and hate that I can't control it.

"Her condition has destabilized. We aren't sure why," he explains. "There are head injury specialists in Seattle with better equipment and technology to treat your mother."

Aunt Daisy cuts in. "We can drive to Seattle to visit her after you graduate. We can stay at Aunt Violet's."

I stare at my mother as tears cloud everything. Nothing makes sense. I hate that the boat accident happened. I hate that storm. I hate the lake. I'll never swim in a lake again.

Aunt Daisy stands. "I'm going down to the smoker's lounge. Give you some time alone with your mom. I'll be back in a bit." She leaves the room.

When the monitor beeps, I make sure the lines keep moving and don't go flat, like what happens on *Dr. Kildare*. I scoot my chair close to my mother and take her hand. It's surprisingly warm.

"They're saying they don't know if you'll wake up, and they might send you away. Mom, please, I really need you to wake up." I sob like a kindergartner. "Please, dammit! Wake the hell up!" I don't care who hears me. I'm way beyond that now.

"There are things I want you to know—that I never said in confession because I was afraid I wouldn't be allowed to graduate. I haven't told you the truth about a lot of stuff." I peer at my mother's peaceful face and note more gray hair.

"The trouble I got into this year wasn't all my fault." I hesitate, wondering how to tell her what I want her to know. "Since I couldn't confess this stuff to Monsignor or Father Murphy, I'll confess it to you. You deserve my honesty, if nothing else." I summon courage with a shaky breath, forcing out the words.

"Bless me, Mother, for I have sinned..." Somehow, it's easier leading off with a little humor.

Chapter 40
The Art of the Atomic Wedgie

January 1968, eighth grade

The Knights of Columbus building on Park Street was the cool place to be on weekends, where the sounds of cheering volleyball games were deafening as the Catholic schools competed against each other. It was a see-and-be-seen kind of deal. We'd painstakingly groom ourselves to make sure we appeared as cool and 'with it' as possible.

We told Rosa we loved her shiny straight hair that looked just like Michelle Philips from the Mamas and the Papas. She said all of us could have hair like that, so she invited us to her house down on Silver Street. We took turns sitting on a chair and leaning next to her ironing board where she'd iron our hair. Cat's and Maggie's waist-long hair looked the coolest, but I hated that Mom made me cut mine whenever it reached my shoulders.

Mom had instructed her hair stylist to cut mine like Barbra Streisand's bob in *Look Magazine,* with sides curled under and bangs on my forehead. Streisand was Mom's favorite singer after seeing her concert at Central Park on TV, so naturally my hair had to look like hers—except I wasn't a rich movie-star singer. Mom probably figured if I looked like Streisand, maybe I'd become rich and famous like her and earn wads of cash.

Danica wore her hair in a flip, and she teased it so much it looked like a bird's nest. She said there was an art to back-combing hair, then pulling a few strands over it so you couldn't see the ratted hair. It seemed like too much work to me.

We each bought Frost and Tip hair kits from Skaggs to add blond streaks to our hair and gathered at Danica's house for the operation. We spent hours pulling our hair through impossibly tiny holes with a crochet hook—like tugging an elephant through a mouse hole. Our scalps throbbed, and we grew tired of yelping in pain, so we made the holes bigger, and yanked our hair through. The streaks were wider, but after torturing our scalps, we didn't care. We used our allowances to run over to Woolworth's to buy tie-dyed t-shirts and badgered our moms to get us bell bottom hip-hugger jeans, since they were all the rage.

We spent Saturday afternoons playing volleyball games against the other Catholic schools. Danica, Mikey Ann, Rosa, and Cat were our all-stars. They got to have fancy letters and white stripes on the sleeves of their St. Michael's school sweaters. I could serve the ball to the back row, but I was too short to spike the ball over the net. The coach would let me serve, then rotate me out. I eventually lost interest and told the coach I was tired of sitting on the bench. She understood and let me quit.

I was more interested in swimming after Maggie and I had qualified for the Junior Swim Team last summer at camp. After school on weekdays, we had swim team practice at the Y. On Saturdays, we cheered for St. Mike's volleyball team from the running track up on the balcony overlooking the volleyball court.

Maggie and I made it a point this Saturday to attend the game with the Immaculate Conception girls. It was the highlight of our season because they were a tough team to beat. After St. Mike's won, Maggie and I watched from the balcony as Cat, Mikey Ann, Danica, and Rosa brushed hands with the opposite team. Afterwards, Mikey Ann and Cat came upstairs so we could watch the last game with St. John's. We were extra cool today with our straight, "frosted" hair, like the high school girls at Central and Butte High.

We leaned on the balcony rail watching the volleyball game below when someone hollered, "Hey, Big Boobs Quinn!"

I turned to see a spaghetti body topped off with a meatball head. I hadn't seen Butch McKnight since I jabbed a pencil into his balls in the second grade. His family had moved to The Flats not long after that. He was exactly the same, only taller. Even had those Tiddly Winks freckles still spackled across his face.

"Hey Quinn, shouldn't you be wearing a bra?" shouted McKnight. "Your boobs bounce when you play. Not that we mind." He made a bouncing ball motion while his two crewcut minions snickered.

Maggie elbowed me while Cat folded her arms and unloaded her stink-eye on him. "Thought we threw you out with the garbage years ago."

"Fat chance," he lobbed back.

"I know this kid. Butch McKnight," I shared with Mikey Ann. "Stabbed him in the balls with a pencil in second grade."

"Guess he didn't learn his lesson," muttered Mikey Ann. She'd begrudgingly led our group in chest protrusions, after sprouting overnight, like Jack's Beanstalk, and normally took great pains to hide them... except today, for some reason.

"Hey, bouncy tits!" McKnight taunted with a stupid grin.

"Shut up, moron!" Maggie hollered back, while Cat flipped him off for good measure. The day Cat stops raising her middle finger will be the day the universe implodes, and the human race will have to start over from scratch.

I wanted to stab McKnight in the balls for old times' sake, but no pencils were handy.

Mikey Ann's cheeks bypassed red and went straight to purple. "Hey, McKnight! Care to repeat that?" she hissed, stepping close and towering over him.

Undaunted, McKnight leered at her. "Haven't you looked in the mirror?"

"Well, if *you* did, you'd break it!" she sneered. "Keep your stupid comments to yourself." Shaking her head, she twisted back around to watch the volleyball game below.

Since three of us had dealt with this lame brain in the past, we knew better than to turn our backs on him. Warily, I kept an eye on him.

"What if I don't want to?" McKnight and his weirdo friends cackled like hyenas.

Everyone's gazes swept to Mikey Ann, who twisted back around in a guess-it's-time-to-kick-your-ass move, her gaze narrowing into a Clint Eastwood glower.

We held our collective breath as time stood still for about five seconds.

Then, with lightning speed, Mikey Ann sprang into action. She lunged for McKnight and spun him around, her hand disappearing down the back of his pants. She grabbed two fistfuls of his underwear and yanked upward with such force it would have sent a Sumo wrestler run screaming into the night.

We heard a resounding rip when she tugged McKnight's underwear up and *out* of his pants. He howled in pain, and the boys made retching sounds while we girls recoiled, sucking our teeth.

"Let go of me!" yelled McKnight, trying unsuccessfully to fend off the girl who was torturing him.

Mikey Ann yanked one last time and McKnight howled louder, screaming obscenities that would curl a miner's toes. Everyone's gazes diverted from the volleyball game to the action on the balcony.

"Quinn gave Butch McKnight an *atomic wedgie*!" Cat yelled to the masses. The girls erupted in triumphant cheers while the boys' faces twisted in a mixture of horror and disgust.

Mikey Ann let go and shoved McKnight. He stumbled forward and hit the floor, yelping in pain.

"Time to blow this pop stand!" Mikey Ann shot us all a crazed look and bolted down the stairs two at a time, with us on her heels. Once outside, we laughed so hard our sides ached.

"Quick! Follow me!" Mikey Ann snorted. She took off, half-running and half-sliding on the icy sidewalk down Park Street.

We slid past the toothless man without legs who rolled around on a flat, square board with roller skate wheels; he was well known in uptown Butte. "Wanna buy a pencil, girls?" he shouted as we ran past.

"No, but I might need one later!" I shouted back, glancing to see if Butch McKnight and his merry band of weirdos were giving chase.

Mikey Ann ducked into the Terminal Meat Market with us trailing behind. We scooted across the floor sprinkled with sawdust and stood in front of the glassed-in meat counter.

A tall, burly man broke out in a jovial grin. "Mikey, are you here for hot dogs?"

"Hi Dad! Some kids were chasing us, so we're going to hang out for a while," she panted.

"Take a load off. I'll get you some snacks." Mr. Quinn motioned to a small round table off to the side with four chairs, and we gratefully sank into them.

He brought us four hot dogs wrapped in napkins and put them in the center of the table. He produced four fat pickles and set them down as well, and we pounced on the food.

"Wait until word gets around school what Mikey Ann did to Butch McKnight." Cat bit into her pickle, eyes gleaming. "No one will mess with her or us ever again."

"You can't let boneheads get away with that stuff. It's none of his business if I wear a bra." Mikey Ann shrugged.

Our eyes automatically dropped to Mikey Ann's boobs. We'd all noticed her chest invaders poking at her white uniform blouse, but we didn't point them out for fear she'd pound us. She prided herself as the toughest tomboy in school and sometimes wrapped an Ace bandage around herself to flatten her chest.

"Forgot to put on my bandage to flatten them today," Mikey Ann said defensively, glancing down at herself. She looked up at us with alarm. "Do you guys honestly think I need a bra?"

We avoided her gaze, vigorously chewing our hot dogs and pickles. No one spoke. We didn't want her to pummel us into the floor.

Finally, I ventured, "It wouldn't hurt for you to go to Hennessey's and ask the saleslady."

Mikey Ann folded her arms over her chest in a self-protective posture. "Why didn't any of you tell me?"

All of us resisted puberty like it was grim death, ignoring pesky hair growing on body parts where it hadn't been before. I was 'developing' as Mom called it, but Cat and Mikey Ann's chests had popped out overnight like Jack-in-the-boxes.

"Maybe because we didn't want an atomic wedgie," I said with a lopsided grin. "I know one thing: no boy in this town will ever mess with you."

Maggie swallowed. "Mikey Ann, you're our official bodyguard. Blessed be the atomic wedgie-givers!"

We laughed as Cat joined in. "From now on, we'll tell the bullies we have a secret weapon named Mikey Ann Quinn. That'll shut them up!"

Mikey Ann grinned as if we'd laid Butch McKnight's bound and gagged body at her feet. None of us worried about running into him again.

Not with Quick Draw McWedgie on our side.

Chapter 41
This Is How the French Do It

February 1968, eighth grade

Some girls in our class got rings from boys on Valentine's Day. They wrapped mohair around them, wearing them on their fingers or dangling them from chains around their necks. Danica and Rosa changed boyfriends like underwear, wearing a different going-steady ring each week. Maggie thought they did it for all the pretty rings.

Monday morning recesses were like press conferences where we got the latest scoop. We'd huddle in a circle around Danica and Rosa as they described their make-out sessions in vivid detail. Enthralled, we hung onto every word.

The confab that blew our minds the most was when Danica reported she'd French-kissed a high school freshman. Not only that, but he also felt her up at a house party! We figured she and Rosa wanted to get a running jump on all the sex action in high school with the cute boys.

"French kissing is the bomb," Danica claimed matter-of-factly, leaning against St. Mike's brick building. "And if the boy does it right when he feels you up, you get tingly all over."

We gaped at her in disbelief.

"Tingly?" I echoed, recoiling at the thought of a boy with his grubby hands on my chest. I didn't want a boy within five miles of my chest bumps and wished the annoying things would stop growing.

Danica was a *fast girl*, as the saying goes... light years ahead of us geeks blundering along back here in the Stone Age. Overnight, her chest had blown up like birthday balloons. Apparently, Butte's east side girls developed faster than us slow-growers on the west side. Must be something in the water over there.

Since no one else asked, I had to be the one. "Okay, I give. What's French kissing?"

Danica shot me a shocked look. Then she and Rosa burst out laughing.

"What's so funny?" asked Maggie, frowning.

"You guys don't know what French kissing is!" Rosa swiped tears from her cheeks.

"Of course we do. We just want to hear *you* explain it." Maggie tapped her glasses and tilted her head. Scholastic pride was a big deal to her. Maggie would rather kiss a monkey than admit she didn't know something.

"All right then, *you* explain it first." Rosa challenged, eyeing the four of us.

We swiveled our heads toward Maggie.

Cat rolled her eyes. "It's that tongue thing the boys go on about."

I grimaced. "What tongue thing?"

Danica's jaw dropped. "You honest-to-God don't know what French kissing is?"

"How am I supposed to know that?" I demanded. "None of us have kissed boys. Not yet, anyway." I wasn't embarrassed to admit it. Boys were doofuses.

Cat flashed me an insulted look. "Speak for yourself!"

My jaw dropped, and I gave her an accusing stare. "Wait a sec. Why am I not surprised? You are always holding out on us, Delaney."

Cat cupped my ear and whispered, "My cousin Frenched me. You tell anyone and you're dead meat!"

I swallowed hard and parked my face in neutral and kept it there as best I could while my brain screamed how gross that was. *Kissing a cousin? Blech!*

Danica folded her arms. "Okay, Wolohan, explain what French kissing is."

My mind roamed all things French: French fries, French toast, French braids. I drew a blank and threw up my arms in exasperation. "Okay, you got me!"

"I knew as much." Danica shook her head. "I'll have to show you. It's too hard to explain."

I backed up. "*Show* me? Whoa, wait a sec—uh—that's not—that isn't—I don't want..."

"Oh, brother. Get your butt over here!" Danica grabbed my coat sleeve and pulled me to a corner behind the stairs. Cat, Maggie, and Rosa followed like paparazzi. Mikey Ann had picked the wrong day to be absent—or the right one, depending on one's point of view.

Rosa smirked. "This I gotta see."

"Stand still." Danica sprayed a quick squirt of Binaca into her mouth, then grabbed my shoulders and pulled me close. "Open your mouth," she commanded.

"Why?" I shot her a distrustful look.

"Just do it." She gripped my chin and covered my mouth with hers. Then she wormed her cherry Binaca tongue between my lips and wiggled it inside my mouth like a garter snake with claustrophobia.

I shoved her away, wiping my tongue while spasmodically hopping around and spitting. "Ach! What the heck was *that*?"

Cat was amused, but Maggie appeared horrified, her hand over her nose and mouth. "Eew!" she shrieked through her fingers. "That's disgustingly gross!"

"That's not kissing!" I choked out. "That's like tongue-wrestling with an earthworm!"

Danica shrugged. "Well, you wanted to know." She squirted another blast of Binaca into her mouth.

"Where did you learn to do that?" I asked, doing my best to recover from her gross tongue invasion.

"I read an article in *Seventeen* magazine that advised practicing with cupcake frosting to learn the technique." Danica smeared her lips with a Chapstick. "You stab the frosting with your tongue."

"Cupcake frosting?" I shrieked. That was just—wrong.

Danica demonstrated with an imaginary cupcake in her hand. "You scoop the frosting with your tongue, then swirl it around the cupcake like this." She flicked her tongue out to show us.

"Next time you frost cupcakes, practice," suggested Danica. "The frosting has to be soft, and you need gobs of it on the cupcake. Sing la-la-la-la-la as you lick the frosting. My big sister gave me that juicy tip."

I was hung up on what flavor of cupcake I'd make, not tips on how to French kiss one. I decided mine would be chocolate.

"Why do you sing la-la-la la-la?" asked Maggie, wrinkling her nose.

"To practice moving your tongue. Duh," replied Danica impatiently, like we should already know this stuff.

I had so many questions. "Do we move the tongue in a certain way? Do you spray that cherry Binaca in a boy's mouth before you do that tongue thing?"

Rosa chortled, shaking her head. "You guys crack me up."

"You poor, naïve children." Danica sounded like Sister Alex. "Today's lesson is over. Tune in tomorrow for tips on heavy petting." She flashed a self-satisfied smile and strode across the playground, giggling with Rosa.

We made a note to show up for tomorrow's lesson on petting. None of us knew what that was exactly, but we suspected it had nothing to do with dogs and cats. Under Danica's detailed instruction, I'm sure we'll find out.

Something tells me I shouldn't let her use me to demonstrate tomorrow's lesson.

That evening when Mom left to go bowling, I made a batch of chocolate cupcakes and slathered them with whipped chocolate frosting. I practiced French kissing my cupcakes. Mack suddenly jumped into my brain, and I wondered what it would be like to French kiss him. He probably knew which way to move his tongue.

"La-la-la la-la," I sang, swirling the frosting with my tongue. I wondered how the French came up with the weird ritual of tongue wrestling. The only problem was, I lost count of how many cupcakes I ate and ended up with a stomachache.

I guess it was worth it, because now I was prepared for the real deal when and if I'm ever with a boy in the far-off future... like when I'm thirty-five or when robots learn to drive cars.

Chapter 42
My Name Is Para Normal

April 1968, eighth grade

Maggie and I had thrown ourselves into swim team practice so we could qualify for a heat in our first swim meet with the Helena Junior Swim Team. We liked getting to know kids from other schools: McKinley, Lincoln, Franklin, and East Junior High. The city was building a new West Junior High for kids on the hill and the west side, but it wouldn't open until next year.

It didn't take long to find out which strokes I excelled in. Breaststroke was my fastest, while Maggie's fastest times were with butterfly and freestyle. We were fast sprinters on the relay team, but I wasn't as fast in the 200 and 400-yard races.

Our swim team coach was Eleanor Murphy, whom we called Coach Murph. She decided which events we were to enter. I was envious that Maggie swam the individual medley with fast times, but my butterfly stroke wasn't as fast, so Coach Murph didn't enter me in the IM.

Our first swim meet was in Helena, and Coach Murph entered me in the one-hundred-yard breaststroke and Maggie in the two-hundred-yard individual medley. During my first competition, I was disqualified because my heel broke the surface of the water. The awful part was that I touched the wall first.

All the way to Butte I cried on the bus, while Maggie and others who'd won ribbons cheered. Maggie had landed a second-place ribbon for the IM, which wasn't bad for her first swim meet. Though envious, I was also proud of her and told her so.

The weekend after our last swim meet, Cat invited the Clover Girls to a slumber party for her fourteenth birthday. She also invited Rosa, Danica, and a new girl, Colleen, who'd transferred into our class after Christmas.

Colleen was from Deer Lodge, where her dad had quit his prison guard job at the state penitentiary to drive the big ukes in the Berkeley Pit, which was gobbling streets and buildings like a greedy monster. She told us her dad enjoyed working in the Berkely Pit because there were no rapists or murderers, plus it paid more.... not that any of us had given it much thought.

She was into fortune telling and talking to dead people in seances, so she brought a Ouija board and a black 8-Ball to the slumber party. Colleen said she and her friends had summoned Walt Disney during a seance last summer, and he told them about Disneyland's Tomorrowland renovation. We were fascinated by this, and I asked her if she could summon him again to tell us the movies he'd be releasing.

After dinner, we got into our pajamas, and Cat brought out a makeup kit her mom bought her. I'd never seen so many colors of eye shadow, with ten shades of each color on a huge white plastic pallet. We crowded into Cat's bathroom, putting on eyeliner and brushing rainbows on our lids.

Cat's brothers teased we looked like ladies-of-the-evening at The Dumas.

Cat yelled, "Get the hell out!" and chased them to their room, slamming the door. Despite their peskiness, I couldn't help wishing I had brothers, too. They came in handy for when we needed rescuing from gallus frames or we wanted to know stuff about sex and puberty.

Cat had been wearing her hair down, and when she pulled it back into a ponytail, I noticed tiny silver posts in her earlobes.

"You pierced your ears! Why didn't you tell us?" I demanded, leaning closer.

"My cousin did it last weekend and taught me how. Want me to pierce yours?" Cat left the room and came back holding a peeled raw potato and a thick needle with dark blue thread in it. "Who's first?"

"Not me!" Maggie covered her ears. "The nuns will say it's the work of the devil, you guys."

Ignoring Maggie's nun forecast, the rest of us exchanged nervous glances until I shocked myself by raising my hand. "I'll go first!"

"Don't worry, I'm good at this," Cat reassured me. "I pierced my other cousin's ears, and they turned out good. Now sit still. Mikey Ann will hold the potato behind your ear." She waved Mikey Ann over and handed her the raw potato.

As I sat on the toilet with the lid down, I noticed a magazine rolled up behind it. I pulled it out and unrolled a *Playboy* magazine. "What's this?"

"Oh, my God! What's *that* doing in here?" shrieked Cat, snatching it from my hands.

"*Playboy?* Ooh, lemme see!" I snatched it back and fanned it to the centerfold, holding it sideways. "Wow, look at this. February's Playmate of the Month is Nancy Burns."

"What do you mean, playmates?" asked Maggie, while everyone crowded around. I thumbed through the pages as we scrutinized the topless blondes and brunettes.

"Wait, what does that say?" Maggie flipped a page backwards and read, "Ten Ways to Masturbate? Are you kidding me?" She flipped to another section. "Here's one on The Miss Nude Universe Contest." Maggie's cow eyes grew wide. "Women prance around naked on a pageant stage? What about the gown and swimsuit competition?"

"Give me that, you guys." Cat descended on us, confiscating the magazine. "My brothers must have left this in here. If my mom finds out, she'll have a cow." She rolled it up with a rubber band and tossed it in a wastebasket under the sink.

"My brothers have those, too," laughed Mikey Ann.

"Well, that was entertaining," I chirped, staring up at Cat. "Are you going to pierce my ears or not? Get with the program."

"All right, already! You'll feel a little sting." Cat rubbed my earlobe with an ice cube, then came at me with a needle and thread. She rammed that sucker so hard, I heard the needle scrunch as it tore through skin and landed in the potato Mikey Ann pressed to the back of my ear. I screamed bloody murder as my earlobe lit on fire.

"A little *sting*? Felt like you ram-rodded a railroad spike through my ear!" I squealed, my eyes watering. I reached up to touch it.

Cat slapped my hand away. "Don't touch, or it'll get infected."

Mikey Ann eased the potato off the needle and Cat shoved the threaded needle all the way through. I yelped when she leaned in and cut the thread with her teeth. Then she knotted the ends together to make a loop and wiped it with more rubbing alcohol on a cotton ball.

"Yow!" I howled in pain.

"Move the thread back and forth to keep the piercing open. Now the other one. I love sticking people with needles. I should be a nurse." Cat's brows jumped up and down.

"Maybe on *General Hospital*. Take it easy on the next one, will ya?" I held my breath and tried not to squeal when Cat shoved the needle through and tied off the thread.

Both earlobes throbbed, so Cat handed me ice cubes encased in two washcloths. "Hold these to your ears to lessen the pain."

Cat glanced around with a wicked grin. "Who's my next victim?" She waggled her finger at Maggie. "Come on, it only hurts for a sec. Trust me."

"Famous last words," I muttered as Maggie shot me a nervous glance. I peered at her as Cat and Mikey positioned themselves to pierce Maggie's ears. "You look like Elizabeth Taylor with that heavy eye makeup."

Maggie squealed louder than I had when Cat jabbed her earlobes.

Mikey Ann volunteered next. "Hurry up and get it over with." She handed me the raw potato, then stuck a dry washcloth between her teeth while Cat pierced both ears. Mikey Ann let out a muffled yell into the washcloth with each poke. Even tough girls have moments of vulnerability, so I gave her a reassuring smile.

As we took turns getting our ears pierced, we entertained ourselves with the black 8-Ball fortune teller that Colleen had brought. We shook the black 8-Ball, but we could only ask yes or no questions. No matter how much I shook it, the triangle display in the tiny window always said 'Maybe.' When Maggie asked it questions, it repeatedly floated up a 'No,' even when she asked if she would graduate. That one freaked her out, and she fretted about it until we shushed her.

When Cat finished up, she herded us all downstairs into the living room, where we watched TV for a while. When Cat's mom and brothers went upstairs to bed, Colleen instructed us to sit on the floor in a circle, then she set the Ouija board in the center. Cat switched off the lights, then lit candles and arranged them around the room. The flames flickered, casting eerie shadows on the walls and on our faces. Our fancy makeup made us all look creepy.

Colleen rubbed her hands together. "Alright, everyone, prepare to summon the spirits. Rest your fingertips lightly on this planchette."

The four of us together placed our fingertips on the white heart-shaped plastic with the little round window.

Colleen glanced around. "It works best if you ask it a question."

Maggie grimaced. "I've heard these things are rigged."

"How can it be rigged if we're the ones moving this white thing around?" I nervously tugged the thread in my ear.

Colleen let out an impatient sigh. "Jo, keep your fingers on it or it won't move. Ask a yes or no question or ask it to spell something." Colleen closed her eyes. "Spirits, if you can hear us, give us a sign!"

"Let's summon Disney," I suggested. "I want to know why the little deer's mom had to die in the forest fire cartoon movie. It was way too sad. I want to tell Disney to only make fun movies, like *Mary Poppins*. No more scary stuff."

Maggie gave me a dour look. "Do you need psychotherapy? You still seem traumatized."

I stuck my tongue out at her.

Mikey Ann squirmed with uneasiness. "I'm not a fan of ghosts."

"Relax, most of them are friendly," said Colleen.

"Okay, spirits, get a move on," I joked. Everyone waited, but the planchette didn't move.

A tense silence rolled around the room. When a bird popped out of a house clock to cuckoo eleven times, we gasped with fright, then laughed to break the tension.

"Maybe the cuckoo has a dead relative he wants to talk to," whispered Maggie.

We fell silent as the planchette inched across the board.

"Look, it's moving!" squealed Cat.

Mikey Ann rolled her eyes. "Well, duh, because you're pushing it."

Breathless with anticipation, we all leaned closer.

"Where's it going?" whispered Rosa.

The planchette slid to the letter "H."

I scanned my brain. "Are you Hayley Mills?" I asked Ouija.

Danica scoffed. "She's not dead!"

"Maybe she has ESP," I sniffed. "Takes forever for this thing to spell out a word."

The planchette moved four more times. "H-E-L-L-O."

"That's lame," quipped Maggie. "Well, hello to you, too." She waved at the Ouija board.

"Give it a minute," cautioned Colleen.

"I know what to ask," said Cat. "Hey Ouija, who does Jo like?"

"No! I don't like anyone," I protested. "Ask it who Cat likes."

Cat flashed me a coy smile. "Who does Jo like?" She emphasized each word.

The planchette hesitated, then it moved to the M and the A.

Mikey Ann groaned. "Not Mary again."

The planchette moved, this time faster. It spelled a 'C' and a 'K.'

"Mack? Son of a beeswax!" Cat squealed. "You mean Thomas MacGregor?" she asked Ouija.

"Y-E-S," the planchette spelled. Everyone whistled and teased me, like I'd been holding out on them.

My face burned with sudden heat. "Uncool, you guys!" I spat out.

"Aha!" Maggie pointed at me. "I knew you still liked him!"

"Nuh-uh! I do not!" I lied, hoping I sounded convincing. I didn't want to be teased into oblivion.

"Liar!" accused Maggie. "You're always moony around him." She put her hands on her cheeks and batted her eyelashes.

I narrowed my eyes. "One of you did that on purpose."

"Nope," insisted Colleen. "Ouija took over, and it doesn't lie."

I sat back, recalling how I'd thought of Mack when I was French kissing a cupcake. I didn't *really* like him, did I? I recalled the hurt look on his face when I said he was a loser in class and my gut twisted with guilt. *Smooth move, Ex-Lax.*

"Josephina!" Cat's voice snapped me back to the present. "Your turn to ask it a question."

I placed my fingertips on the planchette. "Will we all graduate?"

The planchette inched around the board. "M-A-Y-B-E."

Everyone's breath caught at the unsettling revelation.

Maggie's expression registered horror, magnified by the flickering shadows on her face. "I can't be a maybe! I have to graduate!" She got to her feet and paced, clearly agitated. "This is the second fortune-teller that said maybe!"

"Come on, Mags, don't have a conniption fit. Sit back down." I patted the spot next to me.

Cat whispered, "Which of us won't graduate?"

Mikey Ann snorted. "I'm not sure I want to know."

The planchette moved erratically, spelling "S-T-O-P."

"Stop what?" asked Cat.

The planchette spelled, "W-O-R-R-Y-I-N-G."

Maggie sank down and scooted next to me. "That's good news, right?"

We looked around at each other exchanging this-is-creeping-us-out looks.

"Let's do a séance." Colleen lifted the Ouija board and set it behind her. "I'll be the medium who summons the spirits from beyond."

The candlelight flickered the edges of the room as we scooted in and held hands.

Colleen's voice took on a spooky quality. "Gentle spirits, move among us. We're calling upon you..."

"Tell the spirits we have cookies," whispered Cat.

"Get serious, or the spirits won't come." Colleen gave her a stern look, then glanced around. "Who do you want to summon?" The flickering candlelight danced spooky shadows on everyone's faces.

"Let's summon JFK." Maggie's coke-bottle glasses magnified her eyeballs like googly eyes on a blowfish.

"Kennedy is all the way back in Arlington Cemetery," I pointed out.

Colleen shook her head. "Doesn't matter where they're buried. Their spirits travel around."

I hoped that wasn't true. The thought of my dad zipping around, spying on the bad stuff I'd done in the last six years, creeped me out.

"How will we know if Kennedy is here?" Mikey Ann glanced nervously around the room.

"Trust me, you'll know. Stay calm when the spirit responds, and only ask it yes or no questions," instructed Colleen. She called out, "John Fitzgerald Kennedy! We are summoning you. Are you with us? Inform us of your presence by snuffing a candle."

My gaze immediately darted to the flickering candles. Suddenly, a flame went out, and a shiver spider-walked up my spine.

"Jeepers creepers, he's here!" Maggie squeaked out.

"Hot damn!" Cat glanced around at the dark shadows.

"Don't cuss in front of the President." I intended it as a joke, but Cat was focused on the candle that went out.

Colleen raised her arms. "President Kennedy, we acknowledge your presence."

"Ask him who's gonna win the world series this year," Mikey Ann whispered.

"How would he know that?" Cat whispered back.

"Ask him if he wants a cookie," I joked.

Mikey Ann giggled. "That would be funny if he came and chowed down on a cookie."

"You guys, ghosts can't eat. They're transparent." Maggie rolled her eyes. "Jeez!"

"She's right. The cookie would drop right through him," reasoned Cat.

"Shh!" Colleen lowered her arms, irritated. "You guys, if you're not serious, he'll leave. President Kennedy, are you still with us? If yes, extinguish another candle," she called out.

When the next candle snuffed out, everyone screamed. I took a long, shuddering breath when I spotted a dark form scurry around a corner into the other room. "Cat, are your brothers down here, by any chance?"

The overhead lights flicked on. "BOO!" yelled Cat's brothers, Micky and Dan, hooting and cackling.

We groaned. "You guys! Now you scared Kennedy away!"

"We had you going, didn't we?" Dan picked up a chocolate chip cookie from a plate next to the candles. "I'll bet Kennedy would have loved these!" He bit into the cookie and grinned.

Cat's brothers were cute, but they were sixth and seventh graders. Dan could pass for a freshman since he was tall. He'd be a heartbreaker someday.

Nope, too young, and he's my best friend's brother.

My thoughts shifted to Mack, and I wondered if he'd notice my pierced ears on Monday.

The next morning at breakfast, Colleen made an announcement. "I have a cousin that does palm readings. She's available this afternoon, if anyone is interested." She glanced around.

Curious to know what my life would be like, I volunteered. "My mom will be gone this afternoon. We can do it at my house."

Everyone's eyes turned into saucers. "Really?"

"I don't know about you guys, but I want to know my fortune," I said, my excitement growing over knowing my future. "Come over around two, after my mom leaves."

"My cousin charges a buck per read," said Colleen. "So, bring some money."

We all dressed and hurried home to get ready for this afternoon.

A LITTLE AFTER TWO, Colleen and her cousin Destiny arrived at my house. Mom had gone to Whitehall with Roy the Rancher, so we had our big apartment to ourselves. I'd made buttered popcorn and cherry Kool-Aid and set up the card table in the living room.

Destiny was dressed like a hippie. She wore pink and green paisley bell bottoms that hung low on her hips, revealing her belly button. A white embroidered belt held them up. An off the shoulder, long sleeve peasant blouse with embroidered flowers on the sleeves showed her midriff. A matching paisley headscarf covered her head down to her eyebrows.

"Okay, my mercurial friend, you're first." Colleen waved me over to the card table, where Destiny was seated.

I followed her, disliking the word mercurial—it felt like she insinuated I hung out on Mercury Street with the ladies of the evening.

Destiny nodded thanks as I slipped two dollars into her hand. She stuffed the two bills into a macrame purse on the floor next to her, then took my hand and rested it on the table. She ran her fingers smoothly across my palm and leaned over it.

"You have a strong lifeline. Your heart line will lead you along many romance paths." She glanced up at me. "You won't have luck with dark-haired males, so stay clear of them. Stick with the fair-haired ones." She returned her gaze to my hand. "Your sun line says you will see much success in your life, but you will work hard for it. You also have a solid health line. Good for avoiding illness."

"What else?" I asked timidly. "Will I be leaving Butte?"

"I can't say. But I see a land surrounded by water in your future. Be patient. You'll know it when you see it." She let go of my hand and sat back.

I didn't want to ask how long I would live. Not after what happened to my dad. But I wanted to know about my future.

"Will I be a writer?"

She shrugged. "If you work hard. Is that what you want?"

"I don't know. I think so." I pointed at my palm. "But does this say I'll be one?"

She ran a finger along another line. "This is your Head Line. It is deep and heavily creased, meaning you'll accomplish most of what you set out to do."

That was good enough for me. There could be hope for me, yet.

As Maggie would say, blessed be the troublemakers, for someday they shall write about it.

Chapter 43
The Great Nun Robbery

May 1968, eighth grade

Thursday after school, I hurried the four blocks to Woolworth's new photo booth. For a quarter, I sat inside while it snapped four black and white photos that popped out in a single strip. I stuck out my tongue, crossed my eyes, and made funny faces. Satisfied, I went home, cut the strip into four separate photos—each one and a half by two inches—then shoved them into my sweater pocket. I wanted to give each Clover Girl a signed photo.

Friday at lunch, Mikey Ann confided she knew how to sneak into the nun convent to get loads of free candy. She made it sound like we could get away with stealing gold from Fort Knox. Naturally, we were interested.

"Yesterday, when Sister Alex had me carry boxes to the convent for her, I used their bathroom. On the way out, I saw a gigantic cupboard with the door open. You should have seen all the chocolate candy bars and penny candy!" Mikey Ann leaned in. "I think we should sneak in and get some."

We stared at her as if she'd sprouted Butterfingers from her ears.

"How do we do that without getting caught?" asked Maggie, looking skeptical.

Mikey Ann eyed Maggie, her eyes gleaming. "I have a plan."

"Okay, what is it?" I asked.

Mikey Ann gave us the lowdown: Every Saturday afternoon, the nuns cleared out for church and shopping. The convent was vacant because their housekeeper only worked weekdays. Mikey Ann suggested posting her little brother, Benny, as a lookout to alert us when the nuns were heading back to the convent. He'd give us a loud whistle through the window we planned to leave open after going in. Benny had sneaked around the building, trying the windows. He'd discovered one that was unlocked and opened to the basement. It was conveniently hidden behind thick pine trees so no one would see us.

On Saturday afternoon, we nonchalantly entered the playground and darted over to the side of the convent, behind the trees. Mikey Ann lifted the small window that Benny had found unlocked, and she, Cat, and I crawled through and lowered ourselves down to the couch directly below.

Maggie squatted, peeking down at us. "I'll have to say a thousand Hail Marys as penance for this one."

"Mags, we can't confess this," I blurted. "We'll all be expelled. Come on, it'll be okay if we just follow Mikey's plan." I motioned her to follow.

"What if we get caught?" asked Maggie for the millionth time.

"We won't!" All of us shouted in unison.

"But what if we do?"

"We will if you keep standing there." Cat gritted her teeth and imitated Sister Alex. "Mary Margaret Houlihan, get your butt down here *right now!*"

"I'll for sure go to hell for this," whined Maggie. While she was the voice of reason out of our group, she drove us nuts with Catholic guilt.

"Nah, you'll just do some light purgatory time," I joked. "Don't worry, you'll have plenty of company. Mikey Ann will be there, since this was her idea."

Mikey Ann jabbed me with her elbow, and I muffled a yell, rubbing my ribs.

"Jeez Louise, what the heck," mumbled Maggie, rolling her eyes. "Why do I hang out with you guys? You're all a bad influence."

"Good girl, Mags," I called out as she crawled through the window, lowered herself to the couch, and jumped to the floor.

Mikey Ann shoved a pillowcase at Maggie. "You be the smuggler. Carrying the candy is technically not stealing." She gave Maggie a healthy slap on the back. Leave it to Mikey Ann to make it sound like Maggie wasn't doing anything wrong, like stealing from the nuns.

"Now that you put it that way." Maggie slung the pillowcase over her shoulder and gripped it with both hands.

"You look like a hobo on a freight train," I jibed.

"Come on, we're burning daylight, sports fans!" Mikey Ann sprinted up the narrow stairs to the main floor and raced through two rooms with squeaky hardwood floors.

We followed on her heels until Mikey Ann stopped in one room with a huge, braided throw rug. There were floor-to-ceiling oak cabinets along one wall, and she flung one open.

"Look what's behind door number one!" Mikey Ann swept her arm out in a Monty Hall gesture from *Let's Make a Deal*.

We were mesmerized, gazing upon several shelves brimming with every imaginable candy ever invented, from edible necklaces and whopper sticks to M&M's, Neccos, and chocolate candy bars such as Payday, Baby Ruth, and Butterfingers. We'd found a candy lover's dream, and it felt like we'd struck gold in a copper mine.

"Mags, this is like the Fizzies at camp!" I exclaimed.

Maggie peeked inside the cupboard. "Holy mother of Joseph! You're right, except our camp escapade didn't turn out so well."

"This is like Halloween on LSD!" Cat jammed candy in her pockets, her tongue on the side of her mouth like an excited puppy.

"How would you know? Have you dropped acid?" I recalled Flower-Child-Susan talking about her friends on acid trips when I stayed with the Jones family down on The Flats.

"This is big time paydirt!" Mikey Ann pawed through the cupboard and tossed out goodies like she was burglarizing a bank vault.

Maggie caught them and dutifully stuffed our booty inside the pillowcase, while she sang an old tune, "Candy Kisses."

Cat wandered around ogling nun stuff like she was in a museum. "Whoa—check this out!" She held up a huge black girdle, laughing hysterically.

"Nuns wear black underwear?" Mikey Ann snorted, then erupted with a coughing spasm of laughing. The rest of us stared at the weird black girdle as if it was a farting Snickers bar.

"Are you kidding me?" Cat picked up an enormous black bra, held it up to her chest, then twirled it over her head. She imitated a stripper singing, "Let Me Entertain You."

We laughed so loud we barely heard the whistles from Mikey Ann's little brother at his lookout post outside the basement window.

"Shh, listen!" I commanded, arms spread, ready for fight or flight. "Was that Benny whistling?"

Everyone froze. Sure enough, another shrill whistle echoed, and we exchanged horrified looks.

"The nuns are coming!" I ran back and forth, flapping my arms like a rubber ducky at a carnival midway.

"Sonofabitch!" Cat tossed the fish-out-of-water girdle onto a table and fled the room, with Mikey Ann on her heels.

I pushed the tall cupboard doors closed, but one kept swinging open. I tried closing it, but it wouldn't latch. "Maggie, it won't close!"

"Who cares! Not enough time!" Maggie grabbed my arm and pulled me after her.

The ginormous black bra dangled from Cat's arm as we scurried toward the basement door.

"Cat, lose the damn bra!" I barked out, frantic to get to the basement window where we came in. "Go-go-go!"

We stampeded down the stairs and I nearly tripped on the bra Cat dropped in her haste to escape. Once in the basement, we raced to the room where we'd come in. Mikey Ann and Cat jumped up and hoisted themselves through the open window. They reached down to pull Maggie up. When it was my turn, doors opened and slammed, footsteps sounding above me.

The nuns were inside the convent!

My stomach plummeted to the floor.

"You guys, help me get out!" I stretched my arms up for my friends to grab me. "Hurry, pull me up!"

Cat reached down through the window as footsteps sounded on the basement stairs.

"Someone's coming!" Panicked, I jumped off the couch, frantic to find a hiding place.

"Jo, grab hold! Get the heck out of there!" Maggie's arms reached down to hoist me up.

It was too late. "No time—I can't! You guys, get out of here!" I whispered, almost in tears.

"Find somewhere to hide!" Mikey Ann pulled the window closed and my friends disappeared.

I gulped. I was on my own.

Frantic, I glanced around and spotted a tall piano sitting diagonally in a corner. I spied a small space between the piano and the wall, so I squeezed my bony frame through the tight space. I slid down the wall, with my back pressed to the corner. I hugged my knees, holding my red Keds close, while my heart jack-hammered. Dust bunnies floated up, and I had the urge to sneeze. I covered my mouth and nose to suppress it as a multitude of footsteps clomped down the wooden stairs.

"What's this brassiere doing on the stairs?" Sister Alex's voice called out.

Sister Bertie's voice. "I must have dropped it on my way to the laundry room."

That's all I need is for the principal to catch me behind this piano. Dear God, please don't let anyone else come down here.

Does God listen to your prayers when you're robbing the nuns of candy and making fun of their underwear? More feet pounded down the staircase and I buried my face in my cradled knees.

"Sisters, we need to practice our songs for Sunday Mass." Sister Bertie sounded too close for comfort. Sure enough, the piano bench scraped the floor, and she grunted, plopping down and banging on the keys. My eardrums exploded and my hands flew to my ears as Sister Bertie hammered on the piano.

When Sister Bertie stops playing, every nun will hear my heart beating itself to death.

The nuns sang one song after another in a deafening concert, like a stereo turned up full blast. The out of tune keys reverberated through me, vibrating my chest.

A voice cut in from upstairs. "Sisters! Supper is ready!"

Boom! Down slammed the piano guard over the keyboard, and I jumped. The bench squeaked back out and the noisy nun shoes clattered back up the stairs. At long last, the basement door slammed shut.

Like a flash, I squeezed out and climbed onto the worn couch. Adrenaline shot through me as I stood on my tiptoes to lift the window open. It would be just my luck to get caught now.

How was I going to hoist myself up? No one was here to give me a boost.

Suddenly, two pairs of hands thrust through the window, and Mikey Ann and Cat's faces appeared. "We thought they caught you and you were being tortured. Come on, get out of there!"

They hoisted me up and out. We closed the window and inched our way around the building so no one would see us skulking around outside.

"We thought you were a goner," said Mikey Ann, her voice wiggling as we rushed to get out of there before someone spotted us.

"I hid behind the piano," I panted, as I ran alongside her.

We ran through the tall chain-link gate, down the alley, and up the front steps of my house. One of our tenants came up the steps after his shift working in the mines. His face was grimy, along with his clothes.

"Hello girls, how is your day going?" Our new tenant, Mr. Duffy, was a jovial guy.

Maggie swung the pillowcase full of candy behind her. "We're uh—doing laundry," she lied, her cheeks turning into tomatoes. I changed my mind about Maggie becoming a lawyer. She was a terrible liar.

"That's wonderful, kids. See ya's later." Mr. Duffy opened the front door and disappeared inside.

Luckily, my mother wasn't home, so we scurried to my room and divvied up our loot.

"We can't believe you made it out." Maggie chomped on a Nestlé Crunch. "If you got caught, we hoped you wouldn't nark on us."

"That's an unwritten Clover Girls rule." I gave her a solemn look. "Even if I got caught, I would never nark on you guys. It was loud behind that piano with the nuns singing their lungs out."

"You were lucky to find somewhere to hide." Cat munched a Butterfinger.

"It was super dusty. If I'd sneezed, I wouldn't be here right now. Sister Bertie pounded that piano like the blonde lady on *Lawrence Welk*. It was like firecrackers inside my ears."

"Better you than me," Mikey Ann grinned. "We thought you were up Silver Bow Crick without a paddle."

Cat gazed at me as if I'd parted the waters of our local creek. "You lucky duck! Had the nuns caught you, you would've been screwed, blued, and tattooed." She popped a tan Necco in her mouth.

Maggie chimed in. "I hope they don't notice the missing candy, with the stupid cupboard door that wouldn't close." She covered her face and groaned. "I knew this was a bad idea."

"Yeah, but how many can say they snuck into a nun's convent?" Mikey Ann shot us a devilish grin, then popped a Jolly Rancher into her mouth.

I gulped. "Yeah, how many can say *that*?"

I thought we were cool for pulling this off. Yep, we were really hot stuff.

Chapter 44
The Come to Jesus Meeting

May 1968, eighth grade

Monday after school, I came home to find Mom glaring at me with our pink princess phone receiver in her hand. "That was your school principal. She has things to discuss with you kids this Saturday at the convent."

"What for?" I replied way too fast, sure to arouse suspicion. I slowed my words. "Do the parents have to go?"

"No. She only wants to talk to you kids."

"What's it about?" I asked, dreading the answer.

"She said you'll tell me afterwards. Is there something I should know?" Mom's tone was accusatory, and it made me uneasy.

If Sister Alex knew what we'd done, I was surprised she hadn't ratted us out.

"Nah, it's probably stuff about graduation." I feigned innocence, but the way my mother's eyes narrowed told me it wouldn't do any good.

"Tell me what's going on."

"I want to talk to Sister first," I insisted. "It might not be a bad thing," I chirped, trying to sound upbeat.

Mom stared at me for a long moment. "If you've done anything to prevent you from graduating from St. Michael's, there will be hell to pay."

"It's not. It won't," I assured her, hoping beyond hope it wasn't the case.

"I'll say this about your principal. She's the best nun I've seen come through this school. She's a sharpie. You won't get away with much." Mom called all intelligent people sharpies.

When I compared notes with the Clover Girls the next day at school, their moms told them the same thing. Sister Alex remained tight-lipped about why she was summoning us to the convent.

The entire week dragged by in torturous suspense. Each day after school, the four of us sat on the apartment house steps, fretting about the possibilities.

"Sister Alex knows we snuck in and got the candy," Maggie declared, solemn-faced.

"Or maybe because we talked to dead people in our seances," suggested Cat.

"Or the Ouija board," said Mikey Ann. "Maybe Colleen narked on us."

"Anyone could have narked on us. The entire school knows about our seances and the Ouija board." I threw up my hands. "Or she found out about the atomic wedgie at the KC game...or someone saw Danica French kissing me on the playground..." I trailed off. There were too many infractions to list.

Maggie heaved out a sigh. "What did your mom say when Sister Alex called?"

"If I don't graduate, there'll be hell to pay." Just saying it raced my pulse.

"Hell to pay as in when you lost your Christmas seals in second grade, or hell to pay when you almost burned down your mom's apartment house or when you told your mother you got stuck on a hundred-foot headframe?" Maggie spilled it out all in one breath.

"Hell to pay, as in I'll be grounded until the day I die," I said flatly.

"Yeah, that's bad." Maggie stared at an ant struggling to crawl up a concrete stair wall.

"Mom knew about the Fizzies and the frogs, but I didn't tell her about Sister Alex's dead goldfish," I said.

Cat whistled, shaking her head. "Jeez, Jo, you and Maggie are hard on the environment."

"Don't go near any more frogs and fish," cautioned Mikey Ann.

I slapped a hand to my forehead. "Oh man, this got way out of hand. Do you think anyone saw us?" I glanced around our circle.

Maggie shrugged. "Maybe a nun looked out the window and saw us running away."

"Oh, man, don't say that! I wonder if Sister Alex noticed the missing candy." My insides jumped around. "Sneaking into the convent was probably not one of our best decisions."

"Well, D.U.H.!" Maggie spelled out emphatically. "I'll bet a million bucks that's why she called this meeting." We were all sure of it, too, but hoped for a miracle.

Even a million bucks wouldn't be enough to get us out of this one.

TWO WEEKS BEFORE GRADUATION

At ten minutes to one on Saturday, I reluctantly crossed the alley, my stomach dragging on the asphalt. It was a warm, sunny day, and the chirping birds in our lilac bushes mocked me because I couldn't stay outside to enjoy it.

I walked up the wide concrete steps to the front door of the convent just as Cat and Maggie strolled down Washington Street. Mikey Ann's dad dropped her off and the other eighth-grade girls had arrived. Now I was curious: why were all the girls in our class coming to this?

The housekeeper ushered us all into the old-fashioned parlor, with flowery wallpaper and dark furniture. The Clover Girls sat together in four of the fancy brocaded chairs arranged in a large circle. Our nerves had ratcheted up, and we weren't as gabby as the rest of the girls talking and laughing.

As we waited to get our heads handed to us on a platter, I nibbled the side of my thumb. Maggie's head jerked around like a frightened chicken on the lookout for a ravenous eagle, Cat toyed with her hair, and Mikey Ann quietly hummed Elvis's "Jailhouse Rock" which did little to soothe our nerves.

Sister Alex breezed into the room with her effervescent smile. "Hello, ladies. Thank you for coming. I am sure you are curious why I have asked you all here today."

"Oh boy, here we go," I breathed to Maggie, who elbowed me in response.

"I will get right to it. The Sisters have asked me to talk with all of you. We know that someone entered our home while we were gone, and not only invaded our privacy, but stole from us as well. There are rumors that eighth-grade girls were involved." Sister Alex glanced around the room.

"I haven't told your parents. I wanted to give you the chance to come forward and admit to what you did." She flashed us another broad smile. "I trust the candy was delicious."

My eyes darted to the other Clover Girls, and we locked gazes. Maggie was right. Again. We stayed silent, listening.

"Why do you think you must steal to get what you want?" Sister asked, studying each of us. "I would have given you the candy. All you had to do was ask."

We lowered our heads, staring at our hands in our laps.

"But why?" She gave us each an accusing stare. "Why did you do it?"

Maggie burst into tears while Cat, Mikey Ann and I froze.

Sister turned her attention to the four of us sitting together, her sharp brown eyes sucking away any hope of salvation. I fixated on a sunbeam slicing through the window, illuminating the crimson rose patterns in the carpet. I wished it would turn into a magic carpet and fly me the heck out of here. My chest was about to explode as my heart walloped it.

Sister's pained expression undid me. Her trust in us was broken, and I was ashamed. I couldn't take it any longer.

"I don't know why we did it!" I blurted, tears welling.

Sister's stare drilled into me. She was the one person in my life right now I hadn't wanted to disappoint. Too late for that.

"Tell me why you did it." Sister's tone was quiet, which unnerved me. "Explain yourself."

What should I say?

Sister patiently waited for me to collect myself, but my shame choked back my words. "I guess—I did it because—I was—"

Cat cut in. "Jo wasn't the only one, Sister. I was with her, too."

"Me, too, Sister," Mikey Ann piped up in a valiant tone. "It was my idea."

Stunned silence as all eyes snapped to Mikey Ann, who'd seemed willing to take the heat.

God love Mikey Ann for saying that, but she doesn't want that kind of heat.

"Thank you, Miss Quinn, but every person who took part is equally guilty," replied Sister.

Maggie sat crying. I couldn't fault her. She'd tried talking us out of sneaking into the convent, and we'd convinced her, anyway. I understood the pressure she faced from her mother, who disapproved of most things she did.

"Maggie?" Sister Alex looked at her.

Maggie lifted her chin, tears streaking her face. "Please don't tell my mother."

"All of you girls remain here after we finish today." Sister looked at each of us. "In the meantime, it has come to my attention some of you have been consulting dirty magazines." She held up her hand. "I am not interested in who has been doing it. But I think it is time we discuss the birds and the bees. You are obviously curious."

The room fell silent as we Clover Girls exchanged stunned looks.

Who ratted us out for looking at Playboy at Cat's house?

Sister Bertie entered the room with a tray of freshly baked cookies and passed them around, while Sister Alex stood and pulled a flip board to one end of the room, with "Sex Education Instruction" in bold letters on the top, and male and female symbols under it.

I choked on my cookie.

We shifted in our chairs, and throats began clearing. The last thing we expected today was Sister Alex giving us the dreaded sex talk.

I thought back to when Cat told us about their husky getting loose and got humped by a German shepherd. Mrs. Delaney ran outside screaming, "A stray dog is fucking Ginger!" The kids were all shocked by their mother's 'F' word, but when she launched into a dog-sex talk, Cat said it blew their minds. She had us in stitches until we almost peed our pants. We couldn't picture sweet Mrs. Delaney saying the 'F' word.

"You looked through those magazines for a reason," began Sister Alex with a plaintive expression. "Is there anything of a sexual nature you want to ask me?"

A sexual nature?

The room instantly quieted. Funeral home quiet. No one uttered a word. No one breathed. We couldn't—a *nun* was talking to us about sex.

"Sister, can you have sexual intercourse during your period?" Danica blurted, her face the color of rubies.

Silence bounced around as her words dripped like acid rain. Embarrassed, Cat and I slid down in our chairs. Maggie's hands covered her face, and Mikey Ann looked as though she'd been smacked by a two-by-four. Asking a nun questions about sex was like asking an aardvark about nuclear physics.

Sister lifted the first page of the flip chart to show illustrated displays of the female and male anatomies and began her talk like we were in science class. She talked about human courtship, mating rituals, and menstrual cycles. Sister Alex left no stone unturned, and we cringed when she said 'penis' and 'vagina.' Sensing our discomfort and much to her credit, Sister did her best to make us feel at ease.

I thought of Pepper showing us the boy and girl parts in her *Gray's Anatomy* book, back in the sixth grade, and how it all paid off for her since she now wrote sex stories for a living.

When it was time to go, everyone was dismissed except for the Clover Girls. She pulled her chair closer to us, sat back, and folded her arms.

"You know what you did was wrong. I will not lecture you about breaking the Seventh Commandment," she began. "Thank you for admitting to what you did. I suspected the four of you were involved. I respect you for admitting to it."

"Yes, Sister," we each mumbled.

"You girls have so much potential, so much promise. Do not do things you know are wrong just to impress your friends. Promise me in the future you will say no to such sinful things." Her brown eyes pierced my soul. "I want each of you to promise me."

One by one, we promised, crossed our hearts and hoped to die.

Tears welled, and I couldn't stop the flood. Neither could Maggie. Cat and Mikey Ann sat still with solemn faces.

Sister took a deep breath. "You are on your way to becoming women. Next fall, when you move into your freshman year, please remember what we taught you here at St. Michael School."

"Who told you, Sister?" asked Cat, always the brave one.

Sister's face remained impassive. "Who told me is not the issue. What is important is that you look to your hearts and pray for the right path to follow. You will not find answers from a Ouija board. Nor will you find answers from seances or from those who fill your heads with gibberish they think you want to hear."

Cat leaned toward me and whispered, "I bet it was Colleen."

Sister shook her head. "A little red birdie told me."

Maggie's fear was written all over her face. "Will you let us graduate, Sister?"

"You will all graduate." Sister rose from her chair. "We are finished here. You can go now."

Mixtures of relief and guilt washed over us because we'd let Sister Alex down.

I stood to go. "I'm sorry, Sister. We'll never do it again." She hadn't mentioned me hiding behind the piano. At least there was *one* thing she didn't know.

"Music to our ears. Repent, my dear little sinners," Sister Bertie interjected from the doorway, smiling. We hadn't noticed her there and once again my face heated with more humiliation and remorse.

"I'll leave it to you to tell your parents. See you on Monday." Sister motioned us to the front doors leading to the street. "Remember what I said."

"Yes, Sister." We mumbled our goodbyes and filed out like penitent little sinners.

"Heavens to Murgatroyd!" shouted Cat when we were a safe distance from the convent.

"Talk about a shocker! I thought we'd have detention for the rest of the year, or worse, we'd be expelled." Maggie tapped her glasses higher. "See you guys at school. I have to get home." She and the rest hurried up Washington Street as I headed to the apartment house.

A lead weight pushed down on me on what I would tell Mom. I spared her the excruciating details and just said Sister called us to the convent to give us a sex education talk because she heard we were curious about sex. I didn't mention our candy caper. Moms don't need to know everything.

Besides, she and Rancher Roy were taking me on a camping trip up to Canyon Ferry Lake this weekend and he promised to teach me how to drive his boat.

I couldn't wait.

Chapter 45
Day Twelve of Lilly's Coma

June 5, 1968, three days before graduation

Today we learned the shocking news that Bobby Kennedy was shot by a guy named Sirhan Sirhan. Three months ago, on April fourth, Martin Luther King was shot at a motel in Tennessee. Sister had taught us about him as a prominent leader in the civil rights movement. People around the country were sad and fearful of who would be next.

And now this.

Tonight, after dinner at the Silver Bow Homes apartment, Aunt Daisy, Aunt Violet and I watch the evening news where Walter Cronkite announces, "The assassination of Robert Francis Kennedy, a United States Senator, took place shortly after midnight in Los Angeles, California. Kennedy was shot as he walked through the kitchen of the Ambassador Hotel."

As he lay dying on the kitchen floor, his last words were, "Is everybody okay?"

No, Bobby, we aren't okay. Fear and anxiety have taken up residence in our confused minds once again after our nation lost your brother five years ago. At school, Sister Bertie hadn't taken this news well, after teaching us about Robert Kennedy. The morning after he was shot, I passed her in the hall, and her eyes were red, like everyone else's. The nuns were still devastated after Martin Luther King was shot back in April.

Since Aunt Daisy had given me Mom's key to our apartment, after school I cross the alley and go to my bedroom. I stand there, studying the framed black-and-white photo of Bobby on my wall I'd hung two years ago. I reach for my large jewelry box and take out the blue envelope with my crinkled pink tissue: a reminder of happier times, when we'd all shown support for a man determined to do good things for America, and who led us to believe in the greater good.

He'd talked to us like we mattered. He gave us young people hope.

I remove the tissue and smooth my fingers over it, trying to understand why these things happen. I want to undo the heartbreak of this awful tragedy, but all I can do is stand here and mourn for someone who tried to make a better world.

I'm standing at the threshold of the next chapter of my life, my heart full of gratitude. For my Clover Girls, whose laughter had carried me through the darkest days; for Aunt Daisy, whose hugs were my sanctuary, and for my mother. That camping trip—that one choice—would haunt me forever if my mother is forever stolen from me.

How many nights had we Clover Girls lain awake during our sleepovers, trusting each other with our dreams for the future? With graduation just a few days away, our lives stretch before us with endless possibility. Hope was especially high on our list these days at St. Michael School. Bobby Kennedy had planted that seed back in 1966 on the steps of the Miners' Union Hall when his words gave us hope for a better world.

I wouldn't talk about the chaos sweeping our country during my next hospital visit. Mom didn't need to hear about sadness and civil unrest. Telling her about my ill-behaved shenanigans was bad enough. The one and only thing in this whole wide world that mattered was that Lilly Wolohan would open her eyes and find me smiling at her.

Nothing else mattered. Not one single thing.

Chapter 46
Day Fifteen of Lilly's Coma

Graduation Day

Early this morning, the phone rings in my aunt's apartment. I'm half awake and don't hear the conversation Aunt Daisy has on the phone. I hear her rushing around before she pokes her head into my bedroom.

"I'm dropping you off early for your graduation. Hurry." Her tone is urgent. Something is out of kilter.

"What's going on?" I bolt out of bed.

"Tell you later. This is a big day for you. Best get going," Aunt Daisy says distractedly.

I pull on my dress, part my hair in the middle, letting it fall around my shoulders. Next, I pat on pink lipstick, like Aunt Daisy had showed me. I work my new metal posts through my earlobes for the first time—it hurts like crazy, but I finally get them in. The Clover Girls had gone to Ben Franklin on Park Street to buy our first pair of pierced earrings and we'd squealed upon finding four identical pairs of green four-leaf clover posts.

I dash around to gather my prayer book and the green-and-white satin ribbon with "Class of '68' embossed in gold, that we'll pin to our dresses. Aunt Daisy drops me off, and when I enter our eighth-grade classroom for the last time, I'm shocked by how amazing everyone looks, dressed to the nines.

My three best friends look like high schoolers in nylons and short heels. Maggie's bright green dress is gorgeous, with ruffled bell sleeves that cover the healing cut on her forearm. We all have our four-leaf clover earrings in our ears.

The boys in their new suits raise our eyebrows, and I fight the urge to gawk at Mack's handsome transformation. I sit next to my three best friends, and we buzz like happy honeybees. Aunt Daisy had gotten me nylons with the torturesome garter belt to hold them up. The wretched elastic straps pinch me when I sit.

Despite all the excitement of graduating today, it hits home about Mom possibly not waking from her coma. I pull my three best friends aside because I can't hold it inside any longer.

"I'm bummed my mother won't be at my graduation," I blurt. "They're sending her to the Seattle brain center tomorrow."

An awkward silence follows as my friends give me an empathetic look.

"I know how you feel," says Cat. "My dad isn't here to see me graduate, either. Mom and I are sad about it, but she said Dad will see me graduate from heaven."

"I guess mine will, too," I say. "I know the nuns and priests have taught about heaven and all, but do you truly believe there's a heaven and hell?" I glance at my circle of friends.

"Yeah, I believe it," says Cat. "I can't bear the thought of never again seeing the ones I love after we die. There has to be a heaven where we can all be together."

"I hope so," I reply. "I talk to my dad when I'm alone, like I'm praying to him."

"I do that, too," seconds Cat.

Maggie grasps my hand and Cat's. "Mikey Ann and I will be cheering for you both, along with everyone else. Even though my parents are divorced, I'm thankful that they'll both be there."

"Me, too." Mikey Ann places her hand on my shoulder. "The Clover Girls have each other and that's enough, right?"

"Right!" we all chorus.

"Thanks, you guys. You're the best," I say, taking a deep breath to hold back my swirling emotions.

"I'm sure your mom liked the stories about your uncles, the spelling bee, and summer camp up at Camp Elkhorn," says Mikey Ann. "You guys are candidates for some serious purgatory time for what you did to those frogs."

Cat laughs as Maggie and I exchange uneasy looks. "Yeah, well, nobody's perfect," I mutter.

Maggie chortles. "You'll be in the doghouse when Lilly wakes up."

I like that she says 'when' and not 'if,' but I'm not holding out much hope right now.

"Can you believe all the trouble we got into this year?" says Cat, laughing. "And we lived to talk about it."

"I'd say we've had an action-packed year," I reply. It feels good knowing we'd survived it.

"Congratulations, eighth graders!" Sister Alex calls out to get everyone's attention. "You made it to graduation. All right, everyone, let's get ready!"

"It's a miracle, considering." Sister Bertie leans against a doorway, nodding emphatically as we all laugh. It was a miracle, indeed.

"This is St. Michael's graduation gift to you." Both nuns distribute rosaries in small plastic containers while Sister Alex speaks about our journey into the brave new world of high school. She chokes up—unusual since she rarely shows emotion—then straightens and hands us our keepsake programs with St. Michael the Archangel on the front, our names embossed in gold with matching tassels inside.

Maggie elbows me, pointing to our names. "We did it, Jo."

I tear up and blink it back fast, knowing I must keep it together. I have too much to cry about. If I start, I might never quit.

Sister addresses us. "Make sure your graduation ribbons are pinned to your left shoulder. And ladies, it's time to put on your white mantillas."

I take the white lace veil from its plastic snap case, unfold it, and drape it over my head. Sister Bertie hands out bobby pins to pin the triangular veils to our hair so they won't slide off.

Out of the corner of my eye, I watch Mack pin his ribbon to the lapel of his navy-blue suit jacket. When he turns his back to talk to someone, I notice his hair creeping onto his shirt collar, and I like how it looks. He turns back around and catches me staring at him. I'd never thought of him as handsome before. Or maybe I had. My cheeks warm, and I drop my gaze to the graduation program in my hand.

"All right, everyone, time to line up in alphabetical order," Sister calls out, clapping over all of us talking at once. "When I call your name, get in line. Girls in one line and boys in the other."

Dutifully, we fall in line like innocent angels wearing our shiny little halos. We leave our classroom for the last time and proceed out of St. Michael

School and down Washington Street to St. Michael Church. Cars honk as our two straight lines head to the main entrance.

Once we are up the steps, Sister Bertie opens one of the bronze doors and announces it's time to begin. Sister Alex opens the other door and holds it open for our graduation procession. The nuns smile and nod at each of us as we enter the church. We smile back, and Maggie gives the Sisters a little wave. I shock myself to realize I'll miss them.

Organ music plays while we walk up the wide center aisle with folded hands, as we have hundreds of times since kindergarten. Cat's and Mikey Ann's families fill two pews, and Mrs. Houlihan stands alone off to one side.

Maggie's face explodes with a smile at seeing her dad standing across the aisle from her mother. I'm so happy he showed up for her after the messy divorce.

Where are Aunt Violet and Aunt Daisy?

I scan the pews, but I don't see them. My heart stutters.

Our class fills the front pews, and we remain standing until the processional music stops. Monsignor and Father Murphy stand side by side in front of the altar in their shiny green and gold vestments, the four of us had laid out in Sacristy for the last time. Maggie had gotten sentimental and blubbery, while the rest of us took one last swig from the wine bottle before filling the cruets.

"Welcome to the liturgy for the St. Michael's class of 1968. First, we will say Mass, then we will have the graduation proceedings." Monsignor motions us to sit.

While I'm happy to graduate, I'm also sad to leave St. Michael's behind.

I crane my neck for a glimpse of Aunt Daisy or Aunt Violet, but I still don't see them. I fidget as sorrow sinks to the bottom of my soul. My heart rips apart—I want to run screaming out of the church that life isn't fair because no one in my family is here to see me graduate.

Finally, Mass ends and an altar boy brings out a basket containing our five by seven-inch diplomas. He sets it on a small round table next to Father Murphy, who will call our names to approach the altar. Monsignor stands next to him, in the center.

When Maggie, Cat, and Mikey Ann's names are called, I clap as hard as I can as they each rise to accept their diplomas. Since we're in church, we aren't allowed to whoop and holler, so I wave wildly and give them a thumbs-up as they return to their seats.

We finally reach the end of the alphabet. As a 'W' I'm always last.

"Mary Josephina Wolohan," announces Father Murphy.

I can't contain the tears that blur my vision as I stand for my big moment. For a brief second, I think about my mom and dad. I swallow hard, swiping away a tear as I move to the center aisle and up to Father Murphy. His well-known grin lights up his face, and I bet he's counting down the minutes until he's rid of our class.

"Congratulations." He smiles and offers me my diploma.

I accept it and Monsignor Coyle takes over. "Mary Josephina. May the Lord bless and keep you," he says, waving the sign of the cross over my head, the subtle scent of incense clinging to his vestments.

When I turn around, my heart thrums and my feet root to the floor. My lungs forget how to work as I stand there, blinking repeatedly.

Have I wished for this so hard that I'm seeing things?

A nurse pushes a wheelchair up the center aisle, with Aunt Daisy practically floating alongside, smiling through happy tears. Aunt Violet walks on the other side, doing the same. My hands fly to my face, covering my nose and mouth as I watch my mother come toward me, eyes open and fully awake! The nurse stops the wheelchair in front of me as happy tears trickle down Aunt Daisy's cheeks.

My vision tunnels until all I can see is Lilly Rose Wolohan's face. The church quiets except for gasps of disbelief.

Dark circles shadow my mother's face, and she seems smaller, as if the coma had been slowly shrinking her. She lifts her hand to reach out, but it flutters to her lap. I can see that she is weak.

Church etiquette flies out the window. "Oh my God, you're awake, you're awake!" I shriek, the words tearing from my throat as my legs catapult me forward. I take Mom's hand with both of mine. "I can't believe you're here." My voice cracks on the last word.

"Made it... to your... graduation," she rasps haltingly. Her smile is wobbly, but it's the most beautiful thing I've ever seen.

"Can I hug her?" I ask the nurse, who nods, my heart hammering so hard I'm sure everyone in the church can hear it.

"Oh, Mom, I'm so happy you're here!" I bend to give her a gentle hug, her hospital smell mingling with the Chanel No. 5 Aunt Daisy must have dabbed on her. I straighten, suddenly aware of the eyes on us.

Father Murphy claps, and the entire church erupts in applause as Cat, Maggie, and Mikey Ann let out jubilant squeals. To say I am overwhelmed is an understatement.

Aunt Daisy pats Mom's shoulder. "She woke up during the night. When she learned today was your graduation, she insisted Dr. Madison let her come. She wanted to surprise you, and it killed me not to say anything this morning." Her words tumble out, breathless with excitement.

I drop beside her wheelchair. "Thank you for coming, Mom. I love you so much." It occurs to me I haven't said this to her in a long time.

"Love you, too... wouldn't miss this." Each word costs Mom an effort, her chest rising and falling with shallow breaths.

"Congratulations, honey." Aunt Daisy's arms envelop me, and I get a whiff of her Shalimar.

Aunt Violet hugs me, too. "We're all so proud of you, Jo." This is the first time I remember my other aunt ever hugging me, and it feels wonderful.

"Thanks, Aunt Violet." And I mean it.

Father Murphy steps up to the altar, arms spread. "All right, everyone, our graduation ceremony has ended. Head on up to the reception at the school gymnasium. Graduates, remain here for the class photo, then you may go."

Father Murphy and Monsignor Coyle step down from the altar to talk to my mother as the church empties.

"Glory be to God that you are with us again, Mrs. Wolohan," says Monsignor. He leans forward, his eyes crinkling at the corners. "I didn't have to give you last rites."

My mother lifts her chin, a spark of her old fire on her tired face. "I'm too... ornery to die. But thanks... me being a sinner and all," she forces out.

Monsignor chuckles. "Welcome back and may you have a speedy recovery." He dips a nod, then returns to the altar to finish cleaning up.

"Mrs. Wolohan, praise the Lord you could come today," says Father Murphy. "Before you go, I'll give you a blessing, in the name of the Father, the Son, and the Holy Ghost." He makes the sign of the cross with his hand.

"Thanks, Father," Mom whispers, her head falling back, clearly fatigued.

"I must get your mother back to the hospital," says the nurse, gripping the handles of the wheelchair. "Dr. Madison was strict about that."

Mom gives me a weak smile. "Later, alligator."

"When your legs are straighter!" I hug her goodbye, blinking back happy tears.

Mom squints. "You pierced your ears?"

"Oh, right." My hand touches my earlobe. "Cat did it at our sleepover."

Mom's mouth lifts. "Clovers... for Clover Girls?"

My stomach somersaults. "That's our secret code name. How do you know about that?"

"Must have dreamed it," says Mom, her voice fading. "See you later, honey."

As the nurse wheels Mom out, goosebumps stick up all over me, like chicken skin. The realization hits like a thunderclap that I told her about the Clover Girls while she was in her coma. I touched my earring like it was a talisman.

She must have heard me!

"Jo, I'm so happy for you!" Maggie throws her arms around me in a bear hug. "I knew she'd be okay. I just knew it!"

Cat and Mikey Ann rush over, and we entangle ourselves in a four-way hug.

"It's the best graduation present ever." I let go when Sister Alex tells us to get on the altar for our class photo.

Our class photographer, Mr. Withers, arranges us by height. The short girls sit on a bench in the front row, then the next tallest girls behind them. The boys line up two rows behind us. It's weird to be on this sacred altar with its floor pattern of marbled diamonds and zigzag lines in beige and brown. I stand in the second row with Maggie on one side and Cat on the other. Mikey Ann is behind us, doing her best to make us laugh.

She leans forward and whispers, "Hey, there's a turtle in here!"

I turn my head to the side. "Where?"

"Right here!" Mikey Ann snaps the back of my bra through my dress. It seems to reverberate around the church, and I swear everyone hears it.

"Ow!" I squeal, just as the photographer takes the photo.

Heads turn toward me as Mr. Withers shoots me a displeased look. Sister Alex and Father Murphy both frown.

I clear my throat. "Uh, sorry." I'm not about to nark on Mikey Ann.

Maggie squeezes my hand. "Can you believe this is actually happening?"

I shake my head, dazed. "Seems like a dream. Pinch me! I was so scared about Mom."

"I know you were. I was scared for you," confides Maggie, squeezing my elbow.

I cup my hand around Maggie's ear. "Mom knows our secret Clover Girl's name. I've never told her, so that means she heard me talk about it when she was in her coma." A shiver flies up my spine.

Maggie pulls back, open-mouthed. "Wow, Dr. Madison was right. Holy smokes, it's a miracle!"

Mr. Withers commands our attention for more photos, and I snap my head forward.

I sense an unspoken truth hanging in the air—these moments will soon become cherished memories. Nearly losing my mother drives home the importance of not holding back when there are words to be said. I make a mental note to tell my three best friends how much I treasure them—and how much their friendships mean to me.

We make faces at each other like kindergartners. Cat sticks out her tongue while Mikey Ann crosses her eyes. *She's actually wearing a bra!*

I glance at Rosa, Danica, and the rest...and in that moment, I know we've all shared something special.

My gaze rests on Mack, looking grown up and handsome in his snazzy suit and skinny tie. His longer hair makes him look like a Scottish Paul McCartney. Remorse runs through me when I realize I probably won't see him after graduation. I want to thank him again for helping me the other morning and I want to apologize for calling him a loser.

As we grin at the camera and wait for another flash, I remember those who taught me things... Pepper the Porno Nanny, Susan the Flower Child, and especially Aunt Daisy, who has and will forever be a second mother to me. Mostly, I'm grateful to my three best friends for showing me what loyalty and resilience look like.

All. These. Years. I really am a lucky girl, after all.

Chapter 47
We've Only Just Begun

June 8, 1968, Graduation Day

The Clover Girls and I walk up the hill back to St. Michael's School for the graduation reception party in the school gymnasium. We arrive to see festive crepe paper decorations and ornamental tables with cake and punch. One dad brought in a high-fidelity stereo, and Sister Alex told us to bring in our favorite records with our names on them.

The four of us had carefully coordinated ahead of time to make sure we didn't bring in the same 45's. Cat brought "Jumping Jack Flash" by the Rolling Stones, and Mikey Ann brought in "Born to Be Wild" by Steppenwolf.

Danica and Rosa are in charge of the music and stack the 45's on the thick pedestal, where they drop one at a time onto the turntable. After bombarding them with song requests, we dance together, loving that our generation is different, and this is our "Happening." When Sister Alex flashes us her tone-it-down stare, we laugh and move to the punch table.

I open the small purse Aunt Daisy bought me and pull out the envelope containing the photos I had signed to give to Cat, Mikey Ann, and Maggie. There were only three photos I'd found in my sweater. I couldn't find the fourth that I'd saved for my photo album. I give them to my friends, and they laugh at the funny faces I made. We make a date to go to Woolworth's together for more goofy photos.

"Bend Me, Shape Me" plays as Mack McGregor ambles toward me while I eat a piece of vanilla cake. When this song first came out, Cat informed me it was about sex. I don't know why I think of this as Mack approaches, but I'm reluctant to admit that I do.

"Hey, want to sign my autograph booklet?" Mack stands before me in his fine-looking suit and holds out his booklet. He gives me a once-over. "Nice threads."

I swallow my bite of cake. "Thanks. You look nice, too," I say, suddenly shy.

His gaze drops to my chest, and I want to *die.* I'm self-conscious about the new bra Aunt Daisy forced me to get when she'd rushed me to Hennessy's. The saleslady had insisted I needed a Playtex Living Bra, which makes my chest stick out like two Big M's. The blasted thing feels like a horse harness.

My head spins as I accept Mack's autograph booklet. What should I write? What amazing, witty sentiment can I write so he would remember me? My mind blanks. All I can think of is to scribble, *Don't 4 get me, you'll go far! XOXO, Jo Wolohan.*

I scribble it in cursive with my green ink pen with the daisy on top I'd saved for this occasion. He signs mine, and he takes a lot longer. I'm dying to see what he's writing, but I stay casual.

"Where are you going to school freshman year? Girls Central or junior high?" he asks.

"Girls Central," I answer. "How about you?"

"Boys Central. If I can afford the tuition." He gives me a lopsided grin.

"I hear the Brothers can be mean." I parrot what I'd heard from friends whose brothers and cousins have gone there.

"Not all of them," says Mack. "Besides, I can handle it." His confident manner has me believing him. If he said we'd be landing on the moon today, I'd believe that, too.

"I've always wanted to ask you, why were you held back two grades?" I venture.

"You want the long or short version?" he asks with a half-smile.

"I'll take the long," I say, wanting to know all I can about this boy, who is far more mature than the rest of us put together.

Mack chuckles. "Everyone wants that story. After we moved to Butte, my mom died, and my dad went off the deep end. He drank himself sick and couldn't take care of my two sisters and two brothers. Instead, I did it to keep our family together, working odd jobs to pay the bills. When family services called, I'd pretend to be my dad. I'd bullshit them into believing everything was hunky dory."

I wasn't expecting anything like that and stand glued to the floor, astounded. All I do is stare back at him, groping for words. "Oh, my God, Mack, that's incredible."

"That was the lead-in to why I dropped out of school that year. After that, I had a tough time catching up, so the nuns held me back another grade. I plan to test into the sophomore class so I can be with kids my own age."

What another unexpected earful. "Jeez, I had no idea. I'm so sorry that happened to your family." It made my past problems pale by comparison. I kick myself for not asking him before. I would have been nicer... I wouldn't have called him a loser.

"Things are better now." He shrugs. "Dad stopped drinking, and we're doing okay. My grandparents are coming from Scotland next month. If you think I talk funny, you should hear *them*."

It feels good to laugh, and it occurs to me I haven't laughed much since the boat accident.

"It would be fun to meet your grandparents," I gush.

"That's so cool that your mom could make it today. I'm happy for you, Jo."

His words warmed me so much I had to tell him. "Mack, I've been wanting to tell you..."

Two boys rush over, asking him to sign their autograph booklet. Mack has become like a rock star to the boys in our class.

I wait awkwardly while he finishes talking to them. Danica and Rosa had turned up the music, and "I Say a Little Prayer" by Dionne Warwick played. I wonder if that was a Sister Alex choice.

"What did you say?" Mack shouts over the music. He jerks his head toward the double doors leading out to Park Street. "Let's go outside where we can hear better."

I follow him out to where kids stand around, laughing and eating cake off small paper plates. Parents snap photos of graduates on the front steps of the school under the St. Michael banner.

Mack waggles his finger for me to follow. He rounds the corner of the school, stepping into the alley. When he turns to me, we talk at the same time, then we both laugh.

"You go first. Lay it on me. Then I have something to tell you." He runs his fingers through his auburn hair, and his bangs flop forward.

I trace the cracks in the alley with the toe of my dress heels. "I want you to know how sorry I am for—for—what I said a few weeks ago when you had that—you know, that—when you ran out of class..." My cheeks heat as I grope for any word other than 'boner.'

He says nothing, only waits with an amused expression. It seems he's enjoying my awkward squirming as I fidget with my hands.

I continue. "I didn't mean to call you a loser. It was thoughtless, and I was showing off. I really didn't mean it. You've always been nice to me, and you helped me when I heard about my mom and you helped me catch my breath and calmed me down..." My rambling trails off when he steps closer.

His height had shot up these past few months, and he looks every bit the high schooler he should have been two years ago. "Hey, it's okay. We all show off for our friends. I've done my share of that." He unbuttoned his navy-blue suit jacket and slid his hands into his pants pockets.

"I know, but I didn't want us—I mean me—me and you—you mostly... to go off thinking I was a mean person." Flustered, I fiddled with the green and white ribbon I'd pinned to my dress.

"I'm glad your mom is okay, and she got to see you graduate." He scans me from head to toe, then squints at my ear. "You pierced your ears and look so grown up. Far out, Wolly."

His noticing that detail hitches my breath, and I nervously step back. "Thanks. You clean up good, too." Regret splays my insides at having underestimated him all this time.

"What was it you wanted to tell me?" I ask.

He grins. "I've had a thing for you since I first came to this school. I liked how you choked on your first cigarette, then acted like you'd smoked for years."

"A thing?" My cheeks burn. "Wow—you mean you—liked me?"

"Want to know how much?"

Stupefied, I force my head to move up and down and wait for his explanation.

Mack steps closer, lifts my chin, and rests his other hand on my shoulder. He leans down and his mouth lowers to mine. I stand still, unsure of what to do. While the sensation is new, it isn't altogether unpleasant.

What is a person supposed to do during their first actual kiss? It's an unfamiliar feeling, but oddly, I like how it tingles through me.

He lifts away and a heady rush speeds through me, leaving me giddy.

"Mack, I, uh..." I lick my lips where he'd left the sweet taste of chocolate frosting.

"Yeah?" He grins.

I'd not noticed his deep blue eyes before. Or maybe I had, I don't know. Right now, I don't know anything. I think of the chocolate cupcakes I'd practiced on and it was now or never. I'm not sure I'd be seeing Mack again. Butte isn't a big town, but we'd be at different schools.

"Wait, can we do that again?" Taken aback by my own brashness, I place his hand back on my shoulder. I was nervous, but for the first time ever, I didn't need to chew my thumbnail.

I almost laugh outright at his astonished expression, but he does what I say and leans in a second time. I cradle his face to hold it still, then I slip my tongue between his lips, and he jerks a little in surprise. Then he slides his tongue into my mouth. It's weird when he swirls it, and I'm not sure how to move mine. So, I copy-cat what he does.

Then a strange thing happens...I don't want this to stop.

Am I supposed to hold my breath?

Danica didn't cover the breathing angle. I'm super-tuned-in to my heartbeat, my speeding pulse, and the air moving in and out of my lungs.

After a while, Mack backs up with a hand to his lips. "Holy smokes, Wolly! Where'd you learn to kiss like that?"

"I practiced French kissing with cupcakes," I blurt.

He gazes at me intently, like I'd just returned from the moon. Then he bursts out laughing. "How the heck does a person do that? You're joking, right?"

"No, I'm serious," I say in an uncertain voice.

Mack tosses back his head and laughs some more. "Well, whatever you did, it sure paid off. You're good at it! You're a trip, man."

I'm proud I'd pulled it off successfully. "You're the first boy I've ever kissed." I shouldn't be so honest. I remember Mom saying, *never lay your cards on the table with the opposite sex—shroud yourself in mystery and keep them guessing.*

Mack's grin widens. "I'm honored to be the first, but I won't be the last. Not when you kiss like that. You'll break a lot of hearts, Josephina Wolohan." He points at me. "Don't forget me. Promise?"

"How could I forget *you*?" I let out a giggle as warmth rushes into my soul. "I promise."

"Good. I better go," says Mack with a wide smile. "Don't want rumors that I'm robbing the cradle. Check you later, Wolly."

"Okay, see ya," I say in a cheerful voice, telling myself not to be smitten.

Mack walks around the corner, leaving me gaping after him. My head is spinning, and I hesitate for a moment to process what just happened.

That was more than just a first kiss—it was the promise of untold possibilities that lie ahead. I can't help chuckling as I step out of the alley to find Maggie standing on the sidewalk.

"There you are! Cat's mom wants a photo of our Butte Girls' Club. She likes that name better than the Clover Girls. I told her our secret name. Come on!" She waves me to the front of the school, where Mikey Ann and Cat wait on the steps.

"Where the heck were you?" demands Cat.

"Jo was in the alley," announces Maggie in a teasing sing-song voice.

"What were you doing in the alley? Having a smoke?" teases Cat.

"Kissing Mack MacGregor," I say offhandedly, waiting for my friends to explode.

Cat snorts. "Gimme a break. Mack has a high school girlfriend. He doesn't mess around with eighth graders."

"Want to make a bet? We're freshmen now, remember?" I point out.

"Not yet," sniffs Maggie with a sophisticated air. "Technically, not until next fall."

Mikey Ann steps in close and peers at me. "She's not lying. Just *look* at her."

My three friends scrutinize me like I'm under a microscope.

Right then, Mack bursts through the front door. "Excuse me, ladies," he hollers, tapping down the steps. He pauses, spins around, and points to me.

"You're a fox, Josephina Wolohan. And quite the kisser. Watch yourself with the fast guys in high school. Tap 'er light." He gives a flirty wink, then clambers into a shiny red Chevy full of cute high school boys.

"Tap 'er light," I respond with a flirty wave.

"Take it easy, cupcake girl!" Mack hollers out the window as the Chevy peels out and speeds along Park Street.

Slack-jawed, Maggie turns to face me. "You actually, really, honest-to-God kissed him?"

"Ha, why else would he say Jo was a good kisser?" quips Cat, then turns to me with a mischievous look. "You sly dog! You're the one that's been holding out on *me!*"

"I take it you told him you French-kissed cupcakes?" Mikey Ann asks with an impish grin.

I nod slowly, still in a daze. "I can't wait for high school," I murmur, breaking into a wide smile. "Did you hear that? He called me a fox!" My ego orbits the moon like an Apollo spacecraft.

Cat nods emphatically. "In boy talk, saying you're a fox is a gargantuan compliment. I'm ninety-eight percent jealous."

Mikey Ann grins. "Wolohan, I knew you liked him!"

"You made out in front of God and everybody? Have you no shame?" Maggie's voice rose an octave as she sweeps her arm to indicate all of Park Street.

"We didn't make out. It was only one kiss." I avoided her gaze. "Or two. Besides, we were in the alley," I added.

"Oh my God, that's worse!" Maggie shoves her glasses higher on her nose, her cow eyes piercing mine. "This is how it starts. You don't want to start your high school career as a slut." She folds her arms in a Sister Alex pose. "So, what was it like, French-kissing the sex maniac?"

I sense a whisper of jealousy. Maggie and I had made a solemn vow to experience everything *together*. "First of all, I'm not a slut. And second of all, Mack isn't a sex maniac. He just talks like he is. I must admit, Frenching is kind of cool." I love this cloud I'm floating on.

"Your first kiss was in an alley," teases Cat. "How romantic. That's such a Butte thing."

"Who's first kiss was in an alley?" echoes Mrs. Delaney, stepping outside with a Brownie camera.

"Whoops," Cat says under her breath. "No one, Mom. We were talking about someone."

I turn away with heated cheeks as Cat smirks at me.

"Okay, Butte Girls' Club, let's see those pearly whites. Now yell, 'we did it!'" instructs Mrs. Delaney, holding the Brownie camera up to her eye.

The four of us stand close and chorus in unison, tossing our arms up. "We did it!"

"And we're off like a turd of hurdles!" wisecracks Mikey Ann.

I keep my hands raised to the sky, gazing upwards.

I did it, Dad. Wish you were here to see this. I promise I'll make you proud.

Cat claps her hands, snapping me back to the present. "I can't wait for the prom! I want to try out for cheerleading."

I look at Maggie. "Maybe we could try out for the swim team?"

Maggie peers over her glasses. "Then we'd better go to team practice this summer."

What I didn't say was, *I want to find out where Mack hangs out.*

No one has to know I have a tiny crush on him, despite my ongoing denials. I open my autograph booklet to see what Mack wrote, noting Andy O'Neil's scribble.

To a good kid, good luck with the boys, Mrs. Loverboy!

I chuckle, turning the page. Mack's is at the bottom in perfect penmanship:

Dear Wolly, you're the reason I looked forward to school every day. You're really cute, so go easy on the boys. Don't 4get me! XOXO Mack

My breath hitches and I can't believe my eyes. I read it again. And again... and again.

Finally, I close my autograph booklet and clutch it to my chest. With my other hand, I absentmindedly flutter the pages of my prayer book the Sisters had given us for graduation. A folded slip of paper falls out, and I bend to pick it up. Unfolding it, I read in beautiful, loopy cursive:

Next time you hide behind a piano, be sure to wear earplugs. Good luck in high school–Sister Alexandria

"You guys!" I shriek, recoiling with horror, as if aliens are poking at my body.

"What is it?" asks Maggie, squinting at the note in my hand. "You look like you've seen one of Colleen's ghosts."

I hand her the note, and my friends bend to read it. They flash me a horrified look to match my own. "How did Sister Alex find out you were behind the piano? Why didn't she say anything?"

Bewildered, I shrug and shake my head when something else falls from my prayer book and flutters to the sidewalk. I bend to pick up a tiny black-and-white photo, and I stare at it. It was the photo I couldn't find that had been in my sweater pocket—the same sweater I'd worn the day we sneaked into the convent.

"My photo must have fallen out when I hid behind the piano!" I say, the puzzle pieces falling into place. "Remember Sister Alex saying a little red birdie that told her who snuck into the convent? Maybe she saw my red tennis shoes when I hid behind the piano? Or when she looked back there later and found this photo."

"Why didn't she say anything?" asks Maggie, stupefied.

"Maybe because we were in enough trouble as it was," says Cat. "For whatever reason, she took pity on Jo and waited until after graduation."

"Sister Alex is the coolest nun of them all," says Mikey Ann, and we all nod in agreement.

I smile at the goofy photo and shove it back inside my prayer book.

A car double honks and I glance up to see Aunt Daisy pull up to the curb in her blue Chevy.

"Whoops, I forgot. I told my aunt to pick me up after the reception to go see Mom," I say, a hand to my forehead. "I have to tell her all about our reception."

Maggie sidles up. "Are you going to tell her about making out with Mack in the alley? Hmm?" She puckers her lips, making kissing noises.

"Told you! We didn't make out!" I say, laughing, as I head to the car.

Now I wish we had after Mack's killer kiss. My bargain with God rushes back—if Mom wakes up, no more secrets.

"Yeah, I'll tell her one of these days… just not yet." I waggle my fingers next to my lips and jump my eyebrows up and down like Groucho Marx.

Right on cue, the Clover Girls crack up and split a gut, just as I want them to.

One thing I know for sure: I'll forever cherish this moment: the four of us together, ready to take on the next four years of high school. I stand back to observe my best friends. Maggie, my loyal companion through thick and thin, and I love her habit of tapping her glasses higher on her nose; Mikey Ann, our loyal protector, snorting her chuckles with her lopsided grin; and bold and resilient Cat, punctuating her convictions with her defiant middle finger.

I wouldn't have made it this far without them.

When our parents couldn't keep our heads above water, our friends did. From each other, we gained strength and confidence, clinging together for survival so we wouldn't face this wild and scary world alone. Our bonds are strong enough to last the rest of our lives… or so we hope. I close my eyes and cross my fingers.

But the best thing of all?

We are just getting started.

Author's Note

Much has been written about Butte, but there's still plenty left to say. At least life is mostly predictable; everyone knows what to expect when they live in Butte (unless one encounters Helen Mirren at Walmart or Harrison Ford at the M&M eating steak and eggs).

It wasn't until I'd moved away and returned home to research my family at the Butte Archives did I appreciate the diverse town where I grew up. If you delve into the complex, fascinating history of Butte, you'll see why. Early in the last century, copper became an invaluable resource as America's electrification expanded rapidly, and two world wars increased industrial demands. The city's population exploded as miners and others arrived to live and work in the harsh winter climate of this mining town nestled in the Rockies.

There's something unique about Butte's people you won't find anywhere else. The friendships I formed as a kid have lasted my entire life. Our memories are doorways to the past, and when I walked through them to write this story, I immersed myself in the 1960s. Butte was like many places in America, with civil unrest over the Vietnam War and rebellion against "The Establishment."

We grew up in a time where hiding under our desks in the event of a nuclear bomb attack became routine. I did my best, like everyone else, not to give in to our unspoken fears back then. I remember thinking, how could I possibly look forward to the future? Thankfully, life went on as it always had.

The friendships we formed as young people in the 1960s are as solid today as they were back then. This is where the genuine gold lies—not in the ground, but in the hearts of Butte's people. Each time I return, a warm blanket caresses me as I crest the hill on I-90 and see the Lady of the Rockies on the East Ridge, welcoming me home.

With a Butte person, you always pick up where you left off. No judgment, no criticism, only welcome acceptance and lifelong friendship. If I've learned anything from the wild and woolly people of Butte, it's this: Keep your heart open and cherish every relationship, whether good or bad—because friends are vital while navigating this thing called life.

Historical figures in this book are loosely based on personal diary accounts from the 1960s and bear no relation to current political figures. The Sisters of Charity from Leavenworth were intelligent, courageous women who took their educational mission seriously. These nuns shaped us in life-altering ways, teaching us right from wrong and how to be honest, kind, and generous. They never gave up on us, no matter how much trouble we caused, and I'll forever be grateful for the education and guidance they provided.

There's another phrase for resilience: Butte Tough. I've experienced it with my family and friends and have sensed it in myself through the years. Some say we should embrace the past to move forward. There is some truth to that. Others say we can never go home again. I disagree. I *have* gone home again. My Butte family and friends are the *real* gold—the *real* copper.

For this reason, Butte will always be home to me.

Thanks so much for reading The Butte Girls' Club! If you enjoyed this book, please tell your friends and family, and please post a review on Amazon. Reviews make an enormous difference for my success as a writer and help other readers discover the story!

Stay tuned for the sequel, *Butte Girls' Club Two, Class of 1972!* Email me at lolo@lolopaige.com and I'll add you to my newsletter, where I keep readers up to date about my upcoming books.

IF YOU'RE INTERESTED in reading about the history of Butte, Montana, *The War of the Copper Kings,* by C.B. Glasscock is an excellent resource about the three men who vied for control of the copper industry at the dawn of the 20th century.

In the fall of 1976 at the University of Montana, I was fortunate enough to have taken a class taught by K. Ross Toole, called "Montana and the West." His classes were standing room only and students crowded the aisles of the large lecture hall because of his animated, high-spirited lectures. His texts for the class were two books he'd written, *Twentieth-century Montana: A State of Extremes and Montana, An Uncommon Land*. I recommend both to read about Butte and Montana's histories.

Acknowledgments

I OWE A GREAT DEAL of gratitude to Lorrie Henrie-Koski, my superhero editor, also from Butte, who had faith in this book from the very beginning back when it was only rolling around in my head. Lorrie helped me breathe life into Jo and her friends. She kept me on track in the 1960s whenever a modern phrase leaked into my dialogue. She stuck with me these past few years, working tirelessly as we went back and forth with edits. This book would not have happened without Lorrie's help.

My lifelong partner and love of my life, Marc Simenson, is another superstar who kept me in the saddle to write this story. He made countless suggestions for what to include and how to flush out my characters. After a lifetime of listening to my real-life stories, he advised me which ones to include. This book wouldn't have happened without him, either.

Daughters Katy Simenson Nerlfi and Rebecca Simenson, who encouraged me for decades: "Mom you should write stories about your stories!" Thanks for your confidence in me, Katy and Becca.

Milana Marsenich is another superstar. A successful Montana author in her own right, we became fast friends after we did a book signing together at Isle of Books in Butte a few years ago. Ever since, Milana has supported and encouraged me and listened to me whine and vent when the going got tough...reminding me I was "Butte tough." Thank you, Milana.

So many Butte friends helped me along the way, with random suggestions: Christine Carney Hardesty, who read my early drafts; Russ Lawrence, who has always said he wanted to read this book; Nerlfi, Pamela McDonnell Showers, Ellen Dowling, Patty Edwards, Steve Wing, Maureen Robinson, Yvonne-Hurd Cappellano, Paulette Scherr, Ruth VanDyke, Billie Lou Barker, April Maye, Christine Muth, Charlotte Walsh Trudgeon, who have supported and encouraged me on from day one; and so many others who got excited whenever I talked about writing this book at our Class of 1972 high school reunion.

Heaps of thanks to The Butte Archives superstars, Shannon Hopewell and Aubrey Jaap, who found answers to my many questions: everything from

Butte breweries to when Harrison Avenue became four lanes, and when the Lexington mine shut down. They were patient with my sometimes-weird questions. Thank you, ladies!

Other resources I used for my research: *Butte: The Original*, a film by Dick Maney & BJ McKenzie, © 2010 Maney Telefilm; The Montana Standard, *Robert F. Kennedy's Visit to Butte*, October 1968 and the Los Angeles Times article, *Kennedy Shot,* on June 5, 1968; *Remembering Butte, Montana's Richest City*, © Butte-Silver Bow Archives; and the many Facebook pages about Butte.

A few good childhood friends inspired me to write this story but didn't live long enough to read it: Paula Waddell Parini and Candice Ann Burns. I'll remember you always. And my eighth-grade class of 1968, who inspired me to come up with the fictional characters. That was the fun part.

Another thank you to historical fiction author Kathleen Grissom, who graciously responded to my email, advising me how to approach researching history for novels set in certain periods. She also told me to "get busy writing it!"

My goldens, the Mandy Lorian and Rooby Doo, who traded loves for treats, and the wildlife that showed up outside my Eagle River window each day as I worked. Mr. Raven, who perched on top of the spruce, cawed at me like he was telling me to keep writing! (I'd like to think so, anyway) And the mama moose and her two calves, who wandered through our yard around the same time each day.

Also By the Author, as LoLo Paige

Check out my romantic suspense novels about wildland firefighting:
The Blazing Hearts Wildfire Series
Alaska Spark
Alaska Inferno
Alaska Blaze
Alaska Firestorm
Alaska Flame (novella)

LoLo Paige Romantic Comedies
The Polar-Paired Series
Cupid's Kerfuffle (novella)
Everybody Loves Polar Bears
Flights, Fights, and Christmas Lights
The Wandering Hearts Series
Hello Spain, Goodbye Heart (A later in life romance)
Irish Thunder (Ever been on a male stripper cruise? Now's your chance!)

About the Author

AS A HYBRID AUTHOR, Lois Paige has published a dozen titles in the romance genre under the pen name LoLo Paige. Her writing has appeared in *Alaska Magazine, The Anchorage Press, Alaska Star, Erma Bombeck Humor-Writers.org, Anchorage Daily News, Alaska Magazine, Washington D.C. Metro Bugle, The Hill Congress Blog*, and the *Santa Fe Writers Project*. In 2016, her true story about wildland firefighting received an Alaska Press Club award. Her romance novels have topped Amazon bestseller lists in the U.S., Canada, and Australia. Several have received awards for best indie-published romances, and *Publishers Weekly* has featured her novels in their *Booklife* section. Born in Butte, Montana, she currently lives in Eagle River, Alaska.

This is her first historical fiction novel. And it won't be her last.

Follow me on Amazon,[1] Facebook,[2] and Instagram![3]

---

1. https://www.amazon.com/stores/LoLo-Paige/author/B0872KT8QS

2. https://www.facebook.com/LoLoPaigewildlandfire/

3. https://www.instagram.com/lolopaige/

Lilly Rose's Pasties

For six medium-sized pasties. Adjust ingredients as needed.

FILLING

1 1/2 pounds raw, tender steak, cut into small cubes. (Or use ground sirloin for tenderness)

1 cup chopped sweet onion (optional)

1 cup grated carrot

3 medium-sized potatoes, peeled and diced

Salt and pepper to taste

Pie Dough – (Use your favorite recipe, or if pressed for time, get the ready-made pie dough)

3 cups all-purpose flour

1 teaspoon salt

1 cup (2 sticks) cold unsalted butter, cubed or use shortening

6-8 tablespoons ice water

Instructions

Combine pie dough ingredients, then divide dough into six balls. Roll each portion into a six-inch diameter circle. For each pasty, mound meat and potato mixture on half the circle away from the edge. Dot with one or two tablespoons of margarine or butter.

Fold the other half of dough over the filling. Moisten edges and crimp together to seal. Cut a small slit in the top of each to let steam escape. Brush dough with a beaten egg to help it brown. Place pasties on greased baking sheet and bake at 350°F for one hour. Pour a teaspoon of hot water into the slit as needed during baking to prevent the inside from drying out. Serve them hot or cold with catsup, brown gravy, or both.

Cocktail pasties are miniature versions of regular sized pasties, served as appetizers. You can make them ahead of time to stick in the freezer. Use a wide-rimmed drinking glass to cut out the dough, and put a small amount of the potato-meat mixture on each and fold them over, same as you would the larger pasties. Ground sirloin is perfect for these smaller ones. Bake them at 375°F degrees for 30 minutes. Make sure they're cooled before freezing.

Lilly Rose's Sweet Potato Salad

2 POUNDS OF SWEET POTATOES, peeled, boiled, and mashed

3 stalks celery, finely chopped

4 green onions, finely chopped

6 hard-boiled eggs. Dice the egg whites and mash yolks until smooth.

Combine all ingredients with the sweet potatoes and add enough mayonnaise for desired consistency. Chill before serving. Can add Pimento for color when serving. The green onion bits and red pimento give this yummy salad a festive touch for the Christmas holidays.